The Hoarder's Widow

Book One in the *Widows* Series

By

Allie Cresswell

This book is dedicated
to my grandchildren,
Molly, Zack, Parker and Ivy
with love from Granny

PART ONE
Chapter One

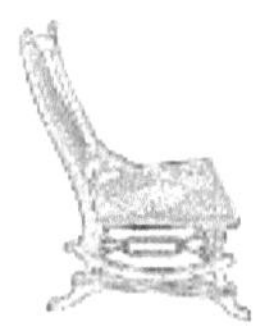

Clifford Wilde died on 14th October. He was 61 years old. According to the coroner, the primary cause of his death was electrocution by a short circuit in the hot water geyser he was repairing. The shock threw him across the garage into a lop-sided rack of metal shelving that had been haphazardly stacked with a plethora of unwieldy planes, obsolete routers and rusty chisels. These, dislodged by the impact, rained down onto Clifford's body as he lay prone on the oily floor, causing severe crush injuries to the chest, multiple cranial fractures and dislodging his dental palette. A bradawl had impaled itself into his left eye socket. The coroner opines these injuries would probably have been sufficient to cause death, notwithstanding the electrocution. A conflagration, triggered by the close juxtaposition of the overheated faulty element of the geyser and a bundle of oily rags on the work bench would certainly have rendered Mr Wilde beyond help had life not already been extinct. On discovering the fire, Mr Wilde's wife, Maisie, had called the emergency services, but no action either on her part or theirs could possibly have altered the outcome of what the coroner describes as an escalation of tragic accidents.

In addition to his widow, Mr Wilde leaves two sons, a daughter and three grandchildren, to whom the coroner extends his most sincere condolences, having pronounced the cause of death as accidental and released the body for burial.

" "

I got that geyser on Freecycle. You wouldn't believe what good stuff people give away for nothing. I've managed to get quite a few beauties, but you have to be on the ball and reply quickly when they get listed. Usually people pick the first person to get back to them. Other times they choose the one who says, 'This will be perfect for my daughter; she's just setting up home for herself and the baby.' Or, 'This will make life so much easier for my disabled wife.' I've tried coming up with a hard-luck tale once or twice, but it didn't feel right. On the whole I don't think people care much. They just want to get rid of things without the guilt of having thrown them away. That suits me fine. My philosophy is that we should never miss an opportunity to save things, if we can.

I knew as soon as I saw the geyser that we could make use of it. Maisie is always complaining about how long it takes the back boiler to heat water for washing up. She's a stickler for washing up, that woman. 'Hot, soapy water,' is her mantra.

'I'll mount it over the sink,' I thought to myself. 'It'll save on water as well as fuel, and Maisie can wash up to her heart's content.'

I went after work to collect it from this bloke. He'd taken it out of his gran's place, he said. Got the impression they'd put her in a home. To be fair, he told me it was broken. 'Something wrong with the element,' he said. 'Keeps shorting out. She'd stopped using it.'

'Probably just a wiring problem,' I told him. 'Fixed in a jiffy if you know what you're doing.'

Of course, on Freecycle, you have to give things away as well. It can't all be one way. That was tricky at first, until I got talking to Ted at the dump about it. Ted and me go back a long way. Time was when you could help yourself to stuff from the dump. I got a perfectly good record player and some speakers and some natural history books for the children. One time, the blokes there were digging out the bank to make room for more skips and they found hundreds of old glass bottles—all colours and shapes, some of them embossed with the names of quack medicines. The blue ones were used for poison. I got a load of them. They're in a box in the attic waiting to be cleaned up. Those are the kinds of things that will make money.

You're not allowed to help yourself now; everything is strictly controlled for health and safety. Well, *officially* you're not allowed.

Anyway, Ted stroked his chin and sucked his teeth and stared into the distance in that way he has when he's mulling something over. 'You don't want to be giving your stuff away,' he said at last. 'Much too good, most of it.'

I nodded. That was exactly what I thought. I had plans for my stuff. But then again, I'd have to offer something on Freecycle if I wanted to qualify to get things.

Then Ted tipped me the wink and said, 'Drop by on Sunday. People bring all kinds of stuff on Sunday and the supervisor never turns in. You never know, something might find its way into the boot of your car.'

So, on the Sunday I got a few bits and pieces that were quite good in themselves but no earthly good to me—a smoked glass and chrome coffee table, an old ironing board, an exercise machine—and I was away.

It was my son Dominic who got me online, back in about 2005. 'What's "online"?' I asked him. 'What's "www dot"? It's all you ever hear about these days.'

'You need a computer, Dad,' he told me.

'Oh!' I said, 'I can get one of those.' They were upgrading the systems at work; there was a whole skip full of monitors and keyboards and boxes of kit at the back of the warehouse. When I got it all home Dominic had a bit of a snigger about it—said it was "steam-powered"—but he got it to work, and once he'd sent off for a box thing with flashing lights from BT and got all that hooked up I was online. I didn't tell Maisie about it. Didn't want to worry her. You hear such stories about viruses and hacking and identity theft. She'd never have slept again if I'd told her we were on the net!

Before Freecycle I got a lot on eBay. That's better in a way because you don't have to sell things or give anything away, you can just buy stuff. Some goes for a pound! You have to watch and bid at the last minute. Then your things arrive and you open the parcel and look them over and decide where they will go, how you can use them. Some of it doesn't look very auspicious at first, but that doesn't stop me. It's a challenge, isn't it? Fixing things and making them better?

Chapter Two

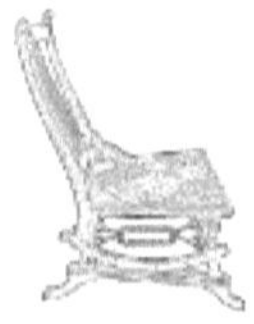

Between the death and the inquest, Maisie is in a kind of limbo. Nothing can be decided, no progress made, no plan sketched out until the coroner's verdict is delivered. For Maisie, who during her twenty-seven-year marriage, had resigned herself to look to Clifford as the instigator of all decisions, progress and planning, this enforced stasis is yet another appalling reminder of his demise. Time, which has always moved very slowly anyway in their household, seems to have stopped altogether. For reassurance, she checks the clocks. They have several, all showing different times. Some of them chime at odd junctures: ten past the hour, twenty-five-to. Pendulums swing lugubriously to and fro. From within, a muffled, dusty tick suggests time passing but, to Maisie, standing with breath held before them, their hands don't seem to move.

She wonders, perhaps it's me who's dead.

Maisie brings to mind some ancient burial ritual—Egyptian, she thinks—which involved the incarceration of the wives and chattels along with the deceased. That's how she feels; immured in this mausoleum of a house. Clifford had been its sole architect, the only one with an overarching scheme. For all she might have felt—during his life—bewildered and lost within its complexities, she had at least felt certain that, with his guiding hand, she would eventually emerge.

Their daughter Frances arrives from Oxford, supposedly to offer support, but it is very much of the school of Job's comforters. She alternates between hand-wringing despair, moaning, 'What on earth, what on *earth* are you going to do, Mum? How in God's name will you manage?' and hand-washing denigration, cawing, 'Well what did you expect? When you let things get so out of hand? You made your own bed, that's all I have to say.' The overwhelming sense—that nothing can be done—assaults Maisie with awful hopelessness hour by hour, like a dull but persistent tooth ache that cannot be eased or escaped from. Occasionally though, sharp new evidence of Clifford's sudden and permanent absence stabs through: his empty place at the table gives her a wincing shock each day. The solid fuel range goes out for lack of wood. It was Clifford's job to chop it and bring it in. The cold and frustration add new layers to her pain. She finds that his socks—when all assembled in one place as opposed to being variously distributed between his feet, the bedroom floor, the laundry basket, the wash and the maiden— won't all fit into their allocated drawer. This tiny circumstance seems like the last straw. She lies on the bedroom carpet amongst the socks—paired and carefully rolled, as he had shown her—and howls.

There are questions that need answers: what is the PIN for the cash card? Has he written a Will and if so, where is it? When is the MOT due on the car? Why, oh why, did he have to buy that stupid geyser? Could he not have given her just a second's warning, to say goodbye?

Between the inquest and the funeral, things are a little easier. There are decisions to be taken, things to discuss. They provide a vocabulary to occupy the mouth—words like casket and cremation, hearse, hymns, eulogy, committal—to take the place of the words that can't be spoken: loss, loneliness, widowhood, death, ashes, and the most dreadful of all—future. There are things to do: a funeral director to select, a black suit to buy, orders of service to compile. These are all displacement activities; mechanical actions that give the hands and the mind purpose, things to do that put off the towering, tottering unmanageable heap of things that *will* have to be done, the reality that will have to be faced, afterwards.

She visits Clifford in the Chapel of Rest, where his body has been arranged on a dais and covered with a sky-blue satin shroud. He looks remarkably well, considering. What arts the embalmers must have employed! His hair is more neatly combed than it ever was in life. He is implacable on the subject of PINs, MOTs and so forth. When she whispers her goodbye, it doesn't feel final. There is no closure, no neat sewing up. The end is jagged and raw and untidy.

Chapter Three

The funeral finally takes place on a dismal Thursday in early November.

When Maisie opens the curtains that morning the windows are lashed with squally rain. The trees across the lane thrash and throw the last of their leaves like insults onto the cobbles. The town, down the distant incline, is a grey vaporous bowl.

Oh well, at least we didn't opt for a burial.

The period of stultifying inertia, followed by the pointless busyness of funeral arrangements, have done their work. She is used to the shock now. Rather than coating the world in bristling needles that draw grief like blood from every common place, the reality has sunk in. It is part of her now, something she must carry—like a deformity. It is a terrible, wearing burden, an annoyance, a frustration that makes her at times very angry, at other times almost inconsolable; at still others she feels strangely distanced and numb.

Clifford's absence from the places where he belongs does not assault her now like it did. She doesn't expect him home at six. She will not make the mistake of cooking too many pork chops for dinner. And because this new reality has become part of her, it is gradually melding itself with her other characteristics: her good humour, her resilience, her loving kindness. The result is a dry, wry, ironical outlook, and a bleak, almost black humour that casts the whole thing in a light she can handle. Apart from all the obvious things that a sudden death is—tragic, shocking, appalling—with all its attendant ramifications, Clifford's death and the situation in which it leaves Maisie is actually, in a skewed, off-key way, rather funny—farcically, bitterly laughable.

She dresses in the new suit. It was ordered from a catalogue and was too big—a last minute panic about its return and replacement giving the past two days a frisson she hadn't really needed. She notes her loss of weight with a distracted satisfaction; bereavement, clearly, is even more efficacious than Weightwatchers.

Her hair is going grey—was it, before? She can't remember having looked at herself for long enough to notice. She drags a brush through it. It is no kind of style. Its curls have a mind of their own anyway. Her eyes are grey, too, their usual softness is muted to sad. When she looks herself in the eye she sees a glimmer of despair which was never there before. Her face is also grey, pallid with shock and weariness. She has makeup somewhere, in a drawer, but never bothers with it as a rule. Perhaps today makeup will be in order. Clifford, after all, will be wearing it. His colour, in the chill atmosphere of the Chapel of Rest, had been oddly high. While she thinks about this she smears Nivea over her face and neck—all the skincare she has ever bothered with, the routine instigated years ago by her aunt Sarah. It seems to have worked. Maisie she has escaped the tell-tale scoring between nostril and mouth that marks so many women of her age. Her forehead is without furrows. There are lines around her eyes—she tries a smile, they concertina obediently—laughter lines. Simultaneously, as though connected by an invisible thread, a dimple puckers in her cheek. She brightens the smile until it becomes a rictus, her lips stretched almost painfully over her teeth.

There now, she snarls, through the grimace. Put on a brave face, Maisie.

By mid-morning the squall has passed but the air is still filled with fine rain that hovers in the air like spray. At the crematorium it acts like a wet blanket draped over everything. In an instant coats, hats, faces are soaked, beaded with silver. The floral tributes left by grievers at earlier services are weighed down, their petals translucent and bruised. A small cluster of soggy mourners waits at the crematorium door where the funeral director's flunkey hands out Orders of Service. They are limp and grey and ink-smudged by the damp.

The hearse is late. The group mills awkwardly, surreptitiously checking their watches. On the tip of each tongue is the caustic observation, 'late for his own funeral,' but good manners prevent anyone from letting it slip out.

Maisie recognises Ted from the municipal dump, Cyril from the auction house and Val, the woman from the farm behind the house. There are a few others she doesn't recognise. She assumes they are from Clifford's place of work.

Maisie is conscious of an on-going altercation between her son Dominic and his wife Pamela. They stand to one side in deeply charged conference. Even though Dominic speaks with flaccid, barely mobile lips, as though practising for a ventriloquism act, and Pamela presses a crumpled handkerchief to her mouth, it is not enough to prevent Maisie from gathering the gist of their disagreement. Pamela does not want to stay the night. Even though they have driven up this morning from Nottingham—a good three-hour drive—she wants to set off straight back home as soon as the funeral is over. Even amidst the emotional turmoil engendered by the occasion of the funeral itself, and the non-appearance of the hearse, Maisie is annoyed; she has gone to the trouble of making up the beds in Dominic's old room and erected two fiendishly stiff and uncooperative canvas camp beds for the little girls. She needn't have bothered, if she had known. But then again, she knows very well that in Pamela's opinion the accommodation back at the house is less than ideal. Apparently, the bulbous shadows of the over-furnished room and the draughty passageway to the toilet make for night time terrors for Jessica and bedwetting for poor little Edmé, who has only just come out of nappies. Only the baby, in his carry-cot, is—as yet—oblivious.

Maisie had been amazed, and frankly appalled that Dominic and Pamela had wanted the children to attend the funeral at all, and had lined up somebody's teenage daughter to look after them for the duration of the service. But Pamela had been adamant. 'They could be *anybody,*' she had cried, meaning the teenage daughter—'a *stranger.*' In her mouth, the word had all the chilling connotations of 'paedophile.' 'And in any case,' she had gone on, 'the girls need to be able to say goodbye to Granddad properly.' They had not been fussed about saying goodbye to Granddad while he was alive, Maisie reflected privately, although she didn't blame them for that, crotchety old sod that he was at times. But in fact, so far, give them their due; the children are behaving very well. They are soberly dressed in suitable pinafores and dark cardigans under their duffel coats. Even Jessica, a determined tomboy aged five, has submitted to hair-combing and some smart patent leather shoes in place of the trainers she prefers.

Presently Dominic's temper gets the better of him. 'We *can't* leave Mum alone on the night of the funeral!' he hisses in a stage whisper that everyone can hear. 'Gareth only got a two-day pass so he's *got* to go back, and Frances has been here since Dad died, more or less. She's missed dozens of lectures.'

'I know, I know,' Pamela, furious with embarrassment, glances at the on-lookers. 'Let's not discuss this now, Dominic.'

'You brought the subject up,' Dominic snarls.

Pamela calls the two girls back to her side. They have been amusing themselves by scrambling onto a nearby tomb, and jumping off again. She takes out her angst on them. 'Look at your coat, Jessica,' she scolds. 'It's covered in moss-stains.'

'Granddad's late for his own funeral!' Jessica quips.

'Here we go, Mum.' Gareth, Maisie's younger son, draws her arm through his. 'Here comes the hearse.'

The 'premium hearse' promised turns out to be a low-slung jalopy with a dodgy exhaust and a missing bumper. It arrives at a less than sedate speed, rattling ominously and trailing fumes. The funeral director, when he climbs out, has oily hands. 'Had to do a running repair on the fan belt,' he explains apologetically, indicating his female assistant, who wears no tights.

On the whole, Maisie muses, Clifford would probably have approved.

Inside, there is a mix-up. Of the front rows either side of the aisle reserved for immediate family, one is inadvertently occupied by the delegation from Harrington's, where Clifford has controlled stock levels in the warehouse and distributed parts for more than forty years. The deputation includes old Mr Harrington himself, who, for some reason not quite clear, has been brought out from retirement to attend, so nobody likes to object. As a consequence, Maisie and the family have to split up. She takes the front pew along with Gareth, her daughter Frances and granddaughter Jessica. Dominic, Pamela and their other little girl squash into the one behind them, which is already occupied by two mourners. The pram sits in the aisle, looking for all the world like a second, miniature-sized coffin.

Maisie casts an exasperated eye over the situation. It is ridiculous to be so crammed together; the rest of the chapel is virtually empty.

The family and the meagre congregation stand while the coffin is lowered onto the dais. The vicar makes some opening remarks and mutters a few prayers.

Of all the emotions clamouring for Maisie's attention, the strongest is the one that emanates from behind her, where she knows Dominic is fulminating with a resentful sense of having been side-lined, relegated to what he will see as a second-class status of mourning.

He should have been at the front, next to me. He certainly wants to be. But Pamela won't entertain it. She'll want him next to her.

The back of the pew shifts fractionally, and she thinks for an awful moment that Dominic is going to clamber over and push in next to her. But it is only Pamela trying to grab Jessica's hood and yank her back to join them on the second pew. The child is having none of it though. She snuggles smugly next to her granny, seeming to feel—like the Harrington's contingent—that she has gained a ringside seat in what promises to be an entertaining spectacle.

Maisie leans over and whispers into Jessica's ear, 'It's only Granddad's body in the box you know, darling,' hoping to comfort the child with an image of a contented spiritual Granddad tinkering eternally in some glowing celestial workshop.

'Why?' Jessica replies, turning saucer-shaped eyes towards Maisie, 'What have they done with his head?'

They are invited to sit down. Heaven knows why. Within seconds they are back on their feet and tuning up for the first verse of *The Lord's My Shepherd*. In the brief interlude however, Maisie hears Dominic gulping and sniffing.

'Use your handkerchief,' she hears Pamela mutter as they stand to sing.

'I can't. I used it this morning when the baby was sick,' Dominic croaks beneath the organ's preamble.

Maisie struggles fruitlessly with her jacket pocket before remembering that it is a new suit and the pocket is still sewn shut. She reaches for her bag, extracting a fistful of tissues which she passes surreptitiously back to Dominic. Dominic is unmanned for the duration of the Psalm. His dismay at being separated from Maisie, his sense of being usurped by his siblings and, most of all, at his mother's intuition—of course, she knows exactly what and how he is feeling—plus a little sadness for his father. It is not until "Goodness and mercy have surely followed him and he is dwelling in the house of the Lord forever" that he manages to get a grip of himself.

Standing between Gareth and Frances, Maisie is somewhat dwarfed, her five-foot-three or -four seems much smaller. To her right, Frances keeps her bony back rigidly straight, and stares sightlessly at a point above the vicar's head. She has thin, sharp shoulders and reminds Maisie of one of Clifford's excruciatingly uncomfortable ladder-back chairs, but dressed in a gabardine. Gareth, on the other hand, is broad and well-made. His dress uniform enhances the thick set of his shoulders, the narrow, nipped-in waist, the sturdy legs used to yomping. He has all his hair, something poor Dominic can't claim even at only twenty-seven. Gareth's presence next to her is very reassuring. He has found a packet of chewy mints in his pocket and is supplying them to Jessica to keep her jaws busy.

Pamela clearly wishes to continue the debate from earlier. Under cover of the vicar's rambling address she murmurs, 'We *don't* need to stay. Your mother's coping perfectly well.' Her words, though slightly muffled by the Order of Service, are clearly audible to Maisie.

'That's Mum all over though, isn't? *I* think she's amazing,' Dominic asserts in a low voice. 'Anyway, there'll be paperwork to look into. I'm bound to be the Executor. It'll be down to me to apply for Probate.'

'I shouldn't think there'll be any need for that,' Pamela mumbles sourly.

'Who knows what's hidden away amongst all that junk?' Dominic whispers.

Who knows indeed? Maisie wants to put in. Rats, probably. But the conclusion of the sermon precludes further comment.

After the service Pamela takes the children for a walk round the garden of remembrance. She struggles to get the wheels of the pram through the thick gravel whilst the girls caper amongst the memorials. They had become bored and fidgety towards the end of the service and the baby had started to grizzle during the committal, all of which had detracted from both the solemnity and the finality of the drawing curtains.

Maisie shakes hands with the departing mourners on the steps of the crematorium. They voice vague consolations and make non-specific remarks about Clifford. Only Mr Harrington, in a surprisingly commanding voice, is able to speak of him with unambiguity. 'A loyal colleague,' he pronounces. 'Worked for me man and boy. I took a special, on-going interest in him, you know, for obvious reasons.'

'Of course. Of course,' Maisie agrees vaguely. She has no clue what he might mean.

'But Clifford was never one to presume,' Mr Harrington concludes. 'He had a very proper understanding of his place in … in the scheme of things.'

'You're very kind,' Maisie replies coldly. She feels rather patronised by this last assertion. But Mr Harrington is one of the town's movers and shakers, as Clifford always told her—its largest employer, a town Councillor, local philanthropist—not a man of whom to make an enemy. She can almost hear Clifford saying, 'Let it go, Maisie. Now, now, let it go.'

But Mr Harrington is speaking again. 'I wonder if you would think it impertinent of me to introduce … er … my grandson, Michael?' There is something weighted about his question, something portentous and significant, and indeed as the old man takes a step to one side he ushers forward a younger man with a sort of semi-flourish, as though conjuring a rabbit from a hat. She almost expects him to exclaim, 'Ta DAH!' Is she supposed to recognise him? Off the television perhaps? She scans his face. He is perhaps in his early thirties, soberly dressed, an ordinary-looking young man … she is at a loss. He too seems uncomfortable, wrong-footed. He holds out a stiff, cold hand. His mouth says 'My sincere condolences,' but his voice fails to contribute. His face, like his hand, is taut with strain, his eyes almost panicked, his pallor pronounced. Maisie is aware of a rope of expectant tension, like a lasso encircling the two of them. Mr Harrington and the rest of the Harrington's deputation wait for her to do, or say, something. But she has no idea what.

In this situation she reverts to a kind of default setting she has of warmth and nurturing care. 'Your poor hand is frozen!' she exclaims, taking it in both of hers and rubbing it briskly. 'Please do join us at the Masonic Hall for hot tea. Dominic—this is my son, Dominic—you'll direct them, won't you?'

But the introduction of Dominic seems, if anything, to disturb the young man even further. His complexion turns from white to ashen. Mr Harrington steps in. As eager as he had seemed to introduce Michael, he is now as keen to remove him. 'Thank you so much. Michael, we must move on. There are others who want to pay their respects.'

Dominic has taken up a position just behind his mother's right shoulder, at once proprietorial and protected. 'What does he mean?' he asks after the Harrington group has departed. 'What on earth was all that about?'

'I have no idea, darling. Perhaps he's being groomed to take over as chairman. This might be his "Employee Relations and Social Responsibility" training. Where has Pamela gone to?'

'Oh. She's taken the children off somewhere.'

Harrington's personnel director returns momentarily. 'Just to mention,' she says, 'Mr Harrington says you must send the bill for the reception to him. At the Masonic did you say? Mention Mr Harrington's name to the steward.'

'That's very kind,' Maisie says.

'There's a reception?' Dominic queries.

'Just a few sandwiches and a cup of tea. You have to offer people something. So you'll be very late setting off, I'm afraid.'

'We won't be setting off anywhere,' Dominic says staunchly. 'We're going to stay with you. Gareth's *got* to leave. And Frances has that tutorial she's so anxious about tomorrow, but *I'm* not going to leave you on your own on the night of the funeral.'

'Pamela won't be pleased.' Maisie throws Dominic a playful look.

'She'll get over it,' Dominic says, but his frown suggests he doubts it.

Chapter Four

'I presume Dad left a Will,' Dominic says later. 'There'll be insurance papers too somewhere, I suppose.' His apparent nonchalance belies an undertow of eagerness. Maisie is amazed he's managed to restrain himself as long as he has. She felt the enquiry pressing behind his every standard solicitude throughout the inquest and while the funeral arrangements were in train. It reminds her of a contained puppy—sometimes frenzied with impatience, sometimes imperative with a sad, woebegone appeal, but thoroughly restrained. Perhaps it is natural he assumes these matters will fall into his remit; he is the oldest child and the elder son and now, presumably, considers himself the head of the family. And he is an articled solicitor, au fait with the paper-shuffling and legal hoop-jumping attendant on a death. And he is officious; he will enjoy the weight of responsibility.

'Oh, I suppose, *somewhere*,' Maisie says, raising an ironical eyebrow over a mischievous eye and indicating the chaos of the kitchen—teetering stacks of yellowing newspapers in the alcove behind the door; the chair by the ancient Aga engulfed by weeks of unsorted junk mail; the innards of a broken clock strewn across the dresser; the box of electrical entrails under the table. Her gesture, by extension, encompasses the entire house—rooms stacked with *stuff*—Clifford's Collection, the ever-encroaching tide of his hoard. From above, the creak and complaint of floorboards, the rusty whinge of an unoiled hinge, could have been the collection girding itself for the intrusion of a search, or the ghost of Clifford himself moving possessively amongst the towers of broken furniture and bales of dusty fabric; but in is fact only Pamela settling the children for the night.

Presently she appears in the kitchen. The overwhelming gloom of the room—barely kept at bay by the single overhead light bulb and the slight dash of bluish brightness from the fluorescent tube over the Baby Belling—

seems to advance with her across the flagstone floor, emboldened by her mourning clothes and her air of sulky discontent.

'I don't think they're going to settle,' she sighs, with an accusing glance at Dominic that carries with it the full narrative of the time she has had trying to cajole the children into the narrow camp beds. She fills hot water bottles from the kettle on the Aga hotplate. 'I told them you'd go up in five minutes, Dominic.'

'I'll be going up myself before then,' Maisie says, yawning. 'Perhaps they'll settle better if they know we're all turning in.'

'Perhaps,' Pamela agrees, but in a doubtful tone.

'It's been a long and difficult day for them,' Maisie observes, instinctively discounting any toll it might have taken on herself. She knows it will count for nothing anyway, with Pamela; it's all about the children with her. 'And I must say, they did behave so well.'

'I'll have a rummage for Dad's papers tomorrow,' Dominic announces, rekindling the question. 'I don't want you bothered with any admin. You'll be too busy.'

'Busy?'

'Well,' it is Dominic's turn to indicate the miscellaneous lengths of timber leaning in the corner, the jumble of screws littering the worktop, the cluster of paintbrushes sprouting from jam jars on the window ledge, all stiff and gluey and beyond any kind of use. As Maisie's had earlier, his gesture incorporates the entire house too—its rooms crammed with the remnants of Clifford's repair projects, his innumerable caches of assorted tools, his waste-not way of thinking that prevented anything from ever being thrown away. 'Won't you want to have,' he pauses, reluctant to touch a raw nerve, 'a bit of a sort out?' he concludes lamely.

His mother picks up one of the hot water bottles and checks its stopper. 'I think that's a bit of an understatement, Dominic,' she says grimly.

Chapter Five

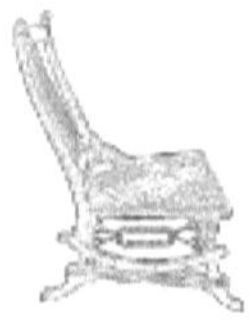

Being alone in the bed is very strange. Maisie keeps scrupulously to her own side, curled around her hot water bottle, but the chill of Clifford's absence creeps across the sheets like icy water. Since Frances' arrival on the night of his death, she had occupied the space. Not particularly to give emotional support but because, she said bitterly, 'My room has been taken over by Dad's stuff and, in any case, it's bloody freezing.' Not that this room has escaped invasion or, frankly, is much warmer. But, over the years, Maisie has managed to pressgang the interloping trappings into use—arranging, for example, her toiletries along the treads of a wonky set of ladders that has leant for ten years against the chimney breast—so that it appears marginally less like a bric-a-brac shop and more like a proper room. The shared companionship in the bed with Frances had generated a kind of warmth. But Frances is gone now, back to Oxford on the evening train and Maisie is alone, really alone, for the first time since Clifford's demise.

It isn't just the heat of his corporeal presence she misses. Lying now amongst the odd assortment of broken chairs and spatchcock candelabra and boxes of bits and pieces bought at auction for a song, without the clear projection of Clifford's vision to light up for her what they *could be*, they appear more grimly than ever as what they *are*: junk, utterly worthless tat. The white elephant in the room—in the whole house—is depressing beyond words; as cold and inescapable and appalling as a pool of vomit, and her stomach lurches and turns when she thinks of it.

Impatiently, she turns over in the bed, shifting the hot water bottle down to her feet where the sheets seem at their most arctic. She won't think of it, she tells herself. Best not to. Try to stay positive.

But the image won't be shut out. The awkward, tumbled shadows of queer accumulations seem to press down on her. The whispers of dusty trappings drift and swirl in the air and cling to her, as the rain had at the funeral.

In the beginning it had been the sheer intensity of Clifford's vision that made it impossible for her to arrest the tide of his acquisitions. He believed in his vision as ardently as any mystic in his holy revelation: Old Farm Hall, beautifully restored, sumptuously furnished with authentic pieces, a living testimony to his skill and patience and taste, the envy of all. Its eventual realisation had been perfectly vivid to him—his own capacity to bring it into being unquestioned. And, in spite of initial misgiving, Maisie too had found her doubt bowing to the ardour of his faith. She had become an acolyte—albeit an agnostic one—carried along by the ferocity of his passion. Apart from the fact that she had been too kind to disabuse him—she simply didn't have it in her to tell him that his vision was a hollow, unachievable fantasy—she had been desperate to believe it herself. To believe that, against all odds somehow, someday, Clifford's dream would become a reality. Ridiculous, she now sees. Like a theatre set with the house lights up, the illusion is revealed as so much paint-daubed plywood: insubstantial, unreliable, temporary. A not-very-clever artifice designed to trick and beguile, but not to last.

She reaches across and pulls Clifford's pillow a bit closer. His pyjamas, which she ironed earlier and placed, without thinking, underneath it, feel comforting under her hand. There is no use denying it. Clifford isn't the only one who has passed away. His dream has gone too and with it, her power to believe. As she committed his bodily remains earlier to the flames, so it is left to her now to consign the tattered remnants of his delusion to rest.

Chapter Six

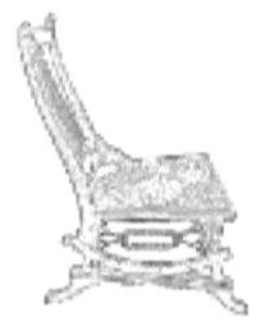

Clifford had bought the house at an auction. He hadn't told Maisie beforehand that he was going, let alone that he intended bidding, and the legalities were all tied up before he took her to view it.

'It was an absolute steal,' was all he would say. 'Nobody else wanted it. I got it for the reserve.' He was almost intoxicated with glee. The triumph of having got a bargain had been potently mixed with the satisfaction of having done it entirely on his own—those two ingredients proof of his unshakeable belief in himself as a maverick high-flier shamefully overlooked by the world at large.

'But where is it, Clifford?' she'd asked, shifting the infant Dominic from one shoulder to the other. 'Are there any shops nearby? And what about school, for when Dominic is older?'

'In the ordinary run of things we'd never be able to afford a place like this,' Clifford replied, ignoring her questions. 'It's detached, in its own grounds, completely private. Nobody will bother us.'

'It sounds lonely. Is it in the country?' Maisie, who did not drive at that time, and who was by nature a sociable creature, dreaded such isolation.

'It might as well be. You'll be the lady of the manor. We'll have a better house than anyone we know. Get yourself ready quickly or we'll hit the traffic.'

'We don't *know* anyone,' Maisie muttered under her breath, sliding Dominic into his pram suit. Clifford's standoffish nature had made developing friendships very troublesome.

'What's that?'

'I said we won't know anyone.'

'It's only on the other side of town, Maisie; we're not emigrating!'

He drove her across town into a semi-industrialised area she wasn't familiar with. The mills and factories looked in poor shape.

'They all look empty,' she commented, trying to hold back a tide of gloom. Dominic had fallen asleep. A nap now would take the edge off his weariness and make his sleeping through the night a remote probability.

'Of course they do!' Clifford cried. 'It's gone six. Everyone's gone home. But as a matter of fact, this is a regeneration area, earmarked for millions of pounds' input from the EU. This is the way I come to work,' he went on, 'so apart from anything else, it's going to make my commute a good deal easier.'

'Oh?' Maisie's interest was piqued. She had never seen Clifford's workplace. She indicated the dour warehouses around them. 'In one of these buildings?'

'No. Over this hill the road drops down to the quays. They're being regenerated too, partly, into a marina with some posh apartments and shops. Harrington's is beyond there, near the docks.'

The road started to climb. Below them, the lights of town began to flicker into life. Looked at through narrowed eyes they looked fantastical, like a faerie encampment. It was a technique Maisie was finding more and more useful; squinted at, life's hard edges and chasms of disappointment seemed less severe.

At the top of the hill a development of new houses brightened the prospect and Maisie wondered—but briefly—if all Clifford's talk had been a joke and they were to move to a nice estate of new homes where other young mothers like herself would become her friends. But before the site could be reached Clifford swung the car abruptly off the main road and they plunged down what seemed like a narrow ravine, the car jolting over cobbles and potholes, its sides scraped by reaching branches from the hedge.

'See! See!' Clifford crowed. 'Didn't expect *that* did you?'

Dominic, thrown around in his car seat, woke and began to cry.

'No.' Maisie said it automatically, but it was a lie. This, in all its bleakness, was *exactly* what she had expected.

The house, when they reached it with a sharp right turn through iron gates held akimbo by moss-encrusted boulders, was large—she had to give him that—although, in the gloaming, it was hard to make it out properly, and no glimmer of light shone from within.

'Are the owners out?' she asked, stepping timidly across the uneven surface of the drive.

'It's empty,' Clifford replied, shining a powerful torch across its frontage. It was drear indeed, rendered in forbidding grey, like a Victorian correctional institution. There were two deep bay windows on either side of an arched porch. One of the panes was broken; a board, roughly nailed over the frame, had a rude word scrawled across it. Maisie grimaced. 'Anyway,' Clifford added pedantically, '*we're* the owners now.'

'Oughtn't we to look around outside, while there's still a bit of light?' Maisie asked, but Clifford was already up the three shallow steps to the porch and pulling a bunch of keys from his jacket pocket. The door was warped. He had to wrestle with the handle and eventually give it a sharp kick before it opened. They stepped in, onto floorboards that were bare apart from strewn sheets of newspaper and a lot of mouse droppings. Clifford flicked the light switch several times in an attempt to wear down its recalcitrance, but clearly the power was off.

'How long is it since anyone lived here?' Maisie asked in a hushed, museum voice.

'Years and years.'

'It'll be damp. It may even be structurally unsafe …' She began to back out of the door, clutching Dominic to her body.

'Now, now, Maisie. Don't start,' Clifford warned sharply, 'you haven't even looked at it, yet,' although she had already come to terms with the absolute redundancy of raising objections,

He walked away from her into one of the rooms, taking the torch with him and leaving her in the semi-darkness. Dominic, awake now but, like his mother, awed into silence by the eerie hush and heavy gloom, gave her a baleful stare.

'It's a project,' Clifford said, with a determinedly positive tone from the other room. '*I* can't wait to get going.' In the stillness Maisie could hear the dry rasp of Clifford's hands being rubbed together in glee. His slight emphasis suggested to her that she ought not to allow herself to lag behind in her enthusiasm. There was no point anyway, was there? It was a done deal. She would have to make the best of it; a talent with which, thankfully, she was abundantly blessed.

What light there was filtered through the glazed panels on either side of the door. They were thick with dust and laced with cobwebs but through the murk she could just see the outlines of tulips and frondy greenery worked in stained glass. To her own surprise the word, 'pretty,' bubbled to her lips.

From the hall a wide bare stair rose to the first floor. On either side of the hall reception rooms would have views over the town if the stiff shutters were pushed back, and the last rays of evening light would perhaps have softened their dismal, neglected appearance. But as it was, only the yellow eye of Clifford's torch gave her any sense of their accommodations. The ceilings were high, and elaborate cornices and ceiling roses spoke of a past time of elegance and quality.

'This was the Armstrongs' place,' Clifford said, with a note of awe in his voice. 'You must have heard of the Armstrongs. At one time, they had a hand in nearly everything that went on in this town: haulage, metal fabrication, several pubs. Old man Armstrong built this place for himself when he was in his heyday. It was the envy of all his competitors …' But whatever élan the rooms had had in their prime was now all but obliterated by patches of flaking plaster and dark blooms of mould.

'Is that who you bought it from? Mr Armstrong?'

'Not the old man. He's long dead. The two sons let things slide. There's a grandson now, a whippersnapper—hardly any older than you. He's selling off all the property bit by bit. It's a mistake. *I* wouldn't be so quick to offload property. But if *he's* daft enough …' Clifford played his torch across the space. A thick network of dusty cobwebs and a heavy fall of soot in the fireplace were briefly illuminated. In the bay window, a drift of dead leaves crackled under Maisie's feet. An ancient nylon sleeping bag, a dozen rusty beer cans and some other bits and pieces that Clifford quickly kicked out of view suggested that squatters or a tramp had been using the place at some point.

'I suppose they came in before they boarded up the window,' she muttered, referring equally to the leaves and the homeless people.

'Yes, yes, I expect so,' Clifford agreed briskly. 'Let's find the kitchen, shall we?'

The kitchen showed further evidence of illicit occupation: empty food tins rimed with mould and an old burned saucepan on a wobbly table; a blackened kettle on a huge, greasy range; graffiti scrawled across the wall. But it was a large room and, although north-facing, had two wide windows that would make it pleasantly light. The windowsills were deep and filled with dead bluebottles, but Maisie had a sudden vision of them lined with pots of growing herbs. Their fresh greenness and pungent smell somehow pressed the shadows and filth back. She looked around the room again, allowing the image to lighten its grimness. Once properly fitted out, it would certainly be a splendid place to cook and serve the family's meals. She crossed the floor, feeling the grooves of its ancient flags beneath her thick-soled shoes, and lifted the latch of a narrow door.

'Clifford, shine the torch in here a moment, please.'

Yes, this dank storeroom and that chilly larder would provide even more space—perhaps, Maisie speculated, a dedicated laundry room. 'They would need white-washing,' she said aloud.

'Of course they will, and shelves, too,' Clifford agreed with a smile which, though sly, was not lost on Maisie.

From the other side of the kitchen a passageway gave access to a smaller room with a blocked-up fireplace, and a tiny lavatory. 'According to the sales particulars this was the housekeeper's room,' Clifford said.

'A housekeeper? How old is the house, then? Victorian?'

'Edwardian. But there's been a house on this plot for centuries. It was a farmhouse when Armstrong bought it. He demolished that and built this. That's why it's called Old Farm Hall. Has a good ring to it, doesn't it? We'll be the Wildes of Old Farm Hall.'

'It sounds like something out of Dickens or Bronte,' Maisie said, pushing away the thought that it was pretentious and a bit ridiculous, since the house was neither especially old, nor a farm, nor a hall.

At the end of the passageway was the door through to the garage, but it was padlocked and none of the keys Clifford had would fit. 'Damn!' he grunted. 'Wouldn't you just know it? The *one* thing I especially wanted to see.'

'Did you? Why?' Of all the rooms to explore, the garage was of the least interest to Maisie.

'Because of my *things*,' Clifford mumbled, 'my things from *before*, in the lock-up. They can all go in there, out of the way.' The things from Clifford's early life were a mystery to Maisie, beyond the fact that they existed and were stored for the time being in a storage warehouse somewhere. Clifford went regularly to check on them but had never offered to take her with him. She assumed they consisted of boxes of photographs and perhaps a few heirlooms that had belonged to his parents. But Clifford never spoke of his childhood, and his parents had passed away "long ago." When she enquired about his youth and early adulthood he had brushed her questions away.

'Ah,' she said now, 'yes, your things. I see.'

'And anyway,' Clifford went on more confidently, on surer ground, 'I'll be doing most of the renovations myself. I'll need somewhere to work and keep my tools. A proper workshop.'

In her head—she knew better than to list them out loud—Maisie ran through a list of things that would need to be done to the house: wiring and plumbing; no doubt several structural repairs; window replacement, obviously; damp and woodworm treatment; perhaps also remedies for wet and dry rot; heating; before the cosmetics of decoration and kitchen fittings and sanitaryware for the bathroom. Surely all those things would require professionals. And, she reflected wryly, a good deal of money. Then the place would need furnishing, carpets … The medicinal verdure of fresh herbs faded, leaving her feeling chilled and a bit sick. 'Clifford,' she began hesitantly, 'now you've really had a look at the place, you don't think that maybe it's going to be a bit much?'

'Rubbish. It's just common sense, most of it. Nothing even an averagely able handyman couldn't tackle. And in any case,' he went on, giving Maisie a distinct sense of burnt bridges, 'we can't go back. I've signed the contract. Shall we look upstairs?'

But it was pitch dark when they got upstairs and even Clifford's torch could do no more than establish four good sized bedrooms and a box room on the first floor. The bathroom was large, with antediluvian fittings, but infested with ivy that had encroached through another broken window. The floorboards were spongy with damp. The stairs up to the attics also looked unsafe. Maisie declined to trust them at all and Clifford only reported 'two more good sized rooms and a smaller bathroom,' before they made their wary way back down to the hall.

Standing on the outside steps while Clifford locked the door, Maisie peered into the shadows across the driveway. It was properly dark now. Any possibility of seeing the gardens and the wider environs had disappeared. The thrash and clash of branches in the autumnal winds denoted many trees; *that*, at least, was positive. There would be birds and other wildlife to watch. Maisie like that. Through their canopy, as she had suspected, she could see the wink and glimmer of the town's lights far below, but what lay beyond the boundary of the trees was a mystery. To the left she could just make out the distant growl of traffic passing the end of the lane and heading, she presumed—with an envious stab that took a moment to conquer—to the pristine, orderly homes on the top of the hill. But to the right of her? Further down the steeply sloping lane? What was down there? And behind the house, would there be gardens? Greenhouses? An orchard?

'Is there a garden?' she asked, as Clifford strapped Dominic back into his seat.

'A good acre. You'll have to come back on the bus, now you know where it is, and have a look in the daylight. I won't have time to bring you again until we move in.'

'And when will that be?'

'Oh,' he tilted his head on one side as he groped to get the key in the ignition. 'Christmas?'

Chapter Seven

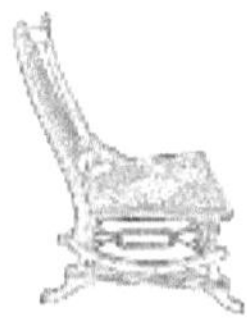

In the morning Dominic and Maisie set about the search for his father's Will. They begin in the garage, which Clifford purported to use as his workshop, although in actuality his numerous ongoing repair projects are spread all over the house. Piles of tacks, the trailing leads of power tools, precarious tins of varnish, missing floor-boards and heaps of rubble tended to spring up overnight, as though placed there by a maintenance team of malicious house-elves.

'Nobody but your father ever came in here,' Maisie says. 'Even I didn't. If I brought him tea or sandwiches, I never ventured further than the door.'

'I was always rather afraid of what might be inside,' Dominic admits. Throughout their childhoods the children had always been strictly debarred with dire warnings of dangerous chemicals and sharp blades. 'I was glad he kept it locked. Gareth always itched to see what was inside though, didn't he?' The prohibition had worked as a powerful draw for the youngest, most adventurous child.

'Oh yes, as a small boy he used to loiter outside the door shouting, 'What are you doing, Dad? Can I come and help? I want to see. I promise I won't touch anything.' Maisie sighs. 'Clifford never would let him in though.'

'Do you know, Gareth once told me that as a teenager he wormed his way through the garage window? I don't believe him though.' The sheer audacity of such an act is far beyond Dominic's own cowardly imagination, but the black irony—that for all the ominous admonitions rained by Clifford upon the children, it has been Clifford himself who met his doom there—is not lost on either of them as they venture over the threshold.

'I hardly know what to expect, do you?' Maisie asks, with a nervous attempt at laughter. 'A collection of porn, perhaps? Whips and shackles?'

'Mother! That's absurd.'

The fluorescent light is defunct, its cover brown and melted in the fire, the tube itself exploded and adding to the litter of soot and ash on the floor. A scorched sheet pinned limply across the window filters out any natural light, but even in the heavy gloom the amorphous collection of tools, boxes of screws and nails, paint tins, buckets, assorted timber—all smoke blackened and charred—are a disappointment. Only an old armchair—its coverings and stuffing gone, its springs exposed—and a small electric heater, give any hint of a pastime other than the relentless repairs and repurposing that Clifford always claimed occupied his time. Fastidiously avoiding the spot on the floor in front of the shelving where the death occurred, they make a cursory search of the drawers of the workbench—empty now, the recalcitrant geyser having been removed for forensic analysis—finding only more tools, tangled nests of wire, various plumbing accessories and an anachronistic jar of marbles, but no Will and no sign of any legal documentation. Suddenly the nauseating smell of burnt debris and the thought of Clifford here in this filthy, ordinary den are insupportable. They turn and hurry out, Dominic wiping his hands on his handkerchief while Maisie secures the padlock.

They have better success in one of the front rooms, which would perhaps in an ordinary house have been a sunny drawing room or comfortable lounge, and in fact Dominic voices a dim memory of this room with proper furniture.

'Didn't we use this room at one time? I seem to remember a Christmas tree in the corner.'

'You would have been very tiny.'

Indeed, the recollection is so distant that it might as well be a dream.

Dominic struggles over an avalanche of Screw-Fix and Machine Mart catalogues to fold back the shutters from the bay window.

'I doubt they'll open,' Maisie warns. 'They've been closed for ...' she considers, '... fifteen years?' But in fact the shutters open without difficulty, revealing a thick mat of cobwebs, but allowing pale winter sunshine to illuminate the room's contents. Maisie stands in a shaft of it, full of dancing motes, seeing the things in the room as though they are a new and appalling revelation. At the same time they are so well-known as to go almost without remark. She struggles with this bizarre familiarity while Dominic clambers over the catalogues to rejoin her. They both know that other people's homes are not like this, of course—Dominic's own home, for example. Although untidy with the children's paraphernalia and in dire need of redecoration that he has neither the time nor the money to tackle, it is nothing at all like this. But for this house, this is normal, and indeed they are as used to these things as other people are to a great-aunt's heirloom whatnot that has stood for time immemorial at the turn on the landing.

Stacks of cardboard boxes, three deep, are ranged against one wall. 'What's in here? I forget …' Dominic lifts a flap on one of the boxes. 'Oh! That's right. Readers' Digest.' A chopper bicycle leans against the boxes alongside a crate of assorted bicycle parts with which Clifford had always intended to repair it, but never had. Both tyres are perished beyond use and the chain is stiff and seized. A heap of black bin liners makes a pyramid against the fireplace; they know without looking that the bags contain a musty jumble of hideous, moth-eaten soft toys. The bags, Dominic points out, are new—evidence of his father's continuous programme of checking, sorting and cataloguing.

'That lot would give Jessica the heebie-jeebies if she was ever to clap eyes on them,' Dominic says. 'Frances had hysterics when Gareth played some trick on her with them one Hallowe'en.'

'They'll all have to go,' Maisie says heavily.

Various road signs—No Entry, Children Crossing, Road Works Ahead—are propped in a corner with a collection of yellow lanterns used to demarcate road works at night, plus a dozen traffic cones and box of cats' eyes. A fan of copper bed-warmers, like a fistful of out-sized lollipops, leans against the chimney. Several chamber pots are stacked nearby. Perhaps twenty tarnished brass oil lamps balance on top of a wrought iron plant stand. God only knows where they came from, or what use they would ever be to anyone, but once acquired they remained—like everything Clifford brought into the house—immovable and inviolable.

Alongside this well-known paraphernalia are some new acquisitions. Items of scratched, wonky furniture, an ugly umbrella stand with various skeletal umbrellas and walking sticks, an old space invaders game, the relic of some pub. Banana boxes stacked eight or ten high contain a cornucopia of tarnished electroplated silver tableware, mis-matched crockery, broken watches, some ugly ornaments, paste jewellery and frames containing photographs of total strangers.

They are both suddenly assaulted with it—the enormity of the task ahead. Impulsively, Dominic says, 'Mum, don't you think it would be a good idea for you to come and stay with us for a while?' He knows as soon as the words are out of his mouth that he shouldn't have said them, at least not before consulting Pamela.

'Don't you think I'd like that?' Maisie says whitely. 'But afterwards, it would still all be here, and still all to do. No, darling. I need to get started with it as soon as possible. But thank you.'

To avoid the bladder of anguish that swells between them, Dominic launches himself into his father's stock, squeezing with difficulty between a section of a bar complete with beer pumps and a scarred upright piano, and climbing over a thick roll of malodourous carpet.

'Here's his desk!'

It is large metal affair pushed into the corner, its surface a litter of old Betamax videos and eight-track tapes and the innards of an archaic telephone answering machine. He pulls the top drawer. It is full of rubber bands, gluey old batteries, paper clips, biros, rolls of Sellotape and blobs of rock-hard Blu-Tak. 'Nothing in this drawer,' he reports. But in the bottom drawer he finds what he is looking for, his father's files, meticulously organised as he always knew they would be. There are much annotated bank statements going back years and years, marked with ticks and crosses and spidery notes, dozens of cheque book stubs tightly bound with elastic bands, the registration documents, MOT certificates and insurance schedules for the current cars and each one they had ever owned in the past, insurance documents for the house and contents and, at the back, a file cryptically labelled "Misc," containing life insurance documents and his father's Will. He flaps it at Maisie across the room, stirring a tornado of dust particles into the air. 'Got it!'

'Good,' she says, wiping her hands on her apron. 'Well that was easier than I expected.'

'I *knew* I'd find it,' Dominic crows as they enter the kitchen. Pamela is occupying the girls with a jigsaw. Maisie picks the whimpering baby up from his rocker and begins to pace the floor with him.

'Are *you* going to make lunch Daddy?' Jessica asks hopefully. She is bored, and food is increasingly becoming her panacea when things become dull.

'I've already told you,' Pamela says tetchily, 'it isn't lunchtime yet.'

'I didn't know he'd made a Will,' Maisie says, shifting the baby from one shoulder to the other.

'You've made one too! Here it is!' Dominic cries, waving a second envelope.

'Have I?'

'You *must* remember signing it, Mum.'

Maisie gives an airy wave. 'Your father did ask me to sign things sometimes. I never asked what they were.'

'Whoever drew these up ought to be stood against a wall and shot for mal-practice, then,' Dominic states authoritatively. 'They're supposed to read them through to you and *watch* you sign—'

'Dominic,' Pamela murmurs, 'don't be so pedantic.'

'Well,' he bites back at her, 'if she doesn't remember doing it, it probably isn't valid.' He inserts his thumb under the seal of one of the envelopes and withdraws its contents.

'Are you going to read that now? Shouldn't the others be here?' Pamela cautions, but Dominic is scanning the paper, a single sheet.

'Hum, well, I suppose that explains it,' he mutters. 'This is a DIY Will, the kind you get from a post office—'

Maisie laughs dryly, 'DIY! What else did you expect, of your father?'

'It's properly witnessed—Cyril Hendrix—was he someone at work? I suppose it's legal, but it'll have to be proved…'

'Proved?'

'By the Courts, for Probate.' Dominic, his face oddly stiff, puts the sheet of paper back in its envelope.

'What does it *say?* Pamela asks irritably. 'Now you've read it, you might as well tell us. Are you the executor?'

'No.' Dominic stares glassily at the jigsaw on the table. Typical of Pamela, it is educational—a map of the British Isles showing points of cultural interest. Jessica is busy trying to force Lindisfarne into the place where St Michael's Mount ought to be. Edmé is sucking York Minster.

Maisie leans over and points to a gap. 'Look, Edmé darling, see if that will go here,' she says gently. Then, in the same tender tone, to Dominic, 'Who *is*, then, if not you? Who else could possibly be up to it? Can you explain what it says to me, please?'

Dominic turns to look at her. His eyes are swollen with hurt tears that his pride will not allow to fall. His upper lip, rather thin, quivers. 'He seems to have expected you to do it all yourself,' he gets out. 'And as far as I can tell, everything he has goes to you.'

'Such as it is,' Pamela puts in.

'Nothing at all for … the children,' Dominic croaks. 'And clearly, he didn't trust … any of us to carry out his wishes.'

'When is it dated? You might all have been children yourselves at the time.' Even as she says it, Maisie is conscious of reverting to a default setting she has of defending Clifford.

I suppose it isn't really necessary anymore.

'Only a year ago, in fact.'

'That will be when we paid off the mortgage.' Maisie perches herself onto one of the kitchen chairs. The baby, who likes to be kept moving, begins to grizzle, but she puts one hand out and soothes Dominic's shoulder as though he is the one whinging. 'Whatever the Will says, sweetheart, I'll need you to help me. As you said last night, I've got enough on my plate here.'

Dominic looks slightly mollified. 'There are some documents here. I don't know what they might be. A lot of them seem to be the things that come through the post offering you free stuff if you take out a policy.'

'Well, you know your father and freebies …' Maisie throws a glance over at the arm-chair. All the junk mail had to be pored over and assessed, vouchers for free things and discounts snipped out, special offers weighed up, prize draws entered … Now she'll be able to chuck it all straight into the recycling like ordinary people.

'If you write me a letter of authority I can find out if there's anything of interest.'

'Of *course*. Whatever you think, sweetheart.'

'Although,' Pamela hisses through pursed lips, 'you do have exams coming up and if you don't pass them *this* time—'

'Oh dear, well …' Maisie looks from one to the other of them. Clearly she can't please both.

Possibly sensing the tension between the adults, the baby begins to cry in earnest, throwing his head back and thrashing his arms. Edmé, who has not slept well and wants to go home, also dissolves into tears and for good measure wets her knickers. Jessica, by dint of bending one of the jigsaw pieces, manages to cram Stonehenge into Scotland. 'It *must* be lunchtime *now*,' she sighs.

Maisie and Jessica make cheese on toast while Dominic leads Edmé upstairs to look for some clean clothes. Pamela takes the baby through to the little sitting room to feed him.

'And are you going to stay in this big house now that Granddad's dead?' asks Jessica, striding out into territory the rest of the family has hesitated to trespass upon. 'Wouldn't you like to live in a little flat like Grandma Brenda, with lots of other old people for company?'

Maisie, who is only forty-six, baulks at the idea. 'I don't think so, sweetheart. But as regards this house, I really haven't decided, yet.'

Chapter Eight

Clifford's estimate of their likely moving-in date had proved wildly optimistic. They had not moved into the house by Christmas, or anytime near it, although Clifford spent every weekend there and some evenings after work as well. He never took Maisie with him, claiming she and Dominic would only get in the way.

However, not very many weeks passed by before Maisie made the first of a number of clandestine visits, changing buses in town, forcing the pushchair with difficulty down the rutted surface of the lane, through the overhanging greenery and between the rusted gates. On the first of these visits she paused on the drive to persuade herself that she had been exaggerating the house's awfulness. In the interim that had passed since their first, twilight visit, the house had assumed in her mind a rather malevolent aspect, featuring as the ghastly, ghostly setting of gothic horror—impossibly derelict, ruined beyond habitation, dangerously unstable and surrounded by dour mills and deserted warehouses. But daylight—particularly the greyish, rain-laden light of winter—did nothing to eradicate her prejudice. Its grey stucco and sagging gutters gave it an intensely forlorn and dismal appearance.

It took all of her courage to put the key into the lock. Without Clifford's pragmatic companionship, the sense of being an interloper was almost overwhelming and she crept warily from room to room, fearing that a vagrant or an addict would emerge from the gloom of one of the shuttered rooms. But all evidence of trespassers was gone and she gained in confidence as she moved through the house. It was true that in daylight the enormity of the task in front of them seemed even more daunting— yellowed, peeling wallpaper, ominous patches of damp where clearly the roof had leaked; outmoded Bakelite plug sockets and light switches; the electrics must be prehistoric. But the actuality was by no means as bad as her imaginings. Already there was evidence of Clifford's industry. Soggy plaster hacked off walls, rotten treads removed from the attic stairs, the invading ivy repulsed from the bathroom. She viewed the stock of building materials he had amassed as a hopeful sign: timber, cement, plaster, paint, not dismayed—as, perhaps, she should have been—by his erratic approach to the works, being a little here, a little there, with many things begun and few things completed. The tap in the kitchen yielded water when she turned it. The toilet in the housekeeper's suite was operational. A meagre heat emanated from one or two of the radiators. The sour smell of damp and decay had virtually disappeared. These things being so, obviously the house was habitable; they would not starve, or freeze, and it seemed sound enough structurally. Clifford was right; there was nothing that diligent repair, hard work and a good scrub could not put right.

And certainly, looked at in terms of its size and style, it was a house which, under ordinary circumstances, they could never have aspired to. She ought to feel proud to own it. And perhaps, she admitted as she leant against the window ledge in the front room and viewed the high skirtings, the ornate cornice, the impressive fireplace, she was beginning to feel that pride a little. It had been—it could be again—a lovely house, a home. She presumed Mr Armstrong had brought his wife there and raised his children—two sons, Clifford said. They had lived elegantly and prosperously. There was no reason why she and Clifford could not do the same.

The front windows of the house remained shuttered. Those giving views to the rear and sides were filthy, and the rain that had threatened earlier now lashed them into opacity so that any view of the garden, let alone the opportunity to explore it, was out of the question. Putting that off for a future visit, she proceeded to the garage where she noted, Clifford's mysterious 'things' had arrived. They were less numerous than Maisie had anticipated—four of the old-fashioned wooden tea chests that people used for moving house before cardboard boxes became the norm. All were tightly packed with items carefully wrapped in newspaper—newspaper that was, interestingly, not many months old. Maisie assumed Clifford had re-packed things in preparation for moving them from the lock-up. There were suitcases also, two of them, old leather ones with reinforced corners, balanced on top of the sort of trunk which, in days gone by, in films and in books, children took to boarding school and aristocrats took on trans-Atlantic steam ships. She resisted the temptation to probe although itching to do so. Perhaps Clifford would ask her to help him unpack, and would tell her about his treasures as they unwrapped them, one by one. All of these items were carefully placed at the foot of a wooden stairway that led to some first-floor accommodations—possibly a chauffeur's quarters—above the garage. There was also a vast array of tools. Some of them looked very antiquated indeed, others brand new: screw-drivers and pliers and socket sets and chisels, a plethora of hammers of every shape and size, spanners ranging from miniscule to enormous, crow-bars and mallets and other implements the purpose of which was beyond Maisie's imagining.

Leaving the house in a lull between showers, she ventured further past the old gates of the house and down the lane to see what lay beyond. The lane—already pot-holed and rutted—became, if possible, worse; cratered with deep, mud-filled chasms, treacherous with broken glass and rusted metal. Finally it petered out altogether into a rubble- and rubbish-strewn wasteland. She worried briefly about fly-tippers or even an influx of Travellers, but a sturdy chain-link fence that protected a collection of derelict single-storey buildings bore dire warnings of twenty-four-hour security patrols, CCTV and guard dogs, so she put her mind at ease on that score—clearly, someone monitored the area. She assuaged the impression of ugliness and neglect by telling herself that there would be no passing traffic; the children, if they were blessed with more, would be able to play out in safety, and the whole area was blocked from view of the house by trees and hedging. So that was good.

To the right of the lane towards the main road, stretching down past the house and beyond, was a narrow but densely planted belt of woodland. It gave privacy and provided a good screening to the urban landscape below. Beyond the trees, the land had been cleared of whatever had been there before—warehouses, perhaps, or mills. The ground was rough with broken bricks and masonry. Clifford had mentioned something about European investment and regeneration. She wondered what would come. But the trees, surely, would remain; and if you looked at them, and listened to the wind in the branches, it created the illusion that you were out in the middle of a vast rural landscape. The muted roar of traffic passing at the top of the lane, the whoosh and swoosh of tyres on the wet road—Maisie cocked her head to listen—sounded like the rush of waves on a shingle beach.

She was suddenly conscious of a torrent of positive energy, a bright buoyancy. 'We'll make it right,' she announced to Dominic, 'we *will*, your daddy and me.'

Chapter Nine

Dominic and Pamela and the children depart for Nottingham and Maisie spends her first night alone in the house. The next day she gets up with something of the same optimistic spirit that had gripped her all those years before. It is a matter, she has decided, of going at it in the same way she always has, with humour and determination, keeping her eye always fixed on a far point of final achievement. She has found that, looked *over,* seen *past,* the impediments are less daunting. And so they will be again. She will just throw herself into turbo-reverse and gradually undo what the years with Clifford and his obsession have accumulated. She will strip it all away, layer by layer, with the same fortitude and sanguinity, until she is back at the start, at the place before things went so awry.

In a victorious metaphor for her plan, she strips the antiquated camp beds of their sheets and blankets, disengaging their awkward catches and stiff hinges before hauling them downstairs and out onto the woodpile for sawing up. Their gangling, dangling wooden struts are like broken bones, their discoloured canvas like leathery hide. They shift and buckle, almost reproachfully.

'There,' she says fiercely, aloud into the wintery day, 'you're for the burner, it's all you're fit for.'

She goes back indoors and puts the sheets in the wash. The little laundry room has been whitewashed once and a shelf or two installed, but without any source of heat and no ventilation it is no place to get anything dry, so she stocks up the solid fuel Aga and drapes the sheets over a maiden in front of it before going out. The house's heating system is at the top of a long list of issues that Clifford never satisfactorily sorted out; satisfactorily to *her,* that is. *He* had been perfectly content, and at times even rather smug about his 'eco-friendly' system of solid fuel stoves with back-boilers, and dismissed her complaints about the lack of adequate hot water and the additional dirt and hard work they entailed as 'environmentally egocentric.'

She has to hand it to him: he has provided her with enough firewood to last a lifetime.

The European millions for regeneration have manifested themselves into a shopping centre on the site of the old quays, past the housing estate and down the hill, and Maisie sets out on the short drive to Tesco's, passing the exclusive car dealership and a collection of business units that the same funding has provided on the sloping land below Old Farm Hall. Driving from the old-fashioned house past these evidences of modernity always makes Maisie feel like a time traveller. She can never decide whether they—with their reinforced steel and acres of plate glass—or Old Farm Hall itself—architecturally obsolete, swathed in ivy and darkly-shuttered—present the oddest anomaly; past and future unaccountably coinciding in the present.

In Tesco, Maisie buys the thickest roll of black bin bags she can find, and several pots of herbs. When she gets home, she clears all the old jam jars from the kitchen window ledges, chucking away the gluey, ruined paint brushes and putting the jars in a box for recycling. She cleans the windows before arranging the herbs along the sills. Then she makes herself a cup of tea and sits at the kitchen table admiring her handiwork.

'It's a start,' she says out loud to the empty, impossibly crowded house.

Chapter Ten

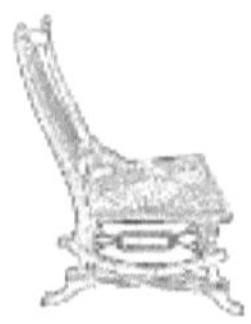

In the attic, the shrill of the telephone from the extension in the bedroom is barely audible. Maisie, who has only just squashed herself with difficulty and some discomfort between an outmoded Singer treadle sewing machine and an eviscerated console radiogram, gives a groan. She looks despairingly at the dusty bolts of fabric that have become wedged behind the machines as the phone rings on and on. The space is laced with sticky cobwebs—a well-stocked larder for some enterprising spider offering a smorgasbord of desiccated bluebottles, butterflies and moths. She is tempted to ignore the call. By the time she clambers over various cardboard boxes, squeezes past a tailor's dummy and moves the elaborate artist's easel in the doorway she feels sure the caller will have given up. Likely as not it is only someone trying to sell her something anyway. As if she needs *more* rubbish! She waits. Surely, *surely* they will give up? But no. The telephone rings relentlessly on and on. Suddenly she has the idea that it might be one of the children, that there could have been an accident, and scrambles over boxes, past jumbled heaps of unidentifiable detritus, negotiates the steep attic stairs and hurries to the phone.

'Hello?' She presses the receiver to her ear with one hand, wiping the other, grey with dust, down the front of her apron.

It is Frances. 'Can I bring a friend home for Christmas?' she asks without preamble. 'Where have you been? I've been ringing and ringing.'

'I was in the attic. Of course you can!' Maisie cries automatically, subconsciously glancing at herself in the square of mirror that she keeps propped behind the—defunct—Teasmade. She notes a smear of dirt across her cheek. Her hair, when she runs her hand through its neglected curls, feels sticky, like the cobwebs. 'And I think, by then, you'll see some improvements—'

'Humph!' Frances says doubtfully.

But in fact there *is* progress, although coming up with a workable system has taken a while. Tackling the hoard by type had seemed a sensible plan. Paper first. The Period Homes magazines and Reader's Digests, the Screw-Fix catalogues, the telephone directories, the newspapers, the junk mail … but it was squirrelled all over the house. Three days of scrambling over furniture and obsolete electricals and bin-bags of God-knew-what to get at the papers, and then struggling to haul them back out again had exhausted her both physically and emotionally. Her determination and good humour all but evaporated, uncovering a raw residue. Her sadness at the ruin—Clifford's devastated vision, and the wreck of her own hopes that were so attendant upon it—has taken on a bitter, almost angry quality, a simmering frustration that brought tears more than once. She finds herself muttering resentful imprecations under her breath directed at *him* as much as at his stuff. It doesn't feel right. For a person so imbued with natural cheer and resilience, these sensations feel foreign and unsettling.

So, she changed tack, and decides to clear a room at a time, starting with the kitchen. Now the work surfaces are free of clutter, the windowsills burgeoning with herbs. The Welsh dresser, usually obscured by Clifford's on-going repair projects, displays a nice collection of Blue Willow crockery that had been Maisie's aunt's, packed away in newspaper since their move to Old Farm Hall. The boxes long incumbent beneath the table have disappeared, their place on the flagged floor taken up by a thick rug in surprisingly good condition discovered rolled up on the landing. The mountain of newspapers behind the door has been reduced by half, revealing a row of coat pegs where Maisie's gardening fleece and everyday Macintosh and apron are neatly hung. The chair by the Aga has been cleared of junk mail and is adorned by a pretty patchwork cushion.

It is a pleasure to return there after a day spent on her hands and knees rummaging amongst Clifford's jumble elsewhere in the house. It is clean and neat, and she can wash her hands and take off her apron and enjoy being free of the nasty, gritty residue that seems to cling to everything. She has taken to sitting there in the late afternoon with a cup of tea and her library book. Quite often—after the exertions of sorting and hauling—she dozes off, but as the comfortable exhaustion overtakes her weary limbs, she likes to look around the newly cleared room. Now the lengths of gash timber habitually stashed in the corner have been sawn up and stacked in the log-store; the plethora of widgets and tools, odd screws and broken hinges have been taken away and the nests of knotted string, gluey jam jars and little heaps of wood shavings have all gone. It is almost like a normal kitchen. 'By Christmas,' she says now, aloud to Frances, 'I hope to give the kitchen walls a coat of emulsion; that will make it a cheery setting for the festive meal, won't it?'

'I'd have thought the state of the décor was the least of your priorities, Mum,' Frances replies drily. 'If it's too much trouble for you, we won't come.'

'Oh! I've been making inroads in other rooms too,' Maisie cries. The sitting room—the room they had always referred to as the housekeeper's parlour—is almost presentable. She had always tried to keep it a clutter-free zone, a place where she could entertain any callers—had there been any—and where she could relax without the impediments of plaster-dust and rubble or the impingement of the encroaching trove. But in spite of her best efforts, Clifford had, from time to time, been successful in inveigling items into it. 'This will be useful for you!' he would say, manoeuvring a superfluous table into a tight space, and, 'This will cheer the place up for you,' laying a balding rug down in front of the hearth. A large set of stamp albums, bought cheaply and brought into the parlour to be examined during the evenings had remained, untouched, totteringly stacked in one corner.

But now these and other items of Clifford's contribution have disappeared. A neat, glass-fronted cabinet that had been pushed into the attic and forgotten about sits against one wall, containing a few cookery and needlecraft books and some framed photographs of the children. The ugly oil paintings hung by Clifford have been replaced by cross-stitched cottages and English country gardens of Maisie's own working. A plain but unobjectionable standard lamp stands in the corner where the stamp albums had been stacked. The frayed fabric of the old settees has been covered with beautifully crocheted afghans unearthed from a crate in the attic and carefully laundered.

'The sitting room is quite presentable, and I've made room for the tree,' she tells Frances, summing up her endeavours over the past few weeks. 'This friend, is it another of the exchange students?' During her first degree course Frances seemed to have befriended—or been saddled with—several foreign students, most with very rudimentary English, some with bizarre dietary requirements. Frances had brought them home from time to time for weekend visits. What these monosyllabic, tofu-eating house guests had made of the peculiar situation at Old Farm Hall Maisie had never known, and certainly they had been too polite —or linguistically unable—to do anything other than express gratitude for such hospitality as the Wildes had meted out. But since Frances embarked on her PhD these visits had ceased. And in any case Clifford's chattels had taken up occupancy of Frances' old bedroom, both beds now covered with antique golfing paraphernalia, box upon box of old vinyl records and a quantity of moth-eaten fur coats. The window ledge, if she recalls correctly, is home to a vast collection of old ordnance survey maps. If Maisie re-directs her efforts from the attic to Frances' room, surely she can make some impact on it. 'Will you mind sharing with her? There isn't really anywhere else I could ask a guest to sleep.'

There is a momentary pause. In her mind's eye, Maisie sees Frances chewing the inside of her cheek, a habit she has when deciding whether to turn awkward. 'We won't mind sharing,' Frances says at last. 'But it isn't one of the overseas students and, well, as a matter of fact, it isn't a girl.'

'Oh!' Maisie is momentarily taken aback. She hasn't expected *that!* Frances has always been of a serious, perhaps even slightly sullen bent, and with her awkward, lanky frame and lack of interest in clothes and make-up, Maisie always thought her rather sexless. But she recovers quickly enough to gush, 'How exciting, Frances! I can't wait to meet him,' as though she has been daily expecting such an announcement. She determines to consider their sleeping arrangements none of her business.

It always amazes me that people are so quick to throw things out. It's as though they don't value them at all. Having things doesn't seem to matter to them, unless they are new things. Don't they know how lucky they are?

When you've never had much of your own, you appreciate things more, I think.

I just knew there would come a point when people would be sorry they had thrown out all their vinyl records. You can usually find a few of them in a box at the back of charity shops, and there is always a man—a bearded, earnest type—crouched over it, flicking the sleeves over one by one. Behind him is usually another, or sometimes two more, politely elbowing each other out of the way, craning over the first chap's head to see.

You see, people *want* things like that. Deep down. They might think they're old hat, too bulky and prone to damage, but when you get down to it records represent things to people—memories. It isn't just the music on them, it's the vinyl, the sleeves, the hiss of the needle in the groove, the ball of fluff that collects behind it. It all takes them back in a way that a row of CDs just won't. By then, when they realise, it's too late. The regret must be almost unbearable.

As I said, I saw it coming, so I took to buying them up from car boot sales and at house clearance auctions. I'd get them for a song. No. Don't laugh. I didn't mean it as a joke. I don't do jokes. And this is no laughing matter. Those records will be worth a fortune one day. In fact I've been thinking I might turn one of the downstairs rooms into a music room. I can set up the record player and speakers in there and Maisie and I can sit in the evenings and listen to the songs we remember from when we were young. Although, of course, she's a lot younger than me so her favourites might not be mine. And now I think about it, she never was much of a one for discos and dancing, and neither was I. So perhaps I *will* sell those records. But I ought to sort through them first. There might be some I want to keep.

I got the fur coats off a woman whose mother had died. 'Nobody wants these nowadays,' she told me. 'It's criminal. They cost hundreds of pounds, and that was years ago. But now people don't want to be seen in real fur. Brigitte Bardot has a lot to answer for.'

I rather thought I'd like to see Maisie in a fur coat. 'I'll take them off your hands,' I said. But when I got them home Maisie wasn't keen. 'They aren't for women like me,' she said, 'and in any case, it's frowned upon now. People prefer fake fur.'

But I think that fake fur will go the same way as the cassette tape and the CD, so I'll hang on to those coats.

The maps? Let me think. They came from an auction along with a few other bits and bobs. Always interesting, aren't they, maps? And you never know when you might be visiting a place … I think it's almost the complete collection too, which is satisfying. I once read about a room that was entirely papered with maps. It was in the *Reader's Digest*. It might have been The White House … I'd have to look it up. I keep all the magazines so I'll have it somewhere. But that's an interesting idea, don't you think?

I keep lots of magazines about houses. They're full of good ideas—things you'd never think of yourself unless you've travelled and seen lots of styles in different houses. When you've got a blank canvas, like we have, you can do anything you want, more or less. It's just a matter of deciding which dream to choose. But there's no rush, is there?

Chapter Eleven

A week before Christmas, Maisie makes a friend, which is something of a new departure. Clifford had not been what you might call a sociable type. He distrusted strangers to the point of paranoia, accusing door-to-door salespeople and canvassers of being thieves and confidence tricksters. 'They're only casing the joint,' he had warned darkly, 'ready to come back when we're out and rob us blind. Some of them will take your purse in front of your very eyes.'

He had disliked casual callers. 'It's rude and inconvenient when people call in unannounced,' he had said once, when the parents of a boy Dominic was friendly with had done exactly that. Maisie's early suggestion that they might invite people over for meals had been met with resistance.

'Who?' he had asked incredulously.

'I don't know,' she had shrugged. 'People from work?'

He'd laughed, a hard bark of humour. 'You must be joking.'

'What about that chap who helped us move. Ted? You seemed very pally with him.'

'Oh yes. Ted's alright. He doesn't do *dinner parties* though Maisie.' Clifford had made it sound as though she was proposing a royal banquet.

'It wouldn't be anything special, just supper,' she'd argued, adding unnecessarily, 'in the kitchen.'

'No, I don't think so, love.'

The children, for a while, had invited school friends over. What tales their friends had carried home—of lavatories out of action and bedrooms accessed via ladders, of inefficient heating and makeshift arrangements for the cooking and consumption of meals—she could not guess. Then, as the children reached their teens and became more observant on their visits to normal homes—and as Clifford's obsession took a stronger hold—they had asked friends in only rarely, leading them apologetically through the canyons carved into the stacked miscellany in order to scale the scree of boxes and tools on the stairs up to their rooms.

Maisie didn't blame them, and in time she too gave up on social aspirations, not wanting to expose their accruing cache to the public eye. As a result, she had become somewhat solitary, making visits to the shops, the library and school events only as necessity demanded. Helping out with PTA events, she had listened to other women making arrangements for lunch and coffee with an envious ear.

Clifford did not like her to be away from home. He would fret if she left him on his own. When she got back, he had always needed her for something—to hold a ladder or fetch a tool. He said her absence held back the works. During the week, while he was at work, he would question her closely. Was she going out? Where to? What for? And afterwards, had she been alright? Had she found somewhere safe to park? Who had she met? The outside world took on a slightly threatening aspect for her. She had caught—from him—the idea that it wasn't quite safe. Now, after his death, she has been forced to overcome this phobia by doing things such as unloading her car at the tip—often the only woman, sometimes the only person apart from the council operatives, or making telephone calls to the utility companies to get the accounts put into her own name, obliged to speak to strangers.

This obligatory therapy has been effective. The outside world, whilst sometimes bewildering, is nothing to fear.

The previous week she staggered into the charity shop with her umpteenth load of donations. By this time she is such a frequent visitor that she is on first-name terms with most of the volunteers. Gwen Barker, the supervisor, is a square, homely woman in her early sixties. A mannish hair style, austerely utilitarian quasi-military clothes and a bluff, no-nonsense manner all disguises a kind heart and sympathetic mien. She took one of the bulging bin bags off Maisie and led her through to the sorting area at the back of the shop where women in bright yellow rubber gloves deftly sorted through the new stock.

'Here I am *again!*' Maisie cried with a half-humorous self-deprecating groan—sure that was what *they* were thinking—hefting the other bin bag onto the table. 'I'm so sorry! You poor things must be sick of the sight of me! I *have tried* to spread it around all the charity shops but yours is the only one with a car park.'

The women in marigolds made gestures of polite denial while Gwen hooted, 'Heavens above! *We* aren't complaining! Those LPs have been flying off the shelves as fast as we can put them out, and I've got a dealer coming in to look at the coats. Apparently she ships them all to the Continent; people there aren't as squeamish about real fur. She's offering very decent money, I must say. What with that and all the other things you've brought, our takings are through the roof!'

'Well, there's plenty more where this came from!' Maisie had laughed recklessly, quelling a sinking sense of having let Clifford down. Perhaps she should have been selling his stuff rather than giving it away? But even that, she realised, was wide of the mark. What *he* would have done with it was precisely nothing at all. She flopped down into a convenient chair with a sigh. 'But I think this will have to be the last until after Christmas.' In truth, the prospect of one more day battling Clifford's trove was more than she could face.

'Look, dear,' Gwen had said gently, 'if there's a lot more you want to donate, we can arrange to collect it. If you wouldn't find it intrusive we could even send volunteers round to sort and pack as well. In some ways, it's easier than doing it here.'

'Oh! I don't know,' Maisie demurred. If there was one thing that would be worse than having to disassemble Clifford's hoard herself it would be watching others do it.

'Why don't I pop round and assess things, at least?' Gwen urged. 'You've been so generous. There must be some way we can help.'

True to her promise Gwen drops in, bringing a dozen homemade mince pies and two jars of bramble jelly. She thrusts these into Maisie's hands with a lack of grace Maisie is to learn is typical with her, but a kind intention that is characteristic also.

Maisie leads her through the hall, past an up-ended, threadbare ottoman, a defunct pinball machine and between teetering stacks of decrepit odds and ends brought from remote corners for sorting, into the kitchen. There she looks Gwen in the eye with an expression look that is an exact balance of courage and shame and says, 'You don't have to pretend. I know what you're thinking.' She has been anticipating the visit with trepidation, as one does an intimate examination at the doctor. It is embarrassing to expose the full horror of it all to a stranger, but necessary.

'Goodness,' Gwen cries, shrugging out of her gabardine and hanging it next to Maisie's Macintosh, 'I'm not thinking *anything*, dear.'

'You *will* do, when you've seen it properly,' Maisie predicts, 'but what the hell? It is what it is. Let me make some tea and then I'll give you the tour.'

Mugs in hands they move from room to room, Maisie like the curator of a mothballed museum of outlandish artefacts, lifting dust sheets and prying open boxes, helping Gwen over impeding remnants to point out particular exhibits in all their marvellous potential and utter uselessness, outlining their place in Clifford's overarching dream which he—and they—have failed to realise. Gwen takes it all in with an awed, sympathetic silence.

On the landing: 'This sideboard—enormous, isn't it? What a struggle we had to get it up here! So cumbersome and heavy! It stood for years in the hall. I'd got quite used to squeezing round it to get to the kitchen. See how the drawers need repairing? And the legs are wonky?'

'Yes. And some of the drawer handles are missing.'

'That's right. Glass. Pretty, aren't they? Clifford wanted to restore it and put it in the dining room. And really, it would have looked very well in there. That's the thing about a large room—you really do need large furniture. Clifford was right about that.'

Gwen beetles a bushy eyebrow, 'So … why didn't you put it straight into the dining room?'

'Ah yes! Well that would have been the obvious course of action, wouldn't it? And we did, at first. But then Clifford started to use that room as his workshop. And then—well, come along and you'll see.'

In the dining room: 'It's a greenhouse, one of the old timber-framed types. You can see the frames all stacked up against the wall, behind the old sinks and that collection of fire irons. All those bricks—in the bay window, there—they're for the base. And in these bags here—all the hinges and window catches. They'll all be there, you can sure of that. Clifford was meticulous. I think he got it on Ebay. I know he had to hire a van and it took three trips to fetch it all from somewhere in Wales. If he'd ever got round to putting it up it would have been enormous, perhaps too big, even for a big garden like ours. But yes, the timber's all rotten.'

'But my dear,' Gwen bursts out, 'why was it ever brought in here? It doesn't belong inside! What were you thinking? Look how it crumbles when you touch it. It's probably riddled with woodworm. Or dry rot.'

Maisie groans, 'Oh God! It doesn't bear thinking about does it? And it's been leaning against this wood panelling all these years! I wonder if he realised. I know. I hear what you're saying, but you didn't know Clifford. There was no arguing with him. He wouldn't listen to reason.'

'Hum, well …' Gwen blows her nose into a man's handkerchief. 'I suppose growing your own veg is very laudable,' she says, to mitigate her earlier outburst.

'Oh yes. He had that idea *years* before all that became fashionable. For an old-fashioned man he was well ahead of his time, in some ways. But as long as it was here in the dining room, there was no point tackling the sideboard. And that's how it was with everything. You couldn't finish one thing before another had been dealt with. And that thing was held up by something else ... so, in the end—'

'Nothing got finished?'

'Yes.'

Somewhere in the house a clock strikes the hour. 'Good Lord, is that the time?' Gwen checks her watch.

'Oh no,' Maisie shakes her head. 'The house is full of clocks but none of them tells the right time!'

Gwen laughs. 'I feel a bit like Alice. Have I fallen down a rabbit hole?'

'How do you think I feel?' Maisie says dolefully.

Gwen stares around the room, stupefied. Looking at it through her eyes, Maisie sees more vividly than ever how bizarre it is. Her explanation of Clifford's rationale sounds ridiculous, but she ploughs on with it, like a confession of dirty secrets. Now she has started, she can't stop.

In the front room: 'Reader's Digest. Yes, *all* of these boxes. They just kept on coming. These are just the magazines. All the books are upstairs in the attic. Clifford never even read them although he always intended to, one day. But you know there's always a prize draw and Clifford said, statistically, the more we ordered, the better chance we stood.'

In the attic: 'These bags? Full of old clothes, I think. Nothing that anyone would want to buy; they're full of moth holes. Clifford planned to use them as insulation. Cheaper than rock wool and more environmentally friendly, he said. Green-thinking again, you see? But they do take up a lot of space, don't they? And they block out all the light from the window so you can't really see that this is actually rather a nice room. But it's junk really. I know that.'

In the garage: 'The fire never really got hold, but you never know, the joists may have been weakened so we'd better not go up those stairs. Clifford brought those crates over when we married. They were in a lock-up before that. I haven't a clue what's in them. No, I never did find out much about his early life. We had a Registry Office wedding, very quiet. Neither of us had any family.'

Afterwards they sit in the housekeeper's parlour. Maisie switches on one bar of the electric fire to keep the chill at bay, and the lights of the little artificial Christmas tree cast a kind of cheer onto a situation which seems unspeakably grim. Gwen manages to command her sense of utter shellshock only by emitting it in controlled explosions of sympathetic amazement. 'Well, well! Did you ever? A heck of a thing! My, my!' before asking, 'Where did it all come from?'

'What you need to understand is that at first it all seemed very reasonable,' Maisie begins. 'We needed furniture. This is a big house and the few bits I got from Aunt Sarah's place just weren't enough. We couldn't afford to buy things new and in any case the age of the house precluded anything modern, so Clifford started going to those house-clearance auctions. It seemed like an ideal solution. It was quite exciting, in fact, to see what he would come home with, and usually it cost next to nothing.' Maisie's eyes shine briefly with the memory. She would be working in the garden, keeping her eye on Dominic who was toddling by then, with Frances asleep in the pram, but her ear cocked for the sound of Clifford's car on the drive. Then, when he arrived, she would hurry round to help him lift things out of the car. Lovely things sometimes, if a little battle-scarred: a drop-leaf table with barely-warped barley-twist legs; a useful dinner wagon that only needed new casters. 'But often,' Maisie goes on, talking almost to herself, 'you couldn't buy just individual items—you had to take a job-lot so we ended up with things we didn't need. How we used to laugh about them! Oh! I don't know, things like flea-riddled taxidermy and hideous hats and one time even an urn of somebody's ashes!' She presses a tissue to her eyes. Gwen laughs too, but doubtfully. 'I expect we've still got it, somewhere,' Maisie shrugs. 'It wouldn't be the worst horror, I can tell you!'

'Really?'

'Well, perhaps the ashes *would* be the worst! But things really hit rock bottom when Clifford started going to car boot sales. He'd go off to look for something quite specific—a washer or fixing he couldn't find in the shops—and come back with the car filled with all kinds of rubbish, I mean really just tat, only fit for the dump. But when you listened to Clifford's rationale, I don't know, he just had a way of making things seem so reasonable. He developed a sort of mantra. "It'll be useful." "We might need it." "People will pay good money for these." And then, increasingly, "I can turn it into something else." Re-purposing, he called it. He liked to think he was saving the planet. You never knew Clifford but he was so determined, so sure about *everything*, that you just got swept along.'

'I just can't imagine how you coped,' Gwen cries, 'let alone brought up a family in the midst of it all. Of course, I've seen this house as I've passed by, and … well, to be frank, I was surprised—and I wasn't the only one—it wasn't compulsorily purchased when they built the pub.'

'Clifford would never have agreed. But it doesn't surprise me that there's local speculation about the place. No doubt we've been labelled as reclusive eccentrics.'

Gwen's blush tells Maisie she is right. To cover their joint embarrassment she makes more tea and does not object when Gwen produces a hip flask from her handbag and laces their cups with a generous dose of spirit. 'You need it,' Gwen declares, 'after all you've had to cope with. In fact I'm surprised you're not a confirmed alcoholic. *I* would be, in your shoes.'

Maisie offers the biscuit tin with a wan smile. 'I can see how odd it all looks from the outside,' she admits, 'but what you need to see—what *I* can see—behind and beneath all the …' she gropes for the word, ' … the *spoils*, is Clifford's intention, his vision, which was always true.'

'True?' Gwen splutters.

'Yes! Well, it *is* wrong just to waste things and throw them away, isn't it?' Maisie replies a little defensively. 'They *might* come in handy at some point. And sometimes unsolicited mail *does* turn out to be interesting or useful, so it's worth keeping just to look ... ' she trails off lamely, realising she is simply reiterating Clifford's arguments. 'But of course I see that it all got out of hand,' she finishes quietly.

'But I wonder,' Gwen muses, almost to herself, 'I wonder what was *behind* it all.'

'So do I, sometimes. Now, I mean, since he died. Now I can see it for what it is.'

Gwen brushes crumbs from her lap and announces, 'What's obvious to me is that you need help sorting it all out. You've got to be practical. There's more here than one person can possibly handle. *Way* more. Do let me help you. I mean as a friend, my dear. I have a couple of days a week when I'm not too busy, and I can commandeer the van from the shop. Also, I know the local auctioneer, he's the church treasurer. You never know, your husband might have been right, some of these things *may* be valuable.'

Maisie, to her own surprise, begins to cry. Gwen launches herself with a shout of concern from the settee and envelopes Maisie in a matronly hug. 'My dear, my dear,' she croons, 'really you mustn't upset yourself over a little offer of help.'

'Oh no,' Maisie manages to hiccough through her tears, 'it isn't the help, it's the friendship.' Although in fact the offer of help has also touched a nerve.

Over the past few weeks she has begun to feel an increasing sense of utter hopelessness which, for a woman who managed to remain positive and ebullient even in the face even of Clifford's mania, is alarming. In response she redoubled her efforts, getting up earlier and working until later into the evening. Her stolid determination metamorphosed into a kind of desperation, at times rabid and all-consuming. She finds herself sometimes heaving furniture and almost hurling boxes with an air of hectic urgency, heedless of her personal safety. She has taken risks by scaling unstable stacks, delving frantically beneath unsteady piles, as though some injured person or a forgotten hostage was trapped beneath, dependent solely on her efforts for release. This sense—non-specific but quite tangible—of rescue, of *saving* something or someone, has become a driving force. But as often as she might pack up the car and trundle off to the tip, as frequent as her visits to charity shops have been, still the hoard shows no signs of shrinking. Every night she goes to bed with a feeling of having failed, of not having grasped the wasted hand that lies somewhere beneath the ruins, of not having heard the parched dry voice that calls from below the surface. Indeed, her burrowing and delving have only shown her that the top layer is merely a constraining lid on a bottomless and ever-expanding interior. Things are contained *within* other things; buttons stored in jars, the jars contained in shoe boxes, the shoe boxes crammed into suitcases, the suitcases draped with layers of old carpet.

Gwen stays for supper. They empty her hip flask and polish off most of a bottle of sherry that Maisie bought for making Christmas trifle. Swept along by the tide of giddiness, the two talk themselves into intimacy. Gwen, it turns out, had married and then divorced five years later, her husband turning out to have a nasty streak she had been unprepared to accommodate.

'I'm thankful there were no children,' she admits, 'at least, most of the time.'

She had worked as a PA to the managing director of an engineering company until taking voluntary redundancy. Since then she has occupied her time with the local scout troop and various charities including one that supports abused women. Now, on a modest pension and with a small inheritance from her father, whom she had brought to live with her and nursed through a protracted illness, she lives frugally but happily, dividing her time between the charity shop where she supervises the volunteers, the local church where she acts as warden and a group of similarly circumstanced women friends with whom she lunches, plays whist and goes on occasional coach holidays.

'You must join us,' she gushes, sloshing the last of the sherry into their glasses as they relax after supper. 'The more the merrier! We've all been through the mill a bit, one way or another. Of course I won't betray any confidences but I'm sure they'll tell you their tales sooner or later.'

'The truth is I'm not sure how I'm placed financially,' Maisie admits. Dominic has still not reported back on his investigations. 'Lunches out and holidays might be beyond me.' She nods at the single bar of the electric fire. 'Even this little luxury might be beyond my means, for all I know.'

'But surely,' Gwen helps herself to another sweet from the tin Maisie has opened, 'surely you'll sell, once you've cleared the place,' she says through chocolate and nougat. 'Is there a big mortgage to pay off?'

'No,' Maisie confesses. 'No mortgage at all. When Clifford was sixty the endowment matured and we paid it off.'

'Well there you are! You'll get a reasonable price for this, buy yourself something small and easy to maintain.'

Maisie smooths the creases from a sweet paper and folds it up into smaller and smaller squares. 'Who'd want to live here?' she objects reasonably. 'I mean, it isn't everyone's cup of tea, is it?'

'A developer would probably pay a mint,' Gwen suggests. 'It's a perfect site for an hotel, I'd have thought. All these businesses round about and, you know, there isn't anywhere decent to stay in town.'

'You might have something there,' Maisie muses, but a niggling disquiet at the suggestion resolves itself into a quick, hot jealousy. She doesn't like the idea of the house being bulldozed and the prospect of her precious garden being turned into a car park is abhorrent. 'Everyone assumes I'll sell up and move. My granddaughter asked me if I was ready for sheltered housing!'

'You aren't old enough,' Gwen puts in. 'They won't look at you until you're fifty-five.'

'Of course selling would be the sensible thing,' Maisie concludes, in a tone that implies that, although sensible, it is by no means a foregone conclusion.

When Gwen has gone, the returning silence in the house is eerie. Maisie has a powerful sense that somewhere in the house Clifford is crossly restoring order to his collection, resentful of her earlier intrusion and feeling betrayed. She moves from room to room, unnerved and a little guilty, folding back into place the lids of the boxes she has disturbed.

" "

EBay is like everything in life—you pick it up as you go along. I got some really good stuff, but I must admit that one or two things were white elephants—even to me; not that I would let Maisie know, she's so easily discouraged. The greenhouse was probably one of those. The pictures the chap put up had been taken years before and when I got to his place he'd already taken it to bits and not as carefully as I would have liked. But what can you do? I'd hired the van by then. So I loaded it up and brought it home. I'm sure I can do something with it, and I will do, in time …

The auctions are better. They generally have a viewing day so you can go and give the stuff a really good look-over. I don't know, I get a sort of feeling about things. They sit there looking all lost and forlorn—abandoned—suddenly up-rooted from the houses where they'd sat for years and years, now unceremoniously jumbled together. No one will ever know their stories. I feel like I'm rescuing them, giving them a new start. I know it's sentimental, but somebody has taken time and trouble to make them—sweated over them, exercised all their skill and patience—and there's still so much use in them …

I don't like the way other bidders look at things—they're cold, somehow, and they narrow their eyes wondering how much money they'll make if they do it up to sell. They yank open the drawers and jiggle the shelves and even turn them upside down, sometimes! Well. It isn't very respectful, is it? Me, I like to run my hand over the wood-grain and stroke the upholstery. I hunker down and give things the gentle once-over.

I know the porters —Cyril Hendrix, he's one of them—and if I can't make it to the auction myself, they'll put a bid in for me, then it will be exciting to drive over after work and see what I've got. There have been one or two surprises, but it doesn't matter—look at all the space we've got! Cyril got the sideboard for me. That was years ago, mind. It's a beauty, isn't it? He borrowed the auction house van to bring it over and helped me get it inside. It started off in the dining room but then we moved it into the hall—I needed the space. It lived there for a while before we moved it somewhere else. I need to make new runners for the drawers and do something with the legs. It isn't a big job, really. It won't be anyway, once I get round to it. But there's no point in starting when I haven't got all the bits. I've been scouring car boots and bric-a-brac shops hoping to find matching handles for the drawers. Something will turn up. Then I'll do it.

Car boot sales can be even worse. I mean, that's the last-chance-saloon, isn't it, for most of that stuff? If it isn't sold it will go straight to the tip. Most of it really is on its last legs. It looks so woebegone and bedraggled. The people who are selling it don't take much time and trouble to present it in its best light, usually. It's just plonked onto trestle tables and picnic rugs. I always think it must be mortified to be exposed in all its tarnish and grime, picked up and sneered at and put down, rummaged amongst. It must feel like those blokes on death row; doomed and hopeless. But if you're like me and have a vision for these things, you'll know that lots and lots of stuff can have years of use if you can turn it into something else. Old clothes, for example—especially woollens—make excellent insulation and are much nicer to work with than rock wool.

I got a letter from Reader's Digest the other day; apparently I'm progressing through the prize draw rounds. It won't be long before my number comes up, I can tell you …

Chapter Twelve

Frances and her friend arrive the day before Christmas Eve. True to her intention, Maisie has cleared Frances' room of all Clifford's things—an even bigger task than she'd anticipated. In addition to the coats, the records, the golf clubs and the maps, the wardrobe was packed to the gunwales with hundreds of jigsaw puzzles. She found several cardboard boxes under the beds filled with old till receipts—all scrupulously arranged in date order—which had to be burned, and about fifty copies of *Period Homes* that she took to the paper recycling dumpster behind Tesco's. Beneath a concertina of continuous computer printout and an avalanche of sewing patterns she unearthed bundles of feathers meticulously sorted and labelled by type—chicken, pheasant, pigeon, crow—counted and tied into sheaths of twenty. There were innumerable margarine cartons containing lolly sticks. He must have been picking them up from the streets, Maisie realises, staring at them in amazement; certainly, we never ate that many ice lollies, even when the children were small. A dozen jam jars crammed with obsolete coinage—also carefully categorised and counted, their contents noted on neatly placed labels—completed the haul.

Maisie laundered the curtains and gave the room a thorough clean, delighting in the floor free of debris and the view over the garden through the unimpeded windows. Making up the beds with freshly ironed sheets, she hesitates about whether to push them together and make them up as a double or leave them as twins. In the end she leaves them separate but removes the small chest of drawers that stands between them.

It isn't up to me to make any assumption, one way or the other, she says to herself as she places a Christmas cactus that has just come into flower on the window ledge, and a bale of clean towels on the chair.

Frances and her friend emerge from the last carriage of the train, both dwarfed by enormous rucksacks and a hefty suitcase that they pull between them. Frances looks flushed and bright-eyed, 'almost pretty,' Maisie thinks as she gives her a hug and tries to commandeer the suitcase.

'It's far too heavy for you. Maxim will manage it,' Frances says, indicating her companion. It is as much of an introduction as they are going to get, clearly.

Maisie smiles and holds out her hand. 'How lovely to meet you. It's so good of your family to spare you over Christmas.'

'Maxim's family is spending Christmas on a yacht in the Caribbean,' Frances puts in, suggesting, rather unkindly Maisie thinks, that Maxim's absence will not be missed amidst such luxury.

'I'm sure they'd have liked him with them, wherever they are,' Maisie retorts. 'Come along then. The car isn't far.'

Maxim grins and grasps the suitcase. He is clearly more than up to the task—tall and thick-set, with a round, cheerful, rather florid face. In Maisie's opinion he wears insufficient clothes for the northern climate in winter: a creased linen jacket over a seersucker shirt and cream chinos more suited to Christmas in the Algarve.

'I hope you've got some thick woollies and thermals in that suitcase, Maxim,' Maisie gushes, deciding that a mother-hen approach is going to be the best way to proceed. 'This is the North, you know!'

'Please, *please* don't say that you're sure there'll be something at home he can borrow,' Frances interrupts. 'Maxim doesn't wear other people's *jumble.*'

'Fran!' Maxim mutters, with mild indignation.

'Of course not,' Maisie cringes. 'I wasn't going to suggest any such thing.'

Maxim's physical capacity notwithstanding, it takes the concerted efforts of all three of them to get the suitcase into the back of Maisie's little hatchback.

'Why didn't you bring Dad's car?' Frances asks testily.

'I never thought about it,' Maisie stammers. 'It's still sitting on the drive where he left it.' True, Clifford's estate car would have been much more practical and now Maisie thinks of it, could have made the process of distributing his damned trophies around easier too. The realisation, as well as the confession, makes her feel inadequate and pathetic. Frances obviously concurs and clearly she is ashamed of the house.

I wonder why she even brought him here, Maisie thinks. Aloud, with a small spark of face-saving retaliation, she says, 'I may not be insured for it.'

'Well *that's* lame,' Fran declares.

'Fran!' Maxim says again, louder this time, and beetles his brows.

'What have you got in the case anyway darling? Presents?' Maisie asks, too brightly, to cover the awkwardness.

'Books,' Frances replies, but with temporarily diminished vehemence. 'I've got *so* much catching up to do, not to mention my doctorate to finish. I'll have to study for most of the vacation, assuming there's a square meter of space for me to do it in. But I'm afraid,' she goes on, with a renewed dash of astringency, 'my bursary hasn't stretched to much in the way of presents.'

'Oh dear,' Maisie murmurs. If Frances is going to be buried in her books then who will entertain Maxim?

Frances wrestles ineffectually with her backpack, her expression morphing from doleful to thunderous as the possibility of getting everything accommodated looks more and more remote, winding herself up into one of her tantrums. Maisie's heart quails at the thought.

But Maxim, undaunted, says, 'Look, Fran, it's no good struggling with it. If we can't get both rucksacks in we can leave one in the ticket office and come back for it later.'

'Good God!' Frances shouts derisively. 'This is Millport, not Adlestrop! Any left luggage will be listed on eBay in twenty minutes!'

But in fact, by folding one of the back seats flat they do manage to finagle all the luggage and the two passengers into the car, with Frances crushed uncomfortably in the back, glowering.

Maxim closes the hatchback with a firm hand. 'We *both* have work to do, Mrs Wilde,' he observes mildly, as though reading Maisie's earlier thought, and with an air of throwing oil on troubled water. 'I've got an interview at the foreign office in February, so I need to get up to speed on international affairs.' His voice, though deep, is pleasantly mellifluous, and his words are accompanied by a meaningful smile that Maisie is unable to misinterpret. 'But it won't all be work and study.' His eyes—iris blue—give a significant glance into the back of the car before he seats himself in the front and settles his rucksack between his knees. 'I'm delighted to be here and determined to enjoy myself.'

As Maisie negotiates her way out of the station car park and enters the one-way system that snakes though the town, he observes the scenery with mild interest, paying no attention to Frances fulminating in the back seat or to Maisie's occasional selection of the wrong gear.

What a nice young man, Maisie thinks; and rather disloyally, I wonder what he sees in Frances?

It is almost dark by the time they get to the house. The fairy lights Maisie struggled to put round the front door cast a feeble cheer. The office blocks opposite—deserted now for the Christmas period but still brightly illuminated—look more festive. As she puts her key in the door she knows with a sinking certainty that Frances being in the mood to find fault, the weeks of work on Clifford's collection will be found wanting—either Maisie has made insufficient progress or, conversely, has gone much too far, wantonly disposing of treasures. Braced herself for criticism, Maisie and is not surprised to hear Fran's bitter salutation, 'Welcome to Steptoe's Yard' as they enter the cluttered hall. Maxim makes no response at all but busies himself with manoeuvring their bags past the paraphernalia on the stairs and through the chicane of assorted furniture, washing machine parts and cast-iron fire surrounds on the landing to their room.

'I'll get the kettle on while you settle in,' Maisie calls after them with forced airiness, resisting the temptation to follow them up the stairs. She will forego witnessing Frances' pleasure—surely?—at finding her room completely free of detritus, in order to avoid overhearing further derogatory remarks.

But when the two descend to the kitchen some ten minutes later it is an altogether different Frances who steps across the scrubbed flagstone floor to gather her mother into an embrace. She is soft and full of comfort, like a cushion that has been plumped, and almost giddy, a dash of high colour illuminating each cheek. 'Mother, you're a marvel!' she exclaims, keeping an arm around Maisie but looking around them at the tidy worktops, the inviting chair, the walls newly painted in soft cream. 'You've done brilliantly!'

Maisie chokes back a tear. 'Do you think so? And your room?'

Frances sighs. 'Our room is wonderful. *Normal.*'

'Very comfortable, thank you Mrs Wilde,' Maxim puts in from the door. The linen jacket has been replaced by a thick Aran sweater. He wears slippers, a sure indication that he means to consider himself thoroughly at home.

He looks down at himself with ironic concern. 'Am I suitably attired for a country house holiday in Northern climes?'

'Hardly,' Maisie jests. 'Where're your flat cap and whippet?'

'I expected to be issued with those at the border,' Maxim rejoins. 'Is that not the procedure, Mrs Wilde?'

'Don't encourage him, Mother,' Frances scolds, but gently.

Maisie beckons Maxim forward, drawing him into their hug. 'Please do stop calling me Mrs Wilde. I'm Maisie.'

Over tea, and then later as they enjoy a meal washed down with a bottle of wine, Frances and Maxim describe their meeting and courtship. 'We locked eyes over a crowded lecture theatre,' Maxim smiles. 'Frances is a creature of habit—you must know that—so she always sits in the same seat. I spent two months moving row by row, seat by seat, until I was sitting next to her; and even then it took me two weeks to get up the courage to actually speak.'

Maisie laughs. 'You don't seem like the shy type.'

'I'm not, ordinarily, but Frances is just terrifying—you must know that too,' he jokes.

'Oh *you.*' Frances shoves him playfully.

Later, Maxim and Maisie wash and dry the dishes while Frances watches the last episode of a documentary series she has been following.

'You have a very beneficial effect on my daughter,' Maisie observes.

'She has a very beneficial effect on me,' Maxim replies chivalrously, but with a twinkle. 'I hope there'll be a chance to look around the garden tomorrow,' he goes on quickly. 'Fran says you've done wonders with it.'

'Oh!' Maisie almost quivers with pleasure. 'Did she? Fancy her even noticing! But yes, if I say so myself, I have worked something of a transformation. When we came it was—well, not to be corny—pretty 'wild!"

'And now it's Wilde,' Maxim laughs. 'And the other thing about tomorrow, I should just mention, is that there's likely to be a delivery.'

'How exciting!' Maisie gasps. 'What of?'

'Well, first of all, my parents are bound to have ordered a few things to contribute to the table. I hope it won't cause an inconvenience. They're the last people to realise that by Christmas Eve you will have planned the menu and stocked the fridge and that an influx of unexpected provisions can only cause problems and duplications.'

'The fridge *is* groaning,' Maisie agrees, 'but fortunately we have a chilly larder where things stay pretty fresh. I'm sure they mean it kindly. What kind of thing will they have sent?'

'Oh, you know, *foie gras*, smoked salmon, brandy butter, champagne truffles … '

'Oh well!' Maisie hoots, 'I think I can safely say there won't be any *duplications*!'

'And there might be a haunch of venison.'

Maisie blanches at that. 'Really? I wouldn't know what to do with that,' she admits.

'I know. I'm sorry. Sheer thoughtlessness on their part. They expect everyone to have a staff of people who can deal with these things.'

'Do *they?*' Maisie squeaks.

'They just don't want me to be a burden on your housekeeping,' Maxim says, diplomatically ignoring her question.

Do they think I'm a pauper then? Maisie wonders. But perhaps I am.

She still has no news from Dominic. But pushing that worry aside she says aloud, 'I'm sure they mean it very kindly and generously, but really it isn't necessary at all. You're very welcome here with us, Maxim, and you must make yourself at home.'

'I *feel* welcome,' he says with a smile, folding the tea towel and hanging on the Aga rail, 'and at home. Thank you.' And then in spite of this assertion, he looks for a moment rather uncomfortable. 'And in addition to the groceries, there will be some gifts that I have taken the liberty of ordering for the family, for the children mainly.'

'Oh but …' Maisie interjects. She has wrapped a couple of things for Maxim, safe—unexceptional things like toiletries and chocolates, but she doesn't think that Pamela will have thought of bringing anything for him.

Maxim holds up his hand, 'Just tokens, nothing embarrassing, but also some things for Frances, which I'd like you to keep hidden, if you can.'

'Oh yes,' Maisie thrills. 'I *love* surprises!'

Chapter Thirteen

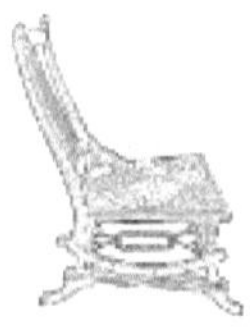

Toddler Dominic had developed bronchitis in February, at the same time Maisie discovered she was two months pregnant with Frances, so it was late March before she managed to make another visit to Old Farm Hall. It was one of those rare but glorious spring days that March sometimes offers, when the high blue sky and pale yellow sun illuminate new leaf growth in such a way that it seems almost incandescent, throwing an emerald aura over woods and hedgerows. On such a day as this, she told herself, as she manoeuvred the pushchair down the lane, even Old Farm Hall would look almost benign. Her optimism seemed justified by the brambles and hawthorns on each side, bursting into life, and a horde of naturalised daffodils that lined the route. Birds were busy nesting in the depths of the bushes. She knelt down and pointed out a robin to Dominic, its beak stuffed with nesting materials.

'It's making a new home for its babies,' she told him, 'like our daddy is for us.' Clifford had been right, she mused, looking around her; you really could believe that you were in the countryside.

She passed a gate and a public footpath sign on the right that she had not noticed on her previous visit. It was swathed by ivy and nettle but seemed to give access into a small copse. Was it *their* copse? Something to explore when she didn't have the pushchair with her.

An arrangement of ladders and a scaffolding tower indicated Clifford had spent the weekend tackling some problem on the roof. A large tarpaulin was stretched over one of the gables. Maisie quailed when she thought of what might have happened if there had been an accident; Clifford could have lain undiscovered for hours. Perhaps she should offer once more to accompany him when he worked on the house—a suggestion made on several occasions but met with grumbled refusal. Two pallets of brick and a stack of rotten floor joists had been placed in front of the garage. She edged past them and along a narrow path, slick with green algae, which led round the side of the house. What had obviously once been a *parterre* garden to the side of the house was now a tangled maze of untrimmed box and weed-infested gravel walkways. At its centre, a shallow stone fountain on an ornate pillar had fallen—or been pushed over —and lay cracked into half a dozen jagged pieces. Beyond, the coppice she had glimpsed from the road—perhaps at one time a shady arbour or romantic grove—made what seemed to be the eastern border to the property.

A wide terrace, treacherous with moss, stretched behind the house. Dominic had fallen asleep so she left him safely parked there while she explored. North-facing, the terrace got hardly any sun, but that made the descent down wide stone steps and out into the light on the lawn somehow more exciting, like stepping out onto a stage. The lawn was infested with rye and clover, clearly not mown for years. She waded through the damp, thigh-high grass as though through water, climbing the gentle slope to a low stone wall, stumbling across formal beds choked with thistle and twitch-grass and vicious with unpruned roses. Over the wall, brambles prevented further exploration of what had once been a vegetable garden, so she followed the wall to the right, passing a sag-roofed summer house that would catch the evening sun, then entering a tangled copse of fruit trees. Leaning for a while against the gnarled trunk of an old apple, she felt breathless and rather overwhelmed. Could all this *really* be theirs? It was her own secret garden! She imagined herself playing hide and seek with the children, serving picnics in summer, making snowmen in winter, a bonfire on Guy Fawkes' night— the thought made her laugh out loud.

The extreme periphery of the garden was demarcated by a thick hawthorn hedge and a gate at one corner gave access onto a ragged field that sloped up towards the top of the hill where the new estate was being constructed. She stepped through tentatively but found in fact a reasonably well-worn track connecting, she speculated, with the public footpath and the gate out onto the lane, so clearly she was not trespassing. Shaggy ponies cropped the balding turf and a gaggle of woebegone chickens scratched in a heap of mucky straw.

Chickens! *I* could keep chickens! And bees!

On the field's eastern border a shambolic collection of tumble-down sheds and stables and an old caravan suggested the spot was some kind of urban farm. As Maisie watched, a thin woman in a filthy anorak came out of one of the sheds and trudged towards the caravan. Maisie raised a faltering hand and waved vaguely back towards the house to indicate where she had come from. The woman, surprised to see anyone emerge from the long-deserted grounds of Old Farm Hall, waved back, and Maisie's heart surged again: a neighbour, a friend!

From this vantage point the house looked solid and almost splendid, set amongst the wide green skirt of garden and bathed in spring sunshine. High above its chimney stacks clouds sailed and birds soared. From here the road, the derelict land, the bulldozed development land and the industrialised town below might as well have not existed. Likewise, in a way she could hardly explain, the past—the sense she had had ever since as a child she was foisted 'for now' on her aunt and uncle—the temporary accommodations and interim arrangements, seemed to loosen its grasp. She was falling—as Clifford had already done—falling in love with the house as it morphed in her mind from just a structure of bricks and timber and a list of jobs to be tackled and hurdles overcome, into a home. She was beginning to see it, to capture his vision, to see—as *he* saw—their future lives here. It was like trying on an outfit in a shop and feeling so marvellous in it that you didn't want to take it off. "Made for you," is what people said when that happened and what Maisie said now with a kind of awe as she stood by the gate and gazed. So much more than those new-builds at the top of the hill, all identical boxes designed to accommodate the notional needs of some theoretical family, this house would really be made for them—for her—her own home. The word 'home' struck such a deep note of emotional need in Maisie that her voice cracked as she spoke it, and an empty space she had hardly known existed suddenly flooded with feel-good endorphins and such overwhelming gratitude that she thought she might cry.

Chapter Fourteen

On the morning of Christmas Eve, Maisie creeps past Frances' room and mounts the stairs to the attic. She has made barely any impression up here; the sheer volume of detritus still to be sorted is depressing and almost overwhelming. There is an enormous accumulation of *Reader's Digest* books, many of them still in their original packaging. There are rolls of carpet, the snarling rictuses of various stuffed creatures, hockey sticks and fishing rods, an ugly twenty-two place setting dinner service, dismembered stereograms and defunct photographic equipment, a collection of dingy oil paintings, a box of gruesome contraptions that might be related to a particularly brutal specialism in dentistry. She has still not decided whether to take up Gwen's offer of assistance, balancing in her mind the relief that having companionship and support would bring, against the shame of having Clifford's secret exposed to public view, although Gwen has tried to reassure her on that point. 'I can promise you the utmost in discretion in the volunteers,' she had said. 'It's part of our training.'

Maisie pushes past a lop-sided bureau and a broken hat stand to peer into the gloom of Gareth's room, She can just make out, between a stack of hat boxes and a pile of ancient camping equipment, that his bed is empty. Every Christmas she hopes he will get leave. Sometimes he arrives just as she has almost given up hope, to devour the plate of Christmas dinner she saved for him and regale them with his story: a last-minute pass, hitching across Europe with a monosyllabic Albanian lorry driver, or getting the last seat on the military transport out of some war-torn desert. His postings are always shrouded in mystery; the delicate, dangerous missions his unit is assigned can never be spoken of and sometimes, when Maisie watches the news, she is almost glad not to know what clandestine involvement her son might play in supressing the latest insurgence in Afghanistan or rescuing hostages from the clutches of Somalian pirates.

Descending the stairs, she loiters for a few moments outside Frances' room. The idea of Frances in there with a man, *sleeping* with him, would have troubled her slightly if it had not been for the instant liking she has taken to Maxim. Nevertheless, she can barely imagine the mechanics of it. Frances was always so stiff and resisting, never enjoying cuddles like the boys. Clifford would not have approved on purely moral grounds, remaining austerely orthodox in the face of every kind of sexual emancipation that the last few decades brought. Of course the fallout should the relationship founder would be immense. Frances, despite a bullish and rather callous demeanour is, at heart, easily bruised and subject to protracted moods of morose self-pity that can manifest in quite nasty outbursts. Maisie does not look forward to dealing with a Frances disappointed in love. But Maisie does not think Maxim will treat Frances in a cavalier fashion. Clearly he is from a very well-heeled family and his employment prospects are more than good; an interview at the Foreign Office bodes particularly well. He has accepted the bizarre situation here at Old Farm Hall without a murmur and has thought to provide gifts which, it seems, even Frances has neglected to do.

Maisie continues downstairs and makes tea. As she often does, she takes her cup out into the garden. No garden is at its best in December and hers is no exception: leafless trees stab the monotonous sky, greyish dew lards the lawn, the herbaceous border is bedraggled with the limp brown remains of last year's growth. But Maisie sees it with a kind of double vision that improves its appearance no end. Over the years, as Clifford's work on the house and his increasing accrual of junk reduced housework to little more than a fruitless exercise in furniture removal, Maisie found herself occupied more and more with the garden. It became her refuge as well as her occupation, and a conduit for the nurturing, creative instinct that was stymied indoors. While progress inside faltered, outdoors she made slow but steady headway. Unhindered—at times, unnoticed—by Clifford, the wild acreage she had inherited was tamed and trimmed into a respectable garden, orchard and vegetable plot. But Maisie likes to retain an image of its unkempt, neglected origins in her mind's eye. The 'before' increases tenfold her pride in the 'after'.

The *parterre*, once so hopelessly scruffy, is now prick-neat—the gravel picked clean of weeds and the box hedging minutely trimmed with a pair of special shears sourced by Clifford from some charity shop and kept just for that purpose. The occasional piece of statuary, bought for a song from a reclamation yard, provides cause to linger along the inter-connected pathways, together with her attempts at topiary; clipped bay trees and conical privet give height and draw the eye. She borrowed Clifford's lump hammer to break up the broken fountain, carrying the pieces to one of the rubble dumps he had insisted on maintaining towards the back of the vegetable garden saying, 'You never know when you might need a bit of good hard-core, Maisie.' Now an elegant stone bird bath discovered lying forgotten behind the summer house stands in its stead. She has placed a stone seat at a point where the first rays of the sun penetrate the branches of the trees across the lane, and just far enough away from the bird bath that its early visitors are not deterred by a silent observer. It is her favourite morning spot although, at this time of year it isn't possible to make use of it every day.

This morning, however, it is already occupied. Maxim sits there warmly dressed against the damp and chill, a book on his knee and a genuine smile on his face as she approaches.

'I'd have brought you tea if I'd known you were up,' she says. 'I didn't expect to see either of you for hours yet!'

Maxim indicates his book. 'The workload is so heavy during term time you get used to early starts and late finishes,' he explains. 'Now I can't sleep beyond six.'

'I got up early to see if Gareth was home. He's managed to creep in and surprise us in previous years. In fact, once Clifford almost brained him with a cricket bat, thinking he was an intruder. But,' she sighs, 'there's no sign of him.'

Maxim nods. 'I'm sure he'll get home if he can. It will be especially important this year.'

'Because of Frances' father, you mean? Clifford was never a particular fan of Christmas.'

'No, because of *you*. They'll want to be here for you. Your loss must still feel very raw.'

Does it? The mass of Clifford's legacy hardly feels like a loss at all, but more like an almost-intolerable burden of gain, his absence translated into a vivid, unwieldy manifestation. The never-ending accumulation of his chattels makes him feel ever-present, but not in a way that comforts or consoles. Her sense of his disapproval as she deconstructs his mass of possessions is increasingly irritating. 'Well? What do you expect?' she has shouted on more than one occasion. 'I can't live like this forever, can I?'

Maisie pushes the memory aside. 'I'd love it if Gareth could get home,' she says. 'He only got a two-day pass for the funeral, and before that I hadn't seen him for months. But don't get me wrong,' she adds quickly, thinking about Frances' future prospects for Christmas in the Caribbean or even installed at some remote Ambassadorial residence, 'I'm not one of those mothers who issues a three line whip every Christmas. Pamela and Dominic were at Pamela's mother's place last Christmas and the Christmas before that. I tell them to live their own lives and not to worry about me.'

'My parents have a similar philosophy,' Maxim remarks with a twinkle in his eye. 'They live their own lives and they don't worry about *me*! Now then,' he stands up and pulls Maisie's arm through his, stifling her half-uttered cry of rebuttal, 'let's tour the garden, shall we? Before all the excitement begins.'

Chapter Fifteen

Dominic, Pamela and the children arrive on Christmas Eve. The adults are in a foul temper. The traffic was terrible and the car conked out halfway up the M1, necessitating a wait of some forty minutes on the windswept embankment pending the arrival of the RAC.

They launch into a volley of complaints before they are properly over the threshold, Pamela apportioning blame with a bitter, self-righteous indignation—'I've been telling you for *weeks* to get it serviced'—before becoming almost hysterical at the idea that the baby may have caught pneumonia or that of one—or both—of the girls might have been sucked into the vortex of a passing lorry.

'You expected *me* to walk along the hard shoulder to the nearest emergency phone though,' Dominic bristles, 'passing lorries notwithstanding.'

'Oh man-up,' Pamela snarls, bustling the baby through to the housekeeper's parlour. 'If you'd keep your phone charged up there would have been no need for you walk anywhere, and if you were any kind of provider at all you'd have bought us a new car by now, one that could be relied upon not to break down, not to mention accommodate us in some kind of comfort!' She flounces away 'to thaw out,' leaving Dominic to unload the car.

Maxim's willingness to help with this task mitigates to a certain extent Dominic's aversion to finding another man in residence. 'Got his slippers on, I see,' Dominic remarks to his mother out of the side of his mouth as Maxim disappears outside to fetch more luggage. 'Feet right under the table, clearly.' However that is not sufficient to allay his shock on discovering that the incomer is sharing his sister's room. 'We don't know a thing about him,' he hisses to Maisie later. 'He could be creeping about at night, robbing us blind.'

'You sound like your father. Believe me, he'd be lucky to find anything worth stealing. *I* haven't, and I've been rummaging through this clutter for weeks,' Maisie soothes. 'Anyway,' she goes on roguishly, 'I think there are more attractions inside the bedroom for him than outside it.'

'Mum!'

'Well! There's no point imagining they're in there playing scrabble, is there? Don't be such a stuffed shirt, Dominic. Anyway,' she changes the subject, 'I hope the girls are more comfortable now they are in their own room.' Maisie has moved mountains, almost literally, to clear an access to the bunk beds in one of the smaller bedrooms. 'I hope you and Pamela will be, too.' Maisie is mulling wine to drink with the midnight chime. 'How's this?' She gives him a taste from the spoon. 'More cloves?'

Dominic shakes his head. 'No. It's good. I can see you've put in a lot of effort since we were last here. I'd have come up to help you, but ...' the inevitable objection of Pamela to such a plan does not need voicing.

'You've been busy with all the admin. *That's* been a full-time job, I'll be bound.' Maisie says, to placate him.

'On that subject, I need to talk to you *privately,* at some stage, or at least only when *proper family* are around,' Dominic says huffily, assembling glasses onto a tray.

'Don't worry, Dominic. There's bound to be an opportunity.'

By the time the turkey is on the table everyone is in good humour. The Christmas hamper containing fine wines sent by Maxim's parents certainly helps, but the effect of Maxim himself is considerable. He has penetrated Dominic's stiff, sniffy façade of distrust by deferring to his age and experience at every juncture, and won Pamela over by entertaining Jessica for hours, helping her construct a mott and bailey out of Lego so Pamela can engross herself in a novel on her new e-reader. Frances has been prised from her books by a mixture of mock-authoritarianism, tickles and kisses, and told in a tone that brooks no denial that she is to take a break from them until the day after Boxing Day.

Maisie herself hasn't needed much more winning over—the hour she spent touring the garden with Maxim established him firmly in her mind as the ideal son-in-law—but if she had done, the fancy Blu-ray player and a selection of classic films on DVD would certainly have done it.

'So thoughtful. So generous,' she says, shiny-eyed amongst the wrapping paper.

'It's from us all. Gareth too,' Frances says, 'although, I must admit it was Maxim's idea.'

'You can catch up on all the TV series that you have missed,' Dominic puts in, 'like *The Tudors*. Or older ones; *Onedin* and *The Forsythe Saga*. You were always telling us about those when we were little. You can get them all as box sets.'

'Fancy you remembering!'

'Didn't Dad bring home a box set of *Onedin* videos once? But none of the ten video players here actually worked! Wasn't *that* just typical of the chief Womble!' Frances cries with perhaps more derision than she had intended. There is an awkward silence.

Then Maxim says, 'I'll connect it to your TV and show you how it works later, Maisie.'

But more influential even than the smoothly diplomatic sway of Maxim on proceedings is—Maisie has to admit—the absence of Clifford, who had found Christmas a needless excuse for expenditure, "on things that would never be useful for anything," and an annoying distraction from the business of husbanding and repairing his collection. His reluctance to join the festivities had made itself uncomfortably felt; his stiff disinterest at the meal table thawing only briefly when the crackers were pulled, when he could garner in the worthless little trinkets that everyone else discarded along with the crepe paper and garish hats. She found them recently, stored in Quality Street tins, another by product of Christmases past: tiny screwdriver sets, dice, plastic key-rings, whistles, miniscule picture frames and dozens of little puzzles. When it came time to open their presents he showed more interest in the wrapping paper—smoothing it out and folding it up with assiduous care—than the gifts, unless they were his and destined to be assimilated into his stockpile. As his hoard became more unwieldy, he increasingly disliked having people—even his own family—in the house in case they moved a vital newspaper clipping to make room for a glass, or spoiled the meticulous organisation of his Machine Mart catalogues to find a place to sit down. Without him, and in the newly uncluttered kitchen and sitting room, the atmosphere is notably more relaxed; they all feel it although of course no one says anything. Indeed, before they eat Dominic raises his glass in a rather pompous, self-important way and says, 'A toast to Dad.'

Gareth does not make it in person, but Maisie manages some Facetime with him via Maxim's iPad so she knows he is safe. As usual he makes no commitments as to when he might next be home he does indicate that, 'it won't be too long,' so she has to be content with that.

'Wasn't that very costly?' she asks anxiously afterwards. 'You must let me reimburse you for the phone call.'

'I've got an unlimited 4G plan,' Maxim assures her.

Maisie frowns. '4G?

'It's the mobile network,' Jessica says, looking up from her Lego.

'Dear me,' Maisie wipes her eyes, 'I must be very out of step with modern technology if I need a five-year-old to explain it to me.'

'You used to have a computer,' Dominic puts in, 'although I must admit a very geriatric one. I set it up for Dad years ago. *I* thought a laptop would be a good Christmas present for you, but I was overruled.'

'I wouldn't even know how to switch one on.'

'There you are,' Pamela crows—clearly, she had been the one to veto the laptop.

'I know, I *know*,' Dominic hisses at her. Obviously this is a subject they have discussed—and disagreed about—at length, 'but there are courses you can go on and really,' he turns to Maisie now, 'Mum, it's easy. Even Edmé can do it.'

'It's time that you joined the rest of us in the twenty-first century,' Frances observes. 'You ought to have a mobile too. You're a bit like Miss Havisham, aren't you? Walled up here while the rest of the world has moved on.'

'I don't suppose it was Maisie's choice,' Maxim puts in gently.

'It was something I had absolutely no power to control,' Maisie says with an edge of anger to her tone that she cannot suppress.

'No. No, we understand that Mum,' Frances replies quietly.

'I've brought *my* computer anyway,' Dominic says heavily, 'and there are some things I need to show you on it, before we go home.'

He takes his opportunity on Boxing Day while the others go out for a good walk across the Country Park. Maisie stays behind to put her feet up and to keep an eye on the baby.

'Gwen is coming over later for a cup of tea. And I've asked Val too,' she tells Dominic as he waits for his laptop to start up.

'Val from the farm?'

'Yes. Well, I do feel for her—having to spend Christmas alone. And I hoped Gareth would be home.'

Of all the children, Gareth is the only one who ever showed any interest in the farm on the hill behind the house, going over most weekends to help with the horses and coming back stinking of dung and horse sweat, and ravenously hungry. Through him, Maisie struck up a halting relationship with Val—friendship would be too strong a word for it. Val is of a taciturn bent, and no waster of words, somehow sad and downtrodden like the neglected donkeys and broken horses that had made their way to the farm. Paid a pittance by the charitable trust that runs the farm, she seems to have no family or friends or any life at all outside of it, and is always to be found—as Maisie did that first day—rain or shine, summer or winter, trudging across the churned yard with buckets of feed and barrows of muck. But after all she is their nearest neighbour, and Maisie makes it a point to invite her over when Gareth is home.

'She isn't still living in that caravan, is she?' Dominic asks.

'No, the Urban Farm Trust had a wooden chalet built for her. It's much nicer. That is,' Maisie qualifies, 'I *presume* it's much nicer. I haven't actually been in.'

'And who is this Gwen?'

'A new friend. I met her at the charity shop.'

'I see. Well now. Here we are. Let me sit next to you and show you these figures.' Dominic settles the laptop onto Maisie's knee. It is warm and purrs faintly, like a cat. Dominic too is simmering with pent up smugness.

'What am I looking at here?' It is a mish-mash of numbers, listed in columns, some of them highlighted in different colours.

'Basically, it's a rough sketch of Dad's assets. Of *your* assets, I ought to say, since you're the sole beneficiary. I've written off, on your behalf, to all the banks and building societies that I found statements for, and also to the life insurance companies. Most of those were a dead end, I'm sorry to say. Dad seems to have taken out numerous policies that offered free cover for a few months, but then he never started the payments. However, there were one or two … I'll come back to those in a moment. Did you know that Dad had a company pension?'

'No.' Maisie shakes her head. The figures on the screen are making her feel dizzy—so many zeros. 'We never discussed those things.'

'He did. And he'd built up a nice pension pot.'

'He'd worked for Harrington's for years and years. As long as I'd known him.'

'Indeed. Well they do seem to have a very sound employee pension scheme, added to which they have a death-in-service lump sum. As Dad was still working, he's entitled to that, see?' Dominic points at one of the figures.

Maisie gasps. 'That's what's in his pension?'

'No.' Dominic points to another number. '*That's* what's in his pension. That's what will provide your income for the rest of your life. The first figure I showed you is just the death-in-service bonus.'

'Good Lord.'

'Good, isn't it? You'll get that as a lump sum, if you want. Or, you can add it to the pension pot and get it as an income, which on the whole is what I would recommend. You won't qualify for your state pension for years. But that isn't the half of it. Have you any idea what Dad's salary was?'

'None.'

'Hmm. Well it was rather good, considering. Remarkably good, for a warehouse manager, and I think it's safe to say that you lived well inside it. There are numerous accounts here with sizeable figures in them. He must just have been stashing surplus cash away. One of them is *years* old. When did you get married?'

'1985.'

'Well, this one is older than that. It was opened in 1981, with a substantial amount of money. Did you know about it?'

'No. We rented our first place and saved up a deposit and then we bought this with a mortgage. We paid the mortgage off quite recently.'

'He didn't touch this lump sum at all then,' Dominic muses. 'Odd, that. I wonder why?'

'I couldn't say.'

'Hmm. Well. The interest rates aren't very good right now but in the past they were excellent, and as he didn't seem to make any withdrawals the accruals are very respectable. See this number here? That's just cash in hand.'

'You're kidding me?' Maisie's hand flies to her mouth. Her eyes are round with disbelief.

'No, Mum. And the best thing about it all is that all these accounts were in your joint names. The money automatically became yours on Dad's death without inheritance tax implications.'

Maisie is flabbergasted. With all Clifford's mend-and-make-do policies she always assumed that money was tight and she kept house accordingly— buying from budget supermarkets what she could not provide from her own garden, rarely buying clothes, and accepting that holidays were beyond their means. And all the time …

'That's not all of it, Mum.' Dominic, though trying to remain calm, is as excited as a boy, his anticipation like an electric current sparking through the fibres of his acrylic Christmas pullover. He wriggles in his seat as he clicks a few keys on the computer. 'Remember those life insurance policies I mentioned before?'

Maisie nods and her lips say 'Yes' although no sound comes out.

'Dad only took them out a few months ago. They were the same kind of thing. Six months free cover. But look what they're worth!' He points. 'This and *this!* And if we do a little macro here—'

'A macro?' It sounds like a South American dance step.

'A sum. If we add those two to the total in the accounts, and then include the death-in-service bonus, and we estimate the value of the house which, even as it stands, or, more importantly *where* it stands, is bound to be of interest to someone.' He sits back and looks with satisfaction at the screen. Maisie can't believe her eyes. 'Suffice it to say,' Dominic concludes, closing the laptop, 'you're an extremely wealthy woman.'

Maisie sits in a stupor while Dominic makes her a cup of tea, lacing it with a generous slug of VSOP cognac from the hamper. 'But what will I *do* with it?' she asks, shaking her head. 'I mean, what do *I* want with all that money?'

'Whatever you like!' Dominic laughs. 'I'll rationalise it all for you into just two or three accounts and then, for once in your life, you can do what *you* like.'

Maisie feels a moment of recoil at the suggestion. 'Oh no! But *you* must have it. You and Frances and Gareth. And the children—'

'No.' Dominic is suddenly grim. 'That won't do. There would be tax implications if you just gave it to us and anyway,' he pauses before blurting out, 'that clearly isn't what Dad wanted. He wanted *you* to have it.'

Maisie isn't so sure; perhaps possession of money had become to Clifford the same as his possession of all his other things—just an end in itself.

'Of course you *will* have it, in time,' Maisie assures him, 'all of it, practically. I won't spend much …'

'That's up to you. You must make a new Will, and I'll help you with that, but then,' he pauses for a moment and Maisie has the impression that his next words will cost him dearly to utter. When he speaks them, it is as though he forces them past some obstruction in his throat. 'Then you must *enjoy* it. God knows, you deserve it.'

Maisie says nothing, but reaches across and takes his hand in hers. It is obvious to her that Dominic was disappointed by his father's Will even before he knew the size of the estate. Now he must feel additionally snubbed. She casts around for something she can offer, some practical and immediate salve she can administer to his wounded feelings. It comes to her like a shot.

'I've been thinking,' she says, 'that when you go home you ought to take your father's car with you. I don't need it, and in any case I never liked driving it—much too big. As far as I know, it's very reliable and I don't think the mileage is very high.'

Dominic looks as though he might cry. 'Oh Mum!' he gasps before mastering himself. 'That would certainly be something I … I'd like to discuss with Pamela,' he falters, 'if Frances and Gareth have no objection.'

'Gareth is the last person to object and a car is a liability in Oxford, so Frances won't want it. In any case, between you and me, I have an idea she'll be going abroad in the not-too-distant future.'

Dominic squeezes her hand. 'Thank you, Mum.' His eyes, always tending to be weak and watery, turn pink. 'I wish … I wish I could do more to help you with things here. What he's left you …' Dominic gestures towards his laptop, 'it hardly compensates, does it, for what he's left you *with*—the fall-out from his … habit. His hoard.'

It is the first time that any of them has put a name on Clifford's obsession, or acknowledged it as such. It had impinged on all the children of course—gradually, insidiously, as his mania got hold. They had realised bit by bit that their house was not the same as their friends', that their lifestyle was not *normal*. But a species of loyalty and Clifford's own unarguable rationale left them all hesitant to address it directly. *He* had seen it in such a clear and reasonable light that his vision had penetrated far beyond the fog of their own confused comprehension and they, like Maisie, in varying degrees, had trusted it. In any case they knew its impact on them could only be temporary. Eventually, they would all leave the massed accumulations of supposed treasures and step into a clutter-free world.

Perhaps it is a sense of guilt about this that makes Dominic say, 'Pamela got some books from the library about it. About compulsive hoarding, mean. Some of it … it made me feel ill. There were cases of canyons of stacked-up junk just collapsing. People were buried alive! Then there were fires … not to mention the financial ruin. Do you know, some people hoard faeces and urine! Imagine the diseases! And I felt guilty, that I'd walked away and left you here … and *now*, I'm not helping …' he dissolves into incoherence.

She takes his hand and pats it. 'I'm getting through it, bit by bit,' Maisie says quietly. 'I'm deconstructing it, hoping to find, somewhere, under all the junk, the good idea your father and I started off with. And when I do, then I'll know which direction to go in.'

Dominic wipes his eyes and blows his nose. 'You'll move, surely? You could find somewhere closer to us.'

'I *could* move house.' Maisie's tone expresses her hesitation to embrace this idea.

'If you wanted to, you could buy a place abroad as well, for holidays. We could all use that.'

'Or I could stay here?'

Dominic sniffs. 'Yes, if you liked. I suppose you could have the place completely made over, although it is big, just for one.'

Maisie indicates the laptop. 'Thank you for all your hard work, Dominic. Is there anything else I need to know?'

He considers. 'Actually, yes. The insurance assessor will be coming sometime in the next couple of weeks.'

'To check that your dad is really dead?'

'No! It's to do with the fire. Your policy was fully paid up and you're covered for fire damage so you might as well have the damage in the garage made good.'

Maisie drinks her tea. The brandy in it is making her stomach glow; she feels flushed and giddy. 'I can't wait to tell Gwen.'

'I don't think you should tell anyone, yet,' Dominic warns darkly. '*I* haven't told a soul, not even Pamela. When a woman suddenly comes into a lot of money, she's likely to attract all kinds of parasites … not that Pamela …'

'Of course not,' Maisie agrees.

'But this new friend. Gwen? What do we know about her?'

'She's sound as a pound,' Maisie says confidently.

Chapter Sixteen

Maisie has always found January a depressing month. With nothing much to be done in the garden she was always confined to the house, which the dark afternoons and inadequate boiler rendered inhospitable. When Clifford was out at work she sat at the kitchen table and did the mending while the *Afternoon Drama* crackled from the wireless. Or she would moon about the rooms, trying to envisage them warm and bright, with comfortable sofas and elegant décor. Sometimes she would pick out a piece of random furniture and try, in her mind's eye, to see where it might fit once refurbished. Or measure up for the curtains she hoped would one day frame the windows. Occasionally she would go out to department stores to look around their home furnishing departments, lingering in the make-believe lounges and pretend bedrooms to admire the pristine fabrics and opulent scatter-cushions.

But this January is different. It flashes past in a whirl of activity and visitors, and a yo-yoing of emotion that leaves her with a sense of vertigo some evenings, sick with fatigue but unable to sleep, enervated and energised all at the same time. The news about the money has still not fully penetrated; the thought of it makes her lightheaded—it doesn't seem real— but then that aura is punctured by a surprising and quite shocking stab of anger when she thinks of the years she spent scrimping by, spreading out visits to the hair-dresser and buying penny-wise clothes in sales. Although the funds are not absolutely at her disposal yet, it is euphoric to think of the possibilities they open up, and sickening to consider the opportunities that have been missed: instrument lessons for Frances, educational trips with school, family holidays. The grind of hauling and sorting and the hundred decisions to be made every day are exhausting, but in spite of them she feels lifted and buoyant, and not overwhelmed.

Two days a week Gwen and a team of discreet, respectful volunteers come in. Whether Gwen has briefed them, Maisie doesn't know, but they never allow themselves so much as a gasp or a raised eyebrow at the state of affairs in the house. They simply remove their coats and pull on their Marigolds, and get to work sorting through the numerous mixed lots of assorted crockery and ornaments bought at auction and the bags of old clothing, deftly categorising them for sale in their network of shops, for recycling or disposal at the tip. Anything potentially valuable they put to one side pending the visit of the auctioneer.

Meanwhile, Gwen has contacted a paper recycling company and arranged for a dumpster to be delivered to the drive. Into it go innumerable Yellow Pages and telephone directories, the entire back catalogue of *Reader's Digest* and *Period Homes* magazines, reams of unintelligible computer print-out, stack upon stack of newspapers, hundreds of Screw-Fix and Machine-Mart brochures, copies of *Auto-Trader* offering models of cars that have been discontinued for years, and fifty-six black bin bags of junk mail. Into a separate container, for shredding, go the endless shoe boxes of till receipts, utility bills and vehicle documentation going back twenty-five years, invoices from *Reader's Digest*, old bank statements and a miscellany of other personal documentation Maisie has sifted through on the days when the volunteers are absent.

It is amazing what a difference that shifting the silos of paper makes to the rooms—clearing floor space as well as removing the oppressive sense of towers about to tumble. The skirting boards in the drawing room see the light of day for the first time in a dozen years.

Gwen brings Mr Sligh, the auctioneer, to view the larger pieces of furniture and the more unusual artefacts. He is a small, stoop-shouldered man with an ill-fitting tweed jacket and an adenoidal voice. His eyes are close-set and beady; they dart acquisitively over Clifford's collection in an unpleasant, rodent-like way. Much of the hoard, in fact, he recognises as Clifford bought it in his saleroom, but he thinks it impolitic to mention that fact at this juncture.

'Will it sell?' Gwen asks him in a business-like manner. 'I mean, for a decent amount of money?'

'Restored, some of these pieces would do nicely, but as they stand,' he points to a slope-shelved bookcase and a dangle-doored armoire, 'their value would be reduced. It would be worth thinking about employing a carpenter to fix them up, perhaps. Do you want to move everything on? I could just treat it as a house clearance.'

'Not everything,' Maisie says, quickly. 'There are some pieces I want to keep.' She laughs. 'They don't all even need repairing! There's a lovely dining table behind that pinball machine; can you see? It's standing on its end. There's nothing wrong with that at all but it got pushed to one side when the room got too full.'

'Yes. Very nice.'

'And there's a rocking chair. That *does* need some work, but it has sentimental value.'

'The best thing to do is buy some little coloured stickers and put them on anything you want to keep, and we'll take the rest. There's a man called Geoff who has the reclamation yard; he'll take those fire surrounds off you, and the butler's sinks, and those Victorian tiles, and pay you good money too. I'll give him a call.'

'I'm ever so grateful.'

'Yes,' Gwen booms, 'thank you Steve. I knew you'd be able to help us.'

'Not at all.' Mr Sligh gives an unctuous smile, revealing pointed yellow teeth. 'Mrs Wilde will be paying seller's commission, and for the men and the van to clear the place, so it will be well worth my while. Church might be church, and all that,' he gives Gwen a thin apologetic smile, 'but business is business. I can assess everything properly when I get it to the warehouse. Some of it might go in the fine art sale, the rest in the household chattels, but one way or another we'll find new homes for it. Then I suppose you'll put the house on the market?'

'Not necessarily,' Maisie demurs.

An insurance assessor calls to inspect the damage to the garage. He is a wobble-paunched, grouchy man with a floppy, stained moustache and a suit long overdue at the dry cleaners. Maisie leads him through the house to the garage where he makes a cursory inspection and says, 'Bet you're sorry the fire didn't get a better hold.'

'I beg your pardon?'

'If it had gone through the house you'd be looking at rebuild value at best, a thorough refurb at least. Bet you'd have liked that, wouldn't you?'

'This is our family home,' Maisie tells him coldly. 'And my husband died in the fire.'

He has the grace to look embarrassed and taps some notes onto his iPad.

'Get some quotes from local builders. Send them in to us,' he says at last. 'I'll just take some snaps. I don't suppose you have a list of what was destroyed.'

'I have no idea what he kept in here,' Maisie says, her eyes straying to the tea chests and suitcases still stacked in the corner at the bottom of the stairs. They are grimy, now, with ash and soot overlaying the dust and cobwebs of years, but undamaged by the fire. 'Some power tools, I think,' she concludes doubtfully.

'See if you can find the receipts, or the instruction manuals. Any proof of ownership.'

'They might be in his desk. Do I have to put it back as it was?' she asks him.

'Good God, no! Find out how much it would cost to reinstate it. We'll give you the money and you can use it how you like. You can hire a demolition machine if you want. That's what I'd do. This place is worth more as plot than a building—'

'Not to me,' Maisie replies sharply.

Chapter Seventeen

Maisie, Clifford and Dominic had eventually moved into Old Farm Hall in September. In the meantime, Maisie made several trips to the house to begin clearing the garden. For two weeks in the summer, she and Clifford went there together instead of on holiday. He worked in the house, she battled the nettles and brambles in the vegetable plot during the day, and in the evenings they picnicked on the terrace while Dominic tottered through the long grass of the lawn or drove his toy trucks long the byways of the *parterre*.

The week before the move, Clifford allowed her to accompany him to the house for some final work before the big move. The final work turned out to be sweeping and cleaning. Maisie, heavily pregnant with Frances, swept the rooms with a languorous broom, gathering sawdust and dust into piles across the floorboards, while Clifford cleaned the windows.

The house appeared sound at least, with a functioning if antiquated bathroom that Maisie cleaned as best she could in her condition. The broken windows had been reglazed and Clifford had refurbished some of the shutters so they folded smoothly back into recesses at either side of the casements. In the kitchen, the range had been cleaned and serviced, and emitted a dull heat. Maisie mopped the stone flagged floor and washed down the shelves beneath the work surface that would hold her crockery and saucepans. She scrubbed the old kitchen table with a bleach solution. Clifford had cured it of its wobble, saying, 'Might as well keep it. It belongs with the house and it's the right size for the room. I expect I'll be able to pick up some chairs somewhere.'

'We will have a proper fitted kitchen at some stage, won't we Clifford?' she asked, looking up from her work, her arms sudsy with lather.

'All in good time,' he replied.

His various theatres of repair had been brought to an interim completion. 'Of course it isn't finished,' he told her, 'but it's good enough for us to move in now, and it's daft to spend money on rent as well as the mortgage.' The areas for re-plastering had been scratch-coated but not top-skimmed. Some walls had been stripped but there was no sign of any replacement paper. Several window ledges and some of the skirtings had been renewed but were yet to be painted. A spaghetti of wires coiled up and taped to the wall above the fuse box suggested that electrical work remained to be done; indeed wires could be seen poking from various holes in the downstairs ceilings. Correspondingly, upstairs Clifford warned her some of the floorboards were loose. There were neither carpets nor curtains in any of the rooms.

The dining room, to the left of the hall, was cluttered with building materials and tools. 'I've brought everything in here for now,' Clifford explained. 'I can use it as a base.'

'I thought you were going to use the garage as your workshop.'

'I will do, when I've fitted it all out. But that isn't a priority, is it?'

'I suppose not.'

The sloping ceilings in both attics had been stripped to the rafters and she could see slithers of sky through the gaps in the slates; old paint tins had been positioned to collect any ingress of water.

'But we won't be using these rooms for ages,' Clifford told her, 'only for storage, after I've made the roof sound. In the meantime, no need to worry about them.'

Maisie supressed her disappointment with a firm hand; the gloriously restored house she anticipated was evidently some way off; the smoothly decorated walls, luxurious carpets and richly draped curtains were clearly unreasonable expectations given the amount of basic repair work Clifford had to undertake.

'When you get here next week there'll be a surprise,' Clifford said, giving her a mysterious look as he locked the door that evening. Maisie felt exhausted and longed for a warm bath. Her back ached. She was anxious about Dominic who had—reluctantly—spent the day with a neighbour.

'A surprise?' she replied, distracted.

'Yes,' Clifford nodded. 'So no sneaking back over here this week.'

'I'll be too busy packing,' Maisie yawned.

But as she wrapped their belongings in newspaper over the next few days, she allowed herself to daydream about what the surprise might be. Carpets throughout seemed unlikely, given the work still to be done under the floorboards, but perhaps Clifford had arranged for carpet to be laid in the bedrooms? Or maybe he had hired a painter and decorator? Or a kitchen fitter—she fancied a Shaker style …

When moving day came Maisie could only watch as Clifford and his friend Ted manhandled their few bits of furniture and cardboard boxes of belongings out of the rental property and into the hired van. She had been having Braxton Hicks contractions all night and was already exhausted. And Dominic was unsettled, tearful and clingy.

'When we get there, don't unpack anything unless you think you'll really need it,' Clifford warned her. 'Your ornaments and so on. They'll only be in the way until we're straight. Tell me which boxes they're in and they can go in the attic for now.'

'The leaky attic? Couldn't they go with your things in the garage, or in the room above?'

'No!' Clifford almost shouted. 'No. I need the space for something else. Pushed up against the walls they'll be perfectly safe in the attic.'

'Alright, Clifford,' she said, too tired to argue.

Ted drove the van and the three of them followed it to Old Farm Hall, but only Clifford seemed genuinely excited.

Maisie bravely summoned what enthusiasm she could as they stepped over the threshold. 'Here we are then,' she said brightly to Dominic, setting him down onto his feet. 'Our new home! Isn't it exciting?' The hall floor was bare and the walls naked. She went into the kitchen to put the kettle on; it was exactly as she had left it.

'I've decided to put the lounge furniture in the back parlour for now,' Clifford told her. 'It's cosy enough in there. Gives me a chance to put the finishing touches to the sitting room.'

'The finishing touches?' Maisie turned to smile at him. 'Is that where my surprise is?'

'No. Try the dining room.' Clifford took the kettle off her as she hurried to see.

The plethora of tools and timber in the dining room had been augmented by two pieces of furniture. Taking pride of place was a long, mahogany dining table, sound as far as she could see, but in need of a good clean and polish. It was large; it could easily seat twelve or fourteen, she guessed, but a perfect proportion for the room. The top had a moulded edge that felt smooth to the touch, with removable leaves meaning it could be reduced in size if required. Underneath, five pairs of reeded legs had recessed castors. It was exceedingly elegant; it took her breath away.

In the corner, a rocking chair lay on its side. Its upholstered seat was threadbare and one scalloped arm had come adrift from its anchor on the seat. Its workings—a twisted metal spring and a metal bracket—lay to one side. It looked like Clifford had already started on the repairs.

Clifford came to stand next to her, bringing her a cup of tea. 'What do you think?' he asked.

'Oh, Clifford,' was all Maisie could say.

'We'll have the whole house furnished like this,' he blurted. 'Authentic pieces. I can restore them. That MFI flat-pack we're bringing in now, that'll all be out of the window before you know it.' He squatted down next to the chair. 'I'm going to have this piece fixed by the time you bring the baby home. Look!' He got up again and crossed quickly to his stash of tools. 'I've been looking at this. It's a magazine for people like us who own period properties.' He brought over a glossy magazine, *Period Living,* and flicked through the pages as she sipped her tea. 'See all the ideas they give you? Colours, fabrics, accessories. I'm going to take out a subscription. This will be our bible! Look at these wall coverings, see? It tells you where you can buy them. Can't you just see that in our sitting room? Look at those ceiling mouldings! They're just like ours! It's the real McCoy we've got here, Maisie, and I'm going to decorate it and furnish it with all the pukka stuff!' His eyes shone as he turned to look at her. Maisie hadn't seen him look so happy since the day they'd got married.

For the rest of the day, as Maisie unpacked her crockery and made up the bed and placed Dominic's clothes back into his little white laminate chest of drawers, she was in a dream of excitement, caught up in Clifford's vision of how it would be. Her eyes scanned the bare walls, imagining richly figured wallpapers. Her feet stepped across rough floorboards, but she felt the soft yield of opulent carpet. That evening, as she struggled to get the range to reheat the casserole she had prepared earlier in the week, her eyes saw copper pans dangling from the ceiling and jars of home preserves lining the high shelves. It was late when they eventually ate, both of them drooping with fatigue and hunger, but almost too happy to eat as they discussed their plans. Even as they lay in bed listening to the seashore noise of the traffic on the road at the end of the lane, and the wind through the branches of the trees opposite, and the strange settling and creaking noises of the unfamiliar house, they continued to talk about the things that needed to be done.

'I'm not sure I'll ever get to grips with the Aga,' Maisie said, snuggling closer into Clifford's side. 'It seems to take such a long time to heat up.'

'You'll get used to it,' he said, rubbing the small of her back in the way that he knew eased the ache. 'And in the meantime, I'll see if I can get hold of a Baby Belling, just as a temporary measure.'

I worked like a slave on that house. Most evenings saw me there after work for an hour or two, and virtually every weekend I was there from dawn to dusk. Not that I'm complaining. I enjoyed it, in fact—the peace and quiet for a start—nobody coming in and disturbing me, asking me for things.

When I was hired I expected working in the stores at Harrington's to be a peaceful sort of job: organising the shelves, keeping the place tidy, checking the stock. But people were in there every minute of the day, waving requisitions at me: 'Can you get me two dozen three-and-three-quarter inch brackets, Cliff?' 'I need a box of number nines, Cliff!' 'Have you got two hundred and fifty manila DL window envelopes, Cliff?' I was scurrying up and down the racks at ninety miles an hour some days! And even after nigh-on forty-five years, they still couldn't get my name right. 'Not Cliff,' I'd tell them, although I suppose that's what had been intended—after the singer. I'm a child of the 50s, you know. I suffered for years because of the way it was embroidered on my school name-labels (Wilde, Cliff) and changed it to Clifford the day I struck out to live on my own.

'Not Cliff,' I'd tell them. 'Clifford.' But they took no notice. Did it for devilment, if you ask me.

'Have you got a sheer face, Cliff?' they'd ask, thinking they were so funny. 'Have you got an eroded bottom?' 'No, but I've got plenty of thick ears, if you want one of them,' I'd reply.

Got the reputation of being a bit of a firebrand at first, but then the time came when people stopped. They treated me with more respect, after that.

There was none of that at Old Farm Hall. It was quiet and I could get on with things in my own way, no one to tell me what to do or how to do it. That was another thing about the warehouse. Always coming up with new systems, they were, forever introducing new procedures that had to be followed and getting all agitated about minimum stock levels. 'I can do it,' I'd say to them. 'I've got a system. I know where everything is, I don't need to fill in a pile of forms.'

'But we need to know as well,' they told me. 'You might not always be here.'

'I expect I will,' I said.

Then they computerised it. Thought I'd give up and leave, I suppose, but not me. I mastered it alright.

Automated picking's the next thing, I hear. Some robot scooting up and down the shelves to fetch the stock. Well, I don't mind. It'll save my legs.

At the house I could look at a job for as long as I wanted, mull it over, like, and think about how it might be done. You could give a thing a try, and if it didn't work, it didn't matter really. Nobody breathing down your neck. Maisie, bless her, she was anxious to get it all done, but she didn't go on about it too much.

'You've got to do these things in their proper order, Maisie,' I told her. 'Preparation is everything; you can't rush the fundamentals. We'll have it just right in the end.'

I bought a book from *Reader's Digest* about home renovations. A leaflet about it came through the door by chance one day, and I sent off for it. It was quite good; it's upstairs right now. I can show you, if you like. They sent me a lot of stuff after that—some quite useful books, and some interesting ones. And they have this prize draw. People win thousands and thousands. It's all genuine because they show you their pictures: 'Mrs W from Caernarfon won £83,000' and 'Mr and Mrs J from Ayr won £146,000'. Mr and Mrs W from Millport, I thought, could do with that kind of windfall. Who couldn't? Although to be fair, Maisie's no spendthrift; she'd understand about the rainy-day money, if she knew about it. No, *Reader's Digest* has some very good offers on things. And they pass your name on to other companies who sell things you might want. Before we knew it we had leaflets and brochures coming through the door all the time for tools and gadgets and all kinds of interesting things. Sometimes there are coupons you can cut out and send off for free things, or get money off. I mean, they're worth having, aren't they, things like that? Maisie called it junk but I told her, 'It's not junk, just because we didn't ask for it. There are some things here which could be very useful. Let's keep it, just in case.' And you know more than once I've had a need for just one of those tools or whatever and I've been able to have a bit of a rummage and then: hey presto! Just the leaflet I need, give them a call, bob's your uncle.

It's like I told them at work: 'I've got a system. I know where everything is.'

But I must admit that doing the house up did prove a lot trickier than I had expected. It was like one of those games of dominoes when you knock one and the whole lot falls down. I know Maisie wanted a new bathroom suite but what was the point in it while the boiler was so unreliable? The ranges you can get nowadays do your hot water and heating but the pipes in the house could never have coped with the pressure, so I had to sort those out before anything. But lifting up the floorboards to get at them revealed a whole world of trouble—rotten joists and what have you. And while I had them up it would have been madness not to tackle the wiring. The wiring in that house was a proper Fred Karno's, I can tell you …

And the lovely thing was, while I was doing all that basic stuff, we didn't have to decide on anything. It was all out there: possibilities, choices. I almost didn't want to choose; picking one thing would kybosh all the others.

I did so want to get it right. This was a whole new ballgame for me: a proper home! The places I'd lived before had only been temporary, and certainly I'd never had any say in what they were like. So this… this was special, and a bit daunting, like landing in a new country.

That table? Oh yes. She's a beauty, isn't she? I knew Maisie would love it. Pity there were no chairs, but I'm sure to come across some sooner or later. The rocking chair, well I did work very hard on that. The mechanism was tricky but I mastered it in the end. I'm planning on taking an upholstery course so I can sort the seat out. A piece like that needs proper skills to do it justice. No point rushing these things, is there?

Chapter Eighteen

February comes, and with it the first snowdrops push up through the frozen ground. Maisie braves the frosty temperatures to prune her raspberry canes. Normally she would have sown cabbages and carrots under a cloche, but she hesitates—she might not even be here by the time they are ready to plant out.

Gwen and her volunteers continue to work their way through the boxes of mixed lots, the books and records and dismal pictures. Maisie looks forward to their coming, baking flapjack and shortbread for them to eat with their morning coffee. Some take to bringing a packed lunch with them; the kitchen rings with their laughter and chat as they take a break at noon. Maisie bustles amongst them, offering a napkin here, the cruet there, topping up teacups and gorging herself on their casual, easy conversation until she feels dizzy with it, almost drunk on social discourse. In the afternoons, when they have gone back to their lives, the silence remains charged with their echoes.

Due to their ministrations the house has a palpably lighter, brighter aspect, as though shrouds have been lifted off the windows. She can simply walk—she does not have to negotiate a route—from one room to another, without fear of tripping, or toppling unsteady heaps. The air, perhaps freer to circulate, shrugs off the musty, slightly fungoid smell that has characterised it for so long. Although there is dust and grime, cobwebs as thick as gauze, balls of amorphous fluff like miniature tumbleweeds and a greyish, gritty, ash-like residue impossible to identify, it is all *accessible,* as it has not been for years, and there seems a point now in attacking it all with the hoover, duster and mop.

Geoff, the genially foul-mouthed owner of the reclamation yard, takes away the architectural hardware, loading it into his lorry with the aid of a monosyllabic but extremely well-muscled trainee. He refuses the greenhouse. 'Only fit for the fire, that,' he says. 'But if you're ripping that panelling out, assuming it hasn't got worm, I'll have that off you.'

'I'll let you know,' Maisie replies.

When it is loaded, to Maisie's amazement, he takes a roll of twenty-pound notes from his pocket and begins to count them out. 'Five hundred alright, is it?' he asks.

'I don't suppose you'd like to have a look in the garden?' Maisie asks him. She leads him round to the scrubby area behind the vegetable garden, where assorted ironmongery and some old stone troughs lie semi-shrouded in nettles, and a dozen pallets of York stone slabs make a palisade against the boundary hedge. Six lichen-encrusted stone gargoyles—relic of some church—gurn through an enormous but filthy stained-glass windowpane. Several stone nymphs, variously amputated, look on through milk-blind eyes. An elaborate, curlicued gazebo is swathed in ivy. Piles of old stock brick and stacks of Welsh slate litter the compound.

'Fuck me,' says Geoff, 'you've got nearly as much stock here as I have!'

A parade of builders comes to weigh up the job in the garage. Some are sharp-suited and business-like; they don't look as though they have picked up a hammer in their lives. They will 'project manage' they say, using a team of trained tradesmen—mainly Polish. Others arrive grimy from some other building site, their hands calloused, pencils sprouting from behind their ears. To a man, they frown at the state of the garage roof, dismiss the timbers as 'unsalvageable,' shake their heads at the parlous condition of the pointing, and issue dire warnings on the subject of damp. 'All in all,' they conclude, 'you'd be better knocking this down and starting again.' None of them inspire Maisie's confidence. Their quotes come in and she forwards them to the insurance company without paying them much attention. She has more pressing matters to attend to.

'Maxim's been accepted by the Foreign Office,' Frances announces via the telephone. 'His interview was last week and we just heard yesterday. They're sending him to Tokyo.'

'When? Oh, darling, that's wonderful news. But what about … what about *you?*'

'I'll go with him of course, or, at least, I'll join him there as soon as I can.' Frances can't appreciate how the news of her removal halfway around the world will affect her mother or, if she does, she gives no sign. 'We'll have to be married of course.' She makes it sound like a mere formality, like having the requisite inoculations.

'Married! Oh Frances! How wonderful! Congratulations! I'm *so* happy for you.' Maisie has a fleeting vision of Frances in a dress like a floating meringue, Jessica and Edmé in pink satin bridesmaid's frocks, cascading flowers and… but reality kicks in abruptly with Frances' warning, 'Stop it, Mother. I know what you're thinking. It won't be anything like that.'

'Oh, but Frances—'

'It will be quiet. A Registry Office probably, or perhaps the College Chapel if Maxim's people really insist. A couple of witnesses. Immediate family only.'

Maisie feels herself deflate like a punctured tyre. 'Well, if that's what you both want …'

'It is. Me particularly.'

'I see. But when, Frances?'

'I don't know. June, perhaps? I have to go. I have a tutorial in ten minutes.'

She rings off. Such a pity, Maisie thinks with a sigh. The garden is so lovely in June.

Chapter Nineteen

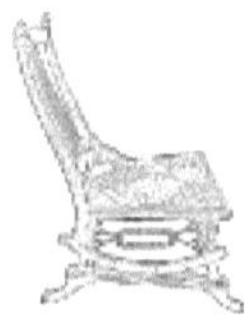

One day towards the beginning of March Maisie crosses the garden. Her wellington boots leave shining trails of dew through the unmown grass. Spring is a while away; the air is chill although the day is fine, the trees and hedges are yet to show that green aura that comes before the new leaves bud, but she is conscious, nonetheless, of a sense of relief. Winter is over; the dark raw days will lighten and lengthen now. Likewise her mourning, as represented by the job of clearing the house, is past its longest night. Since Gwen and the women came to help, the task seems finite: she *will* accomplish it. Her rage and occasional bouts of despair are a thing of half-remembered nightmare. She wakes now each day with a surge of purpose.

Today's purpose is to speak to Val, and accordingly she does not linger in the orchard although it is tempting to do so, but goes straight through the gate and up the field.

She finds Val mucking out one of the dilapidated stables. 'I want to have a bonfire,' Maisie says. 'A big one. Can I use your paddock?'

Val, a diminutive, wirily thin woman with cheeks mapped by bluish thread veins, scratches her head through the grey, hay-encrusted bobble hat she wears throughout the winter months. 'Don't see why not,' she grunts, wheeling a loaded barrow of manure towards a steaming muck heap. It seems amazing to Maisie that the woman can even lift it, so petite is she— hardly five feet tall. But Val empties the barrow with little apparent effort before asking, 'Want a hand?'

'I'm going to need all the help I can get,' Maisie replies with a grin. 'I've a pack of Scouts coming on Saturday and I won't be able to keep them in line on my own.'

Gwen and a dozen of her most trusted Scouts, Val and Maisie labour all day to move the awkward greenhouse frames. Gwen and Maisie, wearing thick gauntlets and protective eyewear, knock out the glass panes into a small skip before the boys carry the frames round the back of the house, up the garden and through the gate into the field. Val supervises the construction of the bonfire. They add other furniture that is broken or warped beyond any kind of use, threadbare rugs and mouldy, moth-infested fabric found festering in corners under jumble that has not been moved for years. Spongy, decomposing chipboard, distorted picture frames and peeling sheets of old laminate, a mildewed mattress and an ancient, buckled door all wind their way like a parade of the halt and lame to their place of final resting. They use the vacated banana boxes and screws of newspaper to ignite the heap, and as dusk falls the Scouts and the women watch in awed silence as the pyre consumes the lot.

'It's very clean and thorough isn't it—fire,' Gwen comments, rubbing her hands together as they watch the flames leap into the darkening sky.

'Yes,' Maisie agrees, 'and final. When I think about all the other stuff—everything I've off-loaded so far and the rest that'll go to the auction—although it won't be *here* anymore it'll be *somewhere*, won't it? being useful—or not! Even the things I've taken to the tip—they'll be recycled, or even if they go to landfill they'll still exist in some form. I mean, I could dig them up and they'd still be there. But these things—by tomorrow, they'll be gone. Ashes carried on the wind.'

'Like Clifford,' Val puts in with morose acuity, wiping her nose with a grubby man's handkerchief.

'Nothing disappears entirely,' Gwen says quickly. 'On a scientific level, everything is energy, and it just gets turned into another form. On a theological one, there's the afterlife. Even if you don't believe in that, we're always left with memories, which last as long as we do. They *can* be comforting.'

'Yes, there's heaven,' Val agrees, 'if you believe in it.'

'Well,' Maisie grins, 'plenty of room *there* for Clifford's collection.'

Three of the oldest and most responsible Scouts wield rakes to keep the smouldering heap in check, while the others caper round the fire, whooping like savages.

'I expect those boys are ravenous,' Gwen says, briskly. 'I know I am.'

'Let's go home,' Maisie agrees. 'I have jacket potatoes and an enormous vat of chilli con carne in the Aga—plenty for everyone.' Noticing her neighbour beginning to shrink into the shadows, Maisie slips her arm into the crook of Val's elbow. 'Oh no you don't, Val. You're coming too.'

'Not dressed for socialising,' Val demurs, indicating her filthy anorak and threadbare corduroys. 'Got holes in my socks.'

'So have I!' Gwen hoots. 'And I didn't like to mention it at the time, but I tore these trews earlier so I expect my rump is hanging out! But I don't care if you don't.'

'What must we *all* look like!' cries Maisie, raking her fingers through her hair: it is crusty with drifted ash and full of burrs from where she has brushed past the hedgerow.

'As a matter of fact,' Gwen observes, 'you look rather lovely. You have a brightness in your eye and a colour in your cheek that I haven't seen since I met you.'

'I know I'm losing weight,' Maisie admits. 'These trousers are falling off me. But I've always been a bit of a roly-poly, so that's probably a good thing. Come on boys! Grub's up!'

When the boys have gorged themselves on chilli and homemade cake and been collected by their parents, the three women remain around the kitchen table enjoying the heat that emanates from the Aga—Maisie keeps it well stocked with anthracite now, careless of the expense—and a glass of vintage port, one of a dozen bottles found stored in a box under the stairs.

Val looks round the kitchen with awed eyes. 'Like what you've done with the place,' she mumbles. 'Been a while since I was in. Looking very tidy.' Even without her bobble hat and disreputable anorak, she looks like a vagrant, her clothes being old and full of holes, although clean enough.

'It looks like a normal kitchen at last,' Maisie laughs. 'In fact, after today, I can almost see the light at the end of the tunnel.'

It is true. Their efforts over the past weeks have worked miracles. They have rationalised the larger artefacts and pieces of furniture, finagling it all into the two downstairs reception rooms. It is a large collection still, and bizarrely assorted: the pinball machine next to a Chinese lacquered cabinet, a set of beer engines atop a dismembered church organ. It jostles and jumbles in the rooms, uneasy in its new juxtaposition, startled and on-edge, like a crowd of delayed passengers in a departure lounge; going back not an option but its onward journey still hindered by unaccountable deferral. This, alongside a few ornate mirrors, several drear but possibly valuable oil paintings, some rolls of surprisingly good handwoven carpet and a few boxes of smaller pieces destined for the fine art sale, are all that remain. Upstairs are only the personal belongings you would find in any ordinary home: the flimsy, utilitarian furniture they had used as a family; clothing; some boxes of toys and mementoes that Maisie thinks the children might like to have; the household linens. Apart from these the rooms are clear— unadorned, unimproved, but clear.

'I forgot to mention: Steve says the van's free on Friday, to clear the remains, if that's convenient,' Gwen announces.

'What's he, then? An undertaker?'

'Sounds like it, doesn't it Val?' Maisie giggles. 'Although in some ways Clifford's collection *is* a kind of a corpse …'

'Stephen Sligh, the auctioneer,' Gwen explains. 'He's going to clear the rest of the stuff for Maisie.'

'Ah.' Val nods and sips her port. 'And then what?'

Maisie shakes her head. 'I still haven't decided.' She sighs. 'But one thing at a time. I'll have to decide what Mr Sligh can take, and what I want to keep.'

'That's the way, dear,' Gwen covers Maisie's small hand with her larger, mannish one. 'Baby steps.'

Later, when Val has disappeared into the chilly star-lit gloom, promising to check the embers on her way, Gwen and Maisie linger in the hall. It is empty now, almost exactly as it had been the day Clifford first brought her to the house, save for the old newspapers and the mouse droppings. Gwen shrugs herself back into her parka. 'Poo!' she sniffs, 'stinks of smoke!' Gwen looks flushed—from the port presumably–but insists she is safe to drive. She rummages her keys from her bag. But on the doorstep she turns unexpectedly and gathers Maisie into a hug. 'I don't know what you'll decide to do, dear,' she says hoarsely, 'but I sort of hope you don't decide to leave …'

'Oh!' Tears spring into Maisie's eyes. 'I *know* … but I'm almost at the end of it now and I'll *have* to decide soon!'

'Yes, yes,' Gwen croons, stroking Maisie's back. 'But there is life *here,* a future … You need to stop looking *back* and look at what there is *here* with new eyes.'

Maisie nods and gently disengages herself. She gropes a tissue from her pocket and mops her eyes. 'I know. I know. And I will do. I think I'll be able to, very soon.'

Gwen gives her a wan smile. 'Good. And look. We've broken the back of this now. No need to flog yourself quite so hard. Why don't you come out for lunch with us on Tuesday? Gloria's back from her latest cruise and wants to tell us all her adventures. We're meeting down the road at the pub. I'll call for you, shall I? About one?'

Maisie quails. 'At the Smithy? Oh dear. I don't know. I've never been in there. Clifford disapproved. He made me promise I'd never—'

'But Clifford's *gone,*' Gwen interrupts, fiercely.

'Well.' Maisie glances through the drawing room door, where Clifford's collection has made its last stand. 'Nearly.'

Chapter Twenty

Clifford hadn't seemed to care about the business units and the car dealership that were built on the sloping land across the lane from Old Farm Hall. The belt of trees shielded it from view for most of the year, and the site had its own access from the main road. Neither the construction nor the business traffic impinged on them in any way, and while the modern plate glass did make an uneasy anachronism to the jutting bays and multiple chimneys of the house, it was no more than the derelict mills had done beforehand.

But the announcement that the tumble-down sheds on the wasteland at the bottom of the road were to be transformed into a public house sent him almost apoplectic with rage.

They'd been living at Old Farm Hall for about five years. 'Living', Maisie used to think wryly, was perhaps poetic licence. *Camping out* would be a more accurate description of their circumstances. Their initial dreams had already been compromised, side-tracked by endless unfinished repair projects and the beginnings of Clifford's acquisitive drive. Life was made awkward and uncomfortable by gaps in the floorboards, draughty window frames and unreliable plumbing. Their budget furniture was flimsy and laughable in the large, high-ceilinged rooms, and the rooms themselves sparsely carpeted with mis-matched strips and squares brought from various sales. Many rooms were without curtains. Everywhere felt chill and eerily echoic. Even back then they tended to spend most of their time in the kitchen. Already an ever-increasing tide of unsolicited mail and newspapers, and the wherewithal of Clifford's various tinkering, were beginning to encroach.

Clifford read about the planning application in the free local paper, one which lay in a heap on a chair awaiting his attention.

'We'll have dray lorries thundering down the lane, music blaring, the smell of chip fat …' he fumed, waving the newspaper at Maisie. 'They'll rip out the hedgerow and you can kiss goodbye to the cobbles!'

'Oh no!' Maisie said, dismayed. 'Our lovely hedgerow? Oh Clifford! We'll have to write and object.'

'Object? I'll say we will! There'll be drunks and ne'er-do-wells stumbling past at all hours, dropping their beer cans and God-only-knows *what* else, and urinating against the gate posts!'

'You could say you're concerned that our privacy will be compromised.'

'Say it? It *will* be! You can forget privacy!' Clifford thundered, pacing vigorously up and down the kitchen flagstones. 'We'll have people *gawping in* at us. People *casing the joint*. We can expect to be robbed blind on a daily basis.'

'Oh Clifford, surely not! What about the children?' Dominic, now aged seven, was not of an adventurous ilk and stayed safely within the precincts of the garden. But Frances, five, had a sly rebellious streak and couldn't be trusted to stay put. She egged on—and then, when they got into trouble, blamed—Gareth who, though only three, was the worst of them all; heedless of personal danger, he was a climber of trees, a ferreter in holes, a curious peeker into things that did not concern him. Val had brought them back from the farm on more than one occasion, as had the security man who made periodic checks on the site at the end of the lane. But in their remote, traffic-free situation, Maisie hadn't been too worried about her children's wander-lust. A pub, with traffic, and strangers, would make things entirely different.

Clifford's fury, effervescent and incendiary only a moment before, concentrated itself down to a white-hot, molten core. 'That's it!' he spat. 'I'm going to the Council offices, *right now.*'

But it was clear, on his return, that opposition was useless. 'The plans were passed last week,' Clifford announced, flinging his jacket over the back of a chair. He snatched up the newspaper and screwed it into a tight ball. 'This,' he said viciously, 'is *weeks* out of date.'

'Put it in the range, Clifford,' said Maisie, abetting his desire to punish the heinous betrayal of the newspaper. Privately, she had a sinking premonition that the pub scheme would not be disposed of so easily.

She was right. A concerted but entirely fruitless campaign ensued: letters to the press, the Council and their local MP were sent off, but yielded nothing. The main problem was that the rest of the community was very much in favour of the pub. The office staff in the business units looked forward to having somewhere within walking distance for lunch. The residents of the estate at the top of the hill likewise liked the idea of a watering hole only a short stroll along the newly refurbished footpaths that had been promised as an addendum to the scheme. The pub was seen both as a community asset and an encouragement to business; it would create employment opportunities for local people. The involvement of the Armstrongs gave the project added appeal. That family was deeply entrenched locally. At one time they had owned all the land in the vicinity including Old Farm Hall itself and they still owned several other public houses as well as other businesses in the town.

In time, despite Clifford's vociferous but impotent objections, the builders' vehicles made their jolting, tortuous way down the lane. Clifford closed the shutters across the bay windows at the front of the house with gloomy ceremony.

'Thank God I repaired these,' he said, grimly. 'They might be all that saves us from being murdered in our beds.'

He omitted giving their front hedge its annual trim and allowed the bramble and nettle within it free rein. 'Got to deter them any way we can,' he muttered. 'Don't let me find you having anything to do with them,' he warned. 'Tea, toilet, anything they ask for, you say no. Best if you don't go into the garden at all; then there's no way they can accost you.' His animosity seemed to stem from an underlying defensiveness, almost a fear, that the building and the builders posed a personal threat.

'Don't worry,' she soothed. But Maisie worried. She regarded his actions and his attitude with a deep sense of disquiet; its vehemence suggested some deeply hidden pain or trauma, an unplumbed geyser of fury and fear. It was an aspect of Clifford she had never seen before; passionate he could be, and very determined to the point of stubbornness, but undergirding these had been a calm self-certainty. His strict interdiction now gave her real cause for concern. In addition, the invasion of Clifford's possessions was at this point beginning to give her an increased feeling of being hemmed in; she needed to feel free to go outdoors, and the garden was her refuge. And her naturally sanguine, easy-going nature baulked at the idea of an ongoing feud. Although by choice she would rather not have the development at the bottom of the lane encroach upon their seclusion, there seemed no point in opposing it once the contractors' vehicles were on site, but bringing Clifford round to this point of view proved dangerous ground. 'The thing is,' she tried explaining one evening as she mashed potatoes for supper, 'what's done is done. We *tried* everything we could—'

'*I* did,' he put in darkly.

'Oh Clifford, we both did! But now it's going to happen, we have to accept it. I mean, presumably, a manager will live in. Maybe a family. We'll be neighbours.'

Her words were drowned by the *scrawp* of his chair on the flagstones as Clifford leapt from the table. 'We'll have *nothing* to do with them,' he repeated angrily.

The construction of the pub restaurant encountered a number of problems. The engines of the dumper trucks were repeatedly sabotaged overnight, necessitating delays and a dozen call-outs to the specialist mechanic. A small fire damaged the stock of new timbers. Tarpaulins covering bags of cement were removed, allowing ingress of moisture that set them as hard as boulders. A hose, unaccountably left running, flooded the foundations and shorted out the first fix electrics.

On several mornings Maisie found muddy footprints tracking across the kitchen floor which she knew had been clean the night before.

At last, they received a visit from Mr Armstrong. He arrived a few minutes after six in the evening. Clifford had only just got home from work. The man who stood on the doorstep when Maisie answered his ring was tall and well-built, about her own age, with a shock of unruly brown hair and a ready smile. He wore a wet florescent jacket over what she took to be a very expensive suit.

'Mrs Wilde?' He proffered a large, warm hand. 'I'm James Armstrong. How lovely to meet you. May I come in? It's raining cats and dogs out here.'

She stepped back into the hall and he came in, removing his sodden jacket and hanging it, as if it were the most natural thing in the world, over the newel post at the bottom of the banister.

'I'm the person who's disturbing your peace down the lane there,' he said with rueful affability. 'We're encountering a few difficulties. Is your husband home?'

Maisie felt her bowels clench with anxiety. Perhaps Clifford had been identified as the perpetrator of the nuisances on the site and was in serious trouble? She showed Mr Armstrong into the drawing room; she had no idea why. The only furniture in there was an up-ended horsehair sofa, a dozen variously broken ladder-backed chairs and an enormous metal desk. A few hundred *Reader's Digest* magazines were stacked along one wall. A stuffed owl—it had come with the chairs—stared glassily from the mantelpiece. The shutters, of course, were tightly fastened, but when she switched on the light the dull glow it threw over the interior enhanced the impression of gloom, deprivation and decay.

'Thank you,' Mr Armstrong said, as if she had shown him into a room glowing with brightness and warmth. Indeed, he rubbed his hands together appreciatively, as though a roaring fire burned in the grate. 'Gosh! What memories!' he exclaimed. 'When Grandpa lived here, this room was—well!'

But Maisie never got the chance to find out what the room had looked like in old Mr Armstrong's time as Clifford then entered it.

'Armstrong,' he said simply. 'What do you want?' He stood with apparent confidence on the threshold of the room, but even in the dimness of the inadequate light Maisie could see his face was white and his Adam's apple bobbed repeatedly in a swallow reflex which, she knew, denoted inner distress.

Mr Armstrong's spiel—and clearly, beneath his veneer of confidence and gush, it *was* a spiel, rehearsed beforehand, its points carefully considered—amounted to much more than simply an appeal from one neighbour to another. It called, bafflingly to Maisie, on what was strongly implied to be a long-standing personal relationship.

'You and I, Mr Wilde, *Clifford*,' he said, more than once, in a tone that was laden with significant import, and yet in some way deliberately obscure. 'Come on. We go back, you and me, don't we?'

The nub of it was, of course, the progress of the project down the lane. It was, according to Mr Armstrong, a project whose completion was inevitable even if just now fraught with avoidable difficulties. He understood that there had been some—possibly quite genuinely held—objections from residents, naming no names, but he sincerely hoped that all concerns would be proved to be without foundation. Short of employing a permanent night watchman … he paused here, and gave Clifford a speaking look, before going on … something he was *more* than prepared to contemplate, *should the current spate of interference continue*, he wondered if he could rely on the Wildes, as neighbours and former close associates, to be his eyes and ears. 'No one better placed than you, Mr Wilde, to keep a wary eye out. And naturally, with your co-operation the funds I'll save on security can be diverted into other projects,' he concluded.

Clifford made no response at all. He regarded Mr Armstrong with a stony eye.

At last, to fill the silence, Maisie stammered, 'Other projects?'

'Mmm.' Mr Armstrong turned towards the shuttered window and, for all the world as though he could see them from where he stood, remarked, 'Those gates at your entrance are *magnificent*, aren't they? Real craftsmanship. They were made at the foundry, you know. Yes, in my grandfather's foundry right there at the bottom of the lane. I'm happy to say that we still keep a few men on who can do work like that. We have a workshop across town, just a small one, *much* more modern of course than the one that used to be down the lane! We do bespoke work and specialist repairs. They're busy making us some railings and a dozen exquisite ornamental iron lamp posts for the restaurant terrace and along the lane here. It would be the simplest thing to have your gates taken over for repair. In fact,' he turned back to face them, 'I can see that you're in the midst of a fairly extensive refurbishment project here yourselves. If there's anything we have on site that you think you could use, or if you needed one of the trades to help you out for half a day,' he glanced at the crumbling plaster cornice, the 'temporary' light fitting, the splintered skirting, 'I'd be more than willing to send them over.'

He smiled at them then, an open-faced, genial smile, and held out both hands as though proffering an invisible gift he was begging them to accept. Clifford remained silent. His eyes, however, had lost their implacable glower but roved restlessly, avoiding their visitor's frank regard. Maisie looked from one to the other of the two men. She said nothing, fighting down a selection of conciliatory phrases with which she felt compelled to fill the silence between them. Mr Armstrong's gesture, surely, ought to be met with some answering demonstration of friendship? He continued to stand before them, his smile unwavering either in expanse or in genial intention, his hands still outstretched in generous supplication. At last Clifford made a noise, somewhere between a cough and a grunt. In no way whatsoever did it articulate an agreement to Mr Armstrong's unspoken yet clearly understood offer, much less a capitulation on the subject of the construction project at the bottom of the lane, and yet tacitly they all understood it in those terms.

Mr Armstrong dropped his hands and made a movement towards the hall. 'Mustn't keep you from your supper,' he said. 'It smells delicious!'

'Thank you so much for calling in,' Maisie offered, following him from the room and watching him shrug his arms into the sleeves of his coat. Clifford remained behind in the drawing room. She opened the door. A gust of rain-laden wind met them with such ferocity that Maisie felt a sudden stab of guilt that she had to turn the man out into it and wondered, wildly, about inviting him to join them for supper.

Mr Armstrong turned and held out his hand to her. 'Goodbye, Mrs Wilde.' His hand held hers firmly, his eyes and slightly contracted brow betraying a mixture of curiosity and mild dissatisfaction and something else that Maisie only identified as his fluorescent coat faded into the thick darkness of the drive—pity.

In the kitchen, Clifford sat at the table reading the paper with concentration. 'What a funny thing,' Maisie wittered, as she probed potatoes and stirred a sauce. 'What can he have meant?'

'Mmm? Who?' Clifford turned a page of the newspaper.

'Mr Armstrong. He seemed to think you two had history. That's odd, isn't it? Don't you think?'

'Not really,' Clifford replied, after a moment. 'When I bought the house, I told you he was the seller. There were legalities. We met a time or two over that.'

'I thought he implied rather more,' Maisie mused. 'As though you two were friends—I don't know—years back, in your younger days.'

'I'm a good deal older than him. He's your age, more or less. If our paths crossed, I don't remember it. Is dinner ready? If not, I can carry on with that grouting.'

After that, work continued on the pub unhindered and their gates were hauled off to be refurbished, although any relationship between these two phenomena remained utterly unacknowledged. Clifford frequently visited the site during the evenings and at weekends, returning with sundry items—lengths of lumber or coils of cabling—adding them to his stockpile without reference to their provenance; they may as well have come from a faerie grotto or magical hardware depository of which only he knew the whereabouts. His capitulation was never mentioned between them, neither was the progress of the building work or the appearance of the finished project. However, Maisie noted to herself with relief that his dire imprecations about the negative impacts of the scheme turned out to be wide of the mark. The landscape contractors did nothing to the hedgerow other than to augment the already quite prolific spread of spring bulbs with several hundred more. The cobbles were removed, but only so that proper drainage and utility services could be installed and the sub-base levelled out, then the cobbles were painstakingly re-laid. A narrow pavement was installed on the far side of the lane, lit by a dozen ornate cast iron streetlights, presumably produced by Armstrong's foundry. A pedestrian access from the commercial estate and another from the housing development intersected with the pavement well below Old Farm Hall, so that there was little passing foot traffic. Clifford's predictions of drunks and ne'er do wells and atrocities committed against their property proved groundless. Vehicular traffic used the lane at sensible speeds, the cobbles and traffic-calming chicanes at the top and bottom of the lane reinforcing the signs that requested a 10mph speed limit and courteous consideration for residents.

Necessarily, in the course of the construction and whilst orchestrating the opening and first few weeks of trading, Mr Armstrong was often on site. He always raised a friendly hand to Maisie if they passed each other on the lane, and called in on the couple of occasions when he felt she needed pre-warning of particularly significant developments—the shutting off, for a period, of water or electricity, or the arrival of a crane that might block their access for a short time. He was genial and enthusiastic in his conversation, had bright, merry eyes, and would lean against the door jamb while he chatted in a way Maisie found familiar and pleasing.

But any friendship that she might feel towards the developer met no echo in Clifford. The Wildes' front shutters remained firmly closed throughout the building work and afterwards, quashing for good any possibility of clearing, decorating and eventually using those rooms. Although invited as VIP guests they did not attend the grand opening, and despite their clamouring importunity the children were debarred from using the pub's play area, although expressly instructed by Mr Armstrong they could do so at any time. It was taken as read that the family would decline to notice the establishment by so much as a glance, let alone patronise it—which was a pity because it became a family-friendly venue for locals and held various community events that Maisie would have liked to attend.

When at last, some weeks after the completion of the building, their gates were returned to them beautifully restored, it was left to Maisie to write a short note of thanks.

What people don't understand—I don't think even Maisie really understands it—was that down at Old Farm Hall we were safe. Well off the beaten track, under the radar. I mean, I don't think many people actually knew there was a house down there at all in those days. I didn't myself until I saw the auction details, and then I knew it would be ideal; no one to trespass—no one to worm their way in, no door-to-door salesmen or Jehovah's Witnesses arriving on the doorstep to soft-soap their way inside. No strangers ever came down there and that's just how I liked it. My Maisie and my children, they were safe.

But the idea of Uncle Tom Cobbley and all coming and going day and night, drunks driving past, snoopers and rubber-neckers gawping in … that threatened everything I'd worked so hard to build up.

I tried everything: letters, visiting the Council offices. I went to our MP's weekend surgery. But none of it did any good. They built the damned place in spite of me.

Well! Let them get on with it, I thought to myself.

I didn't make it easy for them, I can tell you! Oh no! I put more than just one or two spanners in their works! And I made them pay too! Don't think they got off scot free! And as long as there's breath in my body they'll never see a penny of my money in their till.

But doing that created more delays, more distractions for me. Work inside the house had to stop while I turned my attention to security. I had to shore us up, make us safe. Armstrong unwittingly helped me out by fixing those gates. If he was fool enough to do it for nothing, who was I to stop him?

I let the hedge grow thick and high, and I made sure there were always plenty of obstacles littered on the drive—nothing valuable, you know; a wheelbarrow with a punctured tyre, the odd pallet, piles of rubble—anything to make it difficult for people to get near. I bolted the shutters of the front windows so nobody could see in. As a matter of fact, that turned out to be a good move because it meant I could bring those two downstairs rooms into proper play. We didn't need them really, we had plenty of room in the kitchen and in the little sitting room, but I could store a load of good stuff in those rooms. I can show you, if you like. Some really good finds, I had; they only need a bit of work to make them good as new. And when I retire, you'll see proper progress.

Maisie laughs at me sometimes. Says I'm preparing for a siege, or for Armageddon, whichever comes first. Our generation was brought up with that kind of threat hanging over us—nuclear war. People don't talk about it so much nowadays. Global warming, that's what we have to watch out for now. Oh, and terrorists—but they're nothing new, are they? What Maisie doesn't realise is that, at any time, people can take away from you the things you value the most. It isn't big things like wars we have to worry about really; it's the small, seemingly innocuous things you wouldn't glance at twice—double-glazing salesmen, the God-squad, Gypsies selling dusters— they might seem innocent enough at first, but once they get their claws in ... and Maisie would be just gullible enough to fall for them, if I let her.

Chapter Twenty-One

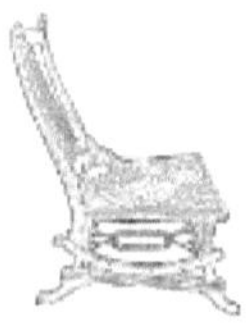

On Monday morning an envelope from the bank welcoming Maisie as a new 'elite' customer, outlining the benefits and privileges of her new standing, which include free travel insurance and access to a Customer Relationship Manager who will be pleased to discuss her needs at any time. The letter includes a new gold debit card and an opening statement. The balance takes Maisie's breath away.

She calls Dominic at work, something she is only supposed to do in an emergency. 'Is this right?' she squeaks.

He laughs. 'Yes Mum, quite right. And there's plenty more to come. Harrington's haven't paid up yet and neither have the insurance policies. Go out and enjoy yourself!'

'Well, as a matter of fact I *am* going out for lunch tomorrow.'

'Good. Treat yourself to something new to wear. Have your hair done. You'll want to make a good impression.'

His words cause Maisie a stab of anxiety. She hasn't given any thought to what "going out to lunch with the girls" actually means: dressing up, choosing from a menu, social intercourse—all things for which her life with Clifford has left her woefully unprepared. AS soon as she puts the phone down she hurries upstairs to see if she has any clothes that might be suitable. It doesn't take long to see that it is hopeless. Her clothes are utilitarian, bought for warmth and practicality—and of course value—rather than appearance or style, and usually from charity shops or off market stalls. Gardening and helping Clifford with DIY has damaged most of them in some way or another—they are variously daubed and torn. Her 'good' clothes, looked at in a critical light—as she instinctively feels they will be by the ladies of Gwen's social circle—seem dowdy and disreputable. Apart from the black suit she bought for Clifford's funeral, her choice is limited to a few pairs of sag-kneed corduroy trousers, a selection of variously pilled and faded fleece tops and a drawer full of matted woollens very much beyond their best. She slips on the suit skirt and the white blouse she wore for the funeral, wondering about adding a cardigan rather than the jacket, but feels hopeless and a bit panicked. Perhaps lunch is a bad idea?

The skirt is much too big on the waist now. And in any case, looking at herself in the mottled mirror, she fears she might be mistaken for one of the waiting staff but for the wild state of her hair and the hunted look in her eye that combine to make her look like an escapee from an institution. She tries other combinations, putting on and taking off trousers and tops, a couple of unseasonal skirts, a track suit, back to the trousers … until the clothes are piled high onto the bed and she is hot and pink with effort and frustration. Nothing is right—too old, too old-fashioned, too shabby, too obviously second hand—and the truth is she has no idea at all what will be appropriate, what will suit her, even what she would *like* to wear. The lunch might as well be a Japanese tea ceremony or a Māori initiation, so foreign, so alien is it to her limited experience. She tries the suit again, pinning the skirt's waistband more tightly, considered sewing in some darts and moving the button, and then, without warning, throws herself onto the bed in a paroxysm of tears. As quickly as it has come, her despair turns to an acrid, appalling resentment against Clifford. 'This is what you have brought me to,' she shouts angrily into the tangled, discarded garments, 'I am one of your wretched *things;* useless and ugly and fit for nothing.'

Both before and after his death, she has been immured in Clifford's stash. Walled-in. Over the years beforehand his parsimony restricted her socially and materially, making her completely out of touch with modern dress code for the middle-aged woman. If she can conjure any image at all, it comes dressed as her Aunt Sarah, wearing tweed skirts and blouses buttoned to the neck, floral-printed, long-sleeved frocks, twin sets, sensible brogues.

The outburst and the ensuing vision shock her into a kind of composure. Spent, and a little traumatised at her outpouring, she climbs off the bed and folds up all the clothes with shaking hands. Then she has a shower, gets dressed into her usual clothes, and takes herself shopping.

Maisie spends an hour in the coffee shop of the local department store simply observing other female customers. It is a revelation! They come and go in a relentless tide, in and out of the coffee shop, meeting friends and drinking lattes, wearing jeans with flattering boots, flowing tunics over leggings, smart tailored trousers and soft, becoming knitwear in pastel colours. Their nails are manicured, their faces discreetly—or, in some cases, not so discreetly—made up. Their hair is every shade except grey, and professionally styled. They are accessorised—that, Maisie realises, is the term—with scarves and jewellery and handbags that match their shoes. Beside them she feels like a country bumpkin, a vagrant, a throw-back from an earlier, savagely puritan age.

Her earlier anger returns briefly; she fulminates over her cup. Where has she been all her life? She is reminded of a film watched one afternoon about a nun who, after thirty years in a convent, renounces her vows and returns to the world to find motor cars where horses had been, men flying in machines, hemlines raised and moral standards relaxed—an entirely different, freer, fresher world to the one she had forsaken, and full of strangeness. But full of possibility also. The nun, after a period of disorientation, found her feet and made something good for herself. This is the recollection that emboldens Maisie to finish her tea, take a firm grip on her handbag, and set forth to trawl the clothing department.

Presently she finds herself ensconced in a changing cubicle while a helpful assistant runs to and fro. It turns out Maisie is two sizes smaller than she believed, but once this error is discovered the assistant brings various styles and colour combinations until they have a wardrobe of coordinated separates suitable for most informal situations—comfortable, stylish, good quality, flattering and—when she takes them to the till and proffers her new debit card—eye-smartingly expensive. Maisie steels herself and jabs in the PIN she has memorised, and returns to the car with a dozen carrier bags in tow.

At home, she empties her wardrobe and drawers with a solemnity that approaches the ceremonial, folding away her old clothes with her old life, squashing them into black bin bags.

Early the following day she returns to the department store wearing a pair of tailored navy trousers, a turquoise and white paisley blouse, a co-ordinating long-line cardigan and a softly knotted scarf for an appointment in the store's hairdressing salon. The time she spends in the hairdresser's chair is probably the longest she has ever spent in contemplation of her own image and, on the whole, it doesn't displease her. Her eyes have lost their sadness, her skin the greyish pallor that had depressed her on the morning of the funeral. Cheek bones and a smooth jaw delineate a face that has always been plump and appley. The stylist admires her natural curls and they agree together on a style that will be practical and easy to maintain without shearing her of this asset. It is shingled up the back but allowed to tumble in riotous disorder over her ears and forehead.

The woman sells her a bottle of styling mousse. 'Towel dry your hair,' she says, 'and stroke a blob of this through it. You'll find it will fall naturally into style, lucky thing. I'd need a perm to achieve this.'

Afterwards she visits one of the cosmetic concessions on the shop floor. 'Tinted moisturiser and some blush, mascara and a new lipstick are all a woman with such excellent skin tone needs,' the assistant advises, 'but we ought to discuss your skincare regime. What are you currently using?'

Maisie tells her.

'I thought so.'

Two hours later she is back at home and ready for Gwen's ring on the doorbell. She feels like a stranger, but a socially acceptable one, and in the time leading up to Gwen's arrival, she alternately preens and picks at the image the mottled mirror reflects back at her. Anxious flutters low in her stomach give way to little trills of excitement that have her rushing to the toilet.

'Get a grip on yourself, Maisie,' she says sternly into the mirror as she washes her hands after her third visit to the toilet.

Gwen is dressed, as usual, in trousers and a shirt and stout shoes, but a dab of lipstick and a couple of grips holding back her fringe indicate that she, too, has made extra preparation for the lunch.

'Goodness me, Maisie,' she whoops as Maisie opens the door, 'what a transformation!'

'Have I overdone it?' Maisie quavers, putting an instinctive hand to her newly-cropped hair.

'Gosh, no! You look fabulous!' Gwen reassures her, 'only, you know, rather different. Is this the new you?'

'I hardly know who I am,' Maisie admits as she collects her handbag and locks the door. 'I was beginning to feel more and more like one of

Clifford's chattels. Perhaps I should just allow Mr Sligh to take me away on Friday and sell me at auction?'

'Well, you don't look like a chattel to me,' Gwen reassures her. 'Not now, anyway.'

'No,' Maisie allows. 'Perhaps I have made some progress in the past twenty-four hours. I went mad at the shops and bought I don't know how many new things.'

'Good for you.' They are walking down the lane towards the Smithy. The car park has few vehicles in it but as they walk a small red car drives past them and parks in one of the disabled spaces. 'There's Amy,' Gwen says, quickening their pace a little. 'She sometimes needs a bit of a hand. Do you mind?'

'Not at all! Is she one of the ladies?'

Gwen fills her in breathlessly as they walk. 'Yes. Amy Snow. Never married. Lives in one of those bungalows round the green. Rather frail in body but don't be fooled. She's sharp as a shard in her mind. Demon bridge and whist player.'

Amy is struggling out of her car seat as they approach. In the time it takes her to extract herself from the vehicle, Gwen has opened the hatchback and taken out a folding walking frame that she erects and secures with expert hands. 'Here you are Amy. Let me take your bag. That's right. I'll lock the car for you.' Gwen quickly takes charge. 'This is my new friend Maisie. Maisie, this is Amy.'

Amy is perhaps in her late-seventies, very slightly built, with white hair showing pink scalp beneath. She is warmly buttoned into a thick woollen coat and has a mohair scarf tucked around her neck. Even so, when she takes one thin, trembly hand from her frame long enough to shake Maisie's, it is icy cold. Her eyes, though deeply hooded by folds of skin, are clear, brilliant blue and give Maisie a look as straight and penetrating as a gimlet.

'Gwen's friend, eh?' She winks. 'Careful where that may lead you!' Maisie expects Amy's voice to have a harsh, carking, corvid quality but it has, in fact, the light musicality of a girl's. When she smiles, it lights her whole face in a thorough-going glee that is almost child-like in its naivety and its naughtiness.

'You mischief-maker,' Gwen remonstrates good-naturedly, steering Amy and her Zimmer frame towards the ramp.

'What do you mean?' Maisie laughs a little nervously, bringing up the rear.

'If you don't know, I can't tell you,' Amy says over her shoulder, giving her another roguish look.

'She means I'll have you volunteering for one of my pet projects,' Gwen explains as she holds the door open for Amy. 'And she's right, of course. I will.'

'There are the others,' Amy says, nodding towards a booth in a room just off the entrance vestibule. 'They're very kind. They always try to get a table that is reasonably accessible.'

'And near the door,' Gwen adds. 'None of us likes walking into these places on our own, even in this day and age. A woman in a bar on her own sends the wrong signals.'

Maisie looks around the interior of the pub while Gwen and the other women get Amy settled and fold away the Zimmer. According to Clifford all those years ago, the Smithy was a place where uncouth, beery louts gathered, a theatre of threatening behaviour and nefarious carryings-on. In actuality the place seems benign, with fresh flowers, a bright, cheery décor and a selection of seating options around a number of open fireplaces. The 'spit and sawdust' he predicted are nowhere to be seen; scrubbed solid wood planks alternate with thick carpet and areas of practical quarry tile. Soothing, non-confrontational music plays discreetly and although there is a pungent smell of food about the place, it is actually very appetising. What few customers there are seem well-to-do: men in business suits eating lunch, a few couples perusing the menu, a smattering of singles reading newspapers or tapping on their laptops. For all the storm clouds and upset it had created on the horizon of Old Farm Hall the place is rather nice. Yet another example, Maisie thinks testily, of Clifford's wrong-headedness that debarred her from something she might have enjoyed.

Maisie's attention is drawn back to their table by Gwen, who is eager to introduce her. 'We usually have a kitty for drinks,' Gwen explains. 'Ten pounds will get you a glass of wine and a fancy coffee at the end, more or less—'

'At *most* places,' one of the women qualifies hurriedly, 'although sometimes, there's an offer. If you buy two glasses you get the rest of the bottle for free. So that's better value. I'm Minnie, by the way.' Minnie has a rapid, breathless, confiding manner of speech, as though communicating secrets as economically as possible on a telephone line that charges by the second. She is perhaps Maisie's age, as plump as Maisie used to be, although considerably taller. She is carefully dressed in painstakingly co-ordinated clothes and accessories, her shoulder-length hair rather lack-lustre but immaculately styled and lacquered into place.

'Minnie?' Maisie repeats, 'as in …'

'Mouse,' interjects one of the other women, derisively.

'Minerva,' Minnie corrects her, 'but I like Minnie, or Min for economy.'

'And economy is Minnie's middle name,' the same woman says more cuttingly still, as they all rummage ten-pound notes from their purses. Gwen takes the money to the bar to order drinks.

'Oh well,' Minnie looks down awkwardly at her hands, which toy restlessly in her lap. 'You know, Viola. "Every little helps."' Maisie feels immediately sorry for her, and conscious of an instant dislike for the woman across the table who has made the remark.

Viola has the pinched, desiccated look of a lifelong smoker. The flesh around her lips is stitched into fine lines, the lips themselves thin and drooping downwards at the corners. Her skin is dull and leathery, her eyes bleary and a little bloodshot, suggesting dissipation. The heavy application of eye makeup does nothing to soften this effect. Everything about her is sharp, from her painted nails to her knife-like nose. Her hair is savagely short, dyed black. She wears weighty, tortuously twisted metallic jewellery including several rings on each finger, giving the impression of a knuckle-duster across her gnarled, claw-like hands. She looks Maisie frankly up and down before introducing herself. 'Viola Cutler,' she says. 'Had your hair done for the occasion?'

Maisie blushes and again lifts her hand to her newly-cut hair but forces herself to return Viola's gaze. 'Yes. Yes,' she admits. 'Just this morning.'

'Where did you go? They haven't brushed you off properly. You have bits of hair in your ears,' Viola remarks.

'Viola!' Amy remonstrates. She has divested herself of her coat and scarf and continues to peel off layers of cardigan and other indeterminate woollens.

'I'm only being helpful,' Viola defends herself huffily. 'I'd want to know, if it was me. Oh, for God's sake, Amy, pass me those clothes. How many layers are you wearing? It isn't *that* cold!'

'You know me,' Amy giggles, 'I'm always frozen.'

'I suppose that's why you read those steamy romances.'

Amy grins again. 'I need *something* to keep me warm at night!'

'I like your cardigan very much, Maisie,' Minnie gushes, reaching out to feel the texture of the yarn. 'Montaray, is it? Or White Stuff?'

'Minnie knows all the designer brands,' says a glamorous woman who hasn't yet introduced herself.

'And the cut-price ones,' Viola adds quietly.

'Oh! Thank you,' Maisie replies quickly, to cover Viola's aside. 'I've no idea what make it is. I just liked the colour and I thought it went with the shirt pretty well. I've been admiring yours, too,' Maisie turns to Minnie, which has the effect of turning her shoulder on Viola. Reciprocally, she puts her hand on Minnie's sleeve. Even Maisie can tell that the material is thin and poor quality. 'You clearly have an eye for colour.'

Minnie brushes invisible crumbs off her bosom. 'Thank you,' she whispers. 'I got it in the sale.'

'Obviously,' Viola mutters under her breath, before announcing, 'I need a smoke. Excuse me, girls.'

'Just when we're all settled,' complains the final occupant of the table, in a ripe, husky voice. Viola has ended up at the back of the booth and in order for Amy to remain undisturbed all the rest of the women have to move so that Viola can get out. When they have reconfigured themselves, Maisie finds herself between Amy and this final member of the luncheon circle. She is blonde, with luxuriant tresses possibly not all indigenous to her head, held in place by a wide diamante headband. Her figure is voluptuous; clad in clothes perhaps a size—or two—too small; blouse buttons strain across an expansive bosom, trousers stretch tightly over ample thighs. She is heavily made-up with blue eye shadow, false eye lashes and bright red lipstick that clashes with the cerise of her blouse. 'I'm Gloria,' she smiles. 'I'm the group's good-time girl. I'm sure you've heard all about me.'

'I don't know anything about any of you,' Maisie says. 'But it's lovely to meet you all and thank you for allowing me to join you.'

Gwen returns with the drinks and some menus. 'Specials today are Pasta Provençale and Fisherman's Pie,' she announces, distributing glasses.

Minnie opens her mouth to ask a question but Gwen, possibly anticipating it, goes on, '£8.99 as a main course, or £10.99 with a pudding if you go for the two-course deal.'

Minnie nods and opens the menu. Maisie does the same. The only thing cheaper than £8.99 is a club sandwich with chips, at £7.99. 'I think I'll have that,' Minnie mutters, almost to herself, 'although usually, puddings are £3.99 so the two-course deal *is* better value, in the long run.'

'Did you happen to see what the roast of the day is?' Amy asks.

'Pork. Shove up, Gloria,' Gwen says, squeezing herself onto the end of the booth. 'Now then, ladies, I hope you've been keeping my friend Maisie entertained?'

'Viola has been her usual charming self,' Gloria smiles, 'but the rest of us, together, have just about managed to counter-balance her negative impact.'

'Where has she gone? Loo?'

Minnie shakes her head. 'Cigarette.'

'Oh. Well, I'll put her wine here, next to you, Amy, shall I?'

'If you must. Will the pork come with Yorkshire Pudding do you think? I'm starving.'

'I don't know where you put all the food you eat,' Gloria says ruefully. She pats the roll of her stomach. 'On the other hand, I know exactly where mine goes!'

'Me too,' agrees Minnie eagerly. 'But on the days when we have lunch, I only have the *lightest* of suppers.'

'You're lucky.' Amy gives a lascivious snigger quite at odds with her spinsterish appearance. 'Men like meat, not skin and bone. That's why I've always struggled to get one interested in me!'

When Viola returns, she seems brighter. 'Just had a chat with the new manager,' she says. 'Seems very nice. Single as well.'

'You must know him,' Gloria turns to Maisie, 'being a neighbour.'

Maisie shakes her head. 'I'm afraid Clifford and I were very unsociable. We haven't mixed with any of the people here. In fact, before today, I hadn't stepped over the threshold here!'

'The previous managers were here for quite a few years. We didn't like them, much, did we?' Gloria looks round the table.

'She was a bit of a slattern,' Viola says. 'Sometimes still in her dressing gown at eleven.'

'I expect they work very late though,' Minnie says quietly. 'A lie-in, sometimes—'

'When were *you* ever down here at eleven, Viola?' Gloria interrupts. 'Don't tell us you're so desperate for a drink that you've taken to queuing outside at opening time?'

'Surely not,' Amy chimes, but in a tone that suggests she could readily believe it.

'Don't be ridiculous!' Viola snaps. 'I left my coat here once and came to collect it, that's all.' She pushes her wine away a little. Half of it is already drunk.

'I was once here earlier than that,' Gloria offers, with a suggestive waggle of her eyebrows. 'Got off with a chap down here one night and went back to his. He brought me back in the morning, for my car.'

'*Did* you?' Amy leans forward eagerly. 'What happened?'

'What do you *think* happened?' Gloria laughs.

'I mean afterwards. Did you see him again?'

'Sadly, no. I think he got back with his wife.'

'Oh, Gloria,' Amy sits back. 'Don't you know the married ones are hopeless? They always do go back, in the end.'

'Says the world's expert in relationships,' Viola sneers, reaching for her glass.

'We ought to order,' Gwen puts in quickly. 'I'm going for the pasta. What about you, Maisie?'

Maisie, who doesn't normally eat much lunch beyond a sandwich or a bowl of soup, says, 'The same, please,' without really knowing what it will be.

Gloria orders something called Strumpet's Chicken—'Made for me!' she laughs—Amy the roast pork, Minnie the club sandwich before at the last minute changing her mind to Fisherman's Pie.

'It's only a pound more,' she says, as though she needs to justify herself, 'and I really will only have a very light supper.'

'I'm not very hungry,' Viola sniffs. 'I'll pass.' She drains her glass. 'I'll have another drink though.'

The others exchange looks across the table but nothing is said. When Gwen returns from the food order point, she puts Viola's wine down and says, 'I've ordered you a bowl of soup, Viola. You've got to have something or you'll be ill,' in a tone that brooks no denial, and when it comes Viola eats it all as well as the roll and butter.

Gloria shows them her holiday photos between lunch and dessert. They are displayed on an iPad. 'Here's the minibus—they pick you up at the door, you know. This is the driver. I forget his name now. This was my cabin. Here I am with Rosario—he was one of the waiters. This is George. He was on holiday with his brother. Here's the brother—very poorly, I gather. You can see by his colour …' Her finger sweeps across the screen. 'Here's me with Nico—gorgeous blue eyes … Oh! This was the night I dined at the captain's table. I was pleased with my dress, I must say. Do you remember, Gwen, I got it from your shop? Minnie altered it for me, bless her. Stuart certainly liked it—he's the second lieutenant, he danced with me ever so many times … I've got a picture of him, somewhere …' The record of her holiday scrolls by with a roll call of names, all male, against, across or on top of whom Gloria is variously lent, draped or perched in assorted states of dress and undress. 'Oh! This was so funny! We were all by the pool …'

'Where was this cruise again?' Minnie asks Amy, aside.

Amy shakes her head. 'Greek Islands?'

'You can't tell, can you, from the pictures?'

'Not too bothered about the *sights*,' Viola says venomously.

Abruptly Gloria's diatribe comes to an end and she snaps the iPad closed. 'You're only jealous,' she says, pouting.

'Humph!' Viola gets up and goes out for a cigarette.

'I don't know why we keep including Viola,' Gloria says in a fierce whisper when the outside door has swung closed. 'She's impossible.'

'Come on. Come on now,' Gwen soothes, 'none of us is perfect. But really ladies,' she goes on brightly, 'we must discuss our next collective adventure—our trip to the Lakes.'

'Why don't you come with us?' Minnie asks, turning to Maisie. 'It isn't expensive, considering, and if you share a room, it's cheaper still.'

'But you don't have to share,' Gwen qualifies. 'Viola's coming with us this time, and she's opted for a single. It costs more, of course, but that won't matter to her.'

'Oh, I …' Maisie stammers, 'so, you're all going?'

'Yes!' Gwen cries. 'The more the merrier.'

'When is it?'

'Next Monday. We get picked up at the coach station at eight and dropped back the following Friday. So it's only four nights. Do say you'll come,' Amy chips in. 'We're doing an overnight at Cartmel, a visit to Holker Hall, Windermere, Keswick and ending up in Kirkby Lonsdale. The hotels aren't always absolutely top notch but the people are usually friendly and the food's always *very* good.'

'It isn't *all* women,' Gloria twinkles. 'Sometimes there are single men—'

'Oh Gloria! Really!' Gwen admonishes. 'Maisie isn't interested in men. She's only just lost her hubby.'

'It's probably booked up, isn't it?' Maisie asks doubtfully.

'A trip away would do you good,' Minnie whispers. 'These women saved me when I lost my husband. They're all ever so nice. Even Viola *can* be, I'm sure, once we get to know her a bit better. The thing you have to remember is that no matter how hard it is, life must go on.'

'I don't know. I'll have to think about it,' Maisie says, feeling a bit harried.

'Time for pudding.' Gwen announces.

Over coffee the women get their diaries out and make their plans for the next few days. It is clear to Maisie that they see a great deal of each other one way or another, getting together socially and coming to one another's aid for practical purposes. Viola, for example, visits Amy weekly to keep the garden tidy.

'She's so green-fingered,' Amy says. 'She's promised to do my hanging baskets for me this year.'

Twice weekly the ladies get together for whist. 'I don't play,' Minnie explains. 'I get all muddled up with the suits. But I like to watch, and I serve the supper, so I try to make myself useful.'

'She also does all our mending,' Gloria puts in. 'She's brilliant with a needle and thread. Zips and everything.'

'Oh!' Minnie blushes crimson, delighted with the compliment, 'Well, really, I—'

'She has a thing going with the dry cleaners,' Viola mentions darkly, as though it is something nefarious. 'They farm out all their alteration work to Minnie.'

'It's just "pin" money, isn't it, Minnie?' Amy quips, pleased with her joke, simultaneously throwing Viola a piercing glance. 'Goodness knows, we all need a bit of help financially these days,' she says, adding, 'not that she charges *us,* of course.'

'You're all so *busy,*' Maisie remarks, 'doing useful things: gardening and sewing and hospital visiting, and you, Gwen, your charity work!' In comparison the weeks in front of her stretch empty and purposeless. How on earth is she going to occupy her time now, without Clifford, and perhaps without the house and garden?

Gwen seems to read her mind. 'There'll be time for you to be busy,' she says kindly, 'but for a while you need time just for you.'

'Oh yes,' Minnie chips in breathlessly. 'That's why I think you should come with us to the Lakes.'

At that moment one of the pub's staff comes to clear away their cups. 'The Lakes?' he echoes.

Viola introduces him. 'This is Oliver, the new man in charge.'

'Oh my,' sighs Gloria, looking him up and down, 'be still, my beating heart.'

Oliver is in his mid-forties, tall and broadly built, without a suggestion of fat or flab—he clearly takes good care of himself. He is very smart in immaculately cut trousers and a crisply ironed shirt open at the neck to show a thick mat of dark hair at his throat. His hands—also rather hairy—are large, the fingers strong, with well-manicured nails. Clean-shaven, he has finely chiselled rather classical features; his mouth is wide-lipped and sensitive, his nose roman, his eyes dark and thickly lashed. An abundance of thick black hair is gelled back off his forehead. But in fact, in spite of its remarkable beauty, it is not his face that immediately draws the attention of the women, but rather a distinctively lithe, restlessly athletic quality of movement. For a large man he is incredibly light on his feet, deft and graceful. The mundane tasks of table-clearing are accomplished with a coiled, contained energy; elevated elbows and precise economy of movement bring to mind the flamboyance of a Flamenco dancer, the power of a *ballerino*.

In contrast, his conversation is genially anodyne. 'One of my favourite places. Glorious scenery. Do I take it you're planning a trip, ladies?' He draws their used tableware towards him almost by telekinesis, and balances it along his forearm like a conjurer, tossing successive teaspoons musically into one of the cups.

'Oh yes,' Gloria recovers herself sufficiently to stammer. 'Next Monday. We're going with O'Keef's.' She gives a lewd, gluey wink with one heavily mascaraed eye, 'one of our *girly jaunts* ... we like to let off steam and, you know, what happens in the Lakes, *stays* in the Lakes!' The debauched implication of her gesture and her remark makes Maisie shudder.

'Take no notice of Gloria, she's incorrigible,' Gwen interjects quickly. 'It's a perfectly respectable trip.'

Oliver diplomatically takes Gwen's cue. 'A walking holiday? Nothing like the Lakeland fells for walking.' With a deft movement, he palms the crumpled napkins and discarded condiment sachets. The cruet and menu cards re-centre themselves on the table as if of their own volition.

'More of a sight-seeing trip,' Gwen qualifies. 'I'm afraid that few of us are up to fell-climbing these days.'

'Speak for yourself,' Gloria replies, desperate to re-establish herself in the conversation. 'Personally, I *love* country activities!'

'I don't think line dancing counts as a country activity, Gloria,' Viola sneers.

'How are you settling in, Oliver?' Gwen says quickly. 'I believe you're new to the area. Mrs Wilde, here—Maisie—is your nearest neighbour.'

'Oh *really?*' In an instant, the pile of cups and saucers has disappeared and Oliver reaches out a hand to Maisie. It is surprisingly cool and its grip firm, and very emphatic. 'I've been meaning to call. Really feeling, under the circumstances that I *ought* to. But one is never sure, is one? Regardless of any prior connection … when there's been a bereavement … I decided it would be better not to intrude.'

'That was thoughtful,' Maisie murmurs.

'*Very* thoughtful,' Gloria repeats unnecessarily, toying with a tendril of hair.

'A 'prior connection'?' Amy ponders with an impish grin, 'sounds *intriguing*—'

'Hush, Amy,' Viola hisses. 'Life isn't a Mills and Boon, you know.'

With a flourish, Oliver produces a card from his shirt pocket. 'Here are my numbers,' he says. 'The pub line, and the flat, which is a private line, and my mobile.' He holds the card out to Maisie. 'In case of nuisance, or if you ever need anything, day or night. My employer, James Armstrong, is quite clear that you're not to be inconvenienced in any way. And on my own account, I'd particularly welcome any opportunity to make myself of use. I mean,' he looks, for a moment, not quite as much master of the situation as he had done a moment before, 'given, you know …'

Maisie looks at him blankly, but then realises he must have been told about the fight Clifford put up to have the pub construction stopped. 'Oh,' she says, 'that's all in the past.'

'Yes,' he says, but with an air of not quite believing it, 'yes, I suppose so.'

Gloria eyes the card enviously, but Maisie slips it into her handbag without examining it. 'Thank you,' she says.

'Won't you join us for a moment?' Gloria edges herself along the banquette to give Oliver half a thigh's purchase on its end.

'Another time, perhaps.' Suddenly two empty beer glasses materialise in Oliver's hand. He swivels on his heel and is gone.

'Ooo, Maisie,' Amy leers, 'he was very attentive, considering you've only just met. I bet he's been worshipping you from afar; that's what he must have meant. You've made a conquest, there.'

Maisie blushes. Gloria sniffs and reaches into her bag for a tissue. Gwen looks absolutely thunderous.

Viola smiles for the first time that day.

Chapter Twenty-Two

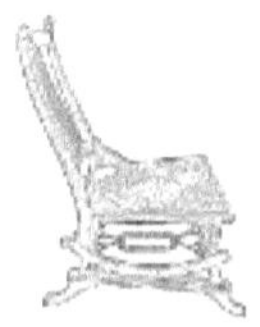

Following the excitement of shopping on Monday and the lunch on Tuesday, Wednesday finds Maisie feeling unsettled. The things that have filled her time for the past years—mending and making do, stretching out minimum ingredients to make maximum meals, reconfiguring stacks of boxes and towers of furniture—are no longer necessary; those days are gone. As pointless as they now seem—and, to be honest, had often seemed at the time—she grieves for the busyness and industry of them. The activity of the months since Clifford's death—clearing and sorting and trips to the tip—is finished too. *That* she does not miss; it had made her feel savage and angry. Now, her overwhelming emotion is one of detachment and a sort of redundancy. She wanders the empty rooms and spends a long time staring out of the windows. The garden, at one time her refuge, and which would usually beckon at this time of year, feels like a no-go area. Until she knows what she is going to do it would be futile to tackle any of the spring jobs that need to be done. What is the point? When, likely, the whole plot will be bulldozed?

Mr Sligh's van is booked for Friday, when he will take the final remnants away. The prospect of witnessing this last exodus weighs heavily upon her—a last, terrible betrayal of Clifford and all he stood for. She has yet to make the selection of furniture she will keep. To do even that much feels wrong—cold and in some way vicious, like a dissection; as though she can pick and choose aspects of Clifford himself when he has been, in everything, so very entire. She can almost feel his rage, and beneath it his hurt, in the floorboards' creak and tremor and in the panicked, importuning rattle of an upper storey window frame.

Throughout the day she roams the rooms, makes tea that she does not drink, tries to watch but cannot settle to one of the DVDs she received for Christmas.

Eventually, once night has fallen, she takes a book of orange stickers and subjects herself one last time to Clifford's hoard. Squeezing amongst the motley jumble that occupies the two downstairs reception rooms, she struggles and clambers, moving one awkward, uncooperative thing to get at another, letting sharp edges and protruding screws bruise and scratch her again, impaling herself on spiteful splinters as she has done for twenty years. It comes to her with a sad, sickening clarity that she has no personal connection whatsoever to anything in the house except the things she has made herself—her pieces of crochet and needlepoint, those bits of furniture bought by Clifford to surprise her on the day they moved in, mementoes from the children, some few items left to her by Aunt Sarah, and the garden, which alone is testament to her own industry, determination and vision. For the rest, it all means nothing, represents nothing more than the sad escalation of Clifford's peculiar, senseless, acquisitive obsession. It is like standing in a room full of strangers.

All at once she scrambles out of the room as though pursued, as though claw feet and curlicues are grasping, as if drawers will fold her up and shut her in. She fights her way out and leans against the door, keeping the demons within at bay. Then she almost rampages through the rest of the house, closing doors right and left. Her book of stickers remains intact.

Let them have it. Let them take it all.

Later, bathed and wearing her new pyjamas, she feels calmer, and makes rational decisions. She will keep a few items purely for practicality's sake—her kitchen utensils, her bedding and towels, the everyday furniture in the little sitting room and the children's beds—pending their replacement. She carefully gathers her personal belongings and mementoes together and puts them in her bedroom, near to the bags of new clothes, which she has not unpacked. She places a single sticker on her bedroom door; the men are not to trespass within.

But the prospect of it—that final disassembling—seems sadder and more final than the consignment of Clifford's bodily remains to the fire; an ultimate ruination of his life's work and the death of her dream.

The telephone rings just as she climbs into bed.

It is Pamela. 'I hope I'm not calling you too late,' she says, and before Maisie can either confirm or deny it, goes on, 'only it's Edmé's birthday next week and you usually ring to ask about what you ought to buy.'

'I have been meaning to call you but …' Maisie hesitates. Pamela is the last person to lend a sympathetic ear to her recent woes. But then a possibility pops into her mind and without stopping to consider she grabs hold of it. 'The fact is, I've been trying to get things organised so that I can come and visit!'

There is a sharp intake of breath. 'Visit? *Here?*'

'Yes dear. Just for a few days. Then I could take Edmé shopping …'

'I see.' Maisie can almost hear the click and whir of Pamela's thought processes as they calculate the inconvenience of having Maisie to stay against the riches that the combination of Edmé, a shop full of toys and a newly affluent Granny are likely to yield. 'I see.'

'I could set off tomorrow afternoon, stay with you tomorrow and Friday, and come back again on Saturday. So it would only just be a couple of days …'

'Just a minute,' Pamela says tersely. 'Let me check with Dominic.'

There is a semi-whispered conference. Maisie catches the phrase, 'Bloody short notice,' before Dominic's voice interjects with a sentence ending in the words, '… able to babysit.'

Then Dominic himself comes on the line. 'Mum? Are you all right? Pammie says you want to come and visit?'

'If it isn't too much trouble, Dominic,' she says, injecting as much brightness as she can into her voice. But it is no good. She can't keep up the pretence. The brightness bursts like a soap bubble. 'The truth is,' she says with a sigh, 'the men are coming on Friday to take your father's things away and I don't think I can stand to be here when they do.'

'Of course. Of *course,*' Dominic murmurs.

And so it is decided. In the morning Maisie packs a selection of her new clothes into a holdall and arranges to drop a key off with Mr Sligh.

She rings Gwen. 'I've decided I *will* come to the Lakes with you,' she says, 'if there's space. But Gwen, I need a single room. Will that be all right?

I know it costs more but I don't feel I know you all well enough yet to be quite happy sharing.'

'That'll be no problem,' Gwen reassures her. 'Viola's having a single room too, for the same reason. I share with Amy so that I can help her with personal care, and Minnie and Gloria go in together. Look, I'm going to call the agent right now and make sure it's going to be ok. Then I'll call you straight back.'

A few moments later she is back on the line. 'Sorted. I had to pay with my credit card but you'll pay me back, won't you?'

'I'm good for it. Shall I drop in a cheque today?'

'No, you'll be too busy and I won't get the statement until the end of the month. Any time before that will be fine, dear. I must say, I *am* pleased you're coming. After what Gloria suggested, I didn't think you'd consider it.'

Maisie laughs. 'I've got the measure of Gloria, I think!'

'She's an absolute floosy and that's all there is to it! There is a little chat I need to have with you about the shared finances. You know, the bar bill and so on, but it'll have to wait. I'm due at the animal rescue in ten minutes. I don't suppose you'd consider adopting a dog, would you? There's an absolute dear of a Doberman just come in …'

After lunch, Maisie walks slowly around the house, checking doors are locked and taps firmly closed. The sound of her footsteps echoes in the empty rooms. Clifford's ghost sulks, but remains silent.

She closes the door and climbs into the car.

Then, at the last possible moment, she re-enters the house and runs through the kitchen, down the corridor past the housekeeper's parlour to the door that leads into the garage. In the far corner, at the bottom of the wooden stairway, Clifford's tea chests and their mysterious contents radiate powerful waves of accusation and intrigue from underneath layers of ash, dust and grime. With a mixture of hopeless resignation, resentment and burning curiosity, Maisie throws a tarpaulin over them and appends an orange sticker.

When she returns on Sunday the house is empty. Those few paltry personal possessions and necessaries that remain seem unspeakably feeble— quite pitiful—but the rooms are vacant and entirely benign. Clifford's hoard is gone, dispersed back into the world from where he collected it, and he himself has shrunk back to the last bastion of his cryptic packing cases where she need not venture soon—or ever, if she doesn't choose.

INTERLUDE

" "

Maisie and I didn't go in for holidays much. There was always the house, you see; so much to get done. I could really make progress in a fortnight. Whiling the days away in tea shops and museums, it felt like such a waste. I'd just get twitchy. And so would Maisie, worrying about the garden; would the woman from the farm have watered the peas?

We tended to have days out, driving to auctions or mooching around bric-a-brac shops. You'd be amazed what we found, just on the off-chance! Maisie would make us a picnic with sandwiches and a thermos. We'd find a park to sit in. It was like the old days, before we were married. The children quite enjoyed it, I think.

On the way home I'd say, 'Shall we stop off somewhere for a bite to eat? It'll be pricey, and we'll get home very late but I don't mind. Or shall we just press on home? Get the car unloaded?'

'Oh yes,' she'd say, 'let's press on home.'

She's a homebody you see, my Maisie.

On occasion, Maisie took it into her head to take the children away for a few days, to a caravan by the sea or a holiday cottage.

'They get bored at home,' she'd say. 'They need occupying.'

'Plenty to do here,' I'd tell her. 'Fences to creosote, wood to chop. I've a box full of old bottles that need cleaning. They'll be worth money. People collect that kind of thing.'

'They're children,' she'd say. 'They need to have fun. They like zoos and theme parks and the seaside.'

Then I'd have to tell her how dangerous all those places were, describe the obsolete machinery and shoddy safety-standards, the rip tides, the fleas and diseases that animals carry, not to mention the pickpockets and kiddy-fiddlers, the confidence-tricksters and perverts that hang around on the lookout for a lone woman or a stray child. I'm quite a few years older than Maisie, you see. I've seen so much more of life than she has. She was as green as grass when I met her and I knew straight away that unless she had someone to look after her, she'd come to grief.

'Much better to stay home,' I'd say. 'Stay at home, where you're safe.'

Chapter Twenty-Three

Flinging caution to the wind, Maisie books a taxi to the coach station. The giddy sense of profligacy that energised her all weekend is only part of a general consciousness of being in some way released.

As—she surmised—their mother had hoped, she took the girls shopping and let them run amok in Toys R Us. For good measure she let them play in all the tents on display in an outdoor equipment emporium while she provided herself with gear for her Lakeland holiday. Afterwards—probably more than Pamela had bargained for but much to the girls' approval—she had treated them to lunch in McDonalds and to the cinema. They floated home on a sugar-induced high, sticky with popcorn residue, their eyes bright and conversation garbled by a heady cocktail of artificial additives. Pamela's disapproval all but wiped out her gratitude for having the day to herself as the children romped and giggled and refused to settle after their bath. Eventually Maisie'd crept into their room and begged them, for her sake, to be good, 'or Granny won't be allowed to take you out again,' she had whispered, as she tucked Edmé in for the fourth time.

Even the drive to Nottingham and back had felt like an exciting foray into unmapped lands, and Maisie herself like a pioneer. She stopped mid-afternoon at a respectable-looking café on a concourse of shops and had tea and a toasted teacake, feeling decadent and daring, at nobody's beck and call—free to spend, to eat, to linger and savour without any sense at all that she ought to be doing something else.

'This is a foretaste,' she told herself, 'of things to come.'

Her trip to the Lakes promises the same flavour of adventure. She packs her new things, plans daytime and evening outfits with changes of footwear, and buys a selection of travel-sized toiletries.

This isn't a cruise, she teases herself, or a safari, or a *trek!* But it feels just as exciting!

They are greeted at the coach station by Monica, the O'Keef's representative who will be their guide. Monica is humourless and dour in a shabby navy suit, and wields a clip-board thick with documentation. Her dark hair is pulled tightly back off her face, the face itself flat and moonish, its monotony relieved only by a slash of red lipstick. But she greets the women courteously enough and immediately sets to work stowing Amy's bags, wheelchair and frame, and helping her into a seat.

'We prefer Mick, really,' Minnie confides as they wait to board. 'He's the other O'Keef's tour guide. Gloria likes him, especially … but no, that's not fair of me to say that. We all do, really. Monica's very efficient, but Mick's more fun. May I sit next to you, Maisie?'

Viola stands apart and smokes a cigarette. Gwen has already boarded with Amy. Gloria has yet to arrive.

'Yes, of course!'

Gradually other passengers assemble. They are mainly women. Two middle-aged widowed sisters, an elderly mother and her daughter, a pair of old friends from school. A larger group turns out to be a Christian Women's Fellowship. They all mill like a flock of anxious chickens around their luggage, gradually inching it closer to the driver as he stows the cases in the hold, and clucking with concern until they have seen it loaded with their own beady eyes. Then, relieved of the worry of it, they turn to greet and scrutinize each other, the squawk of their conversation a cocktail of eager anticipation, apprehension and barely concealed curiosity. They are joined by some married couples, the men proprietorially linked by the wives, and a wholly masculine contingent from a camera club, loaded down with photographic paraphernalia.

Monica begins the boarding procedure, checking names off her list.

'Gloria's late,' Viola complains as she joins them in the queue that is forming at the coach steps. 'It's so rude to keep people waiting.'

'I'm sitting next to Maisie,' Minnie says quickly, like a child bagsing the front seat.

'I thought you'd be next to Amy,' Viola sniffs. 'I hear you're supposed to be her "carer".' Viola makes inverted commas with her fingers.

Minnie flushes. 'I've told them lots of times that isn't necessary.'

'Apparently they always put Minnie down as a carer,' Viola explains. 'Gwen told me. I suppose you've had that little chat, too? That way, she gets reduced entry to everything.'

'Which "little chat"? I don't know what you mean. I never ask them to do it,' Minnie mutters, looking from one to the other. 'In fact, I'd be happy to sit next to Amy, only Gwen always gets there first. I'm sure that overall I do quite my share of the caring.'

They climb the steps and have their names ticked off Monica's list.

Gwen has saved them seats. 'I hope you don't feel I've abandoned you,' she says as she hoists Maisie's hand baggage onto the luggage rack. 'The truth is we always play Amy's Blue Badge status pretty strongly. It gives her all kinds of priorities and privileges. I'd never have got these front seats if I hadn't insisted on helping her up the steps.'

'I like being close to the front,' Minnie says, 'but I don't care about the window. You take it, Maisie. No? Oh well, if you're sure. Oh look! Here's Gloria. Goodness! What an enormous suitcase!'

Amy emerges from a multitude of wraps and coverings to explain, 'Coach tour etiquette dictates that the seats you get at the beginning are the ones you pretty much stick with, so it's worth getting on early.'

They can hear Gloria, still on the concourse, apologising to the driver about the size of her case. 'Is it *very* heavy? Even for a fine figure of a man like you? I know it's naughty of me, but what's a girl to do? I'd hate to run out of shoes. I wonder how I'll manage it when we get to the hotel? Oh well! Not to worry! There's usually a knight to help a damsel in distress!'

There is murmur of objection as she pushes past the people waiting to board. 'Do you mind? Only my party's already seated … thank you so much …' She arrives, breathless and dishevelled, and falls into the seat next to Viola. 'Did you think I wouldn't make it? *I* did. Last minute hoo-ha with the heating thingy. Had to rope in the taxi driver, not that he minded of course! Who wouldn't take the opportunity of a quick tour of my *boudoir*? I thought his eyes were going to pop out of his head! Turned out to be the battery. You should have seen his hands shake while he tried to get them in! Ah! Here we all are then!'

'Gloria,' Gwen says, 'you're hopeless!'

'I know!' Gloria laughs.

Viola hunches down in her seat and stares gloomily out of the window. She looks as though the whole trip is an ordeal she has been press-ganged into.

'She'll cheer up when we get to the stately homes,' Gwen says, following Maisie's thoughts. 'She comes alive in a garden—quite a different person.'

Gloria rummages in her handbag, eventually pulling out her phone and a set of headphones, which she puts in her ears. 'Can't live without my music,' she announces loudly, 'and usually the driver only wants to play Radio 2.'

The driver, who cannot have avoided hearing her comment, stiffens, but responds politely enough to Gwen's enquiries about their route.

Minnie carries on a rambling and mainly one-sided conversation about the arrangements she has had to make for her dog. 'Of course, she *loves* going to stay with Irene and Gordon, and they treat her absolutely like one of the family, and they won't take a penny off me but still, it's difficult, isn't it? You do worry.'

Presently all the passengers are seated. Monica switches on the microphone and introduces herself and Bill, their driver. 'We're waiting for one more guest to come,' she says, glancing at her list, 'a last-minute booking, by the looks of things. Then we'll be on our way. I'll save all my routine announcements and a description of the day's itinerary until we're all aboard.'

'Oh good,' Maisie whispers to Minnie. 'I'm not the only one to have booked late.'

'Time's ticking,' Bill the driver says, giving the engine a little rev. 'Got a schedule to keep to, you know.'

'I know,' Monica replies sharply. She looks at her watch. 'We'll give him five more minutes.'

Three minutes tick by.

One of the Christian women stands up. 'Does anyone mind if I pray?' she asks generally, 'for a safe journey, and opportunities to forge new relationships?'

The passengers not of her party—and some who are—shift uncomfortably, but nobody raises an objection so the woman begins, 'Oh, Lord Jesus, whose ministry involved travelling from place to place in order to reach the lost and broken …'

Ten minutes have elapsed before her prayer comes to a close. 'All right, that's it,' Monica says, almost before the woman has regained her seat. Bill puts the coach into gear and is all but moving off when a cab tears into the station and screeches to a halt practically under its wheels. A man springs out, conjuring a holdall from the seat beside him. He waves presidentially at the coach with one hand while the other dispenses coins like a magic shower into the cab driver's outstretched hand.

'Well look who it is!' Gloria sings out. She whips her compact out to check her face. 'I never knew a prayer to be answered so quickly!'

'Are you lost and broken then?' Viola jeers.

'No, but I'm all for forging new relationships!'

Amy swivels with difficulty in her seat and waggles her eyebrows at Maisie. 'He's come for you,' she mouths.

Maisie frowns and shakes her head.

Bill opens the coach door and Oliver, manager of the Smithy, leaps aboard. 'Good morning, good morning!' He shakes Monica and the bemused Bill by the hand before turning to the rest of the passengers with a flourish. 'So sorry to have kept you waiting, ladies and gentlemen. Oh!' He notices the luncheon ladies for the first time. 'You *are* here. I did wonder.' He gives them a brilliant smile. Gloria gives an audible sigh.

'Can you take a seat please, Mr Harrington? We're behind schedule,' Monica says stiffly, indifferent to his charms. 'You'll have to manage with your bag until the first comfort stop.'

'Of course,' Oliver gives an airy wave, 'I always travel light. "Wherever I lay my hat," and all that.'

Bill lets out the clutch and the coach lurches forward, throwing Monica off balance and causing Gloria to poke herself in the eye with her eyebrow pencil.

Chapter Twenty-Four

Oliver seems keen to attach himself to their party from the start, taking charge of Amy's wheelchair at the first service station stop and shepherding them across the car park as though they are absolutely under his jurisdiction.

'Good grief,' grumbles Viola under her breath, 'we'll look like a bunch of Mormons!'

The women hold a hasty meeting around the hand drier in the ladies' lavatory.

'What shall we do about him?' Minnie asks anxiously. 'Do you think he'll pay his share?'

'I shouldn't think he'll want to be saddled with us,' Gwen opines. 'He'll have his own fish to fry. He'll probably join forces with that group of photographers.'

'We can't leave him on his own,' says Gloria, refreshing her lipstick. 'That would be very unsociable. I think we ought to ask him to join us.'

'Why don't you just cut to the chase Gloria, and ask him if he'd like to have sex with you on the back seat?' Viola carps. 'I notice no one else is using it.'

'Don't be ridiculous, Viola. I know this is all new to you but you forget that I go on these trips all the time,' Gloria snaps back. 'The whole point is to meet new people, to mingle and be sociable. Being all clannish and exclusive just isn't the form.'

'Perhaps we should just wait and see what *he* does,' Maisie advises. 'Gwen might be right; he might want to pal up with the men. On the other hand,' she adds, 'he might just want to be by himself. I should think, with a job like his, he gets rather tired of being sociable all the time. And he did say that he enjoys walking the fells. Maybe that's what he's planning to do.'

'You're quite right,' Gwen agrees. 'The tours of the stately homes aren't compulsory. He may well just want to go off on his own.' She sounds as though she rather hopes this will be the case.

'You tell yourselves that, if you like,' says Amy, winking at Maisie. 'But I saw it coming, just remember that! He's come to sweep Maisie off her feet!'

'If you see any particular partiality,' Maisie replies, 'it will only be because my husband worked for Harrington's. I presume it's the same family. Just a coincidence.'

'He *said* his boss had given him special instructions,' Viola scorns, 'although I must say spending four days with a bunch of menopausal old maids seems beyond the call of duty.'

'Speak for yourself, Viola,' Gloria blusters.

They emerge to find Oliver has reserved a table for them in the café and persuaded the barista to deliver their refreshments on a tray even though, strictly speaking, the café is self-service.

Gloria pours herself into the seat next to his with an oozy lack of ambiguity. 'So, to what,' she croons, 'do we owe this unexpected pleasure?'

'I found I had a week's leave still owing that I had to take before the end of the financial year,' Oliver explains. 'A trip to the Lakes felt like just the thing. You see, you inspired me, ladies!'

'Well, we're very *very* glad,' Gloria declares, which hardly represents the party's unanimous view, but they let it pass. 'And we've been wondering,' she goes on, 'whether you'd like to join our table for dinner this evening.'

'*Some* of us have,' Viola qualifies.

'Indeed,' Gwen agrees. 'Some of us think it's the last thing you'll want. You mustn't feel in any way obliged.'

'Not at all!' Oliver smiles, dealing coffee cups around the table like a croupier. 'I'd be delighted, naturally.'

'Dinner's included, of course,' Minnie puts in quickly, eager to clarify the situation. Heaven forbid Oliver might think they are asking him to be their guest! 'But we usually split the bar and wine bill.'

'What a sensible arrangement. I hope you'll allow me to take charge of the kitty, ladies.'

Gwen bridles, but says nothing.

'Gwen's our treasurer,' Viola states with surprisingly loyal fervour. 'She looks after the finances.'

'By all means,' Oliver says smoothly. 'But these coffees are on me. I ordered a selection of pastries as well. Travelling always makes me hungry.'

Presently Maisie takes the opportunity to say, 'I couldn't help overhearing your surname. Are you related to *the* Harringtons?'

Oliver leans back in his seat and regards her with a narrowed eye before replying, 'Yes. I thought you knew.'

Maisie stammers, 'N … no. I hadn't any idea, until just now.'

'Ah!' Oliver's brow clears. 'That explains things, of course. Yes. I'm the black sheep of the family, I'm afraid. Very much a disappointment to the old man.'

'My late husband worked for the firm all his life.'

Oliver stirs another sachet of sugar into his coffee with a slow spoon, as though concocting a magical brew. 'Yes. I think I knew that. And—forgive me, I find that almost everyone in Millport is connected to us, one way or another—it's just that, is it? I mean, you're not, for instance, connected to the girls in any way? To my sisters?'

'No.' Maisie shakes her head and finishes her shortbread biscuit. 'No. I never met them.'

When they get back on the coach Gloria abandons Viola to sit with Oliver some six or seven rows back. Amy dozes so Gwen moves to sit next to Viola, and the two of them tackle a tricky Sudoku puzzle on Viola's iPad. Minnie, from her window seat, gives a sort of running commentary that includes further details about her dog. She scrolls through many snapshots on the tiny screen of her mobile phone—Dolly in the garden, Dolly at the park, Dolly in her winter coat—until Maisie begins to feel a bit queasy. After that Minnie contents herself with general observations about the passing landscape. She doesn't seem to require much more than the occasional nod or murmur in response and Maisie is able to let her mind tread its own pathways.

Her sense of being more out in the world than she has ever been before sharpens with every motorway mile; the place names and the unfamiliar landscape feed the flame of excitement that uplifted her all the previous weekend, raising her to even greater heights of rashness and adventure.

This, she tells herself, with a mental sweep of her arm across the velvet-draped hills and rugged scree, all this is available to her now—a wider, richer, more fulfilling world with new people and experiences, and the idea that for the first time in her life she is absolutely independent. It might be wrong to feel so upbeat about a situation that has come about as this one has but, after all, life does go on.

Perhaps it would be folly to hold onto the old house—she quells, resolutely, a fleeting, reproving image of Clifford's crates—and even the old town. An entirely new start could be what is needed. She imagines, somewhat romantically, a village green, cricket teas, market stalls with striped awnings, herself with a basket moving amongst a bucolic crowd … she cranes to see the tiny grey settlements just perceptible between the folding hills, reading the names of towns indicated beyond the junctions. Could it be that one day she'll call one of them—or somewhere like them—home? It is intriguing to think that, during the years she has spent in the narrow confines of Old Farm Hall, sequestered behind the shuttered windows and encircled by the thick, high hedges, here or elsewhere may have been waiting—patiently waiting—a life with wide-open windows and a door on the latch.

She is roused from her thoughts by Minnie, who has taken her hand. 'You're feeling a bit agitated,' Minnie misdiagnoses, 'but don't worry. We get looked after every step of the way with O'Keef's. There are do's and don'ts, of course. You learn those, after a while. Let me give you one little hint. Run yourself a nice deep, hot bath *as soon* as you get into your room. I always do. It's one of the treats I look forward to on these holidays. I so rarely allow myself the luxury of a bath at home. But don't delay. If you wait too long other people will have used all the hot water; they can be selfish like that, some people.'

Chapter Twenty-Five

The coach brings them into the outskirts of Cartmel village a little after one in the afternoon and comes to a halt in a large car park adjacent to the racecourse.

'We will disembark here,' Monica announces. 'This is as close to the hotel as Bill can get us. Our rooms won't be ready until three, but the hotel kindly allows us to store luggage securely in the meantime. I'll show you the way in a minute. Then you can have lunch, if you desire. Do take time to see the famous Priory at some point during the afternoon though. If you're booked onto the Holker Hall trip tomorrow, you won't get the opportunity to visit the Priory otherwise.'

The party waits at the side of the coach as Bill unloads their bags. The passengers mill around in the car park, glad to be out of their seats which, for the last hour, have not seemed as comfortable as they had at first. Four or five of them, including Viola, move to a distance and light up cigarettes. Within this clearly demarked sub-group, they begin to introduce themselves.

Monica makes a number of fruitless attempts to use her mobile phone. 'They insist I let them know the second we've arrived,' she complains to no one in particular, 'but they take no account of the atrocious signal here.'

Gloria seems determined to keep close to Oliver, fixing him as often as possible with a gooey gaze from beneath her lashes. As it was the last to be loaded, her suitcase is one of the first out. She makes a number of ineffectual efforts to move it out of the way of the melee, sighing and struggling with affected surprise as though its size and weight have unaccountably increased over the course of their journey. 'My case is terribly heavy,' she remarks—unnecessarily—to Oliver, with a loaded intention in her eye. 'I hope the hotel isn't too far. I might have to ask for your help.'

'I've already volunteered to carry Miss Snow's bag,' Oliver replies promptly. 'I do think the hotel might have sent transport for *her*, at least. I'll speak to the manager about it later. Unless, of course,' he turns to Maisie, 'Mrs Wilde needs any assistance.'

Maisie is too surprised to make any response at all to this enquiry and ignores Amy's knowing wink. Gloria is visibly deflated, and her disappointment lends a churlish tone to her response that she perhaps does not intend.

'I see,' she says coldly. 'Well, I can quite see why Amy might claim your assistance but I don't know why Maisie should be more in need than any of the rest of us.'

'She is only recently widowed,' he explains, 'and she's my neighbour, apart from other considerations.' He gives Maisie a smile with a significance she is unable to decode.

With a gargantuan effort, Gloria tries to reintroduce a flirtatious tone to her banter. 'Oh well,' she says with a gaudy twinkle, '*all* ladies need a man to lean on sometimes you know, regardless of who they happen to live next door to.' Her attempt at coquetry comes across as sadly desperate. Maisie looks away, across the racecourse, disassociating herself from the whole, distasteful exchange, but cannot avoid hearing Oliver' response.

'Indeed. But I have special reasons for wanting to make myself useful to her.'

'Creep!' Gwen, who has also heard the conversation, remarks under her breath but then adds aloud, 'Come on, I'll help you Gloria,' before grasping the case by its strap and hauling it out of the way.

The day, which had earlier promised to be bright, is now overcast. Rain seems more than a possibility. 'Welcome to the Lakes!' some wit remarks, indicating the sky. The photographers' conversation turns to the subject of polarising filters.

The rain notwithstanding, the morning's relative inertia on the coach and her enthusiasm for things new make Maisie restless. The prospect of sitting still for a further period of time is almost insupportable, and she really isn't hungry.

'I don't think I'll bother with lunch,' she says to Amy in a low voice. 'I'll drop off my case and have a walk. No one will mind, will they?'

'Oh! So will I!' chimes Minnie. 'I never can manage two big meals in one day, can you? Let's have a look at the Priory, shall we?'

'I'm famished,' Amy announces. 'I'll have to have something or I'll fade away.'

Gwen, Viola and Gloria all declare in favour of lunch.

'Although mine will be liquid,' Viola asserts.

Presently all the cases are unloaded and Monica leads them, like a crocodile of nursery school children, through the narrow streets of the village to their hotel. Oliver strides along at her side like a martial arts exponent, negotiating street furniture and on-coming pedestrians with timely swerves and athletic feints. He is vociferous in his opinion that the tour company ought to make 'proper and adequate provision' for their disabled guests. Amy's small, wheeled case bounces and jitters over the cobbles behind him like an inept pupil.

'I hope you didn't have anything fragile in there Amy,' Viola smirks. 'If you did, it will be smithereens by the time we get to the hotel.'

'Everything will be sticky with syrup of figs!' Amy laughs. 'If I want to keep my bowels regular this trip, I'll have to suck my medicine out of my corselettes!'

They pile through the doors of their hotel as the first drops of rain begin to fall. It is a tiny space, soon packed to capacity with the crush of guests eager to escape a drenching; they and their luggage occupy every square inch and begin to spill out into other areas, impeding the lunch and bar service by clogging the thoroughfares. In addition to suitcases and holdalls, each member of the camera club contingent has numerous lens bags, tripods and supplementary equipment that increase their mass and poke intrusively into the personal space, backs and bosoms of anyone in the near vicinity. Several of the Christian women have guitars that they wield without consideration for furniture or decorative knick-knacks. One has a tambourine. She jingles it with sickening enthusiasm on the slightest encouragement, making those not of her party—and some who are—shrink with dread of catching her eye. Amy has to abandon her wheelchair whilst she uses the toilet; it gets in everyone's way as a long line of women forms a restive queue outside the lavatory door. In spite of these inconveniences however, the general tone amongst the holiday-makers remains determinedly jocular and up-beat.

Amidst the good-humoured chaos and noise, the manager and Monica try to complete their registration. Meanwhile, a member of the hotel staff collects their luggage and transports it to a storeroom.

Before relinquishing hers, Maisie extracts the pair of sturdy walking boots she purchased from the camping and hiking shop in Nottingham. A public footpath sign at the periphery of the car park pointing up a wooded hillside and promising views over the town and surrounding countryside has appealed to her newly adventurous spirit. With or without Minnie, she is determined to explore it. Just then Minnie yoo-hoos her from near the reception desk. Maisie joins her, squeezing with some difficulty through the crowd.

Before she can explain her intention, Oliver interjects, 'Mrs Wilde, I believe you and I have reserved single rooms. Just to reassure you, I've made the necessary arrangements with the manager.'

'Oh!' Maisie is nonplussed. 'I thought that had all been arranged …'

He leans closer to say, 'So often one is allocated a linen cupboard of a room without private facilities *even though* they charge a supplement. They'd tried to palm you off without a proper bathroom, but I've remedied that.'

'Well, thank you.' Maisie turns to Minnie. 'I do hope you don't mind, Minnie, but I've decided to head out of the village for a good long walk. I think I'll save the Priory for later. Just now, I really feel so fidgety I don't think I could do it justice. And I've got these new boots, you see. I ought to break them in.'

If she had feared Minnie would be disappointed, she'd worried in vain. 'Oh no,' Minnie affirms, breathlessly, 'Mr Harrington has just expressed his intention of skipping lunch in favour of seeing the Priory with us, so I'll walk with him. Great minds, eh?' she looks up at Oliver, '*You* don't mind, do you? If it's only me?'

Oliver gives a stiff nod. 'Not at all,' he says, although he looks as though he minds very much. 'There's sure to be plenty of time for Mrs Wilde and me to get better acquainted.'

Maisie's walk takes her over a stile and up a hill, through a copse of trees. She walks quickly, heedless of the rain that spatters on her new waterproof coat and of the mud that squelches underfoot and smears the new boots. She fills her lungs with the sharp, damp air, and stops often to survey the view of the waterlogged little town below her. The footpath is well signposted, and while she can keep the village in sight, she tells herself there is no fear of getting lost.

I am *exploring,* she tells herself. This is an *adventure.* If the worst comes to the worst, I can just retrace my steps. But I need to be brave; this is nothing, *nothing!* A walk in the English countryside. It might feel like a trek in Uzbekistan but that's because I've just spent too long cooped up.

She walks on, around the perimeter of a field, across a track and through a farmyard, glancing into a barn where sheep are penned, some with lambs. A dog comes to sniff at her and the farmer, appearing suddenly from another building, nods a greeting.

'Good afternoon,' Maisie calls boldly.

He shows her the lambs, explaining—in an accent that is as thick and flat and lugubrious as a cake of liquorice—about their husbandry. She is allowed to hold one, stroking its tight, soft curls as she presses its warm, strong little body close to hers.

'What a shame,' she says, as she relinquishes it.

'That they turn so ugly?' the farmer laughs, showing a row of jagged teeth.

'No, that they're so delicious roasted with a sprig of rosemary!'

When Maisie gets back to the village the steady rain has all but emptied the streets. Tea shops with misted windows are packed with people sheltering within, drinking tea and eating cake they neither need nor want. Maisie passes them all, although in fact the idea of tea is very appealing. Her legs feel heavy with fatigue and inside the coat, although perfectly dry, she is feels a bit chill. But she doesn't want to miss out on seeing the Priory, so she follows the signs through the grey, drizzled streets.

The Priory is deserted. The grey graves within the precincts of the grounds probably have fascinating history to reveal, but they are dark and illegible in the rain and the idea of crouching in front of them to make out their legends seems ghoulish as well as grim. She makes instead for the cloisters, somewhat sheltered from the weather. The shadowed arches conjure shades of ancient monks; the wind around the high masonry is like a whispered call to prayer. Involuntarily, she gives a shiver. Her boots on the flagstones make no sound but leave a wet and muddy wake.

Perhaps I oughtn't go in, she considers. They don't want mud tracked inside.

But the clatter of cups and crockery from an inner room reignites hope for a cup of tea, just what she needs. She presses on until an A board and an apologetic waitress in an apron inform her that the tea rooms are closed.

Defeated, she sinks onto one of the rear pews in the chapel, contemplating the architecture and reading from an information leaflet she finds. As a rule, she has no particularly religious feeling, but the single candle burning so steadily on the altar draws her eye and seems to ignite an answering tremble in her own heart. The air is thick with peaceful, soporific resonance, a thick weft of ancient prayers and faithful observance, something high and holy summoned by sheer and sustained—palpably human—effort. A frocked official moves quietly between the pulpit and the dais, preparing the area for a service which, she presumes, will take place later. She wonders briefly if the Christian women from the coach will come to banish the contemplative silence with strident guitars and the tinny rattle of their tambourine. She hopes not.

If only religion was all *true*, she sighs, wanting with a strength of desire almost spiritual for Clifford to be somewhere comfortable, needing to believe with a passion almost prayerful that he would understand what she has done since his death. But she finds no countering echo to her tentative supplication, has no sense of Clifford anywhere other than crouched irritably over his remaining chattels. Like them, he is reduced—a vestige, a mere shade of his former, dominant self. This unarguable diminution is more puissant to her than any plucked harp string, any feather floating down from the groined roof, any stroke of a ghostly hand.

Chapter Twenty-Six

They have unwittingly chosen the wettest March week on record for their Lakeland holiday. Almost the month's entire quota of rain falls within two days. Roads are flooded. It takes Bill tortuous hours to negotiate detours through lanes that are really too narrow for a coach. Gloria suffers from travel-sickness under such circumstances and sits white-faced beneath her makeup, with a sick bag clutched on her lap.

Their itinerary is soon in tatters. Monica spends a lot of time looking for a mobile phone signal in order to re-arrange their bookings. She scrambles through hedges to stand on small knolls surrounded by dripping sheep, shouting at the top of her voice, her finger in one ear.

There is limited access to the rooms of the stately homes; it is feared wet boots and outerwear will damage the furnishings.

'Really it represents very poor value for money, doesn't it?' Minnie avers. 'I think I'll complain to Monica. We ought to get a refund.'

'Of course, Monica's solely responsible for the rain,' Viola says with barbed sarcasm.

The historic gardens are quagmires and visitors are debarred altogether. Viola is bitterly disappointed; they are what she has most looked forward to, the reason, really, that she has come away at all. Her mood—not sanguine at the best of times—blackens perceptibly. The garden centres they substitute for the formal borders, ancient arbours and famous hot houses of Muncaster, Holker, Levens and Brantwood are poor surrogates, she says.

Tea rooms, restaurants and gift shops do roaring trades; there is nothing else to occupy the visitors. However, their floors—slick with water—are an accident waiting to happen and indeed on the second day the daughter of the elderly mother does turn her ankle and they are both sent all the way home in a taxi at O'Keef's expense.

'Next year's prices will go up,' Minnie predicts, 'to cover the insurance. All this extra expense is more than I'd budgeted for, I don't mind telling you.'

'What do you want us to do?' Viola snaps. 'We can't stay out in the rain all day, cheap as it would be. Amy would catch her death.'

'My waterproof turns out not to be,' Gloria complains. 'I'm so sick of being wet. My hair is a perfect frizz.'

'It isn't as though we can spend the day in the hotel,' Gwen laments. 'That's the downside of moving from place to place. Perhaps next year we'll book ourselves into a central location and do trips out from there. We could manage in two cars. I wouldn't mind driving, for one.'

Although several of them own cars and hold licences, none feels able or willing to volunteer, and so the proposal is dropped.

Later, Gwen tells Maisie, 'These group holidays are usually such fun. I'm so sorry that this one has been a washout. Perhaps you and I might consider going away just the two of us. Taking so many people's needs into consideration does mean less flexibility.'

The photographers are in despair; there are no decent photographs to be had of anything. The fells are permanently shrouded in low cloud and, in any case, their equipment would be ruined by the rain. Boredom and frustration mean that small arguments and disagreements begin to erupt. Two camera enthusiasts have a stand-up row over the likely exposure time of a landscape photograph in a gallery. Morale amongst the fell-walkers is likewise low. Those who do venture out—a few doughty members of the Christian delegation, and one or two of the couples—report conditions ranging from dangerous to impossible. Oliver, who joins their rambles, says he has never known things as bad. Only the Christians manage to maintain a determinedly spirited good humour in the face of the depressing weather and attendant inconveniences. Their camaraderie becomes more effusive with every additional inch of rainfall. In the evenings, when they tend to take up occupancy of an unused function room or deserted lounge, their songs of worship seem designed to court, rather than to discourage, further precipitation. 'Pour over me,' they trill, 'rain down, O Spirit, rain down!'

'Brilliant,' Viola spits.

The rain falls in endless grey sheets. The village streets are a torrent, the lakes almost indistinguishable from the drab landscape and depressing sky. The holiday-makers loiter in out-of-the-way, unexceptional churches and small museums remarkable for their paucity of exhibits in an attempt to while away the time until check-in. Coats and shoes can hardly dry out overnight. The interior of the coach begins to smell foisty with wet wool and saturated leather; the seats are permanently damp.

'My rheumatism is flaring up,' Amy winces.

Maisie, however, finds that she is more than able to put a cheerful face on things. The new locations and experiences, hotel living and varied eating opportunities are all a revelation. She loves her new clothes, choosing outfits and dressing with care each day and evening. Leisure—to sit and read before dinner, to amble and explore, to wallow in deep baths—feeds her parched soul. Every day she manages a walk alone. Her waterproofs and boots are thankfully well up to the task, and her hair is forgiving of the wet-dry-wet-dry regime to which it is subjected. She slips out of the hotel in the late afternoon, while the others bathe and rest, to explore paths glimpsed earlier, crunching along lake-shores beneath the dripping fringe of trees and entering parks deserted except for the odd deliriously happy, saturated dog and its owner. She climbs pot-holed bridleways and pursues paths into woodlands. The rest of the day is a slow, minutely orchestrated shuffle past oil paintings, tombs and tapestries, a repetition of roll call as they climb on and off the coach. There is a good deal of standing around while things are arranged, both by Monica on behalf of the entire group and amongst themselves. Everything is debated endlessly. Will they walk beside the lake— will the rain hold off long enough? Or should they go for coffee? Who wants to explore the shops? Or perhaps the gallery might be of interest? It all makes her feel slightly hampered; the flock-instinct chafes. The call—the boundless opportunities offered on every side—to go out and explore is irresistible. Her solitary rambles give her a sense of independence that is new and satisfying. She is always back at the hotel, showered and changed and down in the bar by seven, when the evening activities begin.

The company of new friends, while occasionally challenging, stimulates a sociable gland that has lain dormant for many years. She finds she is able to connect with all of them on one level or another. She takes her turn in keeping Amy company while the others explore venues inaccessible to wheelchairs; their cosy chats more than compensate for the skipped museums and passed-up view-points. Amy spends one afternoon telling the story of her fiancé, killed in the Sutton Coalfield rail disaster in 1955. 'After I lost him,' she says, 'I more or less buried myself in my work at the library. Old women and pensioners! No wonder I never met anyone else!'

She, Gwen and Minnie enjoy the charity shops—Gwen viewing them with a professional, Minnie with a bargain-hunting eye that is also clever at identifying good quality. Formerly she worked as a specialist machinist making high-class ladies' coats so she knows a superior cut and material when she sees it. 'Of course when I married Peter he made me give it up straight away,' she tells Maisie. She has two step children. 'We aren't close,' she says. 'I married their father when they were grown up. I don't know them very well, really.' Maisie's gratification in the bargain shops comes with the secret relief that they are not now her only resource for shopping. To prove it, she goes wild in the Beatrix Potter gift shop, buying books and toys for the grandchildren at enormous expense.

She spends an extended and interesting period in the horticultural section of a second-hand book shop with Viola long after the others have given up and drifted off. Gwen is right about Viola—she is transformed by an enthusiasm for plants even though it seems she doesn't have a garden. Maisie broaches the topic but Viola immediately diverts the conversation to her son Brian, of whom she is immensely proud. He is a successful stock-broker apparently, much sought-after in the City, a rising star in the mercantile firmament.

In Keswick, Maisie accompanies Gloria on a shopping trip to find a new waterproof. The shopping opportunities for such things are legion in Keswick and Gloria's search is exhaustive—she moves from one outlet to another, trying on and preening briefly in the mirror before casting aside coat after coat.

'This isn't a fashion garment,' Maisie suggests at last.

'Oh no, of course not. But I don't want to look a frump, and all of these look like they were made for Captain Birdseye. I know what I'm talking about, you know; I was a model in my youth. But I wasn't really made for work. Pleasure is my forte.' She has been married three times. 'I was a child bride, the first time. We ran away to Gretna Green. It only lasted eighteen months. The second lasted longer. He was away a lot, so that helped. We're divorced now. The third one died five years ago; he was my sugar daddy. He left me very well provided for. I have a daughter but she hasn't spoken to me in years; she disapproves of my lifestyle.'

At first Maisie is reluctant to spend any time in Oliver's company. His marked attention and odd, veiled remarks make her feel as though he has an alternative agenda. But in fact, as the days progress she finds his partiality less apparent. He turns out to be an attentive companion to the whole group, fending off Gloria's blandishments, indifferent to Viola's spiky humour, patient with Minnie's pettiness. He anticipates every difficulty for Amy and heads them off with ease, manhandling the wheel-chair, the Zimmer and occasionally Amy herself with chivalrous aplomb. He is careful to defer to Gwen as the group's natural leader. From being initially rather alarmed at his appearance on the trip, they all come to appreciate him being there. He is seemingly unfazed by the predominantly feminine nature of their conversation.

'With two sisters,' he says, 'I'd like to think I'm reasonably in touch with my feminine side.' He turns to Maisie. 'I think, Maisie, you said you didn't know my sisters?'

'No. I never met them.'

She feels on occasion that he is observing her rather closely but then more than once he steps to her aid and she is very glad of it. For example, his discreet suggestions and explanations help her through the minefield of unfamiliar dishes presented by the hotel menus and before long she is leaning across the table to ask questions like, 'Oliver? What is a *velouté*?' 'How can a fondant be a potato and also a chocolate pudding?' 'What does *'confit'* mean?' He recommends Dijon mustard with steak, and a dab of cranberry sauce with *pâté*. One night she braves—at his urging—a Thai curry, something she would never have dared without encouragement.

'You're clearly a very seasoned diner-out,' she remarks one evening.

'It's only been a matter of opportunity,' he demurs.

He is less forthcoming on the subject of his past and family.

'I think I might have met your son,' Maisie says, by way of an opening gambit. 'He attended my husband's funeral, with your father.'

'Oh, no,' Oliver gives an odd, strangled laugh. 'That isn't *my* son. But he is very much the golden boy.'

'One of your sisters' children then?'

'Yes.' Oliver looks at her, narrowly. 'You didn't know?'

'No. Why would I? I never went to Harrington's, for all the years Clifford worked there. I think they had Christmas parties, but Clifford wasn't the party-going type. Well, your nephew seemed like a very fine young man. Does your father hope he'll take over the business?'

'We don't discuss it, but I understand he already has more or less taken over the reins. All I know is I'll never be in that happy position.'

He changes the subject to talk about his experiences abroad, about which he is an interesting raconteur. 'I was a merchant seaman for ten years before transferring to cruise liners. Then I did some itinerant travelling here and there,' he says. 'I've worked for James Armstrong for a while, now. The Smithy is just the latest in a line of projects for him. Recently I've been running the whole company, more or less. He's been away all winter on an extended vacation.'

That explains why he didn't come to the funeral, Maisie thinks to herself.

Maisie is rapt in his tales of adventures in exotic places. 'Tell me more about your explorations abroad,' she urges. 'Have you ever been to Venice? That's somewhere I'd like to go.'

'Oh yes,' Minnie puts in. 'Oliver was telling me earlier. He says it's just like stepping into a cannelloni.'

Oliver disguises his amusement with a discreet cough. 'I think I said Canaletto,' he murmurs.

In comparison Maisie feels like a very dull and homely bird. She has not even, like the other women, held down a proper job. Oliver seems interested, nevertheless, and asks how she and Clifford met.

'Oh,' Maisie shakes her head, 'not a very interesting story, really.'

'I'd like to hear it though,' he replies quietly.

I met Maisie because she used to get on the same bus as me. We'd be standing in the queue and she would always smile. Such a lovely smile she has, with that dimple of hers. She wasn't much more than a child really, only twenty or so. She smiled at everyone. She was so trusting. Too trusting. She still is.

One day I got the seat next to her and when her stop came, I pressed the bell and helped her off.

That was it. After that I sat next to her every time, if I could.

One day some blokes at the back started arguing and it turned into a bit of an argy-bargy. The language was blue. Maisie blushed scarlet. I knew the blokes; they worked at Harrington's. I got up and walked to the back of the bus. 'Watch your language,' I said, quiet but firm. 'There are ladies present.' That shut them up. They knew me by then; they knew I wasn't just anybody. Walking back down the bus, I felt ten feet tall.

Maisie and I didn't talk much. Well, *I* didn't. Maisie had a line of chat she kept up. Did I know the bakery sold things off cheap at the end of the day? I didn't. It was handy to know. She worked at the bakery café serving teas and coffees and dainty little sandwiches with the crusts cut off. She liked to tell me about the people who came in, the bits of conversation she'd overheard, the things she'd seen through the big front window. One day she'd seen a funeral cortege, preceded by about twenty motorbikes. Did I like motorbikes? 'Not really,' I told her. Another time a woman on a bike had been knocked over by a taxi. 'A terrible mess,' she said. 'It took three buckets of water to clean the pavement.' I wondered what had happened to the bike. Again, a dog tied up to an A board on the pavement while its owner was inside had taken off across two lanes of traffic, dragging the A board behind it. The dog zig-zagged across the road, terrified by this thing on its tail. The A board slammed into two cars and another swerved into a post box trying to avoid it. In the end the dog and its A board got wrapped round a lamp post. Oh! She had a fund of stories like that.

One day it snowed—one of those freak falls that the forecasters never see coming. The pavements were deadly. I got off with her at her stop and walked her home. She was wearing these little shoes with heels. No grip. Completely unsuitable. They were soaked in no time. It was a wonder she didn't fall. She would have done, if I hadn't been there. 'Hold my arm,' I told her, and she did.

'Come to the pictures with me,' I asked her, when I'd got her to her porch.

'Yes, all right,' she said, straight away.

After that we went out every Friday, usually to the cinema but sometimes we'd go to a Beefeater for a meal. Nothing too fancy—neither of us were used to eating out, but you know where you are with a Beefeater. When the weather got warmer we went for walks in the country park. She'd pack us up a picnic, and I brought a blanket for us to sit on.

I held her hand, and when it was time to say goodbye, she would stand up on her tiptoes and kiss my cheek and say, 'Thank you for a lovely time.'

She was twenty, and I was thirty-two. I told myself she thought of me as a big brother or a kind of uncle. I knew I ought to end it, so she could find someone her own age. Somebody young, who would take her dancing and to parties.

But every Friday I called for her and she'd be waiting for me.

Then her aunt had a fall and Maisie had to give up the café to look after her. Maisie had lived with her aunt from being quite a young girl. I never found out exactly why. I'm sure she did tell me, but when someone talks a lot about random things, it's easy to switch off. Anyway, the aunt had a fall. She'd been a bit twirly-whirly even before that, but after the fall she left the building, as they say, and then she died. I went to the funeral although I'd never met the woman. Afterwards there was tea and cake at their house, and I stood in the corner and watched Maisie as she served the guests, and I watched her uncle, too. He was a small man but very fat, balding, with lots of wobbly chins and a wheezy chest. He had tiny eyes almost buried in the flesh of his face, and all the time he kept them on Maisie as she passed round plates of food and poured tea. As he watched her, a film of perspiration broke out on his lip, and he kept rummaging in his trouser pocket for a handkerchief to wipe it off. Even though he'd only had that handkerchief out moments before, it seemed to be very difficult to locate; his hand delved and plunged and grappled deep in the pocket. I knew what he was up to. It was the most disgusting, smutty thing I had ever seen. At his own wife's funeral, as well.

When the mourners had gone Maisie's uncle took off his shoes and loosened the top buttons of his shirt and his trousers before switching on the television and lowering himself into an easy chair. I helped Maisie wash up the cups and saucers in the kitchen. 'What will you do now?' I asked her.

'What do you mean?' she said, and she looked at me with such innocent eyes.

'Where will you live, now that your aunt has gone?' I dried a saucer, turning it round and round in my hands.

She shrugged. 'I suppose I'll stay here. Uncle Arnold will need somebody to look after him. I might see if they'll have me back at the tea shop.'

'But don't you want to do something else?' I asked her. The saucer was so dry now it squeaked under the tea cloth. 'I mean, go to college or university. Train for something? Travel? You're young. You could do anything.'

She considered this, staring out at the garden as though it bloomed with possibilities, with opportunities. 'People *do*, nowadays, don't they?' she mused.

Perhaps that was my cue to say something like, 'We can find out, if you like, at the library or the careers place.' That's what an older brother would have said, isn't it?

But I said, 'Or, you could marry me.'

I don't know which of us was more shocked, her or me. Anyway, I know I dropped that saucer.

Chapter Twenty-Seven

Despite the challenges of the days Maisie finds the evenings thoroughly pleasant. Monica encourages them in sociable activities like quizzes. One evening she produces a selection of board games and Maisie enjoys Cluedo, a game she hasn't played for years. There is a convivial hub-bub around the bar. Generally, after dinner, the women group around a fire and bring out books or craft projects that lie untouched as they chat the evening away and finish the wine.

Unfortunately, this cordiality is increasingly marred by small eccentricities, easily tolerated at first, but that gain in momentum and intensity. Amongst Maisie's group mild irritation morphs into weary annoyance and eye-rolling turns into head-shaking.

The first issue is Gloria's pronounced propensity to flirt. Her high-spiritedness makes her amusing company and Maisie has to admit that without her mischievous sense of humour they would certainly be a much duller group. Gloria is a social butterfly, flitting between the different groups of holiday-makers, often choosing to sit with different folk and then coming back to the lunch women with snippets of gossip and interesting information.

'Can you believe,' she tells them one day, 'that chap over there with the beard and the Indonesian wife, he has a false leg? You'd never know, would you? Lost it in a motorbike accident.'

By this time Maisie knows all about Gloria's eagerness to form relationships with men and shares the view of the other women that it is harmless if a little tawdry, and hopeless. Gloria's frequent claims to have 'got off' with men are treated with scepticism as embroidered, if not downright fantasy. To Maisie, however, her overt coquetry is rather shocking. Maisie reprimands herself for such an old-fashioned attitude; time has moved on, she tells herself. Aunt Sarah wouldn't have approved but things are different, now. It isn't only young people who can enjoy themselves. But still …

Gloria declares her agenda from the first evening. She appears dressed to the nines in a tight, low-cut cocktail dress, plenty of makeup and very high heels.

'A tad over-dressed, aren't we?' Viola remarks tartly.

Frankly, Maisie agrees; she has opted for flattering black evening trousers and a colourful silk tunic top. She carries a cashmere pashmina, in case of draughts. Viola wears jeans tucked into high boots, a shirt and a black suede waistcoat. The other customers in the bar—a group of walkers—wear muddy walking gear. They are ruddy with exercise and fresh air and gin and tonic. Beside them all, Gloria looks dreadfully out of place.

Gloria looks them—and Viola—over briefly before replying, 'Well, at least I'm still sober. Where are the others?'

'The photographers have gone into dinner already,' Viola tells her. 'They want an early night. They're hoping for some good sunrise shots tomorrow, so sadly no opportunity *there* for you—tonight at least.'

Gloria shakes her curls and smiles brightly at the teenage barman.

'Hello handsome,' she says, leaning perilously over the bar. 'Can you manage a long, slow screw?'

'Jesus! Gloria!' Viola protests. 'You're old enough to be the lad's mother!'

Maisie cringes, thinking the same.

'It's a cocktail!' Gloria cries. She is not a whit deterred.

Later that evening, during dinner, she makes an excuse to approach Monica, who shares a table each evening with Bill, the driver. Bill is a slow, ponderous man with a substantial belly and not much hair, genial enough and a capable driver, but no conversationalist and certainly no Lothario. Gloria, however, claims to have marked him out as having romantic potential from the moment she arrived at the coach station. She leans over Bill's shoulder provocatively while she asks her question. Monica shakes her head 'no', but does not look up from the novel she has propped against the cruet between herself and Bill. Bill blushes and looks uncomfortably around him—at the ceiling, at his plate, at anything other than down Gloria's cleavage, which she presses against his cheek as she steals a chip.

'You'll give that poor man an apoplexy if you carry on like that,' Amy says with a twinkle, when Gloria returns to their table.

'I like them shy,' Gloria declares.

'Are there any other likely bachelors, Gloria?' Gwen enquires. 'I'm not sure I can really approve of you distracting the driver.'

Gloria beams. 'A couple, in fact. Decidedly positive vibes from at least one of the photographers. And one of the couples turns out to be brother and sister, so that's a distinct possibility. Rather nice, in fact; Fair Isle jumper, small moustache ... what? What are you all laughing at?'

'At you, you goose,' Gwen replies indulgently. 'You're man-mad and you don't care who knows it.'

'No, I don't.' Gloria pops a last crust of bread into her mouth. 'I know you find it all very shocking, but with me what you see is what you get. I'm tactile and passionate by nature. I like men. I like sex.' She throws an unambiguous glance in Oliver's direction, but he is busy with the wine list and doesn't notice. 'I'm not keen on my own company,' she goes on, 'and I don't plan on being a lonely old woman. You can bet your bottom dollar that if there's a companion for my old age out there, I'm going to find him. But in the absence of a long-term relationship, I'll take some one-night-only tenderness.' She looks around the table. 'I don't know why you all find it so dreadful! You're all children of the sexual revolution, aren't you?'

'Perhaps,' Minnie agrees, after a few moments, 'but brought up under the shadow of mothers who had different ideas. *My* mother's mantra was that "nice girls didn't".'

Maisie gives a fleeting thought to her mother—flighty and independent and very much frowned upon by the rest of the family.

Amy shakes her head sadly. 'What opportunities you have all wasted in your mothers' names,' she mourns.

'Amy! Don't encourage her,' Gwen warns.

'I can assure you,' Gloria gives a suggestive waggle of her pencil-assisted eyebrows, 'I haven't wasted any opportunities that have come my way.'

They are distracted from their conversation by the arrival of the Christian Women's Fellowship who are dressed in every manner of style, from flowing multi-coloured kaftans to brushed cotton pyjamas and fluffy slippers. They distribute themselves around two large tables. One of them stands and announces to the room at large that after dinner there will be, 'open worship, non-denominational and for all believers of any and every faith and those with enquiring minds,' before she delivers a protracted prayer of humble thanks for the Lord's great bounty. Afterwards the Christian contingent gives detailed instructions to the waiters concerning their various dietary requirements which include veganism, vegetarianism, lactose and gluten intolerance, nut allergies, diabetes and a dislike of, 'fish that look at you.'

'Dear God,' Oliver mutters, 'I don't envy the chef!'

'Will you be attending the worship?' Gloria enquires, leaning close to Oliver.

He shakes his head. He is not, he states, a believer.

'Not even in Aphrodite?' Gloria's question, though whispered, carries to the rest of the table. Maisie is amazed and appalled that Gloria can schmooze one man in one moment and another in the next. It only shows, she thinks, that there can be no real liking, no real attraction to either. Perhaps Oliver feels something similar. He ignores Gloria's question and physically turns in his seat to address a remark to Minnie.

'Look at that little dog down there,' he says, indicating a small, well-behaved dog lying quietly under his master's table. 'What kind is yours?'

'Oh!' Minnie swivels in her seat to see. 'How sweet! Dolly's a white Poodle. I didn't know that we'd be staying in dog-conscious hotels,' she remarks with a note of sadness. 'Perhaps I could have brought Dolly after all?'

For the rest of that evening Gloria mounts a determined assault upon Bill, leaning against him at the bar and then following him to a table where he attempts the crossword in the newspaper. But she does so almost with her head over her shoulder, looking to see how her behaviour affects the other men in the bar. Bill appears embarrassed by her attentions, blushing and awkward.

'Isn't he sweet?' Gloria asks as she re-joins them briefly to refresh her glass from the communal bottle. 'I've got him all in a lather!' She gives Oliver a coy glance over the rim of her glass. Wouldn't *you* like, it says, to be lathered up by me?

Oliver's reply is to excuse himself. 'I think I'll mingle,' he says.

'Gloria!' Gwen remonstrates, when he is out of earshot. 'You can't play one man off against another like that!'

'Why ever not?' Gloria is unrepentant. 'I'm just testing the field anyway, at this point. The *real* assault will come in a day or two.'

'Poor Bill,' Viola sneers. 'He's just cannon fodder, then.'

'Are you sure he's even single?' Minnie whispers.

'Of course!' Gloria is indignant. 'I might be a Jezebel but I'm no marriage-wrecker. He's divorced, has been for fifteen years or more.'

'Sounds to me like he's decided to stay single,' Viola remarks.

'Sounds to me like he's ripe for the picking,' Gloria replies with a tinkling laugh as she heads back to Bill's table.

But soon afterwards Bill says goodnight and goes up to bed, and Gloria returns to the others with a sigh. 'A more difficult nut to crack than I had imagined,' she observes, slumping down into the settee next to Minnie, and kicking off her shoes. 'However,' she adds, 'I am not deterred.'

Subsequent evenings follow more or less the same pattern. Gloria descends in a succession of low-cut, see-through or otherwise provocative outfits, her face and her mind thoroughly made up for conquest. Like one of those jugglers who spin plates on sticks, she goes to work first on Bill but then, as the evening and the week progress, adds other apparently available men. Availability seems to be all the qualification they need to warrant her attraction. A dapper septuagenarian member of the camera club is her second object. He is short—perhaps half a head shorter than Gloria—but very energetic, with bright, intelligent eyes and a fluent line of eager conversation. He wears very well-tailored tweed, various brightly coloured waistcoats and, in the evenings, immaculately neat bow-ties.

'His name is Robin,' Gloria tells them. 'Isn't that appropriate?'

'I rather fancied him myself,' Amy admits. 'Isn't he too old for you, Gloria?'

'Oh! Age is all in the mind,' Gloria says airily. 'I think he's rather well off. Harris tweed doesn't come cheap, does it?'

'Are those his own teeth?' Viola wants to know.

Gloria gives an exaggerated smile. 'Well, these aren't all *mine*,' she says, indicating her veneered incisors, 'so I could hardly complain about that, could I?'

'As a matter of fact,' Gwen puts in, when Gloria is out of earshot, 'we get tweed in the shop all the time. You can pick up very decent suits for next to nothing. He could have got his from a charity shop.'

'Except for the size,' Viola demurs. 'He'd be lucky to find one so small, unless it was one of Ronnie Corbett's castoffs.'

'I get suits to alter quite often, from the dry cleaners,' Minnie says. 'I'm sure that's where they originate most of the time, from charity shops, I mean.'

'If they're good quality and not worn, that's a good thing though, isn't it?' Maisie asks. 'My husband thought so, anyway.'

On the third evening Gloria adds a third man into the mix, the Fair Isle brother, who having said his goodnights once appears back downstairs without the Fair Isle cardigan and also without the sister—'for a night cap,' with something of the attitude of a lamb presenting itself at the abattoir. He orders a large malt whisky and sits at the bar looking spare and uncomfortable, casting furtive glances at the various groups assembled around tables or distributed on sofas.

'Bless!' Gloria croons, and soon swoops upon him.

During the day Gloria is kept increasingly busy shoring up nascent relationships, dividing her time between her women friends and the various romantic prospect—and not neglecting Oliver who, apart from the occasional ramble, keeps himself more or less attached to their party. By Thursday—their final day away—she is a blur as she flits from one to another, sitting with Robin and a couple of the other photographers at breakfast, chatting brightly to Bill as he loads the cases into the coach, sitting next to Oliver as they travel and then pursuing Fair Isle and his sister into a café for mid-morning refreshments.

'I don't suppose any of these liaisons have actually come to anything yet, have they?' Gwen enquires.

'She's spent every night in our room so far,' Minnie replies conspiratorially. 'Although I must say sometimes it's well after one when she comes in.'

'She's making a prize idiot of herself,' Viola says sourly. 'Doesn't she realise how *desperate* she looks?'

'I don't think she cares. At the heart of it, you know,' Gwen says, 'she's just incredibly lonely.'

'Aren't we all?' Viola asks quietly.

Their final night is spent in Kirkby Lonsdale, where the party is divided between two hotels. 'Our original hotel had to close due to water ingress,' Monica explains over the tannoy as they approach the town. 'There isn't another that can accommodate the whole party. I really am very sorry, ladies and gentlemen.'

'We've all become such friends,' complains one of the widowed sisters. Her comment is greeted with a gust of agreement.

'We were going to offer an impromptu communion tonight,' a Christian woman announces, dismayed, 'and an evangelistic invitation to accept the Lord as Saviour.'

The response to this is more muted.

All of the Christian women and the majority of the photographers are dropped off at an hotel on the outskirts of the town before Bill ferries the rest of them to their final destination just off the market square.

The hotel is clearly of a lower standard than they have enjoyed so far. Even the most energetic efforts on Oliver's part fail to get Maisie a decent room. 'They're all pretty poor, I'm afraid,' he reports, having insisted on inspecting a few of them.

The room she is shown into is tiny, the *ensuite* barely more than a cubicle; it is hardly possible to close the door without standing in the shower or on the toilet. Through the paper-thin walls she hears Minnie and Gloria complaining about their room before their words are drowned out by the gush of bath taps. On the other side, there is the creak of someone lowering themselves onto the bed and then the blare of a TV quiz show turned up too loud. Above, she hears the tread of footsteps crossing and re-crossing the room, the squeak of a wardrobe door, the hum of an occasional conversational exchange. Maisie puts the kettle on for tea and changes into her walking gear.

Presently she hears Gloria knocking on the bathroom door and shouting, 'Don't use all the hot water *again,* Minnie, please. Have a thought for the rest of us.' On the other side, loud masculine snores punctuate the tinny, repetitive theme tune of the quiz.

Under the saucer, on the tea tray, Maisie finds a short, curly hair.

In spite of having quite enjoyed her time away, Maisie is suddenly overwhelmed with a longing for home. It swamps her like a cold shower, leaving her sick and oddly trembly. The amorphous trappings of the hotel room—the scorched lamp-shades and limp curtains, the dusty skirtings and worn carpets—make her shudder. She is repelled by the thickly applied sealant in the shower, bloomed with pink mould, the scummy remains of someone else's soap in the dish. The sheets are thin and over-washed, the pillow smells of a stranger's head—greasy hair, she speculates, night-time dribble. She wants, more than anything, to be back at Old Farm Hall where the tattiness is familiar and self-generated and can be repaired. She longs for her own things, the smell of her own pillow, Aunt Sarah's Blue Willow, the blank canvas of the rest of the rooms now, ready for whatever Maisie decides to apply. A simple salad, tea made with fresh milk instead of UHT jiggers, a happy and productive afternoon spent amongst the raised beds— they call to her as articulately as a well-known voice, as Heathcliff called to Cathy, as Rochester called to Jane.

It's all been very nice, she thinks. But such a waste of time and really, now I'd like to go home.

That evening there is a concerted effort all round. Viola officiates at the bar with more than her usual alacrity, fuelling Gloria's last stand so that in addition to being more provocatively dressed than ever and producing a master-class of flirtation—excessive hair-twirling, incessant eye-lash fluttering, a paroxysm of simpering and dimpling, perpetual peals of tinkling laughter and generally signalling sexual availability by the bucket-load—she is also tipsy. She totters between Bill—ensconced at the bar with his newspaper and his pint of shandy—and Robin—seated in an alcove with those few of his photographer friends not banished to the other hotel—with the occasional lurch across the room to Fair Isle and his sister who, as is usual with them, play cribbage before going into the dining room. From time to time she joins the women, perching unsteadily on the arm of Oliver's chair to peruse the menu.

'Mmm,' she says, inhaling his aftershave, 'you do smell absolutely delicious, you know.'

Before the women are summoned to their table—as though she hasn't got enough spinning plates on the go, Gloria adds another to her act, drawing in the O'Keef's Area Manager who has dropped in on the tour as a result of Monica's frequent and increasingly fraught appeals to head office. She, utterly frazzled by the myriad stresses of the trip, has briefed him thoroughly with a long diatribe of the difficulties she has had to overcome; the navigational problems, disrupted tours, restricted attractions, complaints from holiday-makers, requests for refunds and the general air of discontent that has pervaded everything. She has proffered documentary evidence including letters of complaint written on hotel notepaper, some of which have been delivered anonymously, slipped at night under her door, and photographs that she has taken on her iPad. Finally, she has dissolved into tears. Now, placated with a large gin and tonic and officially off duty until the morning, she is left to lick her wounds while the Area Manager does a circuit of the room, introducing himself to the O'Keef's guests.

The Area Manager appears to be in his early fifties, a man of medium height with a figure tending to corpulence and a jaw-line sinking into jowl. But he has a good head of hair—'All his own too,' Amy speculates—and is impressively dressed in an expensive business suit. In ordinary circumstances he would hardly excite interest, being rather plain looking. But a sense of his own authority, and an impression that he by no means seeks to dispel that he has come from Head Office as a trouble-shooter to, 'sort things out,' does lend him an unmistakable attraction and quite palpable sexual appeal. He works the crowd, shaking hands, making assiduous enquiries as to people's satisfaction, handing out business cards so that 'written comments' can be sent directly to him for his personal attention.

'My, my!' Gloria declares when he arrives at their table, frenziedly hair-twirling, eye-lash fluttering, giggling and wiggling and, for good measure, pressing her balconied bosom against him, 'where have *you* been hiding, gorgeous?'

'I have fought my way past dragons and through thickets of thorns to rescue you, my princess,' he replies promptly. He draws Gloria's arm through his. 'Let me escort you to dinner.'

After dinner the other men of Gloria's entourage seem to realise that the Area Manager is about to take the prize unequivocally offered to *them* over the last few days. It galvanises them. To a man, they throw off the limitations of their vintage apparel and past-it attitudes to enter the fray. Suddenly neither beer belly nor bus pass seems any drawback. They might have been bewildered by Gloria's blitzkrieg, perhaps not believing they had read her signals correctly—although, to be fair, a blind man at a great distance could hardly have misinterpreted them. As the days progressed, they might have resented the suspicion that they were not the sole object of her ardour. They gather around Gloria at the bar like rutting stags around the hind. Even Bill, who might well hesitate to challenge his superior, stakes a claim by assisting Gloria onto a bar stool and by taking possession of her handbag—pink, studded with diamantes—holding it defiantly in the face of all comers. Fair Isle abandons his sister and a half-played game of cribbage to claim the honour of buying Gloria a drink, hardly blanching when she asks for a champagne cocktail. Robin fusses with his light meter and tries Gloria in a number of poses before inviting her to his studio, 'to do some glamour shots.' Even Oliver who, up to this point has rather repulsed all Gloria's gambits, joins the jockeying party around Gloria, appearing helplessly drawn by some primitive instinct which, in his rational mind— Maisie tells herself—he would never indulge, and makes his play by telling Robin with scarcely veiled sub-text that his camera equipment isn't up to the task. The Area Manager stands at a little distance and leans nonchalantly against the bar. His eyes are fixed on Gloria. He is patient and deadly, a lion biding his time, deciding when and how he will strike.

In the night, Maisie is awoken by a cacophony, a series of low moans and shrill cries, the rhythmic complaint of bedsprings, a woman's ardent gasps, the percussive thump of a bedhead against a wall. Every guest must likewise be disturbed.

It goes on. And on.

Somewhere not far away, something is dislodged with a thud; a glass, perhaps, from a bedside table, a picture from a wall, some restraint or impediment thrust aside.

Maisie is paralysed with embarrassment. She cringes beneath the thin sheets.

The panting becomes a sequence of ardent squeals and half-articulate chirrups that carry a sense of extreme urgency, of ravening appetite. The tempo increases. The man now contributes the occasional sound: a strangled cough, a grunt of effort.

Somewhere else, a light is snapped on. Irritated feet stamp across a room. A toilet is flushed, fiercely.

From the vortex, there is a sound like furniture moving, like tectonic plates shifting, an awkward, unwieldy juxtaposition of bodies, the grapple and scrabble of perspiring flesh. The sounds are of effort and struggle, almost combative. They take on an edge. The yelps are serrated with frustrated angst.

Then, in desperation, the woman—Gloria, unmistakably—shouts, 'No! Not there, you fool! *There!* Like *this.*' There is a murmur, a pause, a slight readjustment. The bedsprings retune themselves to a different key. The thump of the headboard becomes more complex, syncopated, a sort of grinding flop. 'That's better. Now faster! Faster!' she cries. And presently, 'Harder! Harder!' The walls almost billow, the floor undulates, the fabric of the very building shakes and trembles. 'Don't stop!' she yells, 'don't stop, for God's sake, whatever you do …' Her words disintegrate into an animal cry—a terrible, climactic scream.

Afterwards, Maisie lies sleepless, and thinks about Clifford.

Chapter Twenty-Eight

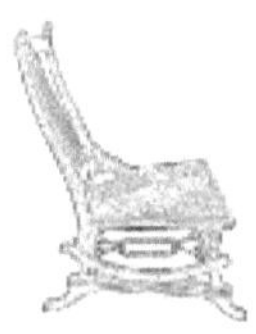

Maisie and Clifford had often laughed about that dropped saucer. Clifford had picked up the pieces and glued them together and it served them over the years as a key dish and a drip tray for plants, a receptacle for mixing small amounts of glue or putty and in many other iterations of usefulness before it was neither use nor ornament but couldn't—of course—be thrown away.

Maisie never knew quite why she agreed to marry Clifford. His proposal had come out of the blue. She had been wondering, truth be told, quite where the relationship was going. He wasn't like the boyfriends that other girls—and girls' magazines—told her to expect. He wasn't romantic, nor did he make sexual advances. He didn't woo her with gifts. But he was trustworthy and kind, and very protective. He turned up, reliably, every day at the bus stop, and without fail on Fridays to take her out.

He had said to her there over the shattered pieces of the saucer and with a sidelong glance through the open kitchen door to where her uncle Arnold's stertorous breathing could be heard above the television's din, 'You need looking after,' and she had realised that of all the things he could have offered her, that was what she most wanted. She had never been 'looked after,' only 'taken in,' first of all by elderly grandparents and then by Aunt Sarah and Uncle Arnold. Her mother's abdication of duty was blamed on a business that demanded all her attention and took her abroad a good deal. The other women of the family—her grandmother and aunt—were darkly disapproving without being specific. The business had folded but its termination had not meant Maisie's to her mother's care. There were occasional postcards from exotic locations, and mention of various male companions during the telephone calls that marked special occasions. In the end Maisie's mother died penniless and alone in a Thai hospital. The news took six months to reach them. Aunt Sarah's response was a sigh that said,

'What else did you expect?' By then, Maisie could hardly recall her mother's face. Of her father she knew nothing. He was never spoken of.

Soon after Maisie's arrival in their home, Aunt Sarah became unwell with a number of non-specific but very debilitating complaints. Gradually Maisie found herself responsible for the running of the household. At eighteen she'd planned on a college course in Hotel and Catering, but Aunt Sarah's increasing incapacity put paid to that, so Maisie got a job at the café instead.

'Then she had her fall. The rest you know,' she told Clifford. 'Now you,' she said. 'Tell me about you.'

He shrugged. 'Nothing to tell. Very ordinary. Parents are dead. No siblings. Work at Harrington's. That's it.'

Maisie was dismayed. 'But who were your parents? What did they do? When did they die, and why? Where did you grow up? Which school did you go to?'

He remained silent, almost as though he had not heard.

'Clifford! I don't really know anything about you,' she insisted.

'Nothing to tell. Nothing to tell,' he said. She had the distinct sense of shutters rolling down.

They married quietly in December, at the Registry Office. Uncle Arnold wasn't able to give her away; he had suffered a massive stroke and been consigned to a bed in a geriatric ward.

Their honeymoon was spent at the seaside in a small private hotel, deserted except for themselves and some elderly, semi-permanent residents who had their own tables in the dining room, which they guarded very fiercely with hisses and gnarled, flapping hands. Their chairs in the lounge were likewise sacrosanct; their reading material, spectacles and indeterminate needlework projects left proprietorially on the seats if they were absent. A dusty Christmas tree occupied one corner of the dining room and, from somewhere very distant—a linen closet, they speculated, or a larder—the choir of King's College warbled carols. Apart from this there was no concession to the season.

Maisie and Clifford had the best room, overlooking the sea. It was quite vast, with a wide expanse of threadbare carpet and some very ornate but sadly dilapidated furniture. A plume of blue-grey dust rose from the top of the wardrobe and hung like a disturbed ghost when Maisie opened the doors to hang up her things. The windows rattled in the constant wind. The radiator emitted a meagre heat. The private bathroom had an enormous claw-footed bath that took an hour to fill from the lime-scale-choked faucet. But the bed was enormous, very soft and heaped with quilts and pillows. They snuggled into it each night like small furry animals into a burrow.

He made love to her almost reverently. 'It's my first time,' she whispered to him unnecessarily, during the preamble.

'I know,' he said.

'Is it yours, too?' She hardly supposed so; he was twelve years older than she was.

'I know what to do,' he reassured her. 'I'll make it all right.'

He did. Afterwards he brought warm flannels and a towel to wash away the mess, and helped her put her nightie back on. He held her tightly all night long, nestling her into the crook of his arm, smoothing the sheets over her shoulder, stroking her hair and making comforting little mewing noises.

The morning after, the stuffy silence of the dining room and the sidelong glances of the crabby residents made her face burn with shame. The very gulping of her throat as she swallowed tea, even the crunch of toast between her teeth felt outrageously personal, explicit and lewd; she blushed furiously, stammered her thanks to the waitress, and scampered away from the table in humiliation.

Clifford laughed when he caught up with her and folded her into an embrace at first paternal but then passionate. They locked the door of their room and did it again amidst the tumbled sheets—with less pain and more pleasure—and ignored the indignant tap of the chamber maid on their door.

During the day the couple walked along the windswept promenade and looked out at the roiling waves pounding the shingle. Clifford held her hand or put his arm around her to pull her close. Sometimes he would turn her to him and check the buttons on her coat.

All of the amusement arcades and most of the shops on the front were closed and tightly shuttered. They found a tearoom in a back street where they sheltered from the worst of the weather and ate toast dripping with butter and lots of hot tea to tide them over between breakfast and dinner at the hotel. Sometimes they drove to neighbouring towns only to find the facilities equally limited, but a different view of the grey, heaving sea.

Maisie was perfectly content. More at peace than she had ever been before. Even in the crusty company at the hotel, amidst the diminished grandeur of the high-ceilinged rooms, she felt at home.

Clifford rented a house for them. It was sparsely but adequately furnished. 'Quite enough to begin with,' Clifford told her. Very soon they were able to augment their belongings with the things from Aunt Sarah's house.

'Where there are duplicates, we can pick and choose,' she said. 'We won't need two dining tables, will we?'

Clifford looked up from the newspaper. 'Why not?'

Chapter Twenty-Nine

That was the beginning, Maisie thinks, as she lies awake, while Gloria and her paramour enter the ring for another round of combative coital encounters.

Although of course not the real beginning, not the origin. *That* must have been much earlier, rooted in some aspect of Clifford's history of which she has no inkling. The 'nothing to tell' and 'nothing to know' that he had claimed was clearly far from nothing. It was 'something,' something sore and precious and jealously guarded. Deeply buried, like the buttons she had found stored in jars, the jars packed into shoe boxes, the shoe boxes hidden inside suitcases, the suitcases buried under old carpet. And now she thinks about it, it was likely that the whole of Clifford's hoard was simply camouflage amassed to disguise and protect some central, vulnerable sanctum where no one, not even Maisie, had been allowed to trespass.

Secrets. He had secrets, or more likely, *a* secret—singular. A dreadful maw of pain too tender to touch.

Why had she never seen it?

Because she needed this week to teach her what secrets look like. They are not cobwebbed caskets located in caves. They are not dusty volumes of hieroglyphs. They do not come scrolled and ribboned, nor locked in drawers. No. They are clothed in manners: odd gestures and peculiar ticks. They propel strange obsessions, irrational aversions, ill temper and unquenchable desires. Like Viola's shrewishness is simply a manifestation of some deep wound or private circumstance, her own barbed stockpile. Likewise, Gloria's promiscuity and Minnie's parsimony are only the paraphernalia they have amassed to disguise inner trauma. She thinks of Oliver, tellingly vague on the subject of family; his very elusiveness suggestive of family feuds, bitter resentment—perhaps even, she speculates, some historic abuse.

And what about herself? Isn't there—flickering dimly beneath the layers of grief and shock and onerous work with which Clifford's death has almost smothered her—a scandalous, unacknowledgeable truth? It is a tiny despicable light, guilty and awful, wholly incompatible with bereavement. She fleetingly glimpsed it between the crates of junk and tumbling piles of dross. A shaft of it from time to time penetrated between moth-eaten curtains or seemed to glimmer through the chink in an ill-fitting floorboard. It should be a widow's anathema, but it is there, undeniable and appalling. Wicked. Disgusting.

It is relief.

Chapter Thirty

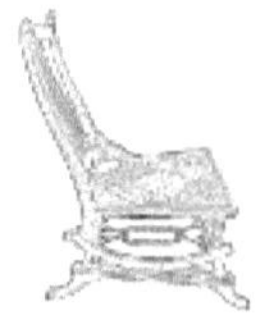

The second source of unpleasantness amongst the ladies stems from a combination of Viola's sour humour and Minnie's marked frugality in matters of money.

The cost of things—value for money—is a constant preoccupation, an understood fixation that needs no reiteration but that is neurotically reprised at any and every juncture. Even Maisie, who until very recently always had an eye on the purse strings and for whom a waste-not way of thinking is deeply ingrained, begins to find Minnie's thrift obsessive. Maisie takes it at face value, assuming it to be evidence of real financial hardship rather than merely a foible or peculiarity of character. But it is relentlessly projected onto every aspect of their trip, injected into every conversation, a light that Minnie has to wearyingly shine on any and every matter. On the whole the others tolerate it. Only Viola is unable to do so. In fact, it is soon clear Viola finds Minnie's preoccupation unbearably irritating. As often as Minnie makes any money-related comment, Viola falls upon it with a caustic, pointed rejoinder like a wild animal falling on a carcass. Viola is an ill-tempered person anyway, liable to criticise and carp either openly or in snide asides. She has an acid tongue that spits impulsive venom. She may regret her words moments after they are spoken—Maisie strongly suspects it—but unfortunately her tendency to over-indulge in alcohol means that more often than not her tongue is unlicensed and her conscience laggardly, a poor keeper of her peace.

The first evening of their trip sets the tone. From Viola's high colour and bright eyes, Maisie infers she has been in the bar for some time. She poo-poos Maisie's tentative suggestion that she might drink sherry and steers her instead towards a white wine spritzer as an aperitif. 'Nobody drinks sherry these days except geriatric old ladies and duffers at the golf club,' she says. 'Good grief, you *are* a greenhorn, aren't you? I shall have to take you in hand. I drink vodka and tonic, but if you're not used to spirits, I wouldn't recommend it straight off.'

Gloria orders a suggestive cocktail. Minnie, of course, is keen to rein in such profligacy. 'Why don't we just stick to wine,' she cries. 'By the bottle it's so much cheaper.'

'But we're not all drinking wine, at the moment,' Viola hisses, with unnecessary vehemence. 'Just have what you *want,* for God's sake.'

Minnie settles for a spritzer, muttering 'Even just between the two of us, Maisie, it would be more economical to buy the whole bottle.'

Viola orders the drinks, including another large vodka and tonic for herself.

Later at the table, Viola insists on seeing the wine list. Naturally, Minnie puts in a plea for economy. 'Hadn't we better just have the house wine?' she asks tremulously. 'It's usually the best value.'

'But it *may* not be,' Viola retorts. 'Sometimes they have some real treasures at the back of the cellar, don't they Oliver? They call them bin-ends and sell them off cheap. It's always worth a look.'

She and Oliver, neighbours at the table, scan the wine list together. 'She can be such a penny-pincher,' Viola complains in a low voice, but quite loud enough for Minnie to hear.

Over the following days poor Minnie can do no right. Viola is poised to pick on her. If she declines lunch, Viola wags her head knowingly and says, 'All right, Paddington,' referring to the bread rolls and marmalade portions they have all seen Minnie filch from the breakfast buffet and know she will consume in some draughty corner on her own.

One day Minnie joins them for morning coffee but asks only for a cup of boiling water, into which she dips a herbal teabag. 'Isn't that the brand they had at the hotel?' Viola asks incredulously. 'Please don't tell me that you took it from there.'

Minnie looks uncomfortable. 'I particularly like them. They really settle my stomach,' she says haltingly.

'You like the fact that you'll only pay for the hot water,' Viola sneers, 'which will probably be nothing. I just can't believe it. You are *such* a skinflint, Minnie.'

Minnie's perpetual vigilance for special offers and sales is a source of uncontrollable annoyance to Viola; likewise the agonised dithering between a £4.99 bowl of soup or a £5.25 toasted sandwich. 'Just decide, can't you, for God's sake?' she snaps one day. 'Have what you want! Just have what you want! Here!' she delves into her coat pocket and brings out a damp five-pound note, '*I'll* pay.'

Eventually Gwen takes Viola to one side. 'Please leave Minnie alone,' she says. 'She's hard up. It isn't her fault. Also, it's making you unpopular. You must know that.'

'As if I care!' Viola throws off. 'But you know, she *isn't* hard up. She lives in that great big house on the Crescent; it must be worth a mint. She's tight. She's just tight. But for God's sake, why does she have to go on and *on* about it?'

'It would go more or less unremarked if you didn't keep harping on about it,' Gwen says. 'I'm not making a fuss about the extra vodka and tonics on the bar bill every night, am I? But don't think I'm not noticing them when I settle up each day. But that's *your* thing, and I accept it. This is hers. Can't you just let her be?'

But Viola's skin is as thick as Minnie's is thin. If anything, her spikiness towards Minnie increases the more the other women upbraid her for it. Gwen's rebuke results in a withering assault upon Minnie that evening during a game of Trivial Pursuit.

'You ought to be called Ninnie instead of Minnie,' Viola jibes when Minnie mistakes Greenland for Iceland. 'I mean, really!'

Snide asides are redoubled, both in and out of Minnie's hearing. 'Free samples of local cheeses, look,' Viola says one day, reading from a poster, 'in the Memorial Hall today. I wonder where that is. Better tell Minnie. Have you seen her, Gloria? No? Oh well, I expect she's there already!'

'I doubt it,' Gloria replies coldly. 'Cheese disagrees with her.'

'Even *free* cheese?' Viola feigns surprise.

'Oh, give it a rest, Viola. This is getting boring.'

The source of her irritation broadens. It isn't just Minnie's cost fixation that annoys Viola, it is also her naivety, her occasional malapropism, her limited general knowledge.

'The Leaning Tower of *Pizza?!*' she hoots on the evening of the quiz, loud enough for everyone in the room to hear. 'Oh Minnie, you are a prize nincompoop.' Minnie can hardly open her mouth to utter a syllable before Viola starts rolling her eyes, tutting and muttering deprecating remarks under her breath.

The effect on Minnie is quite marked. Knowing that Viola is primed to pounce, Minnie grows even more indecisive and faltering. Her agitation causes her to become clumsy and awkward; she scalds Amy with coffee and knocks wine over Gwen. By Thursday she is withdrawn and tearful. In the end she disappears altogether for an hour and a half, to be discovered eventually wandering alone by the lake.

'Very thoughtless and selfish,' Viola declares waspishly as they return, soaked and frazzled from the search. 'I hope you know that Monica was within an ace of calling the police.'

'I seem to irritate you all so much,' Minnie blubs. 'I thought I'd take myself away for a while and give you a break.'

'You don't irritate me,' Gloria says. 'Viola's a nasty witch; you mustn't let her get to you, Minnie.'

'I can't help it,' Minnie sobs.

Amy's predictions about the arrangements on the coach turn out to be correct. Every day Maisie finds herself seated beside Minnie and she gets a clearer impression than anyone else of the effect of Viola's behaviour. The cheerful if undiscriminating narrative with which Minnie observes the passing countryside diminishes as the days pass. She sighs often, and wonders mournfully about her dog. She vacillates between fight and flight; tense and uptight one moment, her hands balled into her lap, then slumped and dejected the next, her face drawn and miserable. From time to time she posts haphazard notes-to-self, showing her mind to be preoccupied with home. 'I really must remember to defrost the freezer when I get home,' she says on one occasion. And, 'My prescription will be due for renewal on the 30th.'

Increasingly as the week progresses Minnie's comments are qualified, their import modified and softened so as to make them less open to criticism. 'That's a splendidly imposing monument,' she might remark, but then, 'I think so, anyway, *quite* remarkable in its way, if you like that kind of thing, given its age of course. Yes, it's reasonably good, of its type, I suppose.'

Her half-whispered conferences with Maisie on the coach are characterised by semi-apologetic self-justification. 'I really wasn't hungry,' she says, white-faced with anxiety on one occasion. 'I didn't mean to make a fuss about it. Did I? Did you think I did? I didn't intend to.' And, 'I truly didn't consider it good value, *for me* I meant, of course. Didn't I make that clear? Of course, I'd never *dream* of dictating what other people spend!' And one afternoon she says, 'Please tell me, Maisie. I mean, let me know with just a wink or a nod, if you think I might be, if you think Viola might …' she trails off. 'I mean you're all very good,' she tries again, 'very patient with me. I know I can be a bit OCDC at times and Viola … well … you know … ' she glances furtively at Viola across the aisle, 'can be very cutting.'

Maisie soothes Minnie's anxieties as best she can. Minnie *is* tiresomely fixated on money, there is no doubt about that. But Viola is unnecessarily cruel.

On the penultimate day of their holiday, as they travel from Keswick to Kirkby Lonsdale, Minnie says nothing at all, her usual torrent of observation and remark dried to silence. She looks out of the window without seeing Shap's Summit or the velvet-draped Howgills, her eyes large with woe. At one point she seems to be sleeping, her head pillowed against the window as the coach crawls through interminable road works. But it is a troubled sleep. She mutters and mumbles a little. Her forehead puckers into a frown, and then her whole face crumples before a tear rolls from the corner of her eye. She wakes as they pull into the village.

'Are you all right, dear?' Maisie places her hand over Minnie's. 'I think you've been dreaming.'

'No, I've been fretting about what to wear,' Minnie says miserably. 'Do you think I can get away with the yellow blouse again tonight? It will be its third outing. I do have another, that jade green one, but it isn't so warm. Last night I was almost perished. Only, you know,' with a rather harried, hunted expression in her eye, 'I don't want to appear … I mean, I wouldn't want people to think … you know, if anyone was to *remark* … well, it would be mortifying.'

'As a matter of fact,' Maisie extemporises, 'I was only thinking last night, I have a cardigan that would look lovely against that green top of yours. I haven't even worn it. Perhaps you'd like to borrow it?'

In fact, she had planned to wear it herself that evening, but she sacrifices it on the fragile altar of Minnie's self-confidence. Clearly, she's at rock bottom.

Minnie's eyes fill with tears. 'You're so very kind,' she says, taking Maisie's hand. 'So *very* kind, and a truly lovely friend.'

Viola's drinking, which has been more excessive with every evening is, on this their last evening, out of control. When Maisie returns from her evening walk Viola is already in situ at the bar, an hour before the time they generally meet. She is resplendent with a tangled noose of jewellery around her neck, her fingers clicking and barbed with rings, a tall glass already half-drained.

Minnie is not even dressed when Maisie takes the cardigan round for her to try on, and threatens not to go down to dinner at all. 'Just a sandwich will do,' she says with a doleful sigh, 'up here, on my own.'

'Of course you must come down!' Maisie says.

'I've said the same,' Gloria agrees from the dressing table, where she is applying false eyelashes, 'again and again. She mustn't let Viola bully her.'

'It won't be the same without you,' Maisie urges.

Between the two of them they manage to overcome Minnie's reluctance, but she enters the bar with dragging steps.

'Have a cocktail, won't you?' Viola cries as they arrive. Her eyes, heavily rimmed with kohl, are glittering. 'It's our last night! Amy and Gwen are drinking dry martinis.' She looks Minnie over critically. 'That's a nice cardigan,' she concedes at last. 'Been keeping it for a special occasion?'

'Maisie lent it to me,' Minnie says in a small voice.

Viola makes a vinegary face. A cutting remark about 'borrowed finery' is on the tip of her tongue.

'You misunderstood, Minnie dear,' Maisie puts in quickly, 'it's a *gift*.' She gives Viola a hard look.

'I'll have champagne,' Gloria declares with a naughty giggle and a swift glance around the room. 'I'm feeling *very* reckless and abandoned tonight.'

Maisie decides she'll have the same. Minnie says in a small, cowed voice, 'I'll have whatever you recommend, Viola,' and fiddles anxiously with the cuff of the cardigan.

Oliver launches himself across the room to carry the drinks. 'We're sitting over here,' he indicates a table in the corner where Gwen and Amy are ensconced. 'Not what we've become used to, I'm afraid.' He indicates the electric fire parked on the hearth. 'No roaring fire tonight. This whole establishment is sadly below par.'

'How's your room?' Gwen asks. 'Ours is in a little sort of shed at the back, isn't it Amy?'

'Perfectly all right if you don't mind the trip past the bins in the dark,' Amy quips.

Minnie excuses herself to make a phone call.

'Calling that damned dog,' Viola remarks witheringly from her bar stool.

'What if she is?' Gloria rejoins.

'I might have another of these cocktails,' Amy says. 'Do you think I should, Gwen?'

'Certainly not. But that won't stop you, you old lush!'

Over dinner, the arrival of the Area Manager gives much cause for comment. 'He's here to smooth things over,' Oliver opines. 'I don't envy him that job. From what I've gathered there are quite a few dissatisfied guests.'

'I shall certainly … that it, I wondered about complaining … possibly,' Minnie hesitantly asserts.

'In the hope of a refund?' Viola jibes.

'Oh no. That is, not necessarily.'

'Of course not,' Viola says archly. 'You could hardly justify it. I think you've had pretty good value for money, all in all, what with all the extra breakfast rolls, and the hot water Gloria tells me you make such free use of every night, and the complimentary toiletries, tea bags and biscuits that I'm certain you've been filching all week. Is your suitcase full of hotel towels?'

'Viola!' Gloria retorts.

The arrival of their starters prevents further discussion of the topic, but Minnie is all-but-undone by Viola's accusation. Her eyes are glassy with tears. She kneads her napkin while the food is distributed. Viola busies herself pouring wine but Maisie sees that she is chewing her cheek and her eyes don't meet anyone else's.

Amy attempts to give Minnie a moment to compose herself by pretending to forget what she has ordered. 'No, no, I do assure you, I'm a prawn cocktail. Gloria here is a goat's cheese, or am I wrong?'

'You *are* wrong. I'm the garlic mushrooms, Gwen is the prawn cocktail and *you're* the goat's cheese. What are *you,* Minnie dear?' Gloria enters into Amy's plan with dry resignation.

'Soup,' Minnie says in a small, choked voice.

'I'm soup too,' Viola offers.

'Nobody cares what you ordered, you old trout,' Gloria declares stoutly.

Viola says nothing, but drains her glass.

She drinks steadily throughout the evening. She has made herself responsible for ordering the wine during the course of the trip, claiming some expert knowledge of viticulture that particularly qualifies her for the task. Flying in the face of—indeed, goaded by—Minnie's initial suggestion that the house wine is usually very palatable as well as being good value, over the course of their holiday they have partaken of numerous unusual grape varietals. Gwen has confided to Maisie that their bar bills, this trip, have been extortionate. 'But don't tell Minnie. I usually make some adjustments anyway for the final reckoning, or she'd never come away with us at all. Gloria and Amy don't mind, but I must say Viola wasn't very amenable when I asked her. *You* don't mind, do you?'

This evening Viola has ordered more wine than usual. Gwen and Amy, perhaps buoyed by their cocktails, drink freely. Gloria also drinks her share, girding herself for her final assault. As a rule, Minnie is not much of a drinker but this evening—possibly as an antidote to misery—she has more than is customary. After the first evening of over-indulging—and a headache all the next day—Maisie has paced herself carefully and alternates a glass of water with every glass of wine, a trick she has observed in Oliver. After the meal Viola insists they move on to port or brandy, 'or at least one of those namby-pamby drinks like Baileys or Kahlua,' she qualifies.

'Oh! In for a penny,' Amy laughs. 'It'll play havoc with my hiatus hernia, but what the hell! I'll have a crème de menthe.'

Under the influence of the alcohol, the atmosphere becomes garrulous. Gwen takes it upon herself to make a speech, struggling to her feet and addressing the table. 'Under the circumstances,' she declares rather drunkenly, 'I think things have gone off passably well. I'm sorry we didn't get to tour many gardens, Viola—'

'We didn't get to tour *any*, properly,' Viola grumbles.

'No, I know,' Gwen continues, 'and I feel in a way I got you here under false pretences. I promised you gardens in abundance—'

'I shall sue,' Viola asserts.

'But the company, I hope, has compensated—'

'*Some* of the company has.'

'For myself, I've been particularly delighted to have new friends amongst us. For people like us, in our golden years—'

'Speak for yourself!' Gloria objects.

'Friendship is the keystone to contentment. Being alone doesn't have to mean being lonely ...' She rummages in her cardigan pocket for a tissue.

Amy, too, dabs her eyes. 'For God's sake,' she says, 'you'll set us all off if you carry on like this, Gwen.'

Gwen raises her glass to each in turn, 'To you, Viola, to Maisie, and to Oliver.'

'New friends,' the others echo.

'I'd like to thank you all for looking after me,' Amy says. 'I know I'm a nuisance and a burden ...' She waves down their choruses of denial. 'No really, I know I am. But *you'll* all be old one day!'

'With any luck,' Gloria shouts. 'The alternative isn't very attractive!'

'Thank you for including me,' Maisie says quietly. 'Getting away was just what I needed.'

'And *me*,' Oliver echoes. 'I must say it's been an unexpected pleasure.'

'Sentimental nonsense,' Viola mutters.

Minnie says nothing at all but after dinner, as they make their way back to their table in the bar, she links Maisie affectionately. 'Such a very kind friend,' she mumbles.

Gloria of course deserts them to hold court at the bar, as does Oliver. Suddenly, with fewer of them to energise it, the atmosphere becomes torpid. They recharge their glasses from the bottles left over from dinner. 'Although really,' Gwen says, 'I've had quite enough and *you,*' she nods at Amy, 'will be ill if you drink any more. I'm sure one of your packets of pills says 'avoid alcohol' on them.'

Amy gives her a look that says, 'What have I got to lose?' before announcing despondently, 'Viola hasn't seen any gardens this week, and I haven't played any whist.'

'We ought to play a round,' Gwen suggests shrilly, pouncing on the idea. 'Minnie, you'll make the fourth, won't you?'

'Oh,' Minnie shakes her head, 'you know I'm no good, Gwen. I only get in a muddle.'

'Well,' Viola sniffs, 'if you *insist* on spoiling everyone's evening …' Alcohol, rather than dulling, has sharpened her. She glitters malevolently.

'It seems rude to exclude Maisie,' Minnie says tremulously.

'She can watch. She might pick it up. We'll just have a couple of hands,' Gwen says, rummaging various items including a packet of corn plasters, a ball of string, her little accounts book and a Swiss army knife from her capacious handbag before unearthing a pack of cards. 'Just a very friendly game or two. Minnie, you can be my partner.'

'That will mean us all moving, and Amy being disturbed,' Viola points out.

'Actually,' Amy slurs, 'I'm not sure I could move if I tried. Those martinis have gone straight to my legs!' Indeed, Amy's habitual bird-like brightness is sadly muted, her eyes' usual acuity glazed.

'Minnie can be *my* partner,' Viola says with a deadly smile. 'You'll be quite all right. I won't bite.'

'Oh dear,' Minnie quavers. 'I really feel I shouldn't. You know I'm hopeless.'

'Oh, don't be pathetic,' Viola snaps. 'Here,' she fills their glasses, 'have another drink.'

Maisie has a gut feeling this is a bad idea. Many hours of playing board games with competitive children tells her that even in very friendly games, things can turn nasty. It seems obvious to her, but then she remembers that Gwen and Amy have no children and Viola only one who, no doubt, was allowed to win at everything. Minnie's step-children would have been too old to fall prey to the vicious squabbling, hair-pulling and fisticuffs that broke out every time Maisie's children got out the Monopoly board. She remembers the Trivial Pursuit and the quiz from earlier in the week.

'Perhaps we should just chat,' she suggests tentatively, but the cards are already being dealt.

Things go as badly as she fears, and over the next half hour Maisie's stomach curdles as she witnesses the coalescence of the week's antipathies. In spite of the amount of alcohol they have consumed, the other women seem able to call on some reserve of innate skill. Viola plays with a focussed, needle-sharp concentration, the energy of her narrow features and thin frame channelled unswervingly to the cards in her claw-like hands. Gwen plays a stolid, almost mechanical game, sorting the cards with perfunctory economy, laying each one down with the precision of an automaton. Even Amy, who only a moment before seemed almost comatose, gathers herself together for the game. But Minnie is all fingers and thumbs, and a hectic rash blooms on her chest and throat. She wriggles in her seat and emits anxious mewing noises. It takes her a long time to get her cards in order; she dithers and prevaricates. Her shuffle is a disaster, the cards get boxed and when it is her turn to deal, she fumbles and forgets the cut.

She replies with a club to Viola's leading spade.

'It's basic courtesy,' Viola spits, 'to return your partner's lead.'

Minnie throws away a boss trump.

'For God's sake, don't you know that hearts are trumps?' Viola yells.

'I thought we were in diamonds,' Minnie whimpers.

Minnie plays a card. 'You could have finessed that!' Viola shouts. 'I led you the six; what were you waiting for?'

'I don't know,' Minnie is almost inaudible.

They play on, the fall of each card like a slap of rebuke.

'You're doing this deliberately,' Viola shouts at one point. She is drinking steadily, finishing first the red and then the white wine. Each glass seems to hone the blade of her contempt.

'No, really,' Minnie stammers. 'I did tell you I was hopeless.'

Viola and Minnie lose hand after hand. 'I'm embarrassed to tell the score,' Gwen admits.

'It doesn't matter,' Maisie reminds them. 'This is just a friendly game, remember?'

'Shame we aren't playing for money,' Amy mumbles, 'we'd be quids-in!'

Viola pounces on her comment and the impending denouement draws closer. 'Perhaps that's it!' she cries. 'This just isn't interesting enough for you, is it Minnie? If we played for money, would that buck your ideas up?'

Minnie blanches. 'Oh no. I'd never dream of—'

'It was a throw-away remark,' Amy protests, but weakly. Now the game is suspended she has lapsed back into torpor.

Viola ignores her. 'But you should, Minnie!' she says, bright with malice. 'Your problem is that you don't *care* about the game, isn't that so?'

'It's only a game,' Minnie says in a small voice.

'But it's like everything in life, Minnie,' Viola caws, 'it's better if it matters. Now this game would matter to you if you stood to, let's say …' she casts round for a moment before her eyes light on Gwen's accounts book where it lies on the table. She snatches it up.

Gwen leaps from her seat. 'Give that back!' she shouts, loudly enough to make both Maisie and Minnie jump. Conversation in the rest of the bar falters as heads turn towards them.

Viola holds the book behind her, out of reach, an archly malicious expression on her face. 'Why?'

'It's private.' Gwen remains standing but is prevented from moving by the impeding furniture.

'Not at all!' Viola replies. 'These are the bar bills, aren't they? They relate to us all, surely?' She begins to flick through the pages.

'Amongst other things,' Gwen says sharply. 'There are personal notes as well, Viola. Give it back.'

Viola smiles dryly. 'Secret sighs and romantic longings?'

'Don't be ridiculous,' Gwen blusters. 'Church matters, prayer requests, things to do with the shop.'

'And our bar bills,' Viola snipes, pointing to a page with columns of figures. 'Oh dear, that night at the hotel in Windermere was a blow out, wasn't it? But I expect tonight will be more.'

'H ... how much was it?' Minnie whispers.

'I haven't added it all up yet,' Gwen says, trying to quell a note of panic in her voice. 'My handwriting's dreadful. I expect Viola mis-read it.'

Viola shakes her head. 'I don't think so. But here's my point Minnie—if we were to play this last hand for your share of this whole week's bar bill, wouldn't that be exciting?'

Poor Minnie is pinned like a butterfly on a board. The idea of having nothing to pay at all is a powerful inducement, if a hopeless one.

'But if I didn't win?' she stammers.

'What *if?* Amy slurs. 'Sweetie, you can hardly—'

But Viola cuts across Amy's words. 'Oh well, of course,' she smiles unctuously, 'in that case you'd have to pay extra. We three players would divide your share between us if you won, and if Gwen won, say, you and Amy and I would divide Gwen's share. That would work, wouldn't it?'

'No, I don't think so,' Gwen says tartly. 'This is a game for partners, for a start. As you well know, there isn't one winner in the sense that you suggest. This is silliness Viola; we never play for money. And it's quite intolerable of you to keep that book from me. I insist that you hand it back.'

'We never have played for money in the past,' Viola ignores her demand, 'but we could agree between us to do so now. Whist *can* be played individually; it *is* commonly played like that. The person who wins the most tricks is the winner.' Viola shuffles the cards.

Minnie looks hesitant. 'And you say that the bar bill is ... how much, did you say?'

Viola leafs through the book again. 'After tonight I'd say it's getting on for a couple of hundred, wouldn't you, Gwen?'

'Each?' Minnie squeaks.

'Nothing like,' Gwen shakes her head vigorously, too vigorously. 'As I say, I haven't sorted it out yet.'

Maisie has a sudden sense of looking down on the scene from a great height, of being in some way distanced. The threadbare furnishings of this seedy hotel lend everything a sordid air. The extravagance of the empty bottles littering the table and, across the bar, Gloria's flagrant and unambiguous exhibitionism makes Maisie feel tainted and ashamed. Viola's malevolence, Gwen's discomfort, even Amy's dissipation all seem appalling, and the threat of the little book that Viola still keeps out of Gwen's reach adds a decidedly incendiary element to the scene whose outcome, even from this elevated perspective, she is unable to see.

She puts her hand firmly on Minnie's arm. 'Let me advise you against this nonsense,' she says. 'Viola's teasing you. We've all had too much wine and this might turn very unpleasant if we aren't sensible.'

Minnie turns to her with round, frightened eyes, 'But Maisie, two hundred pounds! That's more than I spend on groceries in a month! I had no idea! If there's any possibility that I might not have to pay it …!'

Viola picks up a glass and tips it to her lips, but it is already empty. 'I think we should have another bottle,' she says. 'In for a penny, in for a pound, eh?'

'There's no possibility of you paying two hundred pounds, or anything like it,' Gwen tells Minnie with an attempt at confidence. 'I've told you, I haven't worked the figures out yet. Viola! Will you kindly return my book to me?'

'I will in a minute.' Viola hugs the book to her bony chest. 'Let Minnie speak for herself. If she wants to give it a try, I take it you and Amy won't stand in her way?'

Amy yawns and slumps further into her seat. 'Once it strikes midnight I turn into a dribbling geriatric. If Minnie did beat me, I think I'd call foul. It would be an unfair advantage.'

'It struck midnight half an hour ago, you old soak,' Gwen attempts to lighten the atmosphere. 'We certainly all ought to turn in, I think.' She begins to restore her other belongings to her bag.

'Everybody seems very keen to prevent you saving yourself a mint of money, Minnie,' Viola observes archly.

'People are only keen on making sure you aren't taken in,' Maisie urges. 'Look, Minnie, if the bill turns out to be a problem, I can help you out. I'm sure it won't, but if it does ...'

Viola gives Maisie a look of acid contempt and throws the cards and the book onto the table. 'Aren't you heartily sick,' she enunciates, 'of being treated like a child, Minnie?'

'I don't know what you mean,' Minnie replies. 'Who by?'

'These women.' Viola makes a gesture that encompasses the women at the table and also Gloria, who holds court across the room, precariously balanced on a bar stool.

'They're my friends,' Minnie asserts.

Viola leans forwards. Her next words are like poison darts. 'Friends? Friends who *baby* you, Minnie. Friends who *make allowances,* as though you are in some way weak in the head, as though you're delicate or damaged, as though you can't face up to life the way the rest of us have to. They lie to your face and talk behind your back, Minnie, that's the truth of it. I might have been cruel and nasty this week—I'm sure many will say so—but I have been honest, Minnie. With friends like these ...?' she looks from right to left, at Amy and Gwen and Maisie, leaving the rest of her sentence unspoken.

'Viola,' Gwen speaks coldly, but not unkindly, 'why don't you go to your room? We'll all think better of this tomorrow.'

Viola gets to her feet with such violence that the bottles on the table are jolted and fall, one breaking into pieces. 'Don't you *dare* presume to send *me* to bed, Gwen,' she spits, leaning over the table and speaking into Gwen's face. 'The others might all dance to your tune, but I won't. Who the hell do you think you are?' Strangely, this first overtly aggressive move on Viola's part seems to sap her of all the tautly implicit malice that has fuelled her actions for the past hour. She staggers a little and has to clutch the table for support. The hardness of her face morphs from cold cruelty to bleak unhappiness.

Gwen sees the disintegration. 'Someone offering friendly advice, dear girl,' she says airily. She has taken back possession of her book and is stowing it neatly into her bag.

'If you don't believe me,' Viola offers a *coup de grace*, 'have a look in Gwen's precious book. Run your eye over her calculations, Minnie. See how they add up and ask yourself why your share seems so much less than everyone else's.' She stalks unsteadily away from the table and approaches the bar. 'Give me a large vodka and tonic,' she says.

Minnie looks at Gwen. 'Is this true?' she asks. Tears press behind her eyes but they are too viscous to shed. Her dry eyes and thick, rasping voice speak a salty well of weeping.

'Viola is drunk.' Gwen is brisk. 'We all are, a little, and things have been said—'

'But I do need to know.' Minnie is now more forceful than she has been all week. 'Surely you do see that. I need to know.'

'Of course, and we will chat this all over comfortably at home, dear. But now I need to get Amy to bed.'

Indeed, Amy is suddenly limp, like a deflated tyre, her pinkish lids heavy over crazed blue eyes. It takes all three of them to manoeuvre Amy's unresisting body into her wheelchair. She slumps into it, virtually insensible.

'Will you go ahead Minnie, please, and open the double doors at the end of the corridor?'

Minnie scurries to her task. 'That bloody woman,' Gwen hisses to Maisie, indicating Viola. 'Try to get Minnie upstairs, will you? And avoid any more mischief-making?'

'I'll do my best,' Maisie says, 'but the truth will have to come out now, kindly though it was meant.'

Gwen sighs, and tucks Amy's wraps more securely. 'Oh yes, of course. I don't know why Viola had to interfere. I wouldn't have thought it of her. And yet, poor woman, she has her cross to bear, like the rest of us. I hate going to bed on an argument, don't you? I'll just go and say goodnight. You wheel Amy into the hall.'

Maisie pushes the wheelchair across the bar and into the reception area. From the corner of her eye, she sees Gwen say a word to Viola, and put out a conciliatory hand.

Viola recoils so sharply she is dislodged from her stool. 'Get your hands off me, you nasty old dyke,' she yells, loudly enough to cause the rest of the bar to fall silent. Her heavily kohled eyes are smudged, the tracks of tears inked down her cheeks.

Chapter Thirty-One

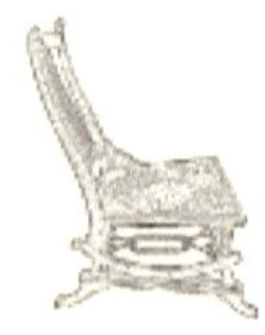

In the morning, at breakfast, there is an atmosphere. The guests help themselves from the breakfast buffet, pass marmalade and stir tea with stiff formality, but do not meet each other's eyes. Their decorum is a veneer, thinly covering the irascibility that accompanies a poor night's sleep.

Gloria is oblivious. She arrives in the dining room with a spritely step, well-coiffed and bright-eyed. Every so often her buoyant mood gives way to periods of dreamy abstraction; she is caught in a reverie over the cereals, and unable to decide between poached and scrambled eggs. She rests her chin on her hand and stares into the middle distance, humming tunelessly, a small smile playing around her lips while the others keep their eyes on their plates and exchange platitudes about the weather. Maisie looks at her with a mixture of revulsion and sorrow. The cheapness with which Gloria has auctioned her body and the recklessly broadcast nature of the encounter is appalling. Surely everybody in the entire hotel heard it; she doesn't know how Gloria can look any of them in the eye. But Gloria is gay and carefree and unashamed.

Until Gloria's blithely abstracted arrival at the table, Viola has been left in sullen and solitary enjoyment of her black coffee at one end. Except for a muttered 'Good morning' she has exchanged no discourse with any of them, ordering 'Coffee, black,' from a passing waitress in a voice that is barely more than a croak. The others have pointedly chosen seats as far away as possible. Minnie is pale and hollow-eyed and eats her breakfast without enjoyment. Gwen pretends absorption in the morning papers. Amy has not appeared at all; Gwen has taken tea and toast to her on a tray.

'Homeward bound today,' Monica announces to the room. 'The coach will depart promptly at ten. Please be sure to clear your rooms of all personal belongings and settle your bar bills before assembling with your luggage in the car park.'

'You must let me know what I owe, Gwen,' Gloria says dreamily. 'I must say, whatever it is, it won't be half enough. I've had a simply wonderful time, haven't you?' She looks around the table.

'I'm going to Reception in a moment,' Gwen says stiffly. 'There wasn't time last night to sort things out. I'll do the sums and let you know.' She throws a significant—almost challenging—glance at Viola, but Viola is busy scratching varnish from her thumb nail and doesn't notice.

Minnie excuses herself. 'I must do my packing,' she says, hurrying towards the door.

'Minnie isn't speaking to me.' Gloria pours herself more tea. 'I'm a very naughty girl. I didn't get in until about five.'

'She isn't speaking to me either,' Viola rouses herself to say. 'I wouldn't worry.'

'*I* would,' Gwen says indignantly. 'I'd be extremely worried if I'd upset a sweet-natured body like Minnie who never did a fly any harm. I'd be ashamed of myself.' She gives both Viola and Gloria a hard look before taking herself off to Reception.

'Oh dear,' Gloria says with an uncertain laugh. 'What on earth has happened? Didn't you have an enjoyable evening, last night?'

'Not as enjoyable as yours,' Viola retorts. 'You kept the whole hotel awake.'

'Oh dear,' Gloria says again, but with the smug, self-satisfied air of a cream-fed cat.

Maisie looks down at her untouched plate of breakfast and is sickened with a visceral, almost physical desire to go home.

'Which one was it, in the end, anyway?' Viola puts a cigarette into her mouth.

Gloria gives a mischievous waggle of her eyebrows. 'I'll let you guess,' she says.

Viola and, in spite of herself, Maisie, survey the room. Gloria's paramours are variously distributed but all look to some degree wan and drawn. Oliver has chosen to eat his eggs with the widowed sisters, a course of action not unprecedented but quite surprising, given that it is their last morning. He is less immaculately groomed than usual; a suggestion of stubble presents the possibility that he has not had time for a shave this morning—had he overslept? But his gestures are characteristically elegant as he passes milk and condiments and the timbre of his voice can be heard over the scrape of cutlery, confidently describing a recent ramble in the Mendips. Nothing in his demeanour suggests a night of energetic intercourse. Fair Isle and his sister eat their muesli and prunes and apply themselves to the Telegraph crossword. Fair Isle is decidedly pallid and clearly restless; constantly on his feet to fetch more juice, a piece of fruit. He spends a long time with his back to the room, adjusting the blinds of the window adjacent to their table. Robin is his usual spritely self, resplendent in velvet waistcoat and decorative bow tie, and very much engaged in a conversation with one of his camera club colleagues. He is already packed for departure; his camera bags and lens cases take up the space underneath their table and he makes frequent forays into the reception area to check on the luggage he has left for collection once the coach comes round. Behind his glasses, his eyes are unnaturally bright. Bill has already taken the coach to collect the contingent from the other hotel. Of the Area Manager there is no sign at all.

When the coach comes around, they are all assembled in the reception area. Minnie contrives to stay away from Viola and Gwen by clinging on to Maisie, but her eyes are drawn again and again to Gwen's bag, and the little accounts book it contains. Gloria stands a little apart, staring dreamily into the distance. Viola stays outside, barely sheltered from the drizzle by an overhanging portico. She smokes cigarette after cigarette.

Bill is unable to load the luggage. It seems an old groin injury has flared up. He limps and stumbles and winces. Monica is left to stow the cases, with help from some of the more able-bodied photographers; she has a face like thunder but there is no help for it as Bill is clearly incapable. He gives what direction he can, his face occasionally going into a spasm of pain. It must have kept him awake all night, poor man; he is grey with weariness, unshaven, and generally dishevelled. He has a livid welt across one cheek—a scratch-mark—and the suggestion of a black eye.

'He looks like he's been in a fight,' someone says, wagging their head knowingly.

Chapter Thirty-Two

After their uneventful trip home, Maisie and Oliver share a cab from the coach station. As always, he is all politeness and charm, lifting her bag into the boot and helping her with her seat belt. 'A most interesting trip,' he says, 'don't you think? Although the weather put a dampener on things.'

'It was an experience,' Maisie agrees, thinking to herself that it isn't one she intends to repeat any time soon.

'How well do you know those other ladies, I wonder?'

'How well do we really know anyone?'

'Indeed. How true.'

There is silence as the cab negotiates some road works in the town centre. During their absence, the trees have taken on a miasma of green, the precursor to leaf.

'Isn't it odd,' Maisie observes, 'how after only a very few days away things can seem so different?'

Oliver laughs. 'I was only thinking that they're *always* digging up this bit of road! So, no change at all there!'

'I wasn't really thinking of physical things,' Maisie says.

'Oh?'

But she declines to explain further, and presently the cab draws into Maisie's drive. 'Well, here we are,' she says, reaching for her purse.

'No,' he lifts his hand and places it on hers, 'please do allow me to settle the fare, Maisie. And let me help you with your bag.'

Maisie finds her keys and opens the door. Oliver pays the driver and dismisses the car. 'I'll walk from here,' he says.

He stands on the threshold for a moment while Maisie clears the post and takes her bag in. She is sure he is eyeing the bare floorboards and dilapidated decor. 'You wouldn't like me to come in and check the place over for you?' he offers.

'Oh no,' she smiles, her hand on the door. 'Everything will be fine, thank you Oliver.'

'Well, I'll say goodbye for now. But I do hope that we'll see a lot of each other from now on. As neighbours, of course, but also, given the circumstances, perhaps as friends? I mean, we've been discreet amongst the others but between ourselves there's no absolute need for reticence, is there?'

Maisie finds herself in something of a fluster. Given *what* circumstances? Discreet about *what?* 'We're bound to see each other,' she says, closing the door an inch.

Oliver takes a step backwards and shifts his bag to the other hand. 'Well.' He gives her a dry smile. 'You know ...' He seems determined to create some opening, but Maisie can only think of him the previous evening, joining the competition for Gloria's favours and, for all she knows, being the monosyllabic, grunting adversary of Gloria's coital encounter. Although it is ridiculous, and she has given no credence to Amy's silly romanticism, the idea of it is galling. And now he seems to be suggesting ... to be inviting ...

Firmly she says, 'Goodbye then.'

But he lingers still. 'Call in any time, if you want to chat,' he says. 'Or come up to the flat if you don't feel comfortable going into the bar. The door is round the side of the building. Ring the bell. We'd be quite private there.'

'I will,' she assures him, closing the door still more, until there is only an eye's breadth remaining. 'Goodbye,' she says again.

He turns and walks away.

She waits only long enough to put on a load of washing and to glance through the post before going out into the garden. It is April now and everything is bursting into life. Some of the perennials are showing signs of growth. In the orchard the naturalised daffodils are prolific. She passes through the gate and climbs the paddock up to the farm where she hopes Val will be able to spare her some milk and a dozen eggs.

Val is mucking out one of the stables. 'Ah, there you are,' she says, pushing her disreputable bobble hat off her forehead and scratching her head with a calloused finger. 'Got something of yours. Turned up yesterday.'

'Oh? What? A parcel?'

'Turn round, and you'll see.'

Maisie turns. On the threshold of Val's chalet, framed by the doorway, is a young man. He wears creased fatigues and is bleary with sleep. There is a week's stubble on his chin and one arm is strapped to his chest.

'Oh! Gareth.' A cold ball-bearing of tension—held perpetually inside all the time Gareth is away on his secret, perilous assignments—dissipates and disappears. Maisie holds out her arms.

He folds her into his good arm. 'Who are you?' he says, 'and what have you done with my mother?'

PART TWO

Chapter Thirty-Three

Gareth sleeps for three days. Every so often Maisie climbs to the attic with food—a plate of toast, a mug of tea, scrambled eggs, orange juice—and manages to rouse him long enough to eat or drink. Periodically she hears the flush of the toilet, and once the tell-tale rattle of the top floor shower pipes suggested he would soon descend, but half an hour later he is flat out on his bed once more, the damp towel around his waist. He is taking strong pain-killers for his injury but she knows his prolonged somnolence is due to utter exhaustion and he is best left to sleep it out.

Meanwhile, she haunts the echoing empty rooms of the house, treading softly across the creaking floorboards and dusting dead flies from the window ledges. She does not know whether it is Gareth she is trying not to disturb or Clifford's ghost. She feels faintly furtive—as though she is trespassing—but while her body might be diffident, her mind is active. It projects flights of fancy across the bare walls, trying to imagine something other, something better than what has gone before: an alternative destiny.

She meets with Gwen for coffee, just the two of them, in a bistro a few doors from the charity shop.

'You haven't seen anything of Minnie, have you?' is Gwen's first question. 'I must say I am worried about her. It was my night for whist last night, but she didn't show up. Amy wasn't up to it either, so we were a player short.'

'I'm sorry to hear about Amy. Is she OK?'

'I think she caught a chill that day we were looking for Minnie by the lake. She says all her bones ache. I'm popping by most days, and so is Viola.'

'Viola?' Viola's aptitude for sick-bed ministration seems doubtful to Maisie. 'So, all's forgiven and forgotten then?'

Gwen stirs sugar into her coffee. 'She behaves as though nothing untoward happened at all. She's like a Russian doll, that woman; she grows a new casing every time the old one gets injured. She has layers and layers of damage, poor thing. That's why I make allowances but,' she makes a zipping motion across her mouth, 'I mustn't say more.'

Maisie takes a sip of her latte. 'I think you're very forbearing Gwen. *You* were the injured party, not her. She was very unkind to you. Cruel wouldn't be too strong a word for it. And rude.'

'Oh,' Gwen does not meet her eye. 'I'm thick-skinned. Water off a duck's back, you know. But Minnie?'

Maisie shakes her head. 'I haven't seen her I'm afraid. Did you ring her?'

Gwen nods. 'She never picks up. I got a cheque for two-hundred pounds through the post though. It's too much. Of course, I shan't cash it.'

'Well, it all seems very strange to me,' Maisie muses. 'Viola says she lives in a big house up by the golf course. Why stay there, if she can't afford to keep body and soul together?'

Gwen leans across the table. 'Maisie dear, I just can't say. If I betray other people's confidences, how can I expect to be entrusted with yours?'

'Oh! I know!' Maisie sighs, 'and I don't expect you to tell me what's going on. But there was me thinking I was the only one to have secret troubles in my life. If only I'd known! Anyway, you've reminded me. I need to write you a cheque.' She opens her cheque book to settle her account. 'I owe you for the whole shebang, don't forget. You paid for my place on your credit card.' Gwen gets out her notebook and names a figure. Without a flicker Maisie writes a cheque. 'Perhaps Minnie's gone away again?' she says, when the transaction is complete.

'I doubt it. You wouldn't go round, would you? Try and explain?'

Maisie hesitates. 'I *could* ...'

'There's a dear. She really took to you. I think you might make better progress than any of us.'

'All right,' Maisie agrees, 'I'll go round in a day or two. And what of Gloria?'

Gwen spreads butter thickly onto her scone. 'The afterglow has worn off, I'm afraid. The itch is beginning to make itself felt again. She was talking about some chap on the hospital visiting team last night. Were you very shocked at her behaviour?'

Maisie shrugs. 'You were in the annex Gwen, so you didn't hear what the rest of us heard. And then, the next morning, the man—whoever he was—just ignored her. She didn't get so much as a smile, let alone a hug or a kiss, out of any of them. There isn't a question of a proper relationship, clearly … But I mustn't judge, I suppose. I only know that *I* couldn't … that *I* would never …'

Gwen interrupts her, 'Of course not, Maisie! No one would presume to think so. You're an old-fashioned girl, like me. Friendship first, then love, then sex.'

'Oh dear,' Maisie says coyly. 'Oliver said something about being friends when he dropped me off.' She girds herself for some teasing rejoinder, but in fact Gwen goes momentarily into what Maisie can only describe as a huff; her face darkens into a scowl and she folds her arms across the chest of her Aran cardigan.

'I hope you told him where to get off,' Gwen snaps.

'Oh!' Maisie sits back in surprise. Gwen's tone—smacking unmistakably of jealousy—gives her pause for thought. Viola's parting jibe to Gwen had been nasty and hurtful, but could it also have been true? Suddenly Maisie is forced to view Gwen's friendship in a new light; it throws a dismaying glow on the cordiality of their relationship. 'Well, no,' she goes on. 'But I didn't encourage the idea either. If there was the least chance that he was the one that Gloria ended up with—'

'You'd be jealous!'

'No,' Maisie denies it. 'But I'd be disappointed.' She gives Gwen a straight look. 'I must admit I've started to think rather well of him.'

Gwen takes her cue. 'We all have,' she agrees. 'A thoroughly nice chap.' She gives herself a sort of shake and unfolds her arms.

'Although, to be fair,' Maisie goes on, 'my money's on Bill, the driver. He looked like he'd done five rounds with Mike Tyson.'

Gwen grins. 'I wondered about the Area Manager chap.'

'He made a quick getaway, certainly. The only thing I'm sure of is that it wasn't Robin. If he'd been party to what I overheard, he'd have needed hospitalising. Now I need to run,' Maisie stands up. 'My boy is home and it's time I administered more sustenance.'

Chapter Thirty-Four

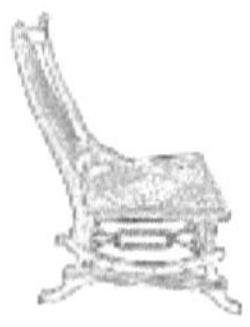

On the fourth morning Gareth appears in the kitchen. To all intents and purposes he is his normal self, dressed and shaved, but Maisie can see that his recuperation is only partial. In his core there is a deeply-seated burden of weariness and perhaps of something else—trauma—not assuaged by his extended rest.

'Like what you've done with the place,' he says, using his good arm to indicate the empty corridors and deserted rooms of the house. 'What is it? Some kind of extreme *feng shui*?'

'Extreme de-cluttering, certainly,' Maisie says with a smile, placing a cereal bowl, spoon and milk on the table. 'What will you have? Cornflakes? Weetabix? Or I could make something hot?'

Gareth opts for Weetabix. Maisie watches him laboriously open the packet and extract the biscuits with his free hand. The buttons of his shirt are done up wrong but she knows she mustn't offer to help.

'And toast?' he suggests. She sets about slicing the bread. 'As a matter of fact,' he goes on, his mouth full of cereal, 'I thought you'd done a runner when I first got home. Moved out without telling me. It was weird. So *weird*, seeing the place all empty. Like stepping into an alternative reality. What is it that Christian sect call it? The Rapture? When they wake up and find everyone has been taken off to heaven but them. But then, these tablets I'm taking make everything seem peculiar. I really did wonder if I was hallucinating at first.'

'In fact, that's how I feel,' Maisie agrees, 'and I don't have the excuse of the painkillers. I felt it all the time I was away—that another life has been out there waiting for me all these years, and now I've stepped into it. At the same time—and this is the really odd part—I feel *guilty,* as though the old life is *still here* somewhere, struggling along without me. As if I've abandoned it.'

'Hum.' He seems to need a long time to assimilate her comments, and to gather his thoughts together in order to make a reply. At last, he says, 'You have nothing to feel guilty about.' Maisie gets out butter and marmalade, peanut butter, Marmite and last year's homemade blackcurrant jam. 'Are you going to move out?' he asks, sliding the empty bowl away.

'At first I thought I would,' she admits. 'But now I'm not sure. Tea? Coffee? After only a few days away I was desperate to get home.'

Gareth spends a while marshalling the jars on the table. 'Tea please. Lots of sugar.' She removes his bowl and substitutes a plate and knife. She thinks the conversation must be over until he asks, 'But how would those two things fit together, Mum? An alternative life in the same place?'

'By being very different. By serving a genuine purpose, for a start. But I must admit, I don't know quite how, or quite what, yet.'

Awkwardly, Gareth smears butter across his toast, which keeps sliding off the plate. He preservers doggedly. He reaches for the peanut butter but at the last minute chooses the jam instead. Maisie smiles. It is the choice that pleases her the most. Perhaps he knew it would be. His next words suggest that he has her feelings uppermost in his mind. 'Were you very unhappy, when Dad was alive?'

'No.' She places his tea on the table, and then pulls out a chair and sits opposite to him with her own cup. 'No, I wasn't unhappy, darling. Frustrated? Yes. Bewildered? Often. Overwhelmed? Almost all of the time. But you see, I believed in your dad, and he believed in what he was doing. It was a sort of temporary madness. It crept up on us very slowly. We started off on the right track but somehow, we went off at a tangent. The more time went by, the further we travelled from the right direction until we were miles and miles off course. Almost as soon as he died, I saw the futility of it. How hopeless it was, and had always been. That's why I've got rid of it all.'

Gareth munches toast. 'Do you think *he* was mad? I mean, he was obsessed, wasn't he? In a way that wasn't rational.'

Maisie laughs out loud. 'To him it was *eminently* rational, but then maybe that's the definition of madness! But no,' she sobers, 'I don't think he was mad. I think he was damaged—hurt—by something we don't know about … yet.'

Gareth nods and licks jam off his fingers. 'And you're going to find out what it was.'

'I hope so. Now you're here, you can help me if you like.'

He nods again and lifts his hand to stroke his injured shoulder. 'I'll be here for a while, I think. Tell me, is today Tuesday?'

'Yes.'

'In that case, I have an appointment at the hospital in an hour. Will you take me?'

'Of course I will.'

At the hospital Maisie accompanies Gareth into the clinic and, when his name is called, into the consulting room, as she would have done if he was a small boy. He does not object, and as a result her suspicions are confirmed. He has a gun-shot wound that necessitated an emergency air-lift from wherever he was engaged in combat, followed by surgery in a field hospital to repair his shattered shoulder joint. The Consultant has X-rays and copious notes and gives the wound a detailed examination before deciding that further surgery on the shoulder joint may be needed.

'They've done a reasonable job of fixing you back together,' he says. 'A cataclysmic injury like yours is tricky though. You won't be deployed again this side of Christmas, if ever. To be frank, the army may invalid you out permanently. I'm not sure we'll ever get full strength or movement back for you, unless we replace the joint altogether.'

'I'm a career soldier,' Gareth states. 'The army is my life, my wife.' Maisie expects him to add, 'my family, father and mother,' but he does not go so far, concluding only, 'There is no other life for me outside of it.'

'All right.' The consultant bundles Gareth's notes together and stretches an elastic band over them. 'We'll have to do our best for you then, won't we? You aren't fit enough for anything at the moment. Let's give it a month, and then I'll see you again. In the meantime, you can leave the dressings off. Let the wound breathe. Keep as active as you can, within comfortable limits. *Don't overdo it.* Do you hear me? I don't want you climbing Snowdon or running marathons. Eat. Sleep. Spend time with your mother. Come off these tablets as soon as you're able; they start to mess with your head after a while. Let me warn you that depression is a common by-product of these situations. Keep busy and stay positive.'

'I will. Thank you, sir.'

When they return home Gareth looks grey with fatigue. 'Go and lie down for a while,' Maisie advises. 'There's no need for you to do anything at all until you feel up to it. But when you do, I have something I want you to help me with.'

He looks ruefully at his useless arm. 'I'm not up to chopping much wood,' he says with a half-smile.

'No need for that. I've got plenty stocked up,' Maisie assures him.

'Just when you thought you were getting your life back,' he sighs, 'now you've got me on your hands, and it doesn't look as though it's going to be a short-term arrangement.'

'Silly billy,' Maisie scolds. 'Don't you know that looking after people is the thing I like best of all?'

Chapter Thirty-Five

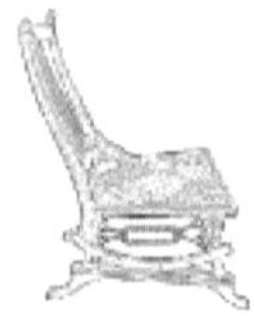

Having Gareth home—even in his incapacitated state—is indeed a joy to Maisie, who mobilises herself into a frenzy of shopping, cooking and baking. It is the end of the week before she remembers her promise to Gwen, and sets off in search of Minnie's house. She finds it situated on a wide, leafy avenue that leads to the imposing gates of the local golf club. All the houses are magnificent, detached, paying lip-service to various styles of architecture: Tudor, Georgian, neo-Classical. One or two very modern, architecturally cutting-edge structures look to Maisie like municipal offices or art galleries. Minnie's house is not one of these, however. It is constructed of old brick, with large mullioned bay windows either side of a porch, twin gables jutting from the roof and several ornately constructed chimneys. A wide gravel sweep is bordered by mature shrubs. A separate garage building looks as though it could accommodate several cars. Down the side of the house, Maisie glimpses extensive lawns and a summer house before what she presumes to be the border with the golf course and a glorious view of the sea beyond. As Viola has suggested, there is absolutely nothing about the house or its location that suggests stretched finances. It is a mystery. Gwen has admitted as much and Maisie ponders it for a few moments as she stands by the ornate wrought iron gates—firmly closed—that debar her from approaching the house.

I suppose it's no different to my situation, she concludes. Anyone looking at Old Farm Hall would think I am as poor as a church mouse whereas, in fact, I'm as rich as Croesus!

An intercom system is mounted on a brick pillar to the side of the gate. She presses the button that displays a bell symbol and waits. There is no reply, but very distantly she can hear the yapping bark of a small dog. She rings again. And again. Finally, she presses the button that shows a mouth with a speech bubble. 'Minnie dear, it's me, Maisie,' she says into the hatched grille. 'Please let me in.' At last, there is a judder and a squeak, and the gates begin to open.

Minnie greets her in an outdoor coat. 'I've just come in,' she says, but Maisie doesn't believe her.

Everything inside the house is exquisite. Pale, thick-piled carpet yields like bowling green turf to the foot. The walls are tastefully decorated with paper, silky to the touch. Elegant pictures and mirrors break up the wider expanses. Large pieces of solid furniture—some clearly antique, all very good quality—display beautiful collections of china and glass and leather-bound books. Nothing is cluttered; while there is opulence, there is never over-abundance. In the lounge, two massive settees sit either side of an ingle nook fireplace, their upholstery plush and splendid but also soft and rather inviting. Magnificent curtains—perfectly draped—frame the windows. Everything is spotlessly clean, polished and gleaming, in excellent taste and of the best possible style.

Maisie finds that the words she has prepared have escaped her. 'What a beautiful home,' she declares instead, shocked to realise that after, surprise— she had expected veneer and flat-pack to proliferate; utilitarian, mass-produced furniture, budget fabrics—the emotion uppermost is envy. Minnie's home is exactly the home she—Maisie—has always craved; a balance of solid quality, good taste, practicality and comfort. And, now she thinks of it, this house shares some characteristics with Old Farm Hall; its size, and the layout of the rooms.

'Let me show you round,' Minnie says with a sort of hopeless resignation. They pass from room to room. A dining room is equipped with a large table and elegant chairs, a study has a leather chair behind an imposing desk. The kitchen is cavernous, very well fitted with bespoke units and has French doors opening onto a terrace. Upstairs, five bedrooms contain beds perfectly dressed with quilts, throws and scatter-cushions, elegant armoires and kidney-shaped dressing tables. Two bathrooms are tiled floor to ceiling and comprehensively equipped with a multiplicity of sprouting shower heads, deep baths, twin sinks, gold taps.

The two women descend the stairs and go back into the lounge. They face each other across the immaculate pale green carpet.

'Perhaps you'd like tea?' Minnie asks at last, but makes no move to make it.

Maisie surveys the room again. The air smells stale and un-breathed and is noticeably chill on this damp April afternoon, which explains Minnie's attire. There is no sign that the fire will be lit later, or indeed has been lit in the recent past. The grate is clean and bare, the log basket empty. The room's appointments, though gorgeous, are impersonal, cold, and in some way artificial, as though posed for an exhibition or set like a stage for a play. There are no personal belongings, no needlework, no reading material, no clothing cast aside, no family photographs. She realises the whole house is the same—unlived in, preserved, for display purposes only. Maisie is reminded powerfully of the mock room arrangements she used to mooch around in department stores. The overwhelming impression, despite the elegance and taste, is one of soullessness. Maisie hesitates to put down her bag, let alone take a seat on one of the cushioned sofas, even though Minnie's gesture invites her to do so. Even Minnie, hovering awkwardly on the threshold of the room, and Dolly, cowering in the hall behind her, have the air of trespassers.

Under the scrutiny of Maisie's gaze, Minnie's eyes flicker momentarily to a large, double-doored cupboard. It is the briefest possible glance, but what she sees there causes a splotchy blush to bloom across her neck. Maisie follows the direction of her look. One door is slightly open. Through the gap flops the corner of a white sheet.

It all falls into place. So that's why she took so long to answer the bell.

Maisie is suddenly brisk, and very confident. 'I'd love some tea please. But could we drink it somewhere else? Show me *your* room. I think I'd feel more comfortable there.'

Minnie's shoulders drop. Behind her, Dolly gives a little whine. 'Oh, all right then,' Minnie says dejectedly, 'follow me.'

There's a room off the kitchen, through a door that had been firmly closed on their tour. Perhaps at one time conceived as a family room, it now comprises Minnie's living space. An old, shabby settee is pushed against the back wall, a piece of crochet abandoned on its arm. Several blankets layer the back cushions. A small table sits in front of the window with Minnie's sewing machine set up on it. The local free papers are stacked on one chair, along with a pair of scissors. A dozen or so coupons have been cut out and carefully kept to one side. A number of cellophane-wrapped garments dangle from hangers hooked over the curtain rail—items for alteration and repair from the dry cleaners. There's a portable TV on a low table opposite the sofa. Dolly's bed and a selection of well-mouthed toys take up the space at one side of an oil-fired radiator. Maisie puts her hand on it—a scanty heat emanates. This room is cluttered and a bit chaotic, but very friendly, in a lived-in way that the rest of the house is not.

Minnie puts the kettle on and then busies herself trying to tidy up. It is a challenge; the room is small and full of the appurtenances of everyday living that most people have spread across the entire house—reading material, outdoor shoes, correspondence, knitting wool, photograph albums, items of clothing, a small maiden festooned with damp washing.

'This is cosy,' Maisie says, pushing aside a hot water bottle—still warm—to sit on the sofa.

'I spend a lot of time in here,' Minnie admits.

'I can tell that. Do you sometimes sleep in here as well?'

'Well,' Minnie hesitates, 'yes, I do, to tell the truth. It's warmer, and Dolly and I like to snuggle up. You won't tell anyone, will you?'

Maisie laughs. 'Of course not. It's nobody's business. But I wish you could have come to my house a few weeks ago. If you think you have irregular living conditions, you should have seen mine!'

'Oh? Really?' Minnie looks mollified. 'I wish I had too, then. What's your house like?'

'As a matter of fact, in some ways, a lot like this one. But an empty shell now, more or less. I've kept just the barest minimum. But it was stuffed with junk, floor to ceiling. Nothing like your lovely things.'

'Are they lovely? I can't see it. I only dust them. They were here when I moved in. My husband and his first wife had chosen them. They mean nothing to me.'

'They are quite lovely, but you can tell nobody loves them. That's the difference I suppose. Our stuff was rubbish but it was loved. Clifford saw the potential of things. He was a compulsive hoarder.' Maisie states this as she presumes members of self-help groups for alcoholics or gamblers might admit their addiction. The thought makes her smile inwardly; it is strangely cathartic. 'My name is Maisie,' she says aloud, with a theatrical accent, 'and my husband was a compulsive hoarder.'

The joke is lost on Minnie. 'Fancy that!' she says. 'Let me get the tea. It'll be brewed by now. It only goes to show you, doesn't it?'

'What's that?'

'Well,' Minnie brings a tray with a teapot, three mugs and a shop-bought cake with a yellow 'reduced for quick sale' sticker on its cellophane. 'It's true what they say, about what goes on behind closed doors. You never know, do you? Are you warm enough? I can turn the heater up if you like. It's very economical, I find.'

Maisie shakes her head and sips her tea. She is unsurprised to see the label of one of the hotel tea bags dangling from the pot. 'So that's *my* explanation,' she says, 'what's yours?'

Chapter Thirty-Six

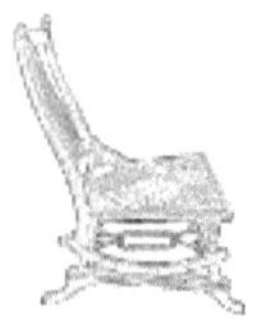

'And so,' Maisie tells Gareth later that evening, 'she poured a third cup that she put down for the dog—only half a teaspoon of sugar, apparently the dog's on a diet—and then proceeded to cut three slices of cake, one of which, you've guessed it, was for the dog!'

'Pampered pooch!' Gareth says with a smile but, to Maisie, there is something automatic, something distracted, as though he has not really engaged with the story.

She is rather worried about him. He isn't sleeping so much but spends many hours on the settee in the housekeeper's parlour staring at asinine quiz shows and back-to-back episodes of Escape to the Country and Heir Hunters. He seems listless and distracted, and Maisie finds herself engineering situations that will bring him out of himself.

The conversation takes place in the *parterre* garden where they rest in the middle of their after-supper stroll. They will not be able to stay out long; the evening is already turning chilly. But Maisie wants to take a good look at the garden to see what needs to be done, and encouraged Gareth to accompany her, 'Otherwise,' she reproached him gently, 'you won't have been outside all day.'

Her brief tour reveals the need for much industry, even if only of a nature to maintain order. The gravel of the *parterre* itself is sprouting with nascent weeds. Soon the box hedging will need trimming. The greenhouse needs a good clear-out and washing with fungicide. The raised beds should be dug over and enriched with the composted manure that was barrowed down from the farm last summer. The flower beds need weeding. The lawn is overdue its first cut of the year. The idea of this excites Maisie momentarily—she will get a ride-on mower, she tells herself, something she has always wanted but which could never be afforded. *Now* … but then she reins herself back. No point in buying one, if she is going to move.

'So, what *was* her explanation?' Gareth asks unexpectedly. 'Why *is* she living like that, in one room of a mansion?'

'Oh!' Maisie is pleased to find that he is still engaged in their discourse. 'Well, come to that, we might ask why *we* are! But I can't really say. I was told in confidence. But it is a tricky situation for her, poor woman. I must say, I do feel for her.'

She is prevented from having to say more by the arrival of Oliver, who appears round the corner of the house, casual in jeans and an open-necked shirt. 'Ah! There you are,' he says genially. 'I rang the bell to no avail, but then I thought I heard voices. Oh!' he checks himself, 'but you have company.'

Maisie's heart sinks. She wonders if he has come for the cosy chat he seems so sure she wants to have. But she quashes the thought. Some masculine company is just what Gareth needs. 'Did you think I was talking to myself?' Maisie laughs. 'This is my son, Gareth, my wounded soldier home to recover. Gareth, this is Mr Harrington—Oliver—he manages the Smithy.'

The two men shake hands. 'It's my night off and I thought I'd stroll up to ask you something,' Oliver says, 'but I don't want to intrude.'

'Ask me something?'

'Yes.' For the first time since she has met him, Oliver looks a trifle unsure of himself. 'Are you busy next Wednesday? There's a trade show up country. It's a nice drive and I wondered if you'd like to come for the run out.'

At her side, Gareth stiffens. Maisie can't tell if it is with outrage or amusement. 'I'm sure visiting a trade show is right up there on my mother's bucket list,' he says with heavy sarcasm.

'It might be, if I knew what a trade show was,' Maisie says with a shrill laugh. 'And I only possess one bucket, so it doesn't need a list.'

'There's sure to be a stand at the show dedicated entirely to buckets,' Oliver says smoothly. 'You can stock up.'

'Hold me back!' Gareth snorts.

'Well, a bucket deficit is a serious matter,' Oliver replies with a glint in his eye. 'In my experience, no lady is content with less than about five.'

Maisie says, 'My bucket requirements are modest.'

Gareth's face cracks and he begins to shake with laughter. 'I never expected to hear my mother being asked on a date,' he guffaws, giving her a nudge with his good arm, 'and, of all places, to a trade show!'

Oliver laughs too. 'Perhaps not the most romantic venue,' he agrees, gamely sharing the joke.

'Oh, stop it, the pair of you,' Maisie scolds. 'Come inside, Oliver, and have some coffee.'

They make their way along the terrace and back into the kitchen. Gareth stoops to whisper into his mother's ear, 'Ah ha! You've made terms with the enemy!'

As they re-enter the house, the telephone is ringing. 'Excuse me,' Maisie cries. 'Gareth, pour Oliver some coffee, will you?' She dashes through to the housekeeper's parlour and snatches up the receiver.

As always, Frances speaks without an opening preface of any kind. 'So, as I suspected, Maxim's people *do* insist on what they call 'proper form and ceremony.'

'Hello darling. How are you?'

'Miffed. I wanted to do it without a fuss. Left to myself I'd have done it already, at the Registry Office, or even driven up to Gretna. But they won't have it.'

Maisie has an image of Frances with a small storm cloud hovering over her head, complete with forks of lightning. She never could handle not getting her own way. Nevertheless, Maisie herself is rather pleased, although the work involved in getting the garden to rights will be enormous …

'Mother, stop it,' Frances cuts into her thoughts. 'I *know* what you're thinking, and I've told you, it won't be anything like that. We've booked the College Chapel. June 21st at noon, and afterwards in the Buttery—or if it's fine weather, in the Rose Garden. No bridesmaids, no speeches, no photographer and most of all, NO FROCK.'

'Oh, but Frances, darling, you'll have to wear *something*. And I think at least one bridesmaid, just a friend from college perhaps, for practicality's sake, to hold your bouquet and so on, and someone to …' she chokes back the words 'give you away' just in time—they would surely infuriate Frances—and substitutes 'walk you down the aisle.'

A burst of masculine laughter erupts from the kitchen. 'Have you got visitors, Mum? I can hear voices.'

'Yes. Gareth's home.'

'Gareth's home? Why wasn't I told? Is he all right?'

'No. Yes. He's been injured, but he's mobile. He's OK.'

There is a pause. 'Was it bad?'

'You know Gareth. He never talks about things, so I don't know the details. I think it could have been a lot worse; God knows, too many of them never come back at all. Between you and me, I am a bit concerned about him. The consultant wasn't sure he'd ever be back to full fitness, and you know what that would mean for him.'

'Oh.' Across the airwaves, Maisie feels Frances cogitating, weighing up the options. 'Perhaps we ought to come up,' she says at last. 'Maxim hasn't met Gareth yet, and I suppose we'll have to talk through some of the detail for the wedding.'

'Oh yes.' Maisie is at a loss to think how Frances' spiky sympathy could in any way assuage Gareth's anxiety over his future career. Maxim, on the other hand, could be a boon. Additionally, a visit might ensure all is not lost in the matter of wedding protocol and accessories. 'Well, you know, whatever I can do. There'll be a lot to organise—'

'The problem is we're so busy just now,' Frances cuts in. 'Maxim has his head down for his finals. My thesis is due by the end of the month.'

'There's no hurry. But when you *can* come, I'll ask Dominic and Pamela too. We're virtually camping here, at the moment. The house is empty of all but the absolute basics, but we'll manage somehow.'

'No change there, then. Staying at Old Farm Hall is always a bit Heath Robinson!'

Maisie steels herself to ignore Frances' jibe. Was it? Is that how it seemed?

'Have you decided what you're going to do, Mum?'

'I'm afraid not.'

Frances never has time for other people's concerns; it's all about Frances, with Frances. Maisie's situation is immediately swept aside. 'At some point you'll have to meet Maxim's people I suppose. They were up here last week, sticking their oar in.'

'You poor girl. You don't need the aggravation,' Maisie says, somewhat automatically. 'What are they like?'

'He's a bit of a stuffed shirt. She's formidable. I hardly like to introduce you at all. She'll make mincemeat of you, I'm afraid. But it has to be done.'

'Oh.' Maisie quails inwardly, but summons up enough gumption to say, 'Don't worry about me. I'm tougher than you think.'

When Maisie gets back to the kitchen the two men have moved on from coffee to whisky. 'You don't mind, do you?' Gareth asks.

'Of course not. I'd forgotten it was in the cupboard. It must be left over from Christmas. What are you up to?'

They are fiddling with an iPad. 'You do have Wi-Fi, don't you, Mum?' Gareth frowns, 'only I can't seem to connect to it.'

'What would it look like?'

Oliver and Gareth exchange a look. 'The Wi-Fi itself doesn't look like anything; it's invisible. But it comes from a sort of plastic box attached to the telephone socket.'

'Oh!' Maisie cries. 'Yes. I did find one of those. But there was a yellow light that kept flashing on and off, so I thought it must be broken. I unplugged it and recycled it in the 'small electricals' skip at the dump.'

Both men roll their eyes. Gareth closes the flap of the iPad. 'Well that explains that,' he says grimly.

'You'll have to come down to the flat,' Oliver offers. 'Use my Wi-Fi. Anytime.'

'As a matter of fact,' Maisie pounces on the opportunity to motivate Gareth. 'I was thinking that I'd like one of those,' she nods at the iPad, 'and a laptop. Everyone seems to have one but me. And a mobile. On holiday I was the only one who didn't have one, wasn't I, Oliver? And I wondered if you could show me how they all work.'

Gareth nods. 'Of course. But first of all, we have to get your broadband sorted. I'll call BT in the morning.'

An unexpected consequence of Oliver's impromptu visit is a decided improvement in Gareth's mood. Their shared experience of exotic travel gives them common ground and, to a lesser degree, Oliver's time in the Merchant Navy. In spite of the difference in their years they seem to hit it off. Gareth is prised away from daytime TV to visit the trade show; Maisie pleads a prior engagement. He takes to sauntering down to the Smithy for a pint in the evening.

Together, the two men set about tackling Maisie's digital education. She is soon the owner of a mobile phone and a tablet computer. Oliver introduces her to the wonders of the internet while Gareth skypes his comrades in Special Ops.

'Muldoon and Fraser are on leave,' he tells her later. 'I told them they could come up, if they wanted. Or I might go and meet up with them.'

'That would be lovely. Don't they have first names, your friends?'

'I suppose they must do. But we never use them. What are you up to?' He leans over Maisie's shoulder, 'Facebook? You've got to be kidding!'

Oliver turns out to be only the first of a number of visitors. Maisie opens the door one day to find Minnie on her doorstep, clutching Dolly in her arms. 'You don't mind, do you? Only it's such a lovely day, and Dolly fancied a walk.'

'Of course not,' Maisie says. 'Come on in. But I warn you, things are very rudimentary here at the moment.'

'You know I don't mind that.' Minnie steps into the hall. 'It really is empty,' she gasps. 'A completely blank canvas. What a perfect opportunity for a new start.'

'That's just the positive way I'm looking at it,' Maisie nods. 'You can put Dolly down, if you like. She can't come to any harm.'

They move through to the kitchen, and Maisie puts the kettle on. 'As a matter of fact,' she says, 'I'm glad you've called. My daughter's getting married in June. I can see we're going to have a battle over the dress. I was wondering if you could make her one. It's going to have to be a wedding dress that looks nothing at all like a wedding dress, if you know what I mean.'

'Oh yes,' Minnie gushes, 'I do. I've dealt with tom-boy-brides before. How would she feel about a really elegant suit, in pearl grey silk? If we can get her to agree to that, it's a very small step to a dress and jacket. Then, in June, of course a jacket won't be required, and voilà! The bride is wearing a dress!'

'Oh Minnie,' Maisie almost stammers, 'do you really think you could get her to agree to it?'

Another day, Viola calls. 'You offered to show me the garden,' she says without any kind of preamble, 'so here I am.'

Viola has been neglecting herself. She looks pale and very thin, even thinner than usual. Her hair is shaved so short it is virtually a crew cut. Her makeup is haphazardly applied. She refuses food of any kind but guzzles cup after cup of strong back coffee. Maisie thinks she discerns a slight tremor in Viola's hand as she lifts her coffee cup.

She gives Viola—as she had given Minnie—a brief tour of the house. Viola has nothing remotely positive or even polite to say. 'Good God,' she exclaims, 'talk about minimalism taken to the extreme! The place is semi-derelict. Look at this bathroom! It's out of the Ark. I'm amazed the Council hasn't slapped on order on you.'

'It isn't that bad,' Maisie retorts. She has decided to take no nonsense from Viola, and to fight fire with fire. 'My husband might have been an amateur but everything he did is sound, pretty much. We're warm and dry, and we have plumbing. There are a few cosmetic issues to be fixed, that's all.'

'But why would you live like this? You haven't any furniture!'

Maisie laughs aloud. 'I haven't any furniture *now*, Viola. But a month ago, you couldn't move for the stuff. On balance, I like this better. You know,' she gives Viola a pointed look, 'it's always a mistake to judge people when you don't know the full story. Come on; let me show you the garden.'

Viola is transformed by the garden. Her spikes and thorns are blunted, her sharp edges smoothed as she exclaims over the herbaceous borders and admires the scope of the vegetable plot. She bends to stroke leaves and smell flowers and to scoop up handfuls of soil to crumble between her palms. Her face and eyes are alight in a way Maisie has never seen them before. The habitual sourness of her tongue is sweetened by praise as she gushes enthusiastically about variety, propagation and cropping. She becomes almost ecstatic in the orchard. 'Some of these trees are very old. What varieties are they? You know I've an idea this is a Deddington Pippin—that's considered heritage nowadays. A specialist grower would probably pay you a mint for grafts.'

They wander through the *parterre* and Viola absent-mindedly begins to pull weeds from the gravel. 'I do envy you,' she admits at last. 'My flat's convenient, and very well appointed, but I do miss a garden.'

'If I decide to stay,' Maisie says, with a sudden gush of warmth, 'you can come and play in mine any time you want.'

Maisie's fourth visitor is unexpected. It is late afternoon. Gareth has gone with Oliver to the cash and carry. Maisie is ironing in the kitchen when the doorbell rings. The sight of James Armstrong on her threshold sweeps her back in time some twenty years, to that rain-lashed night when he had come to reason with Clifford. Now, in the thin sunshine of a late April afternoon, he seems no less burdened than formerly, the reason for his visit equally grim.

'I really must apologise,' he begins. 'I've been abroad. My wife is unwell, and we went away for the winter. I heard about your bereavement of course, but this is the first opportunity I've had to come and pay my respects. It's unpardonably late of me, I know.'

Maisie steps back to admit him to the house, thinking he would see very little difference since his last visit—the same bare walls and uncarpeted hall, the same program of repairs and improvements awaiting commencement. Now—as then—James diplomatically makes no comment at all, and for some reason she can't explain she shows him once more into the empty drawing room as though their movements are prescribed, like dance steps or stage directions over which they have no control and can only repeat, time after time.

But the shutters are open now, and in the light that pours into the room Maisie is able to see that some things have not remained the same. It is the first time Maisie has seen James at close quarters for some time. Once the pub opened and was running smoothly, his visits there became less frequent as, she presumes, other business interests took priority. She has seen him very occasionally, across a street perhaps, and exchanged only a wave or a nod of recognition. On the last few of these occasions Maisie found herself turning to look into a shop window or rummaging furiously in her handbag, to avoid contact. It was hard—no, not hard, painful—to explain the reason why: she felt ashamed. Ashamed of her neglected, bedraggled looks and jumble-sale clothes. Ashamed of their situation at Old Farm Hall, the waste they had made of James' family heritage. Ashamed that Clifford had fallen so very far below whatever equal standing he had at one time shared with James. She found she just couldn't look him in the eye.

Now though, the shame has gone. She looks him over with a bold eye, as his eyes rove the dusty cornices and shabby paintwork of the room, conjuring, she supposes, more auspicious scenes of years gone by. His skin, though tanned, is sallow. His hair, still thick and unruly, is peppered with grey. Time, and perhaps trouble, have scored lines on his face where none were before. His shoulders are as broad as formerly but seem weighted, carrying invisible burdens. The geniality of his eyes is tinged by sadness.

Still, he gathers himself and turns once more to the room to declare 'Ah! This room! What memories!'

'*What* memories?' Maisie can ask now, as she hadn't felt able to before. 'Please, do tell me.'

Together, they walk through the house and for once it is not Maisie who supplies the narrative but her visitor. 'In this room, the drawing room, there was always a fire burning in the grate, no matter what the weather. Grandpa had a huge chair here with a table next to it, and all the newspapers scattered around, and a circle of ash on the carpet from his cigars. I used to imagine it was a fairy-ring, and he enchanted within it. He was often asleep, you see.'

Upstairs, in the front bedroom, 'This was Grandpa's room. He had a high bed in here with a sort of canopy and curtains. I could hardly clamber onto it, but of course I was very small, only two or three. I suppose Grandma shared it, but somehow it was always *his* room. He died in it, in fact. All alone. I think that must be the loneliest thing.'

In Frances' room, 'This was Great Aunt Maud's room. She was an invalid. She never married and although Grandma was the lady of the house, Maud ran it like a military camp. She used to force feed me Fisherman's Friends; she said they kept the evil spirits away—frightened me to death! I almost choked on one once. Mum had hysterics.'

In the garage, 'They had a chauffeur called Johns. Yes, he lived in that loft room, up the stairs. I was never allowed up there. Johns used to carry Maud up to her room and out into the garden, and drive her out to wherever she wanted to go. In fact, I sometimes wonder if there wasn't more to their relationship than they let on—you know, like Queen Victoria and Mr Brown? In fact, in many ways, they lived as though they were still in the Victorian era.'

In Dominic's room, 'This was my dad's room when he was a boy. When I came to visit, I'd stay in here. All his toys were still here; Grandma kept them all as they had been.'

In the kitchen, 'Johns' sister did the cooking and cleaning, but she didn't live in the house. I think this must be the same range cooker she used. Isn't that amazing? She landed me such a slap once, for pinching a rock bun.'

For the time that they tour the house and, afterwards, the garden, whatever worry it is that weighs James down seems dissipated. Afterwards, Maisie pours them each a glass of wine and they sit at the kitchen table.

'I'm sorry to hear your wife is ill,' she says very gently. She supposes this to be the source of his disquiet.

'Ah, yes,' he sighs. 'I never expected it of Elspeth, but there you are: the curse of the Harrington women.'

Maisie gives a shout of dry laughter. 'I might have guessed it!' she says. 'Wherever I turn, the Harringtons seem to be there waiting for me, like an invisible thread through the material of my life.'

James raises an eyebrow. 'What do you mean?'

'Well. All those years Clifford worked at the factory; I suppose there's nothing odd about that. He only worked in the stores, but Mr Harrington himself turned up to the funeral. That seemed odd. It was certainly unexpected. Then, Oliver, down at the Smithy—my nearest neighbour—turns out to be a Harrington! Talk about coincidence! And some fluke books him onto exactly the same coach tour as me! And now you. Married to a Harrington!'

James holds his hands out in front of him and gives a rueful smile. 'What can I say? It's a conspiracy!'

'It seems more than accidental. But I suppose it isn't that surprising. This is a small town after all, and the Harringtons are an influential family.'

He neither confirms nor contradicts her assertion, but gives her a long, direct look. 'So, apart from these quirky coincidences, you don't know *anything* about the Harringtons? About the girls, for example? About Elspeth or,' he swallows, 'about Louisa?'

'Why does everybody keep asking me that?' she bursts out. 'No. Nothing at all. Certainly nothing from Clifford. He hardly ever mentioned work, or his employer, let alone his employer's family. Oliver told us that he has two sisters. And I know there's a grandson—I presume he's your son? A very nice young man.'

'No.' James gives a strangled laugh, exactly like—she now recalls—the one Oliver gave when she suggested the same thing. 'No. Michael isn't ours. Elspeth and I never had children, unfortunately.'

Maisie wants to ask more: about the 'curse' James has mentioned, about the nature of his wife's illness, about the other sister—Louisa—who must, by a process of elimination, be the mother of Michael. But it seems indelicate, and James is speaking now of Clifford's funeral. 'I should have been there. I *would* have been, but I couldn't leave Elspeth.'

'Don't give it a second thought. There was no reason why you should have been there, or why anybody should, come to that. Clifford lived a quiet, very private life. Your place was with your wife. Whereabouts were you?'

'In Italy for a while, and then we went further south still, to Cape Town, trying to escape from the affliction of the British winter. But some afflictions follow you, no matter how far you travel. Luckily, I could leave the business in a safe pair of hands.'

'Oliver?'

'Amongst others, yes. In fact, Oliver has proved a real boon in many ways. Surprisingly, after a feckless start in life, he's come good.'

'He's certainly looked after me—at your behest, I understand.'

'Well, that's good.' James smiles, 'You need looking after, I think.'

Maisie gives an involuntary shiver. 'That's what Clifford told me, when he proposed.'

James nods. 'It was his strength, wasn't it? Taking care of the lost. I'm sure you miss him very much.'

Maisie is too stunned to reply, and presently, James drains his glass and stands up to go. It is as though his worries have been waiting in the air. As he rises, they drape themselves back across his shoulders and settle there, like an old coat; she can almost see them—the dragging weight of them, the irksome fit—as he makes his way across the hall and puts his hand on the door handle.

'Thank you so much,' he says. 'May I call again?'

Maisie just nods and, after he is gone, she leans against the door in a kind of stupor.

How does he know, she asks herself again and again, about Clifford? How on earth does he know?

That night, and for several nights afterwards, she lies awake in her comfortless bedroom. Now that the ladder has gone, her toiletries are assembled on the window ledge. She has added to them, on the recommendation of the woman in the department store: eye balm and lip cream, serum, neck gel, day and night emoluments. They jostle in the draught from the ill-fitting window, an apt metaphor for the thoughts and queries that jockey for position in her head. The Harrington connection continues to intrigue her—the unprecedented appearance of Mr Harrington at Clifford's funeral; the awkward, loaded loop of expectation at the introduction of his grandson, Michael. Whatever is it that Oliver dances round each time they meet—the 'special circumstances', 'other considerations' and 'particular reasons' he hints at but never elucidates? What is the unexplained historical connection between James Armstrong and Clifford? Clearly—and in spite of what Clifford told her—they knew each other, and knew each other well. And why is she repeatedly cross-examined about her association with the Harringtons, in particular, the Harrington girls?

She feels she is playing a fantastical game of musical chairs with the Harringtons and the Armstrongs. She somehow belongs in the game, but every time the music stops, she alone is left without a seat. Clifford plays along with the rest, seeming in some way she cannot fathom to fit in while she trips and stumbles amongst them, out of step with the music and unable to keep up.

She is more and more convinced that the answer is in Clifford's 'things,' the closely-guarded hoard from his previous life that still crouches in the gloom of the garage.

It is galling to contemplate that there is something more to know about the man she thought she knew so well. Anger makes her toss and turn in the bed until the sheets are a tangle and her lovely new night-dress is wet with sweat. Clifford lied to her. There is no getting away from it—lied about his past, about knowing James Armstrong and goodness only knows what else. She can hear his voice now, "If our paths crossed, I don't remember it." "Nothing to tell. Nothing to tell."

The thrashing trees across the lane seem to laugh at her gullibility. Nothing to tell? *Nothing to tell?*

More bleakly than ever, she views the years she struggled to accommodate Clifford's whimsical, obsessive enthusiasms as wasted time— a useless, pointless sacrifice. He had mis-directed her towards some self-sufficient, eco-friendly vision of living, pointing her always to the future potential when all the time he hadn't been driving forwards at all, only running away. Old Farm Hall—the ramshackle, inconvenient, half-baked edifice she had been encouraged to think of as ground-breaking and innovative—had never been about building anything new! It was no more than a mausoleum, a cairn of junk to bury something old!

She is angry, yes, but also sad—sad to think that whatever pain, whatever error or loss or shame Clifford had sought to incarcerate, he had not been able to share it with her. Was it was some fault in herself—some lack of capacity for sympathy or understanding, that had prevented him? Would she, perhaps, have judged him?

As the black sky lightens to grey and the first sparrow tries the opening bars of the dawn chorus, Maisie slips out of bed and stares into the pre-dawn. Over the trees the town wallows in a lagoon of mist, illuminated here and there by strings of orange streetlights, like a topaz necklace nestled in cotton wool. It is sobering, this; the idea that Clifford's secret—whatever it is—is more a result of her failing than of his. After all, she never pursued it, did she? Never probed or queried? It could be that Clifford had been waiting for her to take him by the hand one evening and lead him towards his cache. Perhaps all she had needed to do was to say, 'Clifford, would you show me, please?' She leans against the window, her head on its cold pane. The tears that course down her face mimic the rain drops that bead the other side of the glass.

Chapter Thirty-Seven

One evening after supper, when a squally shower prevents them from going outside and there is nothing on the television to tempt them, Maisie takes Gareth along the passageway that leads to the garage.

He has abandoned the sling now, but she suspects he is still taking the painkillers. He sometimes has a bright, hectic look to his eye, and he is very difficult to rouse in the mornings. He frequently winces and rubs his shoulder. Some evenings while watching television, he throws himself from one place on the settee to another, unable to get comfortable. More than once she has caught him in a sort of dream, staring into the middle distance; perhaps reliving, in slow motion, the flurry of action, the violent exchange that led to his injury? She can hardly imagine what his life is like when he is away from her—what deprivations he has to endure, what extremes of savagery he is called upon to engage in. Of all her children he is the most like her, he has her softness and sense of humour. He looks the most like her. It is inconceivable to her that he could shoot or stab or cut the throat of another person, and yet she knows he has probably done exactly that. That man—that violent, calculating, cold-blooded man—is not her boy but another person altogether. It's the only way she can deal with it.

But of all her children, he is the one she would most wish to share this moment with. She is glad to have him with her.

She pauses outside the door, her hand on the padlock which, from force of habit, she has retained. 'Do you remember,' she asks, 'that there was something I wanted you to help me with?'

'Yes.' Gareth gives an artificial shiver. 'This isn't going to be anything weird, is it Mum? You're not going to try and summon Dad's ghost?'

She grins. 'In a way, perhaps I am.'

She unlocks the door and they step inside. The garage is empty apart from a pall of gloom that hangs almost palpably within. Everything—all Clifford's leftovers of timber and tool, crusted paint tins and buckets of rusty nails—is gone, even the wonky storage racking and the limp, scorched curtain across the window. But there is a chilly presence nonetheless, and Maisie wraps her cardigan more tightly around her body.

'It's only an empty garage,' Gareth remarks reassuringly, and takes a step that brings him closer to her. 'I don't know what I expected, really. I was *desperate* to get in here as a boy.'

'I know. Your father occupied the whole house, but this … here … was his inner sanctum, wasn't it? None of us ever disturbed him here.'

'What *did* he get up to in here?'

'Who knows?'

'Why are you whispering?'

She has been speaking with a lowered, library-voice. She wants to giggle but supresses the urge. It's only nerves, she tells herself, and there needs to be a measure of appropriate decorum. What she is about to do, after all, is to probe somebody's soul. It is a serious, almost a sacred act.

'I think these had something to do with why he liked to keep us out.' Maisie points to the tarpaulin-covered heap in the corner, at the bottom of the wooden staircase. Beneath the tarp they are just as she had left them— just, indeed, as *he* had left them—four wooden tea chests, two leather suitcases and a large trunk. In Maisie's night time cogitations they have assumed an almost awful aspect, concealing unspeakable horrors. At the same time, they have levelled painful accusations against her that have been uncomfortable to contemplate. She summons up her courage now— expecting a reprise of indictment—and lifts off the sheeting. To her surprise, they look both less intimidating than she had feared, and less reproachful. In fact, they are a sorry legacy, crouching here like wounded creatures in their lair. They are grimy with dark, sooty residue and laced with cobwebs. The newspaper visible in the tops of the chests is yellowed, stiff and laminated by successive regimes of damp and dry. Mottled rust lards the metal catches of the cases like ancient lichen.

Gareth bends over to peer at the boxes.

'Your father had these things in a lock-up of some kind when we married,' she tells him. 'He didn't bring them with him to the house we rented. He just referred to them as his "things, from before." When we moved here, they arrived and came straight in here. I don't know what's in them. To my shame, I never enquired. But I think we should look now. Your father didn't tell me a single thing about his life before we met. He said there was nothing to know. But as things turned out I think there *must* have been *something*. Perhaps something terrible, or sad. And I need to know what it was before I can decide how to go on. Do you understand?' She turns to look up into Gareth's face. He has anxious eyes. 'Are you all right, Gareth? You look worried. Would you rather not do this?'

Gareth shakes his head. 'No. It isn't that.' He looks at her, and then back at the things in the corner. 'Don't you think it would be better to let sleeping dogs lie? I just don't want you to feel lumbered with carrying on his crusade—whatever was at the bottom of it. Good God!' he gives a sort of cough of bitter laughter, 'you gave it twenty odd years of your life!'

'But I want at least to understand it, if I can. I *must*, Gareth. It's eating away at me. The further I try to forge on with my life, the more I seem to be hampered by something that went before. There's something I don't know—some key, some mystery, some secret that explains why your father behaved as he did.'

'OK.' Gareth seems to resign himself to the idea. He takes an experimental grip on one of the boxes, testing its weight. 'Shall we take them through to the housekeeper's parlour?'

'Careful, mind your shoulder.' Maisie puts a restraining hand on his arm. 'We'll lift it together But I don't want them in the house. They're his things and this was his domain. I think we should do it here.' They look at each other across the mysterious boxes. The garage is unlit—the fluorescent tube had melted in the fire—and a chill, damp draught blows in under the doors and nips at their ankles.

'All right.' He rubs his hands together. 'Well, we can't do it *here*,' he throws a glance to the spot on the floor where his father met his end. 'It's just too macabre. We'd better try to make ourselves comfortable or we'll have the heebie-jeebies!' He peers up the stairs. 'Let me nip up there,' he says.

'Be careful. The stairs may not be safe, for all I know.'

But the stairs are sound, if filthy, and there is a skylight that admits some light through a moss-encrusted pane. The loft room is large, slope-ceilinged and entirely empty apart from dirt and dead flies. Whatever had been there—if anything—the auctioneer's gang removed. Gareth fetches two garden chairs and a collection of candles, as well as the remains of the wine they had opened for supper. Together they haul the first of the packing cases up and place it between them.

'This is nice,' he says ironically, pouring wine.

'It *is* nice, with you here,' Maisie agrees.

They chink glasses. The candlelight casts eerie shadows across the room. The rain on the slates above them is a soft, incessant crackle of white noise. Maisie reaches for the first newspaper-wrapped parcel. 'Let's begin,' she says.

Do you want me to have a quick rummage through,' he suggests, a little awkwardly, 'in case there's anything—you know—men's stuff?'

Maisie laughs. 'You mean porn? When I suggested that we might find something like that to Dominic, he was very shocked!'

'Dominic's an old woman. He wouldn't recognise a Dominatrix if she stood on his foot with her steel-toe-capped stiletto! But, yes, I was wondering about porn. Or worse.'

'*Worse?* Body parts? Well, I'm fully expecting a skeleton of some sort!'

The idea breaks the thread of tension that has been wrapping them in its silk from the moment they entered the garage, and they begin to lift the newspaper-wrapped items from the box.

An hour later they are surrounded by gifts. Some are still in their elegant wrappings. The tags are missing or too faded to make out. They struggle to undo matted tangles of ribbons and to detach gluey Sellotape from stiff, fly-spotted paper. The gifts are gorgeous relics of a bygone era, artefacts of a lifestyle whose formality and elegance were a thing of the past even at the time they were presented. A dinner service of translucent fine bone china, delicate beyond handling—let alone use—but very beautiful, in an elegant old-world style. A canteen of silver cutlery mottled with tarnish, a lifetime's chore to clean and polish yet heavy and opulent, a pleasure to handle. Decanters it would take two hands to lift, and a bewildering range of cross-hatched crystal glassware that sends rainbows of refracted light shimmering across the bare loft: impractical, cumbersome, but exquisite.

'Surely,' Gareth says at one point, 'surely these are wedding presents, Mum, that you've just forgotten about.'

'No.' Maisie is emphatic. 'Not ours. We didn't receive any gifts. We hadn't any guests. If I'd had things like these,' she looks them over with a kind of awe, 'don't you think I would have remembered?'

There is a silver tea service, an array of platters and tureens, pictures, mirrors, porcelain figurines, paperweights, hors d'oeuvre trays, rose bowls. The haul seems endless, the cases bottomless pits of precious, useless objects. When they finish, the entire floor of the loft is covered.

'Hum,' Gareth gives a wry smile, 'rather a sense of *déjà vu*! Looks like we've set them out for a car boot sale!'

'I feel as though a fairy godmother has touched all your dad's old bits of tat and dross with her wand, and turned them into treasures.'

'There's only one conclusion,' Gareth says airily, 'these are just more of Dad's collection. Random stuff he's picked up. Someone's unwanted wedding gifts.'

Maisie takes a gulp of wine. 'Maybe,' she says.

But in the last packing case they find a photograph album.

'Now then,' Gareth says, laying it on his lap, 'this will throw some light on things.'

Maisie shifts her chair closer to his. Gareth opens the album. Any hope that the contents of the boxes are no more than additional items of Clifford's inventory is immediately quashed. It contains a dozen shots of a bride and groom and assorted guests. They are colour prints in pristine condition—never looked at, never enjoyed. The faces that look out from beneath the brims of formal hats are sombre, the poses stiff and uncomfortable. Maisie gives a little cry. Gareth takes her hand in his and squeezes it tightly. Clifford—it is undoubtedly he, a younger, unfamiliar Clifford, a stranger to them both—holds himself ramrod straight, his facial expression one of astonished panic, his eyes wide and dazed, his jaw tight. His arms are clamped to his sides, hands clenched into fists. He and the bride do not touch. She has very dark hair, lots of it, parted in the centre and falling in lustrous tresses over her shoulders and down her back. She wears a loose, many-layered gown, draped and nebulous, with wide, flowing sleeves. A flower-studded veil is secured by a circlet of flowers across her brow. At her side stands the grim, soldierly figure of her father.

'That's Mr Harrington,' Maisie gasps.

That wedding—my first wedding—was as different to my second as chalk and cheese. The Harringtons arranged it all and paid for it too. They invited the guests and chose the hymns and arranged for the reception. I was given a Best Man—young Oliver—hardly out of short trousers he was, at the time. They even provided the ring—a gold band that had been in the family for years. Oliver handed it to me when the priest gave him the cue; I was never more pleased to see anything in my life! It hadn't occurred to me to get one, you see. It fitted all right. They'd made sure of that, too.

It was big, formal affair. You'd have thought that under the circumstances they'd have wanted to keep things very quiet—a small, private ceremony. But no. That isn't the Harrington way. So we had the whole caboodle—morning suits and top hats and several cars to ferry the bridal party backwards and forwards between the church and the hotel where the reception was held. There were printed invitations, embossed with gold and tied with white ribbon, and orders of service to match. Dozens of guests. I don't know where they found them all. At first, they filled up the left-hand side of the church but then someone pointed out that things were going to be very unbalanced so the ushers—more Harrington men—started directing people to the right to even things up. It was the same at the reception. Some senior Harrington relatives sat at the top table, where my parents would have been, if I'd had any.

To be honest with you, the whole day went by in a sort of daze. It was like a dream—one of those where you find yourself on a stage in the middle of a play, and you have to speak the lines, but you don't know what they are, or what's going on. I stood where I was told, repeated the words, took her hand when they said, put the ring on it, smiled, kissed the bride. Outside the church, various combinations of Harrington relatives and hangers-on came and stood on either side of us for photographs.

'Smile!' they told me. 'Smile for the camera,' but I'm not sure that I did. I think I was in shock.

Afterwards, at the reception, there was a line up. The guests filed past and shook my hand, told me how lucky I was, and didn't the bride look radiant; and I nodded and said yes, again and again. At the end of that I caught her eye. I think she was as dazed as me, and we gave each other a sad sort of smile. That was the first genuinely honest thing we had ever shared, come to think of it.

There was food—I couldn't tell you what—and champagne, and then speeches. At first Mr Harrington, talked about 'a very promising young man at the company, who had impressed from the start, a bright future ahead of him, a welcome addition to the family.' That was me, apparently.

Then it was my turn. I didn't think my legs would support me. All those faces turned towards me, red and shiny with drink and stuffed full of food, the women's hats like fruit bowls and flower baskets. The silence. Everybody waited. My mouth, dry as crackers. My head, empty. Mr Harrington's fingers drummed on the table. The silence grew wider and deeper and more awkward. Then she slipped her hand into mine and gave it a squeeze—it was cool and dry, where mine was sweaty—and she whispered, 'Toast the bridesmaid,' so I raised my glass—champagne slopped out of it, it was shaking so much—and raised it up and held it out towards where she sat a couple of places down the table. That seemed to do it.

'The bridesmaid,' everyone chorused, raising their glasses, as I had. And I sat down.

There was dancing, and then it was time to go. Nobody made a fuss; we just slipped out of a side door and there was a taxi waiting. Last things I saw were Mr Harrington—he had Oliver by the collar—the lad was drunk as a skunk—and the bridesmaid, crying as if her whole world had come tumbling down.

We went to London for the honeymoon. I'll draw a veil over that. But when we got back to the house—a new house, bought and paid for with Harrington money—there were presents, things we would never need: sherry glasses and soup tureens, cut glass vases, a china tea service, silver candelabra.

'What kind of a life do they think we're going to live?' I asked her. 'Wouldn't a few saucepans and some bed linens have been more useful?'

She gave me a sharp look. 'If you think you're going to get any input from me in either of those two departments,' she said, 'you can think again.' She started to put her coat back on.

'Where are you going?' I asked her. 'What about the unpacking, the washing? We've only been home an hour!'

'Do it yourself,' she shouted.

'And what about all this?' I indicated the glassware and crockery and all the other stuff strewn across the carpet, and the things we hadn't even got round to opening.

'Do what you like,' she said. 'Pack it all back up. Throw it all out, for all I care.'

I heard the door slam. I packed everything away, back into its bubble wrap and boxes.

But somehow, I couldn't bring myself to throw it away.

Chapter Thirty-Eight

Maisie hammers on the door to Oliver's flat. It is still early—perhaps too early? She doesn't care. She has been up and dressed and pacing the kitchen floor since five. Eventually he answers the door. He is dishevelled, his dark hair wild and unfettered as she has never seen it before, his chin shadowed by stubble, a tracksuit hastily thrown on.

'Oh,' he says when he sees her, but he doesn't ask why she's come. He knows. She realises he has been expecting it. He steps back into the little vestibule at the bottom of the stairs and beckons her in.

He shows her into a small living room with kitchenette off. The room is rather sparsely furnished, which allows it to accommodate the bulk and presence of Oliver himself. The furniture is square and modern. The whole room is very masculine, without ornament or frippery of any kind. An enormous TV and assorted accessories take up one corner.

She perches on the edge of a latte-coloured settee while he puts the kettle on. 'Now I'm here,' she says, with an awkward laugh, 'I don't know quite how to begin. I suppose I want to know how *on earth* … I mean, how *come* …? And then, of course, what happened? Where is she now?' From shock and denial, Maisie has moved on to a ravening desire for details. Acrid jealously kept her awake all night, burning like gall in the back of her throat. Was *she*—this other, this *first* bride—the love of Clifford's life? Had Maisie herself been only some poor substitute? Is this very surprising, clearly secret, obviously doomed marriage of Clifford's the root cause of the obsessive hoarding that has blighted her own?

Oliver grins. 'Well, that's fairly comprehensive,' he says. 'Have you really only now found out?'

Maisie takes a sip of her tea before placing the cup carefully down on the low table in front of her. Her hands are shaking; she can't be sure she will not spill. 'Yes. Only last night. Gareth and I were looking through some boxes of Clifford's and we found—amongst other things—a photograph album. A wedding album.'

Oliver takes an armchair across the room. Perhaps it isn't his usual seat or isn't very comfortable. At any rate, he seems unable to settle, constantly crossing and uncrossing his legs, and fussing with the cushion. 'It seemed impossible to us that you didn't know,' he muses, 'and yet, when you had the opportunity, you didn't refer to it and so we drew the conclusion—'

Maisie interrupts him. 'We?'

'James and me. We drew the conclusion that you didn't know or that you absolutely adamantly didn't want to discuss it.'

'I didn't know,' she confirms, 'although, with hindsight, I must have been a complete ninny to think a man of thirty-three—which he was, when we married—had no history, as if he'd just materialised out of thin air.'

'You mustn't blame yourself,' Oliver soothes. 'We Harringtons did our best to bury the whole matter in obscurity, during and afterwards.'

'The wedding didn't look very hole-in-corner,' Maisie retorts. 'From what I could see it was a big, formal affair!' That has been a bitter pill for Maisie swallow. How pallid, how measly her own seems, in comparison. Had Clifford thought so?

'Ah well, appearances can be deceiving you know, Maisie.' Oliver rakes his fingers through his hair.

'Well, yes,' Maisie mutters, 'I suppose I *do* know that.'

'It *looks* like a really big, swanky affair, doesn't it? I was best man, if you can believe it. I was—I don't know—fifteen or so? I think I'll make some toast. Would you like some?'

Maisie shakes her head. Oliver moves into the kitchen. She can hear the rasp of a serrated knife on a rustic crust—she could have guessed that Oliver would never touch a packaged, sliced loaf—but he continues to speak. 'That wedding was a Harrington show from start to finish. *I* had a splendid day, as I recall, until the old man caught me helping myself to the champagne. *Then* I was in for it, I can tell you! Anyway. I was the best man and Elspeth was the bridesmaid, so that was all in the family. Every guest was a Harrington by name or marriage, or some associated flunkey of Father's. The priest was a Harrington cousin, brought in from down south somewhere. The reception was at a private hotel closed to the public for the day. An uncle took the photographs. Two aunts did the flowers. Even the chauffeurs were Harrington men. I don't know if Clifford had much family?'

Maisie shakes her head. 'No. None at all.'

'I suppose that made things easier. But even if he had, they wouldn't have been invited.'

'So,' Maisie is confused, 'so, are you telling me it was all a charade? Were they not really married at all? Poor Clifford! Was he just a pawn in a game?'

'Oh no.' Oliver returns with a plate of toast. 'It was real all right. But it wasn't what the Harringtons thought of as desirable. It wasn't—forgive me, I don't mean to be disrespectful—but Clifford wasn't at all what was expected for a Harrington girl. It was done, and properly done. But outside the family, it wasn't broadcast.'

'But she—Louisa?' Maisie asks wonderingly. 'She wanted him? She insisted?'

Oliver shifts in his seat. 'Louisa was very hot-blooded, very wilful.'

Maisie gives a dry laugh. 'Poor Clifford,' she says again. 'He wouldn't have known what hit him! To be swept off his feet like that.'

'Indeed, no. I don't think he knew what day it was. His feet never touched the ground. He got sucked into the Harrington damage-limitation machine, processed and spat out again.'

Maisie ponders what she is hearing. 'It just doesn't add up,' she murmurs at last. 'The Harringtons didn't consider Clifford a suitable match, but they allowed the marriage with every appearance of what my daughter's prospective in-laws would call 'proper form and ceremony.' Clifford himself, according to you, hardly had any say in the matter. But just because a girl—I mean, what age was she? Eighteen? Nineteen?—had set her mind to something, everyone danced to her tune.'

'She was seventeen. As I say, she was wilful.'

'*Seventeen?* She *must* have been.'

There is silence for a while. Oliver finishes his toast and reaches for his tea. Maisie's is going cold on the table—after her first sip she forgot about it. Almost to herself she says, 'So he really was married before,' and then, addressing Oliver, 'how long did it last? I mean, where is she now? Does she live locally?' The idea that Maisie might have seen Louisa, even spoken to her, is disturbing. She swallows. 'Did she and Clifford keep in touch?'

'No. No chance of that at all,' Oliver sighs. 'It didn't last long, only a few years. She was long gone when I came out of the Merchant Navy.' He puts his mug down, and then picks it up again, even though it's empty. He swivels awkwardly in his seat in order to stare out of the window, biting the rim of the empty cup.

'Gone? Do you mean she *died?*'

The word seems to galvanise Oliver. Suddenly he is on his feet, collecting crockery, gathering together the few sheets of newspaper that lie on the coffee table. 'You'll have to forgive me,' he says, striding into the kitchen. 'I ought to get ready for work.'

Maisie stands. 'You don't want to talk about it?'

Oliver opens both taps at full force. 'It's the Harrington skeleton,' he tells her over the sound of running water. 'We're not supposed to mention it. But I will tell you this: it's the reason I fell out with my father. When I came home and found out … found out how they'd treated her.' He almost throws their cups into the sink.

'They?'

'Oh! Not Clifford! He behaved like a saint, by all accounts. No. The Harrington machine.' The bitterness in his tone is quite caustic. It is Maisie's first indication that, as unexpected as this turn of events has been to *her*, it also represents a painful episode in Oliver's archive.

She recalls his words from earlier. 'The damage-limitation machine?'

He nods and turns off the taps. When he lifts his head, she can see that his eyes are glassy. 'James will tell you how it all ended,' he says. 'I'm afraid I can't. It's too painful and it makes me too angry.' He looks at her in mute, anguished appeal. For the self-controlled, poised and capable man she has come to know, the depth of his distress alarms Maisie. 'I think I've probably told you all I can. I'm sorry. I didn't expect to be affected like this. It's been so long, but now I think about it, it all comes flooding back.'

Maisie's pre-set instinct—to nurture and reassure—kicks in. She crosses the room and enfolds him in an embrace. It is awkward; he is head and shoulders taller than she. In addition, he seems nonplussed by her action, unable to read the nature of it: a motherly gesture? A romantic impulse? A sexual advance? Whilst he does not resist, neither does he reciprocate, but stands rather woodenly in her arms. 'You've been very kind, and patient and honest with me,' she says at last, stepping back. 'I wonder if you will do one more thing. Please ask James to come and see me.'

He nods. 'I will,' he croaks. 'He's very caught up in ... in a personal matter at the moment, but—'

'His wife? Your sister?'

Oliver nods again, beyond words now.

'Oh well,' Maisie says gently, 'in his own time.'

Back at home, Maisie goes through the motions of her day: washing, baking, a little gardening. The rain has cleared. The day is fresh and bright, but a chill wind blows. She feels lightheaded, tired, but too restless to sleep. The odd situation goes round and round in her head—that Clifford allowed himself to be used by the Harrington family, compelled by the Harrington girl, almost against his will ... and then that she, Maisie, was deliberately kept in the dark, lied to ... she feels patronised and belittled, treated as though she somehow lacked the capacity to understand, to forgive ...

'I think I'll walk up to the farm and help Val out for a while,' Gareth announces after lunch. 'She's got some bales she wants moving, and I'm running to seed.' He slaps his belly; it is perhaps not quite as taut as it had been.

'Don't overdo it,' Maisie warns, but half-automatically. Her thoughts are elsewhere.

Alone in the house, she is drawn to the garage and to the attic, where the gorgeous wedding gifts are anachronistically arrayed on the grubby, bare boards.

Fit for Miss Havisham, she thinks.

The wedding album is on one of the garden chairs. She leafs through it again, scrutinising the faces—especially Clifford's—seeking with a jealous eye any spark of affection there for the dark-haired girl at his side. She finds only pure bewilderment. He looks stupid with shock, very pale, almost as though at any minute he might be sick.

It is so hard to fathom. What on earth was going on? Why would Clifford—such a determined, decided person—have bowed to the whims of a wilful girl?

The bride—Louisa—is a riddle, with dark enigmatic eyes and an unreadable expression. She is beautiful—no getting away from that—a feminine version of Oliver. 'Hot-blooded.' Oliver's description comes back to mind. Only seventeen, Maisie muses. So young to know her own mind so certainly. Maisie sees no sign of adoration in her demeanour; she doesn't stare at Clifford with loving eyes, there is no sense of doting. But neither is there any suggestion of smugness in the girl, nor of triumph at having got her own way. She does not lay, for example, a proprietorial hand on Clifford's sleeve; she does not thread a possessive arm through his. On the other hand, there is nothing cowed about her either. She is not doing this against her will. She faces the camera and looks directly into the lens, although she does not smile. Gutsy, Maisie decides, is the impression that comes across most strongly. Gutsy and defiant.

There are no pictures of the bride and groom alone.

In them all, Mr Harrington stands resolutely at his daughter's side, grim and sombre, his height and severe demeanour dominating every shot. There is no one clearly identifiable as the bride's mother and, now she comes to think of it, Maisie doesn't recall ever hearing of a Mrs Harrington. Perhaps she too fell victim to what James described as "the curse of the Harrington women."

The other people in the photographs are an assortment of older couples, the men sober and upright in morning dress, the women capaciously girdled and redoubtable. One or two manage a polite curl of the mouth but in the main they look serious, conscious of doing their duty, bearing witness. The words "what is done cannot be undone" come powerfully to Maisie's recollection, as well as something her aunt Sarah once said about Maisie's errant mother. "She's made her bed. Now let her lie on it."

It had been late when Gareth and Maisie finished unpacking and examining the contents of the wooden crates. They had decided to leave the other things for another time. The trunk and two suitcases sit in a shaft of greenish sunlight that penetrates the grimy rooflight. A flame of curiosity burns in Maisie. She knows she ought to wait; wait perhaps quite a few days, until the shock has subsided and she has spoken to James Armstrong. But the need to know burns inside her—not with the jealous, caustic heat that had flared up overnight, but with a purer, righteous desire for truth.

I have a right to know.

She reaches for the larger of the two leather cases. It belongs to an era before suitcases had wheels, expanding gussets or extraneous pockets and compartments; these must have been heavy and unwieldy to carry around. This one has a single handle on its narrow edge and two solid lockable metal clasps. It is sturdily constructed, with reinforced corners. On its lid are embossed the initials L.H.

Inside are Louisa's wedding clothes. Her wedding dress, diaphanous and fine; layers of slithery silk and feather-light chiffon appliqued with flowers. Not white but a delicate shade somewhere between peach and apricot that the photographs had not done justice to. It is very beautiful— much nicer than the simple A line dress Maisie had worn to the brief, impersonal ceremony at the Registry Office. As Maisie lifts the gown clear of the case a shower of confetti flutters free and drifts across the loft. She brings the fabric towards her face—she can't help herself—and inhales, but the only smell that lingers is stale, very faint and mercifully impersonal: cigarettes. Beneath the dress is the veil, the silk flowers of the headdress crushed and spoiled. A pair of peach satin pumps is wrapped in tissue paper; they are pristine, evidence of a single wearing. Beneath that, shockingly anachronistic, are baggy dungarees and capacious t-shirts, socks, bras and pants. They are not clean—one t-shirt has a coffee stain down the front, the trousers have a muddy hem—but they have been folded carefully; Maisie sees Clifford's hand at work. Louisa does not come across as the type to fold her clothes. Beneath the clothes are toiletries and make-up, a paperback book, a hairbrush—the predictable accessories of a short break away.

This is Louisa's honeymoon case, Maisie realises, although there is no sign of the seductive nightie and frilly undies that Maisie herself had packed with shaking hands—almost bilious with anticipation, fear and a scandalous, overwhelming, melting lustfulness—a day or so before her own wedding. She is besieged with images of her Clifford with another youthful virgin— hesitant, yielding, moist with eagerness and tight with terror.

'I know what to do,' he had told her. Of course he did! The thought makes her want to weep with sick betrayal. She wonders how many other girls he had deflowered, but immediately knows the thought to be unworthy of her, and of him, and also—probably—of this poor girl who has gone now, like Clifford himself—disintegrated to a drift of ashes.

I'm poking and prying where I have no right to. And suddenly Maisie bundles the things away again, stuffing them back into the case and closing the lid.

Anyway, there's nothing here to tell me anything useful—like what on earth became of her, which is what I need to know most of all.

The other case is smaller, more of a briefcase really, with a flap and single metal clasp. Inside, the contents are meticulously ordered, filed chronologically—again, Clifford's influence. Wedding cards addressed to Clifford and Louisa Wilde are tied together with a piece of peach-coloured ribbon. Some are still in their envelopes, but most have been opened and—she presumes—read. A marriage certificate confirms the validity of the ceremony. Clifford's signature is the same as she has seen it countless times. Louisa's is a round, childish hand. Her occupation is stated to be 'student.' Next, a sheath of newspaper clippings, perhaps a dozen or so, fastened with an old bull-dog clip. The paper is ochre-coloured with age. The clippings are adverts, presumably placed in the personal columns of various newspapers. Some have been taken from foreign publications; the notices above and below the relevant insertions are in languages Maisie doesn't know. The wording in each is the same. 'Information is sought regarding LOUISA WILDE, née HARRINGTON, last seen in Millport, UK. Reward for genuine news. Louisa, please come home. C.

Maisie gasps. She ran away! She disappeared! Poor girl! Oh, the poor, poor thing!

A Decree Absolute tells that the marriage of Clifford and Louisa ended in divorce a couple of years before Maisie met Clifford. The last document in the case is a letter, written by hand in a flowing script on thick linen stationery. The address is a Carmelite Mission in Mexico. The writer informs Mr Wilde that his wife is a patient at the Mission, gravely ill, and that he should send funds for the care and repatriation of mother and child, or go himself to collect them.

A child, Maisie murmurs. Oh! Of course. Michael.

Living with Louisa was like living with a bag of feral cats: scratchy and screechy, angry and wild—full of hackles and spit and flying fur. She was hopeless round the house and likely to fly into a temper if I mentioned it. Meals on the table? Clean shirts? Forget any of that.

'I'm a free spirit,' she told me. 'I can't be contained. I can't be tamed.' And one day, in a paroxysm of laughter that went on and on so long it was like a hysterical fit, 'I really am a 'Wilde child' now!'

She was helpless with it—stumbling round the room, clutching on to the curtains, bent over double with tears streaming down her face.

'You're not a child,' I told her. 'You're a grown woman and a wife. You have responsibilities.'

It just made her laugh more. I thought I was going to have to slap her, to shock her out of it, but I couldn't do it. No matter how riled she got me, I could never hurt her.

She wet herself in the end. Literally wet herself. I could see the dark of it, seeping down her jeans.

She was like that sometimes: uncontrollable, hysterical, a complete harridan. Some evenings I'd get home from work and sit in the car wondering what I'd find when I went inside. There was really no telling. Opening that door was like opening Pandora's box; she might be inside waiting to throw things at me—physical things, like cups or shoes or knives, or just words in a tirade of abuse and angst that she'd been simmering all day like toxic soup, and brought to the boil just in time for my arrival. Or, she might just be sitting there, mild as a mouse, reading a magazine or painting her nails.

I never knew which it would be. I think she liked to keep me guessing.

Sometimes when I got home, she'd be gone. The door wouldn't even be locked. Once it was left wide open. There would be records strewn around the floor, cigarettes left burning in the ash tray, the kettle boiling itself dry. Any whim that took her, and she was off. If she found out a group were off on a trip, she'd bag a seat and go with them. Just like that, not a thought for anyone. And be gone for days. She rode pillion to Loch Ness once, on the back of some lad's scooter. She phoned me from a phone box using a fake Scottish accent, saying she was very sorry but my wife had been eaten by the Loch Ness monster. She liked festivals and pop concerts and protests. She'd come back smelling funny—rank, like an animal, and filthy with twigs in her hair; white and wiped-out with tiredness. She'd let me look after her then, bathe her and feed her nursery food—rice pudding, scrambled eggs—and carry her to bed in my arms. She would curl into me and purr as she drifted off to sleep. Like a cat. Yes, she was like a cat in lots of ways.

'Let me fix the place up for you,' I'd say. I mean, it was a nice enough little house in its way, but nothing special. I had in mind some improvements, a bit of decorating.

'No! No!' she'd shout. 'You'll make it into a prison. You'll put bars on the windows and locks on the doors. I'll be a prisoner!'

'You won't, Louisa,' I'd say. 'You'll be safe.'

She needed keeping safe—she was so gullible, so trusting, easy prey to every Tom, Dick and Harry that happened by. She was absolutely careless about who she let into the house. If people came to the door, she'd let them in: Jehovah's witnesses, Gypsies selling heather and telling fortunes, salesmen toting insulation or timber cladding, beggars and ne'er-do-wells, confidence tricksters—opportunists one and all. I can't tell you how many times I'd come home to find the lounge full of strangers, and she'd be poring over their brochures or looking through their wares as though she was really interested, and nodding to the religious fanatics, 'Yes, yes, she wanted to go to heaven, and yes she was sorry for her sins,' and holding the salesmen's tape measures while they measured up for something we didn't need. She'd throw me a look and I'd know it was all for devilment, and it would be up to me to get rid of them.

She was a night-owl. I often woke to find the bed empty beside me, the car gone off the drive. Where she went, who she saw, I don't know. I was beside myself with worry about it.

'Who hurt you, Louisa,' I'd ask her, dabbing Savlon and arnica on her cuts and bruises. People hurt her. Blokes in night clubs, strangers in cars, down-and-outs down on the quays? Who knows? When I first saw the marks on her arms, I thought they were the same ilk—bruises where she'd been roughly handled. But they weren't.

It pains me to say it but I know she had other men. Even in the house. There were clues. The bed not made right, too many dirty cups in the sink, the toilet seat left up.

'Oh, Louisa,' I'd say, 'Louisa, why won't you let me keep you safe?'

And she'd look at me all helpless and shake her head. She didn't deny it. It was a kind of compulsion. She was as much a victim of it as I was.

Then the disappearances started lasting longer. She'd be gone weeks, then months. I'd ask around but no one had seen her. I took to placing adverts, hoping she'd see them, or that someone else would. Occasionally it worked. I'd get a call from someone. She'd been seen in London. A sighting at Penzance. Someone had met her at the summer solstice at Stonehenge. Word was she'd joined a band, a commune, a kibbutz, a cult.

She might come home and walk in as though nothing had happened, smelling of foreign places and strangers, her hair in braids, or on one occasion shaved off altogether, dressed in rags or peculiar robes with ropes of beads and filthy bare feet. We might have a period of calm then, an attempt at housekeeping. But that restless, reckless spirit couldn't be stilled. It was killing her from the inside, eating away at her, whispering into her ear like a demon, goading her into more and more danger, and she'd be off again.

That last time she went off, it was for good. I knew it in my heart although I kept on with the adverts. Mr Harrington knew it too. After a while he came to see me. 'A quiet divorce,' he said. 'Keep the house. It's the least we can offer you, after what you've been through. We'll relieve you of all responsibility.'

So we were divorced. I don't know how they arranged it, but they did. I sold the house and banked the money for a rainy day and went back into digs. Really, it was as if the past few years, like Louisa herself, had been a dream—a bad dream, one that stayed with me and made me ask what I had done wrong, how I had let it all slip through my fingers. I re-ran it over and over in my head until I thought I'd go mad.

Then the letter came from the Mission in Mexico. She was there, ill, and there was a child. I showed the letter to Mr Harrington. 'I'll deal with it,' he said, no emotion at all. Cold as a tomb. 'This is no longer your responsibility.'

So I left it to him. But as it turns out, his way of dealing with it was to do nothing at all.

And then it was too late.

That worries me too. It eats away at me, to tell the truth.

Chapter Thirty-Nine

Maisie fills her days with activity—it helps assuage her impatience to hear from James. Having Gareth at home is a welcome distraction; she goes to endless trouble cooking his favourite meals and spoils him with homemade cakes and pastries.

'I'll be as fat as a pig,' he says, helping himself to more brownie.

Focussing on him helps take her mind off the astonishing revelations and unanswered questions presented by the things in the attic.

'You don't need to iron socks, Mum,' Gareth scolds gently, one day, 'even the RSM doesn't insist on that.'

'I do,' she assures him. 'I'm exorcising all the mothering I can't do while you're away.'

But the cooking and laundry are only displacement activities as the same queries chase each other round her mind. How had Clifford come to marry the Harrington girl? Why hadn't he told her? What had she been running away from? Or who? What connection was there, if any, with the strange behavioural traits Clifford had developed in later life?

The only antidote Maisie can administer to herself is to tap the nurturing, loving gland that is intrinsic to her nature and pour out care onto others. If Gareth begins to feel swamped by her fussing affection, he is too patient and intuitive to say so. His tendency to vegetate in front of mindless television is less apparent, but still present. He good-naturedly accompanies his mother to the supermarket where he is a god-send, reaching things from high shelves, pushing the trolley and carrying the bags. But it isn't the kind of occupation calculated to satisfy a man used to an active, adrenalin-rich lifestyle, so when Gwen has the brilliant idea of getting him involved in her scout troop, he readily agrees.

'The lads will love it,' she cries, 'knowing a real military man. You'll be able to teach them a thing or two, especially the older ones.'

Gareth is soon co-opted onto the team organising the up-coming summer camp. 'I'm going to take some of the older lads backwoodsing,' he tells Maisie, 'teach them some survival skills.'

'Oh? Like Bear Grylls?'

He laughs. 'Not quite that extreme, perhaps. I shan't require them to drink their own piss.'

'I should hope not! But what about your shoulder?'

He waves away her concerns with a dismissive hand. 'I'll manage. I'm going to teach them to build a bivvy and set a rabbit snare. I might even see if Muldoon and Fraser want to come. We might do some mock night–ops.'

'I expect some of those boys have *pet* rabbits,' Maisie remarks.

'Well, they won't view them in quite the same way when I've finished with them!'

Perhaps to compensate Maisie for his inability to enlighten her on the subject of Clifford's first marriage, or possibly tuning into her desire to see Gareth's rehabilitation progress, Oliver throws himself into the campaign to get Gareth out and about more, inviting him on various jaunts. They use Armstrong's VIP box at the local football club and gate-crash Harrington's hospitality tent at the races.

'You've made some very influential friends,' Gareth says one evening, returning drunk from one of these sprees. 'I approve.'

As his shoulder improves, Gareth even begins to work a couple of shifts behind the bar at the Smithy.

'Dad wouldn't have agreed to it,' he says to her, 'would he? Although I must say that now I don't feel he was quite as qualified to take the moral high ground as he seemed to think.'

'You're a grown man,' she tells him. 'You don't need your father's permission for what you decide to do. But there was nothing shameful about what your dad did, Gareth. I don't want you thinking badly of him. It was odd that he never told us, and the circumstances of how it came about are very perplexing, but it wasn't intrinsically wrong.'

'He wasn't honest about it.'

'No,' Maisie has to agree. 'I can't argue with you there.'

Oliver has still had no word from James. 'He knows you're waiting to see him, but things are difficult at the moment. He hasn't shown his face at work for days.'

'I understand,' Maisie sighs. It is almost a fortnight since she and Gareth opened the crates. The questions remain on a loop in her mind. They chase each other round in endless circles like water in an eddy, carrying her helplessly round on a current from which only James, it seems, can rescue her.

Whatever the motivation behind Oliver's actions, Maisie is keen to reciprocate and includes him in her encompassing circle of care. 'You know where the kettle is,' Maisie says to him on the third or fourth occasion that she finds him in the kitchen. 'Just help yourself.' When she manages to persuade Oliver to stay to supper, the three of them have a jolly time of it round the kitchen table, and Maisie puts out of her mind the awkward moment in his flat when she had offered—and perhaps also sought—a little comfort, but failed in both.

She invites Gwen to join them whenever she can. Their friendship has not cooled but Maisie has altered the focus of it a degree or two until she can be sure of Gwen's sub-text. To this end she includes Minnie in her invitations, who needs no excuse to escape from her drear little room at home.

'And you don't mind my bringing Dolly, do you?' she gushes. Dolly has appropriated the chair by the Aga.

'Of course not. Come as often as you like.'

Viola takes Maisie at her word; she is often to be discovered, unannounced, in the vegetable garden, turning over the soil, or in the greenhouse sowing seeds into trays. 'It's such a waste to leave these beds fallow, and anyway,' she looks up from the potting bench and turns empty, desolate eyes on Maisie, 'it's good therapy for me. I'm mad with boredom at home and you know the devil makes work for idle hands.'

The idea of being bored at home is alien to Maisie, and she says at much.

'Perhaps you'd better pay me a call,' Viola suggests. 'Then you'll see what I mean.'

Carried headlong on a rush of nurturing, Maisie agrees. She is determined to find a way through Viola's quarrelsome, obstreperous shell, and Viola is the only person she feels she can speak to in confidence about Gwen.

Viola's apartment is part of a complex built around the new marina, the marina itself part of the regeneration of derelict old quays and dry-docks that now incorporate the supermarket and a number of other retail outlets. Maisie parks in the private underground carpark and goes up in a lift that clings to the waterside façade of the building, giving vertiginous views over the grey, turgid waves. Viola's apartment is on the exclusive topmost floor. Windows on three sides give uninterrupted views over the sea and the parade of select coffee shops and boutiques below. This splendid outlook has to atone for the unforgiving interior, strictly two-tone—everything is black or white. The open plan living space is void of anything approaching a soft furnishing; glass, wrought iron, stone and bone-cold ceramics proliferate. A small settee and a narrow chair constitute the lounge furniture, rigidly upholstered in slippery white leather.

'Well, you said you were a minimalist,' Maisie remarks, 'and you weren't wrong.'

'I can't stand clutter,' Viola says.

In the corner of the room, a tortured arrangement of black sticks sprouts from a tall, narrow-necked white urn. This, and a number of shards of slate arranged into a jagged pyramid, are the only "decorative"—Maisie's mind places the word in inverted commas—items on view. Certainly nobody could accuse the large canvasses on the walls of being decorative; one is a study of a pedestrian crossing, another is a series of big splodges and random swipes of glutinous black and white paint. Maisie regards them both with a sceptical eye. Edmé could do better. There are no books or photographs, no evidence of needlework or craft activity, no music. The space is sterile, both emotionally and intellectually. No wonder Viola is bored. The flat has all the charisma of a waiting room. 'But where are your things, Viola?'

'Things?' Viola shrugs. 'I haven't got any. I don't know why people get attached to them. Things should be functional, or what's the point of them? Unless they're investments, like art.'

'Well, this flat certainly seems very functional,' Maisie allows. Goodness knows "comfortable" is not a word she could utter in relation to it with any conscience.

It seems to satisfy Viola. 'Thank you,' she says. 'My son arranged the purchase for me—I wasn't well at the time. The place was brand new. But it's turned out to be a good investment. These apartments change hands for a mint of money, nowadays. They're very sought-after. On paper, I'm quids-in.' She speaks from the searing brightness of the kitchen where many halogen bulbs pour intense illumination onto an array of very high gloss white units, polished granite work tops and numerous black, state-of-the-art appliances: a cavernous fridge freezer, double oven, integrated microwave, espresso machine and—naturally—a dedicated wine cooler. In spite of the abundant catering technology, it doesn't look as though much cooking takes place. No foodstuffs whatsoever are in view. No fruit bowl, no biscuit barrel, no breadbin or butter dish. Indeed, the room has such an austere, clinical ambiance that Maisie feels it might be more suitable for minor surgical procedures. The flat is warm, illuminated like a bell-jar by the watery sun that penetrates the grey cloud and bounces back from the steely water below. Even so, Maisie feels unaccountably chilled by the lack of home comforts, the harsh décor and by Viola's suggestion that her home is no more than an asset on a ledger.

Viola makes coffee with a machine that splutters and coughs like an old man with chronic catarrh. 'I haven't any fresh milk, I'm afraid,' she announces, 'will Coffee Mate be all right?'

'Oh yes, anything will do.' Maisie perches on the hard edge of the settee and tries not to look as horrified as she feels. Her natural, glass-half-full instinct kicks in. 'So you were one of the first to move in then? That must have been nice, starting a whole new community from scratch.' The close proximity of neighbours is the only aspect of apartment living that appeals to Maisie.

'Yes,' Viola concedes, 'there is a sort of a community. Well,' she qualifies, 'there's a management committee. We meet once a month to argue about who's parking in the wrong bay and who's surround-sound is being played at an antisocial volume, and whether we should be allowed to put our personal belongings in the communal areas but,' she sighs, 'it isn't much fun.' Viola carries their coffee in from the kitchen. Her high heels make a metallic percussion on the tiled floor that ricochets around the room.

'It sounds very acrimonious.'

'You know me. I don't mind a decent row from time to time, but it gets boring after a while.'

'I can imagine.' Maisie sips her coffee. It is lukewarm and very bitter. 'But there must be some nice people here, people you've made friends with?' she asks, but doubtfully. 'Don't you socialise?'

'We did at first, but it just turned into a hotbed of casual sexual liaisons, and I wasn't interested in that. Most of the original residents have moved away. Lots of the flats were bought as investment properties; they have tenants who never seem to stay long. Some of the flats are only used during the week by people who work in town Monday to Friday and go back to their countryside homes at the weekends. There's a private gym in the basement but nobody seems to use it much. I can go days and days without seeing anyone at all.'

The bleak picture Viola paints fills Maisie with gloom. 'Thank goodness for Gwen and the others,' she says, steering the subject round to a topic that lies heavy on her mind.

'Oh yes,' Viola agrees, 'any port in a storm, as they say.'

A strong hawser of loyalty to Gwen—regardless of any concomitant complications—suggests that as appreciation for Gwen's long-suffering friendship this is rather shabby, but Maisie is reluctant to say as much at this juncture. 'You've known Gwen quite a while, I gather?'

Viola gives her a narrow look. 'Yes. We met some years ago, through one of her charities.'

'Through the shop?' Maisie tries her coffee again, suppressing a shudder.

'No, not through the shop.'

'Oh?'

But it seems that Viola will not be drawn further. 'I think she's the most amazing, generous woman I've ever met,' Maisie declares. 'She's tireless on behalf of all her good causes.'

'Oh yes. She's very keen on her lame ducks.'

This, however, is a jibe too far. 'I'd be sorry to think that's her only interest in *me*,' Maisie retorts.

Viola gives a snort. 'I think I can assure you on *that* point,' she says.

It is exactly what Maisie has feared. 'I feel we're developing a real friendship,' she avers, 'and it's because of that that I'd be very sorry to hurt her feelings, in any way.' She throws Viola what she hopes is a speaking look. 'That's why I'm asking you, who have known her the longest, if you think that might be possible.'

Perhaps Viola recalls her wild words of betrayal, rashly spoken on the last evening of their holiday. She fumbles in her bag for her cigarettes and inserts one between her thin lips. 'It isn't really for me to say,' she mutters, standing up and walking towards the wall of glass in the seaward side of the apartment. She fumbles with a handle mechanism before sliding the pane to one side. A rush of briny air fills the room. It is chill, and carries with it a mournful, hollow note but to Maisie it is welcome. Viola hesitates on the threshold, lighting her cigarette behind a cupped hand before stepping out onto the narrow veranda. When she speaks again, her words are muffled and snatched away by the wind, but Maisie catches them nevertheless. 'But as Gwen's friend, I'd say yes, probably, it would.'

While Viola finishes her cigarette, Maisie takes her cup to the kitchen and throws the coffee down the sink, rinsing the mug and leaving it on the drainer.

'So what do you think of my place then?' Viola asks as she steps back inside. The clang of the sliding window seals the room back into its sterile, oppressive silence.

'Well, it seems very ...' Maisie gropes for some adjective that she can honestly apply, 'conveniently situated and modern and I'm sure, as you say, it represents a good investment, but I can't help wondering ... as you're not friendly with your neighbours and you miss a garden, why don't you find something that suits you better?'

Viola makes an ironic moue. 'I brought you here so that you could see what options might be available to you if you moved out of that old pile of yours,' she says, 'but I can see I haven't sold the idea of penthouse living to you!'

'Oh gosh, no.' Maisie is appalled at the thought. Even a flat decorated to her own tastes would feel oppressive to her. 'Anyway, I'd need somewhere I could put all the children up if they came to stay,' she reasons, 'so a flat wouldn't suit me.'

Old Farm Hall—as empty and austere as it currently is—feels welcoming and comfortable in comparison to Viola's accommodation. Having said that, as Maisie drives towards it, she knows that there is work to do before it can adequately accommodate an influx of visitors. Frances and Maxim, Dominic, Pamela and the children are due to visit for the bank holiday weekend at the beginning of May. While she has retained the beds in Frances' room and the double in Dominic's, the bunk beds the girls used at Christmas have gone. At present, she has nowhere for them to sleep.

As soon as she gets home she mentions the difficulty to Gareth, who she finds munching cornflakes in the kitchen.

'No problem,' he says breezily. 'They can have my room. I can make a bivouac in the orchard. Or I can borrow a tent off the Scouts and the girls can camp out with me in the garden. They'd like that, wouldn't they?'

'Jessica would. In fact, I can't think of anything she'd like better.'

With this solution in hand, Maisie goes out to buy new bedding; everything she has is threadbare and grey, the pillows flat and spent. She knows that tightly-tucked sheets and heavy woollen blankets overlaid by eiderdowns and bedspreads are woefully old hat. She buys duvets instead, and plump, opulent pillows, and delivers all her old bedding to a collection point for victims of an earthquake. But when she has the new linen on the beds, the brightly sprigged covers and trimmed pillows make the remaining appointments of the rooms seem dull and seedy. She itches to peel off faded wallpaper, where there is any, and rip down the thin curtains.

'First things first,' she hears Clifford's voice in her head, and the echo of his dogged, unarguable reasoning stays her hand as it always had done, although now she resents it.

Time, and her instinctive tendency to reach out to others, do their work. The idea that Clifford was married before becomes less raw to her. It helps to think of him as a victim of the Harringtons' machinations, prey to Louisa's youthful passion and helplessly overtaken by events in a way that does not sit at all comfortably with her knowledge of Clifford's character, but which she must accept. The hurt of his keeping it from her remains acute, however; it implies a lack of truth in their marriage that is painful to contemplate. The details of poor Louisa's demise she finds achingly sad. She is reminded of her mother, whose end was so similar; both died alone in a foreign land, far from home and without the comfort of a consoling hand.

The shadow cast by the contents of Clifford's boxes makes a nebulous bridge between the old life and the new that Maisie re-crosses a dozen times in the course of a day. The days of struggling over rubble and managing for prolonged periods without running water or power are a distant memory revitalised by the gloom and chill of the draughty attic. The perpetual drudge, gloom and grime, the mending and the making-do are thrown into sharp relief by the opulence of the gifts spread across the floor. The company of her friends, trips into town, shopping, and now—thanks to Gloria—the occasional visit to a salon for facials and manicures are warm, bright bubbles of pleasure. And yet, in the midst of the socialising, in the heart of the coffee-drinking and chat, the outline of a question mark hovers. It leaves a hollowness she cannot fill: the not-knowing, the inability to understand. She often finds herself in the attic, looking over the wasted gifts. They are bloomed with dust now, their pristine beauty subsumed by their irrelevance. They seem to her more and more part and parcel of Clifford's hoard.

Chapter Forty

'Oliver and Louisa were very close,' James says. He has called at last and they are in the garden. The hedgerows are green with that velvet, baby-soft growth of leaf that glows with a kind of phosphorescence. Within the hedgerow's depths, birds are busy nesting and mating and feeding their chicks. The early evening air is soft all around them, pungent, sweet with the scent of mown grass and acrid with the smell of petrol. James bends over the workings of the lawn mower as he speaks. 'There were only a couple of years between them, and in character they were very similar. They were kindred spirits. Both had the wanderlust. Oliver assuaged his by joining the Merchant Navy. But Louisa—'

'She ran away as well—but not to sea, I presume,' Maisie sniffs. She has been crying. In fact, James discovered her crying on the lawn when he arrived, ostensibly over the mower that had stopped and wouldn't start again, and over the burn it had inflicted on her hand when she accidentally touched the hot motor, but in fact she was crying over the things in the attic—the wonderful, squandered things—and over Clifford, the loneliness his secret had exacted.

'Oh yes, she ran away all right. To sea, to the circus, to Timbuktu, to Never Neverland!' James says, wiggling the wires to check they are properly connected.

'How that must have annoyed Clifford,' Maisie murmurs, 'and frightened him! He was always very protective over me. He worried about me every time I left the house.'

'Perhaps that's why,' James remarks.

'Of course!' The realisation hits Maisie almost between the eyes. That's why he liked to keep his eye on her, why he hadn't wanted her to take a part time job. At the time she'd resented his prohibitions, interpreting them as a lack of trust or even that he thought her in some way incapable of holding down employment. But having lost one wife already, how afraid, how *very* afraid he must have been! Tears spring to her eyes again.

She feels mortified to have been discovered this way—sweaty, dishevelled and snivelling, in her old gardening clothes—but James seems unaffected by it. He has come at last to tell her all he knows about Louisa. She presumes he has come from work—he wears a business suit, smart shoes—but nevertheless has set about checking the mower over for her, waving away her objections as to the deleterious consequences to his suit.

If he realises she is crying again he chivalrously ignores it. 'Louisa was a rebel,' he goes on. 'Old man Harrington was at his wits' end with her. He called her his wild child.'

'So he married her off to Clifford!' Maisie snorts through her tears. 'A neat way of dealing with a problem—palming it off on somebody else.'

'I don't think it was his *ideal* …' James remarks, peering at the dip stick.

'No,' Maisie is mollified. 'Oliver told me that. It was all *her* doing. Why *Clifford*, of all people? Why set her sights on him, and then leave him? I can't make it out. I want to know about their life together. And what happened to her. I presume she died in Mexico?'

James stands up and yanks on the starter cord. The mower roars into life. 'I think you just flooded it,' he shouts over its din, wiping his hands on his handkerchief. After a few moments he switches the machine off again. It sputters and dies. The silence it leaves in his wake is eerie. The birdsong, loud as it is, does not quite fill it. Louisa's story hangs between them, a barrage of unspoken words.

He looks at his watch. 'It's almost seven,' he says, 'and it's quite a long story. Have you eaten?'

'No. And neither have you!' Maisie pulls herself together and struggles to her feet. 'You'll want to get home,' she cries, fighting her disappointment. 'And look at the state of your shirt! You must drop it round for me to launder.'

He shakes his head. Hesitantly, he says, 'I don't know what your evening holds. Mine holds a microwave meal for one. Not a very tempting prospect.'

'For one?' Maisie queries.

A shadow darkens James' features for a moment. 'Elspeth has had to go into …' he hesitates before pronouncing the word, '… care,' he gets out at last. 'It was the best thing, for us both.' He sounds as though he is convincing himself. Then his face clears. 'Anyway. I was wondering if you would think it very inappropriate of me to ask you to have dinner with me.'

Maisie's first instinct is to think it very inappropriate indeed. He is a married man, regardless of the whereabouts or medical status of his wife! And then she … she looks down at herself, at her bobbled trousers and disreputable top … for a moment she is the old Maisie again: harried, timid, socially inexperienced. The impulse to refuse calls strongly, but with a voice that seems superseded, obsolete. The old Maisie would not have contemplated such a thing, but she is not the old Maisie. And he is a respectable acquaintance—a neighbour, after a fashion, almost family—her mind tries to fathom it, but it is too tortured. A sort of step-brother-in-law? The thought makes her smile. Last of all, his appeal is to her nature—her natural sympathy and kindness—and is therefore irresistible. She runs a grass and oil-stained hand through her hair. 'Could you give me half an hour?' she asks. 'I need a shower.'

'I'll nip home for a clean shirt,' he says.

He takes her out into the countryside to a pub perched on a hilltop with views on every side. The bar is lively, with a crowd of motorbikers in creaking leathers drinking soft drinks and comparing motorcycling notes. The dining room is quieter, and the waiter shows Maisie and James to a table by the window.

'We'll be able to see the sun go down from here,' James says, pointing to the west.

She orders a white wine spritzer and picks up the menu offering silent thanks to Gwen, Viola and the others.

I can do this, she tells herself, scanning the dishes.

He orders smoked trout and duck. She requests a terrine to begin, risotto to follow. Then, 'Start from the beginning,' she says.

The story he tells her is sad beyond words. Mrs Harrington had succumbed early to what James calls 'the curse,' a debilitating dementia. 'Old Harrington put her away very early on,' James recalls, 'as soon as she started behaving oddly at Masonic functions and showing him up at the golf club.

Both the girls and Oliver were sent away to school. I mean, we're not talking Dotheboys or anything. I assume things were fairly enlightened at boarding schools in those days, but it must have affected the children. When I met Elspeth at a Young Conservatives dance, Louisa was already married. How is your terrine?'

Maisie swallows a mouthful of it. 'Delicious. Try some?' She loads a piece of toast with a scoop of the terrine and hands it across. 'My aunt developed Alzheimer's, so I do know a little about it,' she says. 'I wasn't very old at the time. I found it hard enough and she was only my aunt. I can only imagine how the Harrington children coped.'

'Elspeth says her mother was a very softening, calming influence in the house, before she went off the rails,' James says. 'God knows they must have needed it. Harrington is a bit of a bloodless stick at the best of times, full of charitable works and good causes of course, but cold. They must have missed her dreadfully.'

'It isn't as though she died,' Maisie muses, 'she was still there *physically*, but the woman they knew had gone.'

'That's how it is with Elspeth,' James says, in a low voice.

Maisie feels a leap of sympathy inside her. She wants to bring it into being with a gesture, but her experience with Oliver makes her hesitate. Instead, she indicates the horizon, where the disc of the sun is sliding between the distant hills, almost as though into a slot. 'The sun is going down.'

They watch in silence. 'Quite beautiful,' James sighs when it is gone.

'And another day is over,' Maisie says quietly.

'Is that how you feel? That life is a succession of days to be struggled through?'

Maisie laughs. 'Not now. I *did* do, at one point. Now I feel as though the days are full of opportunities and I want to take them all, and savour them, and to feel that each one has achieved something good. Trouble is, this thing is hanging over me, and until I understand it, I can't move on.'

'You will do,' James assures her.

He pours wine, and when the waiter brings their main courses Maisie remembers to ask for a glass of water.

'In a briefcase,' Maisie ventures, steering them back to their subject, 'I found a lot of advertisements. Can you explain to me why Louisa ran away such a lot?'

James shrugs. 'She would just take off without a word of warning. Pop concerts, protests, New Age gatherings, Druid festivals. She had serial enthusiasms; one minute it was Apartheid, next minute Buddhism, left wing politics, White Witchery … and she would rant and spout and flap leaflets in your face, but she couldn't reason sensibly. You couldn't debate these things with her rationally. She wasn't rational! These things were just an outlet for an over-arching mania and a course of self-destruction that played a part in everything she did, including constantly going AWOL.'

'She sounds tortured,' Maisie observes.

'She was. I think that today she'd be diagnosed as bi-polar. She seems to have had no discrimination, no instinct for self-preservation. Of course, tied up in all of this there were drugs and alcohol—it goes without saying, the people she was running with, the dives she was hanging out in. She would turn up at places—I mean public places like the Town Hall or the Masonic Lodge or the annual County Show—the places where the Harringtons were known and respected—stoned out of her mind, with people who were just beyond the pale. I'm talking about hoboes and winos, a woman who claimed to be a medium, Travellers, an itinerant Evangelical preacher with a beard like Rasputin and terrible BO … she had them in the house too, by all accounts.'

'Clifford wouldn't have liked me to do that,' Maisie puts in. Then, with another ray of bright understanding, she knew why.

'She was manic, a maelstrom of urges and impulses and energy. Unchanneled, undisciplined; totally out of control. It was as though she had a demon, but whether it pursued her or she pursued it, I couldn't say. In the end …'

James puts down his cutlery and wipes his mouth with his napkin. The contours of the hills seem to distract him momentarily. They have been softened by night, their peaks and escarpments blurred and amorphous; the light is bluish black, in places dark purple. Across the darkened valleys the lights of farms and hamlets shine out, comforting beacons in the strangeness. In answer, the first star comes out. 'Almost fantastical, isn't it?'

he observes, 'when you see it from a height, like this? Those ordinary fields and hills and little farms out there, they look like something out of a fairy story.'

Maisie agrees. They look together out over the shadowy landscape.

'As a youth,' James goes on, 'I read a book. It was French, and I read it *in* French, so I am guessing its finer subtleties evaded me … but it was about a boy who got lost in a landscape like that, deep in the French countryside. He experienced some magical evening in a mysterious old mansion, where he met the love of his life. He was an orphan, and for that night, with that woman, he felt at home for the first time in his life. In the morning, the girl had gone and the mansion was deserted. He almost killed himself trying to find them again, to recapture what he had lost. Louisa was like that; driven by some powerful impulse to find something, or perhaps some state of being, where she could rest and feel at home.'

'I wonder if Clifford wasn't driven by something similar,' Maisie muses.

Their plates are cleared. They both decline dessert and coffee. They hear motor bikes being started up, calls of farewell, and the troop roars off into the distance like a departing dragon.

They are the only clients remaining. The waiter extinguishes some of the lights and they are left in silence.

'And in the end …' Maisie prompts.

'In the end it pursued her to Mexico, where she succumbed to illness. I'm speculating it was AIDS, but I don't know that for a fact.' He sighs and holds out his hands. 'And she died.'

'I saw a letter. The person who ran a Mission wrote to Clifford. He mentioned a child.'

'Yes. Ironic that, wasn't it?'

'How so?'

'Oh well, that after all her rebellion, she should have returned to the church, very *Brideshead*. But anyway, Oliver came home and when he found out, he went berserk. His father had known—I presume Clifford showed him the letter—but done nothing about it; washed his hands of her. Oliver and I went together. The Mission was a sad, dilapidated place. Somehow, I'd imagined whitewashed walls, a patch of garden, the tinkle of water over rocks, the sound of goat bells. You know, somewhere calm and restful. It wasn't like that.'

'And you brought Michael home?'

He looks up at her, sharply. 'No. We didn't take Michael.'

Maisie frowns. 'But the child? Surely, that was Michael?'

'Ah.' Realisation dawns. James reaches out and takes Maisie's hand across the table. 'No. *That* child died. Louisa had already had Michael. In fact, she was expecting Michael when she married. You see, *that's* why Clifford married Louisa.'

Maisie stares at him. Her hand turns cold in his. All of a sudden, her delicious terrine and creamy risotto turn acrid in her stomach. Pennies drop. Things slot into place, like the sun into the hills an hour before. It explains everything. The words of Mr Harrington at the funeral, "special on-going interest ... Clifford was never one to presume ... a very proper understanding of his place in the scheme of things." And that peculiar, portentous way he had brought Michael forward. Michael's obvious emotion—and who can blame him? At his *father's* funeral? Not to mention his reaction at being introduced to Dominic—his *brother*, after all!

'Because he'd got her pregnant? And Michael is his son?' Even saying it out loud doesn't make it seem real to her. She is shaking, and James hands her a handkerchief—not the oily one from earlier she notes, even amidst her distress, but a clean one, crisply ironed—and calls to the waiter to bring some brandy.

But as the first rush of emotion subsides, another—equally strong— rises to meet it.

No, she thinks. Emphatically no. Not Clifford.

She snatches her hand back from James'. 'I don't believe it's true,' she manages to stammer out. 'I don't know why Clifford married Louisa, but I do know this: he would not have fathered a child beforehand. Of all the things I've found out about my husband over the past month—as surprising and unexpected as it has all been—nothing has gone against the fundamental grain of his character which, as you yourself said, James, drove him to protect people and keep them safe. But this does. *This* does. He would *never* be so reckless!'

'All right,' James says, and she has the sense he is humouring her, as perhaps he has grown used to humouring poor, demented Elspeth.

'I want to talk to Mr Harrington,' she says firmly. 'And if necessary, I shall demand a DNA test.'

James looks suddenly very uncomfortable. 'That would be difficult for everyone, wouldn't it? Unpleasant and embarrassing. It doesn't *matter*, Maisie,' he assures her. 'It doesn't make any difference to you, or to your children. Michael won't expect anything—anything, I mean, that would disadvantage them.'

Maisie stiffens. 'It isn't about the money,' she says. 'It's about the truth.'

" "

I first met Louisa and Elspeth when their father brought them to work during the summer holidays. Elspeth had finished her A levels the year before, and done a year at secretarial college, so they put her straight into the typing pool. Louisa still had a year to do at school. She couldn't type and couldn't be trusted not to make a mess of the filing, so she ran errands for people. They were both supposed to stay up in the offices, with the secretaries and the payroll people, and take their lunch in the Board Room with the other white-collar staff, but Louisa was always sneaking downstairs to the production floor and loitering in the canteen. Sometimes she'd make the excuse of bringing a memo or fetching a job sheet, but usually she had no reason at all; she'd just come down in defiance of the rules or her father's wishes.

That was her, all over.

She liked to hang about with the production-line lads and the packers. They were unsuitable company for her, of course. Rough types—ignorant and coarse—from the wrong side of the tracks. The rougher they were, the more she seemed to like them. She was like a moth—drawn to danger. More than once I had to step in. If I saw her father coming down the stairs I'd say, 'Miss Harrington, your father is coming. Now come into the stores and let me give you something to take back to the office.' And I'd give her a packet of paperclips or something.

She liked the stores. She said they were an Aladdin's cave. 'A treasure-house,' she said. She walked between the racks of shelving and looked up into the rafters at the boxes stacked above her. 'All these things …' she'd say, with a kind of wonder. But then she'd want to open up all the boxes and look inside. 'What are these for?' she'd ask. And 'How do these work?' Or 'How many of these have you got, Clifford?'

She was the only one to get my name right. I suppose that's why I had time for her.

She was beautiful, Louisa was, there's no denying that. Lots of dark hair. She wore it wild and mussed up. She had big eyes and thick eye lashes, and skin that was soft, like the skin of a peach. Her mouth was wide and moist. The clothes she wore were wholly unsuitable for the factory—jeans with wide, flapping bottoms and loops of beads that could have got caught in a machine at any moment. She was full of questions and mischief. She got all my paperwork in a muddle and liked to mess up my shelves so that things weren't where they should have been when a requisition came in. I'd hear her giggling while I rummaged through boxes and scoured the racking. She was a nuisance, to be honest.

I liked Elspeth better. A quiet, tidy little body, mousy and pale in comparison to Louisa, but sensible and well organised. She wore modest skirts and blouses done up to the neck, tidy hair. On occasion she'd come down to the stores—on legitimate business, to collect envelopes or staples or the like. She stood and waited patiently while I fetched them for her and took a long, careful time over the paperwork. I asked her to go to the cinema with me once. It was bold, I know that. I mean, who was I? Lowest of the low, scarcely out of my apprenticeship. But she looked sort of helpless and lost. I knew their mum was poorly, and that made me feel sorry for them; it struck a chord, I suppose. So yes, I made so bold. And she looked at me with such … I can hardly describe the look on her face … such longing mixed in with such sadness.

'I wouldn't be allowed,' she said.

But she *wanted* to.

I was lodging down by the quayside back then. They were a bit dodgy, the quays. You got some bad people down there. The pubs were rowdy and people cruised round in their cars looking for drugs, women, trouble in all its forms. Of course, it's all different now—posh apartments and fancy shops. But in those days … I never had any truck with it and normally speaking you wouldn't have caught me out there at night.

But this particular night my landlady had had a funny turn and I'd gone with her in the ambulance to the hospital. They kept her in—it turned out to be a gall stone, I think—but they didn't decide that until after the last bus so I had to walk back through town and down to the quays. It was all over bar the shouting, down there. The pubs were shut and only a few people were still on the streets, mostly the worse for wear.

She called my name. I hardly heard it at first, it was so faint and croaky. I stopped and listened and was about to carry on when she called again.

'Clifford.'

I didn't recognise her. She was slumped against some railings, half hidden by a rubbish bin. Her hair was more wild than usual. Her face was plastered with makeup and the eye stuff had smudged and run down her face. Her clothes were … well, let's just say, more off than on. She only had one shoe. She reeked of cigarettes and alcohol and vomit. To be honest, she looked like a street woman, a common whore. I almost walked away. I didn't want anything to do with that type. She tried to speak but she couldn't make much sense. It was only the fact that she used my name—my proper name—that made me realise who it was. It was Louisa Harrington, incoherent with drink and semi-naked in the street.

I helped her up and took her back to my digs. If my landlady had been home, I never would have got Louisa in; visitors were not allowed, especially those of the opposite sex. But the old girl was laid up at the hospital, so I had the place to myself.

Louisa was sick all over my bedroom rug and then she collapsed. She was in a bad way. I'd say she'd been beaten up, not to mention whatever drink or drugs she'd had. One elbow was grazed and bleeding. Both knees the same. The foot without the shoe was filthy dirty and cut underneath. There was no telling how far she'd walked. The other foot had a blister on the heel. Her fingernails were broken. Such little hands she had, delicate as a geisha's, they were.

I cleaned her up as best I could with a washing-up bowl of warm soapy water and a dash of Dettol in it. I washed her hands and feet and got the grit out of her wounds and put plasters on. I cleaned the sick and makeup off her face. All the time she lay in a stupor on my bed.

When I'd finished, she looked like a little girl, vulnerable and sweet, with her hair tumbled over my pillow. She *was* only a little girl really, I suppose.

I let her sleep for as long as I dared, and then I made a cup of tea and some toast, and woke her up. She didn't say much. She looked like death— pale, hollow-eyed. I gave her one of my jumpers to put on over her clothes, and then I took her home. I carried her, piggy-back; her feet were too sore to walk. She was light. There was no weight to her.

I'd never been to the Harringtons' house before. It was long way out of town, out in the sticks, with a view over the sea. It was getting light by the time we got there. The house was enormous, beautiful and solid, red brick and stone mullions, lots of windows, some of them stained glass, like in a church. It had a wisteria that climbed up one wall and snaked over the upstairs windows. The lawn was covered in beads of dew; it looked like a crop of diamonds.

This is the way to live, I thought to myself.

She gave me a little smile and walked across the gravel of the drive—how her feet must have hurt, but she never so much as winced. She grabbed hold of one of the wisteria's branches and began to climb. Halfway up she cracked open one of the windows and slipped inside.

A few months later I was called up to Mr Harrington's office. It happened from time to time. Those of us who he had taken on as apprentices and trained up, we were used to being summoned for a bit of a chat to see how we were getting on. I thought nothing of it.

When I got into the office Louisa was there. She'd been crying; her eyes were red and raw. Every so often she made a series of little hiccoughing noises like a chain going through a ratchet, the way people do when they've been crying a lot. She was standing to one side of her father's desk. He was behind it, also standing. Don't get me wrong, he was never a very genial bloke—always rather stiff and humourless—but on this occasion, he was as black as thunder.

'Come in Wilde, and sit down,' he said.

I did as I was told. She threw me a look as I took the chair. It had pleading in it, and fear and desperation, but also a glint of devilment. She wore her school uniform but it didn't fit right; too small and too big all at the same time. She held a ball of tissue in her hands. I noticed that her fingernails had grown back.

'Do you recall, Wilde, that little chat we had when you first came here? When we signed your indentures?'

I nodded. I did. It had stayed with me.

'Good. Now, with that in mind, let us proceed. Louisa tells me that while she was working here, in the summer, she asked you to introduce her to the questionable delights of the quays by night,' Mr Harrington said.

I made a sort of noise. Not a 'no' but not a 'yes' either. It seemed to satisfy him.

'In the course of your evening out, she was tricked by some of the disreputable people she met to drink vast quantities of intoxicating liquor. Is this true?'

It seemed a reasonable enough explanation of the facts. 'Yes,' I said, 'I think so.'

'She became drunk and argumentative. She got into a disagreement with one of the local worthies, a female of low morals. You took her back to your place of residence and cleaned her wounds, sobered her up and brought her home. Is that all true?'

I nodded. What else could I do, with Louisa standing there all a-quiver, her face white as ashes and looking at me with those eyes, sending me blazing arrows of messages I couldn't read?

'Good. So you take responsibility, do you?'

I nodded again. I didn't know if I was going to lose my job or get some kind of medal.

'And for the baby, also?'

'The baby?' My head shot up then. In fact, I think I got up from my chair. I looked from Louisa to Mr Harrington, and back again. The torrent of communication from her eyes had increased tenfold; volumes of words poured out of them—urgent, piteous, beseeching reams, but shot through by that white-hot, go-to-the-devil defiance that would be her undoing.

'Say it, say it, please *say it*,' her eyes said to me and, in the same wordless tirade, 'deny it then, if you like, and see if I care. Just see if I care.'

Damned if I do, and damned if I don't, I thought to myself.

And I thought about what happens to babies who aren't wanted.

I sat back down and looked him in the eye. 'Yes,' I said. 'The baby, too.'

So, I got the credit for Michael if I didn't get the pleasure of him, either in the making or in the moulding.

Chapter Forty-One

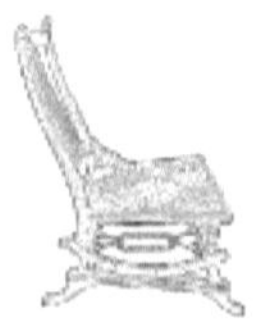

James promises to arrange a meeting with Mr Harrington. 'I can see,' he admits, as he drives her back through the darkling countryside, 'why you need to hear it from his lips. But frankly, I can't see him agreeing to a marriage between Clifford and Louisa for any other reason.'

'I know. Oliver said the same,' Maisie admits. 'Under ordinary circumstances, Clifford wouldn't have been "good enough" for the Harringtons.' She speaks in a snide, mocking tone that she doesn't like but cannot help.

'He was a Catholic. In that sense he was eminently suitable,' James puts in, adjusting the heat control; the atmosphere is a little chilly.

'Was he?' It is news to Maisie. 'He wasn't practicing.'

'That wouldn't matter, really. The Catholic church is like that; once you're in, you're in for keeps, unless you're excommunicated or defect.'

'And the Harringtons are Catholics?'

James inches out of a tricky junction. He doesn't reply for a moment. Then, 'Oh yes. That's why there was no alternative solution for Louisa, you see?'

'How archaic!'

'Yes. They have very old-fashioned values,' James concedes.

'And tastes.' Maisie gives a wry grin into the unlit interior of the car. It is impossible to stay angry at James for long and, after all, it isn't his fault. 'You should see the things they bought as wedding presents.'

'Oh, I know,' James says with a laugh, 'don't you think we have cupboards full of china and silver and cut glass at home, that we never use but daren't throw away?' His laughter dies on his lips as he remembers that

Elspeth isn't there anymore and, likely as not, will never see those white elephants again.

They don't speak for a while. Maisie ponders James' revelation as he drives smoothly along the narrow lanes.

'So,' she begins, 'while Louisa was off on her … jaunts. Clifford …?'

James nods. 'Yes. He took care of Michael.'

'Until she died.'

'Until they were divorced. Harrington arranged that, when it was clear that Louisa couldn't be saved. Afterwards, Michael went to live with him.'

Maisie's heart contracts when she thinks of the loss Clifford must have suffered, but her compassion is soured by cynicism. 'Harrington piety didn't baulk at divorce. Not when it meant he got Michael. A son to replace Oliver. I don't blame Oliver for feeling bitter.'

James says, 'Oliver is like all the Harringtons. He sees things very much from his own point of view.'

Maisie might have forgiven James, but a sense of impotent outrage against the Harringtons galvanises her over the next couple of days while she waits for James to get back in touch. She washes windows and scrubs paintwork, cleans out her kitchen cupboards and defrosts the geriatric freezer.

'Dear me,' Gareth exclaims, coming into the kitchen to find crockery all over the table and tins and packets in the process of being sorted along the worktop, 'is this all going out too? Am I going to have to bring my survival skills into play?'

'Just cleaning,' Maisie mumbles, her head in a cupboard. 'Don't worry. It'll all be back to normal by supper time.'

In addition to a searing, outraged anger at the Harringtons, Maisie is consumed by jealousy for her three children; she wants to gather them in and hold them, to protect them from this interloping fourth, this cuckoo, Michael, the impostor thrust upon their father. She knows it is ridiculous. Michael poses no threat, there is no question of him having any association with her family, let alone making any claims upon them; she'll see to that! Let him just try it! But she cannot help wondering if Michael in some way explains Clifford's stiffness with his children—his *real* children. He had never been a very demonstrative father and she had put it down to the fact that he was older, brought up in the era when men were not expected to be hands-on. He had been busy—always so busy—up ladders or tinkering in the garage, or out attending auctions, and she had been at home so naturally all the childcare had fallen to her. And then there was his nature: shy, prickly, bluff and no-nonsense. *She* had penetrated it, but he had never let the children through his shield, and more than once had recommended she should arm herself in the same way. 'The children aren't ours to keep, Maisie,' he had said to her. 'Don't love them too much. In the end, you know, they'll go away.'

Which—she realises now—is exactly what he had experienced with Michael. Regardless of biology, to all intents and purposes Michael had been Clifford's son until events conspired to take him away. The agony of such a thing is beyond her comprehension.

She calls Dominic. 'Are we still on for the bank holiday?' she asks, struggling to keep a desperate, importuning edge from her voice. 'It seems like so long since I saw you all. Are you alright?'

'Yes, we're all fine. Theo is teething. Poor Pamela isn't getting a wink of sleep. Jessica's landed the part of the Lion in the end of term production of *The Lion, the Witch and the Wardrobe.*'

'How wonderful,' she gushes. She aches to hold him, to hold them all. 'Not about Pamela of course, poor thing,' she qualifies, knowing that their conversation will be repeated word for word. She must not seem to be lacking in due sympathy, 'but what a coup for Jessica.'

'Yes, she's mightily pleased with herself, and practising her roars.'

'And Edmé?'

'She's to be a dryad, or some such. They usually give the pre-schoolers peripheral roles.'

'You've taken your exams?' she asks. 'How do you think you got on?'

'Oh,' he says with a sigh. 'I don't know. Probably not brilliantly.'

'Well, let's just wait and see,' she says airily, as though the result hardly matters but nevertheless she has every confidence. 'When you come up, Dominic, I hope you'll be able to spend some time helping me with my laptop.' That will bolster his ego, she thinks, and she will be careful to defer to his knowledge.

'Of course I will, assuming Gareth hasn't already taught you all you need to know,' Dominic sniffs. 'I did offer, you know, at Christmas.'

'Yes dear, and if you hadn't given me the idea, I'd never have been brave enough.'

It is harder to get hold of Frances. When she eventually manages it, her daughter is terse. 'What can you possibly want?' she asks. 'I was having drinks with the Fellows.'

'Oh, Frances, I am sorry. I didn't realise.'

'Never mind. What did you want? Is it about the weekend?'

'Yes, and I wanted to know how you were, if you'd got your thesis finished, about Maxim …' She quails to admit that she had just wanted to hear Frances' voice.

'I haven't got time to go into all that *now*, Mother.'

'I have email now,' she offers, 'perhaps you might write and fill me in—'

'Good God, you'll be on Facebook next!'

'Well, as a matter of fact—'

'Look I can't talk now. They're going into dinner. I'll see you on the 2nd, as agreed.'

'Yes, all right dear. Goodbye.'

Frances puts the phone down.

A day or so passes and still James doesn't call. To distract herself, Maisie visits Amy with Gwen. On the way Maisie breathlessly pours out her story; the things in Clifford's boxes, the first marriage, the child. She feels, now that she knows the whole—*almost* the whole, what *purports* to be the whole—story, that she must tell someone, or burst.

'What a revelation,' Gwen coos. 'You must tell it all to Amy. It's just the kind of romantic story she loves.'

'*Is* it romantic?' Maisie queries. 'I think it's outrageous. Poor little rich girl finds herself in the family way, nameless underling forced to take responsibility. Disney wedding promises happy-ever-after until the family curse strikes, girl runs mad and dies. Nameless underling returns to obscurity. Prince brought up oblivious.'

'Well, if you tell it like that, it sounds like something straight out of Grimm,' Gwen remarks, 'although in fact it doesn't look like the 'prince' has been brought up oblivious if they presented him at the funeral.'

'No. I hadn't thought of that.'

'Is this all hush-hush?' Gwen asks as they pull up at the kerb.

'The marriage is a matter of public record. But I haven't told the children that they might have a half-brother. Oh!' she bursts out, 'the idea of it is ridiculous! Anyone who knew Clifford even slightly would know that!'

Gwen is doubtful. 'Hum,' she says.

Amy lives in a local authority bungalow for the elderly, one of a small enclave built around a pleasant square of closely-cropped green turf. The bungalows are all very neat, their gardens minutely tended.

When they arrive, Viola is busy dead-heading tulips in Amy's flowerbed. She stands up at their approach. 'She's a little better today,' she tells them. 'She's sitting up in the chair.' Viola points through a patio door to where a strew of pink blankets and soft eiderdowns conceals a chair and the slight form of Amy, waving weakly from their folds.

Inside, the tiny rooms are crowded with twee knick-knacks and frilled doilies. A host of soft toys stares coyly from the back of the sofa, the bookshelves, the pelmets.

'Excuse the children,' Amy says, gesturing towards the toys, 'they've no manners. I've told them a hundred times not to stare!'

Gwen has brought homemade soup and some portions of casserole for Amy's freezer. She bustles into the kitchen to put them away.

Maisie opens a box of flapjack. 'Eat up,' she enjoins Amy. 'These are full of oats—they're good for you and you can eat as much as you like.'

Amy takes a big piece. 'We won't worry about the butter and the syrup, will we?'

'Not at this stage.'

Despite her good humour, Amy doesn't look well. She is thinner and more translucent than ever, her eyes sunk into their sockets, her hands emaciated and skeletal. She puts one of them up to her fine, thistle-down hair. 'I haven't been to the hairdressers,' she remarks, 'I must look a sight.'

'You look fine. What does the doctor say about you?' Maisie enquires.

'Oh! She says it's terminal. Old age, you know. What can I expect?'

'We need to build you up, Amy,' Gwen announces, coming into the room with a tea tray. 'You'll soon bounce back. We need you to. How will we manage for whist?'

Viola, stepping in through the patio door and removing her work boots, mutters, 'Let's not go *there* again.'

'Indeed,' Gwen agrees. 'Moving swiftly on, Maisie has a rather intriguing story to tell …'

Afterwards Viola says, 'The biggest query for me is why he kept it secret from you. I mean, people do marry several times these days. I've been married twice. There's no shame in it. It wouldn't have made any difference, would it? You'd still have married him?'

Maisie thinks about it. 'If I'd known the details, I would have done. If she'd been some paragon of beauty and excellence, probably not; I couldn't have filled those shoes. But Clifford was a very proud man. He wouldn't have wanted me to know that he hadn't made a success of something.'

'I think I might have heard about the Harringtons in a previous life,' Viola ponders. 'He was a big mover and shaker, I recall. He was involved in all kinds of charities and philanthropic organisations. He was always opening fetes and new hospital wards.'

'That's why the Harringtons wanted the business with Louisa kept quiet, I think,' Maisie says. 'And it was in Clifford's interests to oblige. He worked there all his life. His salary paid our bills and put food in our mouths.'

'Do you think they paid him off?'

Maisie thinks of the money in the account that Dominic found, untouched for years.

'I think Maisie is trying to find a link between her hubby's history and the way he developed in later life,' Gwen puts in, 'aren't you, dear?'

Maisie nods.

'The way he developed?'

Maisie steels herself. 'He was quite reclusive, paranoid about strangers coming to the house, and he was a hoarder.'

'So,' Viola helps herself to another piece of flapjack, 'he hoarded rubbish? Like those people you see on the telly?'

'Oh, no! Not rubbish,' Maisie says defensively. 'It was quite specialised. He collected things that were broken but could have been fixed, things that had been wrongly thrown away. It was as though he thought he was their last chance.'

Viola raises an ironical eyebrow, 'So … *not* rubbish, then.'

'*He* didn't think they were rubbish. He saw the potential of things to be repaired or made into something else. To have a new start.'

'He sounds like a cross between a Womble and a Borrower!'

Gwen growls, 'Viola!'

Amy murmurs, 'Ah, well there you are. It's plain as a pikestaff to me. This girl—Louisa?—was broken and she was throwing herself away, and your husband wanted to save her. But he couldn't. He couldn't give *her* a new start. So he started to rescue things instead. It was some kind of replacement activity; he was trying to make good.'

Maisie stands up and walks to Amy's window. Yes, she thinks. Yes. I am beginning to see it. She turns back to face the room. 'He rescued *me*,' she says, her eyes beginning to brim, 'and,' she manages to laugh through her tears, 'I don't know if that makes me really special, or just like a piece of his broken old rubbish!'

Gwen joins her at the window and envelops her in a hug. 'I think you know the answer to that,' she whispers. The gesture and her words, which at one time would have signified no more than warm friendship and sisterly affection, now make Maisie cringe. She struggles out of Gwen's embrace and excuses herself to go to the bathroom. As much as she is in need of reassurance and care just now, Gwen is the one person from whom she cannot accept it.

'Don't you think you'd better warn Maisie what she's about to encounter, Amy?' Viola says with an uncharacteristic brightness. Her words have the effect of turning attention from Gwen, who is left alone—empty-armed and bewildered—by the window.

'Oh, yes. Please excuse the fresheners,' Amy calls after her. 'I have a horror of toilet smells.'

'I have to wait until I get home,' Viola confesses. 'My sphincter absolutely closes up when I'm here! It's no wonder you're constipated, Amy!'

And indeed, in the bathroom Maisie is assaulted by a sickly pall of deodorisers. She counts over twenty different kinds: gel-sticks and oil diffusers crowd the tiny window ledge, scented candles and bowls of potpourri are balanced around the bath, touch dispensers adhere to the tiles and several muslin bags of lavender dangle from a hook on the back of the door. The toilet paper itself is heavily scented, as is the soap.

'My goodness,' she exclaims when she goes back into the sitting room, determinedly bright. 'What a comprehensive array!'

Amy shakes her head sadly, 'But do you know? None of them are effective enough. Just as no amount of hoarding could quite assuage your husband's sense of loss.'

'No amount of perfume can dispel the smell of crap,' Viola remarks. She has drawn Gwen down onto the little pouf at her side, and together they are leafing through a magazine. 'All you can do is open the window and let it out.'

Yes, Maisie agrees privately. If only Clifford had told me, I could have helped him do exactly that.

Gwen begins to clear the tea things. 'You're looking tired, Amy, we should go and leave you in peace,' she says. Viola puts her boots back on and goes out to tidy away her tools.

Maisie sits on a low stool beside Amy and they look out into the tidy square. 'It's lovely here,' she remarks, 'peaceful and quiet. I expect there's a nice community amongst the neighbours?'

'There is,' Amy agrees, but hesitantly. 'During the day, there's a bit of coming and going between the bungalows, and we help each other out where we can. But in the evenings, we're all on our own. There's no fun in preparing a meal if it's just for yourself, and no enjoyment in eating one alone either. We watch the same programmes on our individual televisions, but you don't laugh in the same way when you're alone, and then I miss having someone to turn to afterwards and say, 'What did you make of that?' or 'Wasn't that awful?' Even I miss that, though I've lived alone for all of my adult life, so how you girls feel, having shared a home with someone, I can't imagine. We're just not made to be alone, I don't think. We're communal creatures; we're supposed to live in groups. I do wonder, sometimes, whether a home—you know, a care home—might not be more companionable.'

'It's nice to have your independence,' Maisie suggests.

'Ah yes, but look at me.' Amy indicates her incapacitated state, 'My body just *isn't* independent anymore, and if I'm not careful my mind will stagnate as well.'

'Oh no it won't,' Gwen pronounces, coming in with a tea towel in her hands. 'Not if I can help it.'

Chapter Forty-Two

Late that evening Maisie takes a last stroll along the terrace before bed. Now, at the end of April, the evenings are lighter and longer. The moon is out but birds are still fussing in the hedgerows. An unsettled breeze tugs at her hair and makes the hem of her dressing gown flap, but the air is soft and quite warm on her skin, and laden with the smell of spring. It is energising to be out in it, buffeted and teased without being in any way threatened. The new leaves shiver and dance in a kind of ecstatic frenzy. It is way past her normal hour for bed, but she knows that she will not sleep; her mind is too full.

She paces restlessly, crossing and re-crossing the breadth of the terrace, her slippers making no sound on the old stone slabs. Why had Clifford chosen such an odd way of compensating for his failure to save Louisa? Wouldn't some kind of charitable work have assuaged his conscience more effectively? Isn't an organisation that traces missing relatives? Couldn't he have supported that? Or raised money for AIDS research? Either of those things would seem to offer a more effective, more targeted salve than the random and ultimately pointless accumulation of bric-a-brac. And, as she now knows, he had not been without the means to make a significant donation.

And what about his other foibles? While he had expended a good deal of his drive on the collection and husbandry of his chattels, that exercise had only been ancillary to his obsession with the house itself. His plans—his program of repairs and refurbishment—had characterised his every waking thought; how good it would be, how clever and innovative, what cutting-edge methods and sustainable materials he would employ.

His vision had elevated him, energised and inspired him; it had carried him, but only so far. Hours would be spent "weighing things up" and the rest of the day would disappear in the accumulation of tools, the gathering of equipment and raw materials, detailed measuring and sketches on the backs of envelopes, humming and hawing and scratching the chin, only for the entire project to be abandoned for the want of the right sized screw. Or he would make some progress—hacking, sawing and making a mess—only to lose interest, thus leaving a dozen jobs unfinished. He had been the king of the interim fix, the meanwhile make-do. 'A blind man,' he would often declare, 'would be pleased to see it.' As passionate and eager as he had been to make significant inroads, at the same time he was utterly hamstrung and almost paralysed. Unable either to make a proper start or to see a thing through, the house had become the epicentre of both his boundless energy and some deep-seated insecurity, the two working against each other in perfect counter-balance. The result? Effectively, stasis.

The largeness of his vision had contrasted starkly with the—apparent—smallness of his resources, for a start. The house was to have been an authentic replication of Edwardian style and décor. Those *Period Homes* magazines, how he had scoured and pondered them! But his mend-and-make-do parsimony was never going to achieve that kind of opulence, was it? It was to have been a family home, but his reluctance to properly heat the place, not to mention the interminably slow pace of works, had seriously impinged on home comforts. It was to have been a showpiece, but no one was ever to be allowed inside.

Maisie sighs and turns back to the house; its blank façade and lightless windows offer no solution to the conundrum. She steps back into the kitchen and bolts the door behind her.

Had it all been an elaborate delaying tactic—the collecting, the tinkering, the eco-enthusiasms—the research into rainwater recycling and anaerobic sewage digestion—putting off the terrible day when he would have had to admit … what? That he wasn't up to the task? That he didn't really know where he was heading? Certainly his schemes had been vague when she had asked him *specifically* what he was doing. He had always been 'working through the stages,' or 'completing the preliminaries.' At the time, she had believed him to be working patiently through a series of clearly defined tasks towards a pre-determined end. But now she wonders if he hadn't just been hopelessly floundering, overwhelmed in the pursuit of an end he couldn't really imagine at all.

She climbs the stairs in the dark. Every creaking tread and wobbly piece of banister is intimately known to her. She draws her hand along the wall, feeling the complexion of its plaster—roughly patched 'for now'—as if it were the visage of an old friend.

In the bed, no sleep comes to her. Above, she can hear Gareth playing a computer game, the roar of racing cars along a track. The sound melds with the wind that buffets the slates and thrashes the branches of the trees across the lane. The thin curtains billow in the draught that comes in through the window. Moonlight streams through them, lending the white veneer of the MFI flat-pack furniture a kind of pearlescence, the tarnished mirror a sort of lustre, but it shines no light at all into the disquiet of Maisie's troubled mind.

In the attic, the large trunk remains unopened. In the small sleepless hours Maisie finds herself kneeling before it in her dressing gown and slippers. The moon has gone down; it is the darkest hour of the night. She has lit candles, dozens of them. The light refracts through the dusty miasma in the air and off the glittering surfaces of glass and gilt, throwing rainbows and dancing shadows onto the whitewashed gables and the laths in the eaves. The wind moans through the chinks in the slates like the chant of monks in a cloister. She feels like a priestess in a high, sacred cupola, conducting a religious rite amongst holy relics and consecrated artefacts.

At the same time, she feels like Pandora.

She lifts the lid.

The trunk is a geology of Clifford's childhood, the layers descending to earlier and earlier periods of his pitiful, deprived past. At the top is the institutional, unimaginative clothing of a boy in his early teens; clothing that is provided rather than chosen. Serge shorts, scratchy woollen sweaters, shirts with grubbiness engrained into the collars and cuffs, pyjamas, vests. There are half a dozen pairs of long grey socks rolled into tight balls, the way Clifford had liked, the way he taught her to do it in the first week or so of their marriage. Each garment has a label sewn inside: St Ursula's Children's Home. Wilde, Cliff. The stitching is laboured and uneven.

Beneath the clothes are books: *Treasure Island*, *Kim*, *Kidnapped*. A label is stuck on the flyleaves. 'This book belongs to' and Clifford had written his name and, at the bottom is printed 'resident at St Ursula's Children's Home.'

In the flyleaf of each, 'A gift from Matron' has been boldly written, with a succession of Christmas dates. There is a stack of schoolboy exercise books, laborious with columns of algebra and French vocabulary and a magazine about a football tournament, much-thumbed. A certificate states that Cliff Wilde won 3rd place in the over 15s cross country race. It is signed by G.W. Harrington, Patron of St Ursula's Children's Home, Millport.

A Quality Street tin, pink, with Edwardian ladies riding unicycles round and round its circumference, contains shells and pebbles and some nuggets of sea glass—souvenirs of a day at the beach. There is also a tangled kite string and an old zoo ticket, presumably treasured mementoes of other outings; paltry and pathetic, but precious to a boy whose opportunities for enjoyment must have been so few and far between.

Lower down, the clothes are smaller and less uniform: Fair Isle cardigans depicting pictures of kites and sailing boats, a striped scarf and matching hat. There are a few toys: a picture book, a spinning top, a toy car. The schoolwork is more rudimentary—handwriting exercises, lines and lines of letters inexpertly formed, simple arithmetic, times tables. Some pictures— childishly drawn and ineptly coloured in—and more certificates, for swimming and cycling proficiency, are carefully stored. Beneath these is a box file bearing Clifford's name and a date—the official record of his reception at St Ursula's; he had been less than a month old. Inside are the baby clothes she assumes he was wearing on his arrival, a dog-eared teddy bear, a pilled baby blanket and a tiny scrap of paper, blotched and discoloured, carrying the words 'Your mummy loves you. Sorry.' in shaky, faded juvenile lettering.

The unspeakable sadness of it liquefies Maisie's heart. She gathers the blanket and the teddy bear to her body, and rocks and moans, like the wind without. The pent-up distress of the last few weeks' revelations pours out of her—the shock and surprise, the acrid jealousy, and hot resentment against the Harringtons. Most caustic of all is the startling vehemence of her antagonism to the idea that Michael might be Clifford's son. They coalesce into a molten core of such toxicity that, if she does not exorcise it, will burn her up. She reaches blindly for one of the wedding gifts and hurls it with a force she had not known she possessed against the far gable of the loft. It is a decanter. It hits with a heavy impact and immediately explodes into a million iridescent smithereens. They cascade like shards of ice-fire, ricocheting off the other artefacts, setting up a musical percussion and knocking over one of the candles. The flame immediately ignites whatever dusty, fibrous matter coats the floorboards—old sawdust, perhaps—and travels with alarming speed across the floor towards the strew of ancient wrapping paper and dry newspapers that had protected Clifford's things in the packing cases. Aided by the draughts that penetrate the lathes of the eaves and the shambolic slates above, they flare up in a sheet of yellow heat, illuminating and threatening the disturbing collection of wedding gifts, the piteous annals of Clifford's boyhood, the house—and Maisie herself who remains absolutely paralysed in its lurid light. The heat of it makes her feel as though she is wax and will melt away. She wonders if this had been Clifford's last sight, before his heart had seized.

From behind her there is a roar, the sound of pounding feet. Gareth rampages across the attic, kicking the delicate crockery right and left, crushing porcelain like bones beneath his feet, heedless of smashing crystal. He hurls the tarpaulin that had covered the crates over the conflagration. It is immediately smothered, leaving Maisie feeling weak and oddly bereft, as the shepherds must have done when the angelic host departed. The familiar gloom descends upon the attic, on the broken artworks and on Gareth, stamping down the burning embers. A smouldering fragment descends like a snowflake onto the face of Clifford's sad little teddy bear, and Maisie brushes it off swiftly.

Gareth wrestles with the skylight for a moment, to let the shroud of smoke escape, but it is screwed shut. 'Come on,' he says gently but firmly, with the kind of authority he might use in the field. He is calm, not angry as his father would have been, not hysterical as she had been on discovering the fire in the garage. He raises his mother to her feet. 'Let's get you out of here.'

'Yes, of course,' she says, meek as a child, but points down to a manila envelope that is tucked down the side of the trunk. 'Let's take that with us.'

He leads Maisie through the housekeeper's parlour, peeling one of the crocheted throws off the sofa to wrap round her shoulders, although she insists she isn't cold.

'It isn't for the cold, it's for the shock,' he says, pressing her into the chair by the Aga.

He makes her strong tea with sugar, which she does not normally take, and a good slug of brandy, left over from the Christmas hamper. 'That's twice I've had to resort to brandy in a week,' she says ruefully.

He does not ask her how the fire started or what she had been doing in the attic. He only remarks, 'I broke all those things.'

'It doesn't matter,' she says.

They sit in the quiet of the kitchen. Outside the sky has lightened to a milky opal, and the first birds begin to sing. Gareth sits on a kitchen chair and stares out of the window.

Presently Maisie says, 'You did wonderfully.'

He shrugs and does not reply.

'Your father always told me his parents had died,' Maisie says, 'but that wasn't true. He was brought up in an orphanage from being a tiny baby.'

Gareth nods. 'Figures.'

'Oh?'

'Mmm. Well. He never seemed very comfortable in his role as a father. I suppose it's because he had no role model.'

Maisie feels a fierce flash. 'He loved you all very much.'

'I know, Mum, and we loved him. But he was … strange … wasn't he? Distant?'

Maisie nods. 'Yes.' It is Michael's fault, but she doesn't want to go into that with Gareth. 'Shall we look in the envelope?' It lies on the kitchen table, innocuous enough in itself, but contains who knows what new disclosures?

There are some photographs, a succession of shots in black and white of carefully arranged ranks of boys on a patch of grass in front of a dour, flat-fronted, brick building. The boys at the back are standing on a long gym bench, the ones in the front kneel. They are dressed in identical shorts and jumpers, have the same easily managed, hygienic crew-cut. To a boy, they are scrawny and jangle-jointed, like plants raised without enough light. They squint into the sun waiting for the click of the camera's shutter. Their faces carry a haunted expression—an empty, bereft glaze. None of them smile.

'Which one is Dad?' Gareth wants to know. He has switched on the light but, as always, it casts an insufficient glow.

'I can't tell,' Maisie says, scrutinising the faces. 'They all look alike!'

At one end of the middle row, a bow-legged, hatchet-faced woman in a sober uniform watches over the boys. At the other, a fully frocked nun looks vacantly into the distance. Both women carry two tightly wrapped bundles of baby.

'Perhaps he's one of the infants,' she suggests.

A file contains Clifford's vaccination records and school reports. 'A quiet boy,' they all record, 'averagely able' in all subjects, 'very neat and tidy.'

Gareth and Maisie peruse them one by one with a kind of reverence, these unexpected records giving history to a man who had seemed to have none, almost as though he had fallen to earth fully formed.

Clearly some efforts had been made to place Clifford in foster homes or even to have him adopted. There is a letter from prospective adopters. 'Dear Cliff, we are looking forward to meeting you next weekend. We plan to go to the zoo. Do you like animals? We will make a picnic. Please write back and tell us what your favourite foods are.' Also, a Christmas card with a note inside. 'Happy Christmas from Uncle Adrian and Aunty Deborah. We hope you are well. We have happy memories of our kite-flying in the summertime. We hope you like the book.'

'What a terrible thing,' Gareth gasps, 'to build his hopes up and then let him down. No wonder he couldn't let his guard down! They call it "attachment issues" these days.'

At some point Clifford had been asked to fill out a questionnaire. His writing is painfully neat. Maisie can imagine him taking great trouble over it, wanting to make a good impression. He lists his favourite things: colour, blue; sport, cycling; food, sausages; and pastime, stamp collecting. And then he is asked,

What kind of area would you like to live in? His reply is: the countryside.

Would you like to live in a house with other children? If they were nice, he says.

Would you like to own a pet? No, he says. I would be sad if it died.

What do you want most of all? A proper home, he says, where people are safe and happy.

And there is it. Maisie and Gareth look at each other over the documentation that is now spread over the old table. They are both tremble-lipped.

'That's all he wanted,' Maisie croaks out.

Gareth nods, unable to speak at all.

I have no memory before St Ursula's. I was taken there as a baby. I remember a room with lots of cots in it, and then another with beds, when I got older. There was a big table for eating meals round. It was hard to tell the different nuns apart and anyway they came and went so we didn't get to know them very well, but the matron was easy to recognise, and to hear, and to smell: Senior Service and sherry. She was in charge at St Ursula's all the time that I was there. She wasn't unkind or cruel but she was strict and she never showed us any affection.

We went to the local school but the other kids kept their distance from us. We were accused of having nits and lice and worms. They said we were smelly but it was only the smell of carbolic and maybe of incense, which came from the chapel.

The catholic influence at the home was firm and constant, but it wasn't forced on us. On Sundays we walked to the local catholic church and sat in the pews. I enjoyed it. I liked the idea of Father God and Mother Mary, and being amongst the catholic families. They'd be dressed up to the nines, the girls in smart coats and little hats, the boys in miniature suits. Afterwards we'd play amongst the gravestones while the grown-ups had tea. The same children who were mean to us at school would be nice to us at church. I suppose it was because their parents were watching. See what a good thing it is, for a child to have parents?

Every summer there was a church picnic. We'd go on a coach to a beach up the coast. The dads would organise cricket or rounders. The mums would lay out the food and drink on blankets and tablecloths. The nuns looked like shipwrecked crows, all ruffled and shiny. It must have been so hot, under their habits. I liked beachcombing. I was allowed to keep the things I found. After tea we'd have a sandcastle competition, or we'd build a dam across the stream until it made a pool for paddling in.

Sometimes couples would come to the home looking for a boy to adopt. They might write beforehand and Matron would suggest a boy they might like. I got taken out a couple of times when I was younger but as I got older, I stopped hoping. People wanted babies, not big boys.

At St Ursula's we hardly had anything that was just ours unless it was given specifically to us. Usually, our clothes were handed down. When we got bigger, we had to unpick the old label and sew in our own. I didn't like that I would look after things carefully and then the next boy to have them would tear them and get them filthy. I didn't like giving them up. I wanted them to be mine, even though I knew they weren't. We shared toys and books. There was a toy shop that we all liked to play with. I liked putting all the tiny tins and packets neatly on the shelves, and putting the plastic coins into the till, all the sixpences together in one compartment, and the threepenny bits in another. It infuriated me to come back and find that someone had messed it all up. I stole that toy once and hid it under my bed, to stop the other boys from spoiling it. Matron found it and told me off. She said I was selfish, that things were not for keeping, not just for the having. I didn't understand it. It wasn't for my sake that I'd wanted it; only that it would be looked after.

There are some things in my trunk that are mine. They must have been sent to me from outside, but I don't know who sent them. I suppose it was just kind women who liked knitting things, or charities.

I don't know anything about my father. I know my mother was unmarried and had to give me away. The catholic church organised it all the time for girls like her. I don't blame her. I feel sorry for her. I hope someone looked after her afterwards, but I wish someone had looked after her before, then she could have kept me. But that kind of wishing does no good.

As we got older, we were expected to take more responsibility around the home. We had to make our beds and keep our dormitory tidy, empty the rubbish bins, weed the garden, that kind of thing. I was put in charge of sorting the socks. I had to match up the pairs using the name labels and roll them up and then put them on the right boys' lockers. Sister Margaret was very keen on the rolling; they weren't allowed to flap, and you had to roll them so the label showed on the sole.

At one time the older boys left the home and went off to do National Service, but after that time something else had to be organised to get them out of the home and into independence. Some employers in the town agreed to take the lads on as apprentices. When the time came, I was taken to Harrington's with two other boys. Mr Harrington himself took a look through our reports and decided where he could use us best. One lad was pretty good at maths, and he went to the accounts department until he got a job at the auction house; that was Cyril Hendrix. The other lad, Ted, wasn't much good at anything but he was big and burley, so they put him out in the yard to load the trucks. He didn't stick it with Harrington's either; he ended up working for the Council, at the dump. Anyway, that left me. Mr Harrington looked at me for a minute and said, 'I don't know what to do with you, Wilde. What are you good at?' I was pretty good at cross country running but I didn't think that would be any use to him, so I thought of the only other thing I had been praised for.

'Sister Margaret says I'm well-organised and methodical,' I said. 'She's put me in charge of the socks.'

So he put me in the stores where, as you know, I worked for over forty years.

When we signed our apprenticeship papers, he gave us a little talk. 'Can I rely on you to work diligently, to the best of your capacity and ability, and to loyally serve me, the company and your fellows?' We all nodded, of course.

'For my part,' he went on, 'I commit myself, personally, to your welfare and professionally, to the fulfilment of your potential. As St Ursula's was your home and family up to this time, so Harrington's shall be your home and family in the future, for as long as our association shall last.'

They stuck with me, those words.

Chapter Forty-Three

Maisie wakes up late; after the drama and the discoveries of the night she slept dreamlessly and deeply. She lies in bed, a rare luxury. Ideas are developing in her mind, like a patchwork of impressions from all kinds of odd places and varied situations. They are connecting themselves and forming into something whole and viable. She catches different edges and angles of it as she turns it over; they glint and shimmer. Some of them are to do with Clifford, putting into proper focus the blurry images and ill-defined concepts that had hampered his vision, making good his deficits. But most of what she plans is purely herself.

They'll say I'm crazy. She smiles to herself, thinking of the children. They will absolutely think I've lost my wits. But I don't care.

When she finally gets down to the kitchen Gareth is there before her. 'Goodness!' she exclaims, 'you're up early!'

'You're up late,' he corrects her, pouring tea from the pot he has warming on the Aga. 'But yes. I had a few things I wanted to do before I go away.'

He is meeting up with Fraser and Muldoon for a few days. Before that he has his hospital appointment and Maisie barely has time to finish her tea before they must set off to the hospital. They wait for a long time before being sent down to X-ray, which is populated by old people—legs akimbo from awkward falls, their faces variously gashed and smashed—and children, pale with shock and pain, nursing angular fractures of wrists and ankles. More waiting, until Gareth's turn. Then back to the clinic. The consultant is pleased with Gareth's progress. He manipulates the arm and shoulder carefully and consults the X-rays.

'I think we might try some physio,' he decides. 'Would you be up for that?'

Gareth nods. 'Definitely.'

'All right then.' He clicks the lid of his biro. 'I'll book you in.'

Afterwards Maisie drops her son at the station. 'You'll be back on Friday?' she reminds him as he unloads his pack from the boot. 'Frances and Dominic are coming for the weekend. I'm off to the supermarket now to stock up.'

He nods, but his eyes are on the station entrance, his thoughts already on the days that lie ahead with his mates.

Maisie feels that familiar stretching in her heart as her son pulls away. It releases a little faucet of emotion, of longing and missing, and a species of maternal panic that she knows is ridiculous and mustn't be indulged. The whole thing coalesces into that hard nugget of anxiety she carries around with her whenever Gareth is away. Even after the previous night's outpouring, as copious as it was, an unspent reservoir remains very close to the surface, liable to erupt if not strictly schooled. She feels it now, pressing behind her eyes. 'Text me,' she says, with an attempt at bravery.

That makes him smile. 'Get you,' he says.

When nearly home she sees Minnie and Dolly walking up the lane, away from Old Farm Hall. Maisie lowers her window and Minnie leans in. 'We'd given up on you, hadn't we, Dolly? Just called on the off-chance, you know …'

'Follow me down,' Maisie says. 'You can help me do some batch cooking for the weekend.'

Minnie is making a habit of "just calling by" but Maisie doesn't mind. Now that she understands Minnie's circumstances she is happy to extend hospitality whenever she can. Today their late lunch is interrupted by the other women, who arrive *en masse*. 'We knew you were home,' Gloria cries, lifting Dolly off the armchair where she has taken up residence, and plonking herself down on it. 'There's no escape now you've accepted my *Find My Friends* invitation!'

'No one is safe, in the digital age,' Viola replies darkly. '*I* haven't been stalking you electronically, Maisie,' she adds, 'or *you* Min. I was coming here with a genuine enquiry and just happened to meet these other reprobates.' The animosity that flared up between Viola and Minnie during their holiday seems to have been put behind them or, at least, to be rigidly contained.

During the course of the afternoon Minnie refrains from mentioning sales, coupons and special offers. Viola keeps her tongue in check and even seems to go out of her way to be nice, making a point of enquiring about a soup recipe Minnie has mentioned.

'Oh, yes,' Minnie recalls, 'delicious, actually and very ch ... cheering.'

Amy seems a little improved, although pale. She leans heavily on Gwen when they go into the garden for a stroll in the sunshine.

After that, Maisie gets on with chopping the vegetables for a casserole while the others sit around the table and chat. 'What can I do for you then, Viola?' she asks during a lull in the conversation. The onions are making her eyes stream but behind the onion's sting is a liquid gratitude for her friends.

I would have been on my own, but here they are, and they're just what I needed.

'No need to cry!' Viola jibes. 'I only wondered if it would be OK to plant up and harden off Amy's summer baskets in your greenhouse.'

'Only if you do some for me too,' Maisie says, mopping her eyes.

'Seems like a fair exchange.'

The afternoon cup of tea morphs into a glass of wine before supper, then supper itself. They eat the casserole Maisie has been cooking for the family. 'Back to square one!' she laughs. It doesn't matter to her. It is such a thrill to play the host, to hear her kitchen full of laughter, to ply with food and drink. Surrounded by people she finds she can press down the undercurrent of anger until she is hardly aware of it at all. But when James arrives to tell her that Mr Harrington will see her the following day, it surges back to the surface like a bloated corpse, that bone of contention that lies between her and Mr Harrington. Clifford had been defenceless, alone in the world—too easy a scapegoat for the consequences of Louisa's wildcat behaviour. In those circumstances, Mr Harrington had acted monstrously, abusing his position as Clifford's employer, not to mention his role as patron of the Children's Home. Offering a boy like Clifford—a homeless orphan— a home and family on a plate, exploiting his deepest vulnerability; it was nothing short of bribery. The marriage had been doomed to failure and it had doomed Clifford to failure, landing him with a burden he carried with him throughout his life. She is convinced Clifford's inability to save Louisa is the direct cause of his compulsive hoarding, and *that,* she wants to shout, ruined *all* our lives.

But it is no good blaming James and indeed, as he stands there on her porch step, she finds she has only sympathy for him. He is pale beneath his tan, his eyes dark with shadow, his habitual burden heavy across his shoulders.

She steps back into the hall. 'Thank you,' she says. 'Won't you come in? There's lots of casserole left. I don't suppose you've eaten?'

'No,' he admits. 'I've just come from the home. Elspeth is very unsettled …' He begins to wipe his shoes on the doormat, preparatory to coming in.

Just then a gale of laughter reaches them from the housekeeper's parlour where the women are watching a DVD. Abruptly, James checks his intention. Instead of stepping over the threshold he steps back from it, off the porch and back into the evening twilight. For a fleeting moment Maisie is sorry that her friends are there, sorry that—because of them—he will not come in. Her desire to offer him sanctuary from his troubles is very strong.

'Another time,' he says with a wide, artificial smile. 'I'll call for you tomorrow, shall I? At about two, and take you to Harrington's?'

The following day James drives her not—as she had expected—to the large industrial complex behind the old docks which is the Harrington empire, but to a well-heeled residential area in one of the affluent suburbs across town.

'Harrington hardly ever goes to the factory these days,' James explains. 'He's still the figurehead of the company but he doesn't play much part in the day-to-day running. Michael has taken over most of that.'

'He must be a very capable young man,' Maisie remarks.

'Indeed he is. Of course, he's the apple of the old man's eye. Nothing has been spared in terms of education and travel. He's had every advantage money can buy.'

'What about the advantages that money can't buy?' Maisie retorts. 'A family. A mother and father? How much does he know about his parents? Was he allowed any contact with Clifford?'

James manoeuvres the car through a complicated junction. 'You can't have it both ways, Maisie. If Clifford wasn't his father, what does that matter?'

'History repeats, and so the world limps on,' Maisie replies enigmatically, thinking of Clifford's childhood at the Children's Home, which she imagines to have been not so different to Michael's—the nuns replaced by nannies, the comfortless orphanage traded for some archaic boarding school—as cold, impersonal and lonely as each other.

'As a matter of fact,' James concedes, 'Michael believed his parents had both died until just after Clifford passed away. Then he was told the truth.'

'The truth according to the Harringtons?' Maisie purses her mouth, wondering what self-serving version of it the Harrington damage-limitation machine has served up.

James nods. 'Yes.'

They draw up outside a large bungalow, set amongst lawns and well-tended flower beds on an extensive corner plot.

Maisie says, 'I expected something … grander.'

'Harrington moved here … oh, I don't know … perhaps twenty years ago, now.' James observes. 'This isn't where Oliver and the girls grew up. *That* was grand. But you won't find any ghosts here.' He helps her out of the car and they approach the front door together. James presses the bell. 'I'm not going to come in with you,' he announces. 'This is nothing to do with me, really. I'll go for a walk and come back for you in an hour.'

This news rather panics Maisie. Scrupulous and even-handed, James has felt like an ally, and the idea of facing Mr Harrington without his calming influence is rather frightening. She is determined to defend Clifford, but one-to-one with the old man feels like an unequal contest. 'You're throwing me into the lion's den alone?' she asks.

He nods. 'I'm afraid so.'

Through the obscure glass of the front door, a fractured figure coalesces and Mr Harrington himself opens the door, another surprise to Maisie, who had anticipated a man-servant of some kind. She catches James' eye; it gives her a brief, conspiratorial wink.

Mr Harrington and James shake hands but exchange no word before James walks away down the drive and out into the cul-de-sac.

Mr Harrington is casually dressed in flannel trousers and an open-necked shirt with an expensive sweater over the top. He is a slightly diminished image of Oliver—less tall, not quite so imposing, with a reduced amount of the coiled, tensile energy in his movement and gesture. But he is still vital, by no means looking the eighty or so he must be. His hair is white, but he has a full head of it, as Oliver does, and presumably as Louisa would have had, if she had lived.

He shakes her hand and leads her though a wide hallway into a sunny lounge. The room has large windows looking out onto the garden, but none of them are open and the room is overly warm. Through the windows she sees more neatly-hoed borders, an ornamental pond, a gazebo housing cushioned seating. The lounge itself is traditionally furnished with an old-fashioned but immaculate moquette suite, several plushly upholstered and deeply buttoned occasional chairs, and many display cases. Maisie stifles an amused smile as she recognises what are clearly the requisite artefacts of the Harrington household: silver-plated rose bowls, heavy decanters, a posse of fine china shepherdesses with flounced, impractical dresses revealing layers of white petticoat and bloomer.

'How charming,' she says, taking the seat indicated.

Mr Harrington talks for a while about the house, the improvements he has made over the years, his active involvement in the local neighbourhood watch scheme and residents' committee before bringing their conversation suddenly to the point. 'I believe you wish to speak to me about your husband?'

'Yes.' Maisie nods and swallows. Her mouth has gone rather dry. It isn't going to be easy to say the things she has come here to say, to level the accusations that have been eating away at her since she first heard how he had stitched Clifford up.

Mr Harrington seems to sense her anxiety. He embarks on a potted history of his association with Clifford Wilde. 'Cliff was a boy at St Ursula's,' he says, 'an organisation with which I was closely involved for many years until its closure. The boys there had come for many different reasons but the main one was that their mothers had been unmarried.' He holds up his hand as though some objection has been raised, although Maisie hasn't spoken a word. 'I don't judge,' he says. 'Those were the standards that prevailed at the time. The women were encouraged to give up the babies in the hope they'd have a better life. Many of them did. *Very* many of them. Others were not so fortunate. I undertook to provide training and employment for as many of those less fortunate young men as I could. Cliff came to me that way, as an apprentice. I placed him in the warehouse where he worked loyally and diligently until his untimely demise. I never had any regrets. I hope he did not. Now then, there came a time fairly early on in our association when Cliff became more than just an employee. I believe it is that particular matter you wish to discuss?'

'Yes.' Maisie nods emphatically, too emphatically. She steadies herself. 'I suppose I ought to begin by saying that up until very recently indeed I had no idea of the family relationship between Clifford and yourself. I didn't know of it, for instance, when you kindly attended his funeral last November.'

Mr Harrington places his fingertips together, forming a cathedral with his large, brown-spotted hands. He nods sagely. 'I see.'

'If I *had* known,' Maisie goes on, 'I think I would have come to see you much sooner, to …' she pauses before getting it out, 'ask you to explain your actions.'

Mr Harrington's craggy eyebrows levitate towards his hairline. 'Really?'

'Yes!' She wants to berate the old man, tell him that what he had done hadn't been *fair*; to *foist* a troubled girl like Louisa and someone else's baby onto a lad like Clifford had been nothing less than exploitation. But sitting in Mr Harrington's home, facing him across the hearth rug, her heart quails; Louisa had been his daughter, and she had died.

She softens her line, 'To ask you about … the misunderstanding.'

Mr Harrington is not appeased. He opens his mouth to speak, to question her choice of words and—by association—their import, but Maisie forges on. 'No, let me finish, please. Because what I am sure you don't realise is that *as a consequence* of that …' she hesitates again, to pronounce it, 'of that *mistake*, when you add it to the privations my husband had already endured throughout his childhood, Clifford *suffered*; he suffered a great deal throughout his life and naturally, as *he* suffered, so, as a knock-on, did *we*. I mean *I* did, and his children did.' Maisie's palms are sweaty. She hears the quaver in her voice, feels her quick, shallow breathing.

Mr Harrington leans forward. 'Suffered? Materially?'

Oh God, she groans inwardly, he thinks I've come looking for a pay-out. 'No,' she says out loud, with an emphatic shake of her head. 'I'm not talking about financially. I mean psychologically. He felt he had failed Louisa,' she gropes to explain it. 'Failed in the task he had taken on in marrying her, which was to keep her happy and safe. He hadn't been able to *fix* her and he spent the rest of his life trying to compensate. He had—I recognise them now, it's so clear to me—he had mental health issues that resulted in odd behaviours …' she trails off. This is speculation on her part. She hasn't any proof. She hasn't a proper diagnosis. But she feels so strongly that she's right.

Mr Harrington crosses his legs and then uncrosses them again, a replica of Oliver's movements in his bare little flat. It is sure evidence that, in spite of his apparent ease, Mr Harrington is troubled. 'Could you be specific?' he asks. 'What was the nature of this "misunderstanding" you refer to? This "mistake"?'

Maisie takes a deep breath. 'My understanding is that Clifford married Louisa …' she is about to say, 'over the brush', a phrase of her aunt Sarah's, but it seems too colloquial, too disrespectful to Louisa's memory so she adjusts it, 'because she was pregnant.'

'That's correct,' Mr Harrington speaks from behind the temple of his hands, still pressed together almost as though in prayer. She can see that it is a painful admission, but that does not mitigate the facts.

'But Clifford wasn't the father of Louisa's baby.' There. It is out. It lies on the Turkish rug between them, scandalous and embarrassing.

Mr Harrington stiffens. 'Not the father?'

Maisie shakes her head. 'No. Surely you must know!' she shouts with a sudden explosion of vehemence. His wilful ignorance is infuriating and insulting.

Mr Harrington is visibly shaken by her outburst. Perhaps he isn't used to being shouted at. Or else the truth—now he has been confronted with it—is unsettling. 'How can you possibly know?' he asks.

He is prevaricating. Maisie casts about wildly. Miss Marple, she thinks, or that woman in *Murder She Wrote*, the one played by Angela Lansbury, would pick this moment to announce that Clifford had been infertile and that all our children are adopted. Those ladies would have proof. The people in CSI would have done a DNA test. But all Maisie has is a gut feeling and her knowledge of Clifford. 'I know my husband,' she states with as much conviction as she can muster. 'I know he would never have taken advantage of a girl like Louisa, or *any* girl. I was young when he met me—very impressionable, very innocent. If anyone could have been taken advantage of it was me, but he never so much as laid a finger on me until we were married.'

Maisie is suddenly conscious of noise from another part of the house; someone moving quietly in another room, the soft click of a door opening, the low hum of a radio. Perhaps Mr Harrington hears it too. He rises to his feet. 'I hesitate to question a wife's knowledge of her husband's character,' he begins, 'or, indeed, to impugn incorrectly the actions of a man who I admired and who behaved like a gentleman,' he continues, with a heavy undertow of meaning that Maisie is unable fully to fathom. He moves slowly towards the door and places his hand on the ornately moulded handle. 'Clifford himself accepted responsibility,' he states. 'What I think you need to ask yourself is why he might have done that? I asked Michael to prepare us some tea,' he goes on without a pause. 'I hope that will be agreeable?' He opens the door to reveal Michael on the other side, wheeling a trolley laden with cups and saucers, a silver teapot and a selection of dainty sandwiches and cakes.

Maisie's repost, 'He did it because you asked him to! You put him in an impossible position!' dies on her lips as Michael enters the room. His arrival dispels in an instant the brooding tension that has held them for the past half an hour. The crockery makes a merry clatter as he wheels the trolley across the thick carpet. The open door brings with it a gust of fresh air from the hallway where the front door stands open, alleviating the stuffiness of the lounge. Michael himself is full of bright chatter and smiles. 'It's so good to meet you again, properly this time,' he says enthusiastically, enfolding Maisie's hand with both of his.

He's a Harrington all right, Maisie thinks, looking into his dark eyes. He has the Harrington hair—thick although not so dark, cut very short—and the same energy of movement. He is not a young man, although that is how she has thought of him up until now; he is older than Dominic by some eight years. There is the suggestion of a crinkle at the outer corner of his eye, the slightest peppering of silver at his temple.

She realises—with a frisson of annoyance—she has been stage-managed by Mr Harrington, placed in an impossible position by the entrance of Michael. She throws Mr Harrington an infuriated look. How on earth can their discussion continue *now*? The physical presence of Michael—the flesh and blood reality—gives their conversation a whole new dimension, as doubtless Mr Harrington knew it would. He has challenged her to at least entertain the idea that Clifford might indeed have been the child's father—as aberrant as that might seem—and provided her with the means.

All right, then. She rises to the challenge, keeping hold of Michael's hand and scanning him minutely for the slightest echo, the smallest possible glimmer of Clifford; the shape of his face, the set of his jaw, his posture, the gleam in his eye. But no. There is nothing whatsoever of Clifford. She smiles and releases his hand.

So, if not that, then what?

Mr Harrington has brought forward a low table and Michael begins to decant the contents of the trolley onto it. 'I hope you're hungry,' he remarks, distributing finger sandwiches, crackers loaded with cream cheese and smoked salmon, shortbread, cupcakes. 'We always are, aren't we Grandfather? We tend not to bother with lunch so by the time tea comes around we're famished. Isn't Uncle James here? I hope he joins us. I catered for him too.'

Maisie is pressed back into her seat, handed a thick linen napkin, given tea and offered food. Michael has the grace and dexterity of a *maître d'* at the Ritz. 'You have your uncle Oliver's gift,' she blurts out.

Mr Harrington's face darkens but Michael's is illuminated with pleasure, 'Really? How splendid!'

The older gentleman takes his tea standing, or rather, perambulating around the room holding his cup and saucer, returning now and again to eat his food from a plate that Michael has placed for him on the marble mantelpiece. He speaks little, seeming to feel that, now Michael has arrived, he need have no further part in the discourse; almost as though he is leaving

Michael to speak the words for him, to be the answer to the question: 'why he had done that?'

Michael fills the space between Maisie and his grandfather with talk. He speaks quickly, in a light but not inconsequential manner, his pace suggesting his narrative has been held back for some while. 'At the funeral,' he says, 'I had just found out—only days before—and it was all still a bit of a shock. I didn't know, you see that your husband was … my *dad*. Do you mind my calling him that?'

'No, but—'

'I'd seen him often, of course,' Michael rushes on. 'Won't you have another sandwich? Grandfather especially likes this ham. We get it from a delicatessen in town … there you are. So, of course I've been going to the factory since I was tiny and I'd seen your husband and knew him at work. Everyone knew Cliff in the stores; he was a legend! Although, I think he preferred 'Clifford' didn't he?'

Maisie nods.

'But I had *no idea* until Grandfather told me, after he'd died.'

'That must have been a very difficult piece of news for your grandfather to deliver,' Maisie suggests carefully. 'How did he go about it?'

Across the room, Mr Harrington straightens a piece of Royal Doulton that is out of place. 'Oh, well he explained it, of course, and I do understand that it was all in my best interest, but I do wish …' The older man saunters to a far corner of the room to adjust the arrangement of silk flowers in a heavy cut glass vase. He has his back to them. Michael lowers his voice and reaches across to place his hand over Maisie's, 'I do wish that I had known earlier, *much* earlier,' he whispers emphatically. Maisie cannot misinterpret the note of longing in his voice, the speaking look in his eye. 'I would so like to have *known* him, properly.'

'Didn't you feel …' Maisie approaches it warily, 'wasn't it a bit of a *let down* when you found out? I mean, I expect you'd imagined your father to be someone well-to-do. The kind of person that a Harrington marries—like your uncle James—an important, influential person. Clifford was just an ordinary man.'

Michael looks at her askance. 'Not at all! No! Nobody's 'ordinary,' are they? I didn't feel a bit let down.' He glances across at his grandfather, who is leafing through a *Country Life* magazine he found on a side table. 'I was *frustrated*. That I hadn't known sooner. All those *years* we could have had.' Regardless of his age, his confidence, his competence at the factory, he is the picture of a boy's anguished craving for his father. Maisie saw it in her own boys: in Gareth's frustration and bewilderment at being debarred from the garage; in Dominic's disappointment when Clifford was too preoccupied to take an interest in his academic progress.

'I'm afraid you might have been a bit disappointed,' she says with gentle sadness. 'Fatherhood isn't something he found very easy. You see, he didn't have a father himself—no role model, no example to follow at all.'

'Oh, I know,' Michael is on his feet. 'I've been doing some research.'

He comes back with his laptop. 'Have you heard of *Ancestry*? No? It's a genealogy site—you can trace your family tree back.' He squats by her chair, flicks open the laptop and dances his fingers across the keys. 'Let me show you this ...' He scrolls through copies of censuses, lists of births, deaths and marriages, parish registers, pointing out possible connections. 'His mother is listed in St Ursula's records as Joan Bailey. It's a common name ... there are lots of them, but *this* could have been her ... my father's mother. She was only sixteen, see? I've been looking for a record of her marriage. If I knew her married name, I might be able to find her. I mean it's *possible* she's still alive, isn't it?'

Maisie watches him, only half listening to his words, caught up instead by his manner. He is fired up with enthusiasm, galvanised, full of hope and purpose, like a man who has been marooned but has now been thrown a lifeline, a chance to make sense of who he is and where he comes from. She wants to reach out her hand and put it on his shoulder, pat it and stroke it, show him the only kind of affection—restrained, restricted—that is permitted a mother when her boys are grown. The impulse is as strong as if one of her own boys knelt here beside her.

She knows—with a sudden melting certainty—that she can't tell him Clifford wasn't his father. She can't take away from him something he has only just found, and that he needs so much.

Across the room, Mr Harrington watches her. She meets his eyes. Michael has indeed done the talking for his grandfather. There is no need for him to speak, his expression says it all. Clifford could not deprive this child of a father, and neither can you.

Maisie holds his gaze. No, I won't. But *you* did. At last, Mr Harrington's eyes slide away from hers.

When James returns, he declines to stay for tea; he has things to see to at work, he says, although by now it is past four o'clock. On the doorstep, Mr Harrington shakes Maisie's hand gravely. He has achieved his aim. She has been foiled and wrong-footed, but somehow it doesn't feel like a defeat.

Michael hands her his card. 'I'd so like to keep in touch,' he says, 'if you don't mind. We haven't talked half enough, I don't feel.'

'I'd be delighted,' Maisie assures him, and genuinely means it. 'Come to Old Farm Hall whenever you like, as often as you like.'

'Oh! But what about …'

'I'm going to tell the family everything,' she says, 'and then you can be one of us, as …' she allows herself a fleeting look over his shoulder to where Mr Harrington hovers in the hallway, 'as you always *should* have been.'

Chapter Forty-Four

In the car James says, 'So, you've changed your mind?'

'No. Not a bit. I'm as convinced as ever that Michael isn't Clifford's son.'

'Oh?'

She shifts in her seat—it is leather, very soft and yielding. 'I couldn't do it to him,' she sighs, 'and it occurred to me, if Clifford was prepared to take Michael on in the full knowledge of the facts, so should I.'

James smiles and flicks the indicator. 'I knew it,' he says, almost to himself.

'Knew what?'

'That you were too kind.'

'To disabuse him? So, you've known all along?'

James makes no reply, but throws her a complicit look.

'Well,' she shrugs, a gesture of self-deprecation. 'But not everyone will take the same line.' She is thinking particularly of Dominic, who is going to struggle to come to terms with this turn of events. His one claim to self-importance—faced with the fearsome intelligence of one sibling and the awesome physicality of the other—is that he is the *oldest*. 'So I'm not going to give them any options. As far as they're concerned Michael is Clifford's son, their half-brother. It will shock them. The idea of their father indulging in illicit, extra-marital sex! It impugns Clifford's character. He would *never* have done such a thing. But I have to think of the living. I hope we can keep our reservations between ourselves?'

'Of course!' James throws her a mischievous look. 'I rather like the idea of sharing secrets with you.'

'If only Clifford had shared his with me,' Maisie sighs, 'and with the children, it could all have been so different.' The ramifications of her afternoon are beginning to catch up with her, throwing out connections and drawing truths from the shadows, but they are all jumbled, like a jig saw just tipped from its box.

'How so?' The traffic is choked up through town. They are stranded in a tail-back whose cause they cannot see—an accident perhaps, or more road-works. James keeps his eyes fixed on the traffic but she knows his whole attention is directed towards her, providing a strong-box for whatever deposit she might choose to make.

'On the face of it, Clifford was such a determined, single-minded man,' she begins, 'very sure about everything. The idea of him being coerced or manipulated—even by someone as powerful as Mr Harrington, much less by some slip of a girl in the grip of a crush—it simply doesn't compute. The children wouldn't buy it for a single minute. To them he was … well, the kindest spin I can put on it really is to say that they found him very *consistent*, for which you can read *stubborn*. Nobody could make him do anything he didn't want to do. But underneath that was someone else—a completely different Clifford. I saw it of course, in the beginning anyway. You did, too, James. You described him as someone who took care of the lost. But the children never saw that. If I described Clifford that way to the children, they'd wonder who I was talking about!'

'It's what Elspeth said,' James murmurs. 'He was her first love, you know. She told me that he befriended her, and took notice of her when, all her life, she'd been pushed back into the shadows by her naughty little sister—and of course by Oliver, the golden child, Harrington's hallowed son. It nearly killed her when Louisa married him. I met her two years later and she wasn't really over it.'

'Well, there you are,' Maisie cries, 'another lost soul he tried to rescue. Elspeth, Louisa, Michael, me—'

'He succeeded with you, didn't he?'

The line of cars inches forwards past whatever impediment is up ahead.

'Yes, I suppose he did,' Maisie acknowledges, 'until I was superseded by the house, and his crusade moved on to inanimate objects.'

James throws her a questioning look.

'Oh, you know. You saw Clifford's collection. It was quite embryonic in those days. It got much worse. The house was Clifford's unfinished symphony. But that's the point, really. While he was out rescuing things and being distracted by every eco-fad that caught his attention, he didn't need to face up to the fact that at home, surrounded by his tools and his building materials and his special widgets and important sprockets, he had *no idea* what he was doing, no conception of it at all.'

'No conception of what?'

Up ahead, a police officer directs traffic round an obstruction in the road. Behind them the wail of a siren heralds the arrival of an ambulance. James eases the car onto the kerb to let it past.

'Of what he was trying to create: a home, and a family. He was an orphan, brought up in an institution by strangers. What basis did that give him? He was lost. He himself was just as lost as anything or anyone he ever tried to save.'

The officer waves them forward. In the road the paramedics are bent over the body of a small child. In a nearby shop doorway, the child's distraught mother is comforted by strangers.

'Poor thing. Poor thing,' Maisie murmurs.

James does not ask who she means.

It is well after six when James drops her back at home. 'Surely you won't go back to work now, will you?' she asks, climbing out of the cool, air-conditioned car into the warmth of the spring evening air. 'Is it too early for a glass of wine?'

He shakes his head. 'The factory is closed next week. It's a throw-back from the old Wakes week—we always close down for Whit. So I need to make sure all the orders are going to get completed. I really ought to go in.'

'All right.' Maisie reaches for her keys. On impulse—it seems to be a day of impulsiveness—she says, 'I'm having a party on Saturday—drinks, canapés—starting in the afternoon and going on in the evening for as long as anybody stays. I hope you'll come?'

It is a wild, ridiculous idea. She has never thrown a party. The house is a shell. She has the family coming and now two potentially sensitive pieces of news to broach with them. But she feels the need to celebrate. The afternoon has felt like the closing of an old chapter; it is the terminus of her exploration of Clifford's things. The past is all in focus now. She understands it and can let it go. It has given her the foundation of what she will build—the essence, the core of what Clifford wanted—but failed so spectacularly to bring about. It is all before her. She sees it as clearly as she has ever seen anything.

James agrees to come back on Saturday afternoon. 'I'd be delighted,' he says. 'The weekends do hang heavy, I must admit. Is there anything I can bring?'

Maisie considers. 'Will it be all right if I ask Oliver to supply the drinks from the pub?'

'It will be cheaper if he takes you to the cash and carry,' James says, 'I'll arrange it.'

She waves James off through the gates he repaired for them all those years before. They still stand straight and true.

Chapter Forty-Five

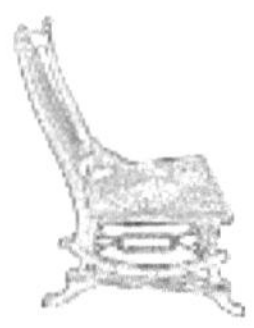

Inside, the house is cool and quiet, waiting, in all its shabby, bodged, beautiful potential. Maisie walks through the blank rooms and loiters on the echoing stairs. It is almost as though the house is unknown to her, and she a stranger, as she had been on that first evening visit with Clifford. The sense of being overwhelmed and daunted is the same, likewise the urgent need of repair and modernisation. She tastes the same doubt and dismay that had assailed her then, but the same vision brightens and lightens it. This had been before and could be again, a lovely home. Clifford's initial instinct had been quite right even if it had gone wildly off kilter.

She finds herself in the dining room, staring absently at the two pieces of furniture she held back from the auction. In the bay window sits the rocking chair. Its mechanism is repaired after a fashion, but Clifford never cured it of a tooth-edge squeak so she had never used it to nurse the babies, as he intended. The upholstery of its seat remains torn and eviscerated; tufts of old horsehair protrude from a slash in the seat and a rip in the seam. One arm still dangles adrift. It's a mess. It's broken, but it says everything there is to say about Clifford—it says safety and shelter, it says protection and love.

The long dining table takes up the majority of the space. Without any chairs it is a white elephant, true—useless for any practical purpose—but it glows with a rich patina. It is sturdy on its reeded legs. This table speaks to her of herself—of hospitality, of nurture, of food for the body and companionship for the soul.

Isn't *that* something to aim for? Something good and worthwhile to offer? Something that people need?

And that, *that*—she cradles it now, and lets it take its first, mewing breath—that's how it will be!

Suddenly she is off, careering round the house. Upstairs, all these rooms. She throws open doors right and left. What's the point in them sitting empty, gathering dust and dead flies? Even if they were beautiful, like Minnie's—decorated, carpeted, nicely furnished—what purpose would they serve? Here's what: people can stay in them, for as long as they like, while they recover, or come to terms with whatever has brought them here. I can put in more bathrooms—people like to have their own bathrooms—like Amy says, people don't like other people's toilet smells. But they won't be like bed-sits. No. We don't want people festering up here all on their own! They need to join in!

Downstairs again. This will be our sitting room; we'll sit in here and talk or watch the television together. I'll place the chairs in little groups—round the fire, or looking out of the window at the trees across the lane. There will be books, and board games, and newspapers. Music, perhaps. The old housekeeper's parlour, I'll keep that for cosy *tête-à-têtes* or for quiet reading. People don't always want to be in company, I suppose. My kitchen … it will be a real hub. People can cook here, for themselves or each other. I don't care. I won't make any hard and fast rules. We'll have to see what suits. And there's the garden. People can help out—gardening's such good therapy—or just sit and admire it.

And here, this will be my room.

She arrives in the garage loft room above the place where Clifford died. All evidence of the recent fire has been cleared away. Gareth must have done it while she slept in the morning after. The floor has been swept of broken crockery and decimated glass, the charred paper and candle stubs have gone. The crates and cases have been repacked, she presumes with whatever could be salvaged, ready to be passed on to Clifford's children—*all* his children. The space is empty and benign, a private eyrie.

An architect can make something of it. All the builders said the whole garage needed rebuilding anyway. What could be simpler than to raise the roof? Extend the footprint little? There'll be plenty of room for a decent sized bedroom and an *ensuite*.

She examines the skylight window. Gareth must have fixed that too, removing the screws. She yanks the handle and the window opens with a yawn, disgorging a shower of desiccated bluebottles and other insect life that must have been trapped in the workings for ever, and stretching a thick mat of cobweb like ectoplasm, thinner and thinner until it breaks and blows away on the wind. By clambering on one of the garden chairs she can see out, right over the garden and the orchard, up to the farm where Val trudges behind her wheelbarrow, and in the other direction—over the trees and office buildings—to the town, spread out below. She gives a little cry of pleasure and excitement. What a view! She must have windows … lots of windows. Perhaps even a balcony.

Now she has seen it, now she has decided, there is no going back. She flies back into the house to phone Gwen. 'Do you know an architect?' she asks breathlessly, 'I'm going to need one. Oh, and Gwen, have you any recipes for canapés? And are you free on Saturday?'

In the garage, the dust and motes disturbed by her passage settle back. A butterfly, roused from its slumber in the rafters, lands on the top of one of Clifford's boxes. It basks there in the light from the window, warming its wings before taking flight. Then it circles upwards in the bright column of air, climbing, climbing until the breeze takes it and whisks it off through the opening and out into the world.

THANKYOU

Thank you for reading this book. I really hope you enjoyed it. As a self-published author I don't have the support of an agent or a huge marketing department behind me. I rely on my readers to spread the word about my books. Please would you consider returning to your purchase platform and leaving a short review? Just a few words to accompany your star rating would mean so much to me.

You can connect with me via Facebook or visit my website at www.allie-cresswell.com where you will find details of my other books and have the opportunity to sign up to receive news and special offers. If you don't live too far away from me, I would be happy to visit your reading club, WI or creative writing group to give a short talk or a reading. On Twitter I am @alliescribbler and on Instagram I am @allienovelist.

I can supply questions to guide your reading group discussions about any of my books.

BIBLIOGRAPHY

Until fairly recently compulsive hoarding was a phenomenon that existed both literally and metaphorically 'behind closed doors.' The Collyer brothers, found immured in their NY apartment, were probably the first publicly acknowledged case. Poor Mr Trebus, who featured in the BBC programme 'A Life of Grime' will be well known to most people. Since then, a considerable number of 'reality' TV programmes have cottoned on to our national predilection for peeking into the private lives of others. Some of this output has had a purely voyeuristic quality—pitting, for example, compulsive cleaners against compulsive hoarders in a competition that can only result in misery for both. Others, though, have attempted a more serious angle on the issue by looking at the psychological factors that invariably undergird this mental health condition.

I read and recommend two personal accounts written by relatives of those affected by the condition.

Packrat by Tom Hixson, 2010, Pub. Tom Hixson, ISBN 978-0-557-70812-3

Dirty Secret by Jessie Sholl, 2011, Gallery Books, ISBN 978-1-4391-9252-8

ABOUT THE AUTHOR

Allie Cresswell was born in Stockport, UK and began writing fiction as soon as she could hold a pencil.

She did a BA in English Literature at Birmingham University and an MA at Queen Mary College, London.

She has been a print-buyer, a pub landlady, a book-keeper, run a B & B and a group of boutique holiday cottages. Nowadays Allie writes full time having retired from teaching literature to lifelong learners.

She has two grown-up children, three granddaughters, two grandsons and two cockapoos but just one husband – Tim. They live in Cumbria, NW England.

The Hoarder's Widow is her fifth novel.

You can contact her via her website at www.allie-cresswell.com or find her on Facebook, Instagram and Twitter.

**Read on for a teaser of book two in the 'Widows' series.
The Widow's Mite - teaser
Chapter One—Minnie**

Nobody expected Minnie Hale to marry. It wasn't that she was ugly. She was quite good-looking—if you liked a classical style—and always nicely turned out. It wasn't her age. She was thirty-eight, which is no age, these days. No, it was her character. She was so shy and jumpy—like a bird, feathers all a-flutter. Just being on the church tea rota brought her out in blotches. More often than not she spilled something or scalded someone, her hands shaking as though palsied. She had no confidence in herself or her own opinions, which made conversation with her quite difficult. She would dither—could never decide, wasn't sure, didn't know—even about straightforward things like whether she wanted tea or coffee to drink. She'd led a sheltered life. She was no judge, certainly not of people. It seemed so likely she would run a mile from any man. On the other hand, she was so gullible, such an innocent, it was something of a miracle she had not already been taken for a ride by one.

But she did marry. To everyone's surprise she married Peter Price. He was a widower, a stalwart of the church. He sat on the Parochial Church Council and read out the notices before the service and could be relied upon to turn up on Saturday mornings to clear litter from the carpark and mow the graveyard. St. Stephen's was the corner-stone of Minnie's life, her social as well as her spiritual home. So if she was going to meet a man anywhere, it was going to be there. She attended everything: Monday night Knit-and-Natter, the midweek Women's Group, Thursday evening Prayer Circle, Saturday's Coffee Morning. If she'd qualified, she would have been at the pensioners' Tea Dance on Tuesdays and Friday's Mums and Tots, too. Suffice it to say that if she wasn't at work she was at church. She worked as a specialist seamstress in a factory full of women, so that was always going to be a non-starter on the romance front.

Peter must have come at her bit by bit, like a stalker, creeping through the long grass of the familiar liturgy, the habitude of hassocks, the predictable prayer books—all the things Minnie felt comfortable with, where she would not be spooked—to gain her trust. Of course, all churches are full of single women: widows, spinsters, women who have been disappointed in earthly love and who turn to God as a substitute for all that life has not supplied. Peter could have taken his pick. He was eminently eligible. His first wife had been wealthy and he himself had been so successful both in his own career and in managing her capital that, at fifty, he was contemplating a comparatively early retirement. His house—The Poplars—was very fine, on easily the best residential road in the most sought-after area and overlooked the golf course to the rear with views of the sea beyond. When a decent interval had elapsed after the death of his first wife there had been some rivalry amongst the devout and righteous singletons of the congregation regarding which of them might take up residence at The Poplars. Minnie Hale had distanced herself from such overtly predatory behaviour. Perhaps that is why she caught his eye.

If she thought of him as a possible suitor, she probably worried that their experiences in life had differed too widely and she might in some way let him down. He had travelled and must have seemed, to her, very worldly wise. In her eyes he was a man of great influence and power, a top executive, a force to be reckoned with. In fact, he was only a sales manager—very successful, but no Lord Sugar. But he was socially confident, considered and sage. He spoke decidedly, pronouncing certainties. To a woman like Minnie he must have seemed a paragon, not so very far removed from God himself.

He broke down her defences pebble by pebble, dispelling the idealised image she had of him by admitting to failings and weaknesses. For all his high-powered professional life, he told her he liked nothing more than a weekend amble round a garden centre or to eat afternoon tea in the quiet lounge of a country hotel, both activities that—he had doubtless apprised himself—Minnie found unthreatening and thoroughly nice. When he discovered Minnie played neither golf nor bridge, he confessed that although he played both—rather well—he enjoyed neither. Really, he had only played to please his wife. He would give up both if he had better ways to eke out the loneliness of widowhood. He owned up to being hopeless in the kitchen and showed her, with shame, a button he had cack-handedly sewn on himself. This was a master stroke. If anything was calculated to move Minnie—accomplished seamstress as she was—it was a badly sewn on button.

Peter was clever in the way he wooed Minnie but there was also kindness in his gentle, sensitive courtship. Through the acknowledgment of his various vulnerabilities, he appealed to her kindness as well as to her keen sense of her own weaknesses. Indeed, their essential altruism finally united them—he asked her on their first date during an evening spent distributing Christian Aid envelopes. From then they found more that united than divided them. They both enjoyed the countryside. Peter inaugurated, and Minnie was the first to sign up for, a church rambling group. Peter had ambitions to conquer Wainwrights and Munroes, to walk the Coast-to-Coast and the Pennine Way. Minnie had never dared aspire to such adventurous pursuits but, with Peter, was emboldened to try. He emboldened her to try many things she would not have contemplated before, notably, at last, matrimony.

'But why?' she asked, as he knelt before her. 'Why would you want to marry me? I'm nothing like your first wife.'

He smiled. 'That's why.'

He wanted no more children. That must have been a sadness to her but it couldn't be helped; Peter had two children already grown and established in life. That was enough, he said.

Peter's affluence was an unlooked-for and naturally a very appealing circumstance to Minnie, who had expected to work up to the point at which she would be entitled to collect her state pension. She had inherited nothing from her parents, owned no property and subsisted on her modest wages. But monetary considerations played no part in her deciding to accept his proposal. Nobody who knew Minnie would suggest such a thing.

Of course she was thrilled by the house, thrilled and perhaps rather awed by it. Her little rented place was nothing in comparison. But any house with Peter would have pleased her just as much. Anyone could see that.

They married. Never was there a more blushing bride or, to be fair, a prouder groom.

Peter's children attended of course. They arrived rather late, bursting through the church doors just as the organ struck up the wedding march, pushing roughly past their prospective step-mother in the vestibule with scarcely a glance, let alone a greeting. They barely stayed beyond the speeches at the reception, keen to get back to London.

So Minnie Hale gave up her job and became Mrs Peter Price, moving into The Poplars, an imposing house on the Crescent, after a short honeymoon motoring in the Cotswolds. If she felt like an impostor sleeping in the very same bed as the late Mrs Price, dusting that woman's furniture or cooking with her choice of saucepans and crockery, Minnie never said so. These chores were done with the assiduousness but essential disinterest of a curator at a museum who cares for artefacts for which she has no particular attachment or antipathy but only because it is her job and they have fallen to her lot. The same could not be said of her husband. Him she loved with great devotion and quiet fervour, and when he died only six years after their marriage she grieved abjectly.

A woman from the church—Gwen—organised the funeral; Minnie was utterly incapable of anything. She was in profound shock, gripped in a vice of devastation that held her so tightly she was numb and dumb; literally she could barely speak, only nod or shake her head. The doctor prescribed medication that relaxed the straitjacket but allowed an onslaught of crying—gulping, choking sobs that wracked her whole body and made her vomit, which was worse. Gwen and the funeral director coaxed the names of Peter's favourite hymns out of her but beyond that she simply agreed to whatever was suggested: a notice in the local paper; a private cremation followed by a service in the church, and a reception with sandwiches, tea and cake in the church rooms afterwards. Throughout the ordeal of the day itself Minnie sat wherever she was put, stiff and awkward, her lips tightly sealed, her eyes bruised with tears. The church was thronged, full of business associates as well as friends. They all had complimentary things to say about Peter but when they approached to offer their condolences Minnie looked at them with a distracted air and made no reply.

Afterwards, Peter's two children followed her back to the house. They were strangers to her; she had only met them a handful of times. She could neither give nor receive comfort but, as it turned out, comfort formed no part of their agenda. The walked into the house with a proprietorial air and hung their coats up in the cloakroom. The daughter removed her high heeled shoes with a sigh of relief and went in stockinged feet through to the kitchen where she put the kettle on and lit a cigarette. The son loosened his black tie and held a small black briefcase out in front of him.

'Where shall we do this?' he asked Minnie. Not waiting for an answer he said, 'In the dining room I suppose.'

Minnie stood uncertainly in the hall, making no move to remove her coat or place her bag in the cubbyhole under the stairs. She looked at them as though she wasn't sure who they were. Taran, the son, was the image of his father, broad set and burly, with the same round face and sandy coloured hair. He did something in the City—Minnie wasn't sure what—and lived in a flat in the Barbican. The woman—Levina—took after her mother. Minnie had only glimpsed the first Mrs Price once or twice. She accompanied Peter to church rarely, sitting sourly on a chair near the door with a fixed expression of disapproval and distaste. Levina was petite, dark-haired, with gimlet eyes. She did something high powered in the broadcasting industry that involved a lot of travel.

In spite of his words Taran walked not into the dining room but into the small room that Peter had used as his study, and began rifling through drawers. Minnie watched appalled, but was unable to say a word of remonstrance.

Then Levina called from the kitchen, 'Minerva, where have you put Mummy's Spode tea service? It used to be in this dresser.'

Minnie moved along the hall and stepped into her kitchen. A number of cupboard doors were open and a few random items had been brought out: a set of Beatrix Potter children's crockery, a tankard-sized mug that Peter had liked to drink his morning tea from, a set of solid silver sugar tongs.

'These are mine,' Levina said, indicating the Beatrix Potter bowl, plate and mug. 'They were a christening present. These tongs are part of a set. It was Mummy's. Where is the rest of it?'

'It's on a tray in the dining room,' Minnie said faintly. She knew the heavy silver teapot, jug and sugar bowl well, having cleaned them with regularity. 'The china is in one of the cupboards of the sideboard.' She reached a tentative hand out to the mug. 'This was your father's—'

'But I bought it for him,' Levina snapped. 'I want it.'

Minnie swallowed hard but made no reply.

'The tea is brewing,' Levina said. She pushed past Minnie and walked along the hall to the front door, thrust her feet back into her shoes and went outside, leaving the door open.

Minnie went through the mechanics of making tea. She noticed with a dull annoyance that Levina had been dropping her cigarette ash into the sink and had squashed the butt there too. There was a small brown scorch-mark on the white resin. She put the cups on a tray and carried it through to the dining room where, by then, Taran had the documents he had found in the study spread across the table, but not in such a way that anyone else could have perused them.

'I suppose you've been through all this?' he asked with a casual tone that rang strangely hollow.

Minnie shook her head. 'No.'

'Oh.' He seemed to digest this for a moment. Then he flapped an envelope at her. 'This is his Will. It all seems in order. I'll deal with it. I'm Dad's Executor.' He tucked the envelope under some other documents.

'I'm … I'm glad,' Minnie got out. She *was* glad. She had some idea of the complications attendant on a death. She had been left to sort out her parents' affairs, though they had left nothing but a Post Office account and a handful of Premium Bonds.

Levina passed the open door of the room, carrying a stack of cardboard boxes and a roll of bubble wrap.

'Livvy, leave that now and come in here,' her brother called. 'There's tea, and some formalities to go through.'

'I don't think I can stand any more tea,' Levina said, but came into the room and took a seat. 'Who thought it was a good idea to hold the reception in that God-awful hall and to serve only tea? You could see people were gagging for Scotch. I know I was. Dad would have been horrified. Wasn't he a member of the golf club? Surely that would have been preferable, at the very least.'

Minnie's hand hovered over one of the cups on the tray. She didn't really want any more tea either, but it was made by then and she didn't want it to go to waste. 'There is whisky in the decanter,' she offered timidly, glancing over at where several heavy lead crystal receptacles sat on the top of a glass-fronted cabinet. Levina followed the direction of Minnie's glance and then swivelled her head back with a pointed look.

She is waiting for me to get up and fetch the decanter and a glass, Minnie thought.

She made a move to oblige, but Levina said, 'Don't bother, I'll do it.'

'Not for me,' Taran said.

'Or me,' Minnie whispered.

'Suit yourselves,' Levina muttered tetchily.

'So, broadly speaking,' Taran said, marshalling the papers together, 'Dad left everything to us—to Livvy and to me. By far the majority of his holdings were inherited from Mum. It goes without saying they come directly to us.' He turned to Minnie and gave her a hard look. Her idea that he resembled his father evaporated. Peter could never have worn a look of such coldness. 'You have no interest in them, morally or legally.'

'No, of course not,' Minnie murmured. She was still wearing her coat. She groped surreptitiously into the pocket for her handkerchief. Tears pressed behind her eyes and in her throat.

'There will be a great deal to be done in respect of them; they're variously tied up. Some funds are offshore. But I'll handle all of that. I must say, by the looks of these statements, Dad has been a conscientious custodian.'

'The values have grown then, have they?' Levina put in. She lit another cigarette but the activity did not disguise the avaricious look in her eye. Minnie regarded the smoke curling up to the ceiling with blank despair.

What a stink there will be in here, she thought. I'll have to take the curtains down and air them.

Taran nodded but showed, by a slight frown, he didn't want to go into details.

'I suppose you discussed financial matters with my father?' Levina said, squinting at Minnie through her cigarette smoke.

Minnie shook her head. 'Not really. He gave me a bank card and said I was to use it for shopping and so on. I was always careful. I always had been and old habits die hard. He used to …' It was no good, she could not hold back her tears. 'He used to laugh at me,' she choked out. A fat tear rolled down her cheek. 'He said I didn't need to penny-pinch.'

Taran regarded her without an iota of sympathy before going on. 'From what I can see there are two joint accounts.' He indicated the documents at his elbow, but made no move to show them to Minnie. 'A current account and a savings account. There's nothing to be done about them. All the funds immediately became yours the moment he died. But the other accounts and investments were in his sole name and naturally form part of his estate. There's no dispute about that, I suppose?'

'Not from me,' Levina said, swallowing her whisky.

Minnie made a noise in her throat, a thick swallow. She could feel her nose beginning to run. It was like drowning from inside. A tide of sorrow was seeping from some spigot at the back of her head, seeking further outlet that her tears of a moment ago had not satisfied. She brought out her handkerchief and blew her nose. The handkerchief was so wet already she could almost have wrung it out. She ought to have got up to find another but did not wish to seem rude to her guests.

Oh, but how long would this go on? How long would they stay? When would she be left alone so she could give way to the paroxysms of anguish that surged in her gullet and behind her aching eyeballs?

'It doesn't look as though Dad put the house in joint names,' Taran ploughed on matter-of-factly.

'She wouldn't want to stay in it, anyway,' Levina asserted, as though Minnie was not even in the room. 'To live alone in a great house like this? Ridiculous to even contemplate it.'

'I ... I don't know,' Minnie croaked through the glutinous mat of heartache that clogged her throat. She thought—but did not voice the thought—that Peter had lived alone there for the time of his widowhood and presumably nobody had thought *that* ridiculous.

Taran fiddled with a paper clip for a few moments, his brow heavily furrowed. At last, he said, 'To be fair, Dad did allow for the possibility.' He uncovered the envelope and withdrew the contents just enough to make out the item he needed. 'The spouse is to have the use and enjoyment of it for as long as she requires.'

'The use and ...?' Levina put her glass down heavily on the table. The movement dislodged the ash from her cigarette. It fell onto the carpet. Minnie rose from her chair and reached for a cut glass bon-bon dish that sat on the window ledge. She placed it down in front of Levina.

'For your cigarette,' she said in a small voice.

Levina looked at her cigarette and then down at the carpet where the worm-cast of ash sat on its pristine buttercream-coloured surface, but made no move to do anything about it. 'But that could be forever,' she spat out. 'All that capital tied up indefinitely. I am certain that isn't what Daddy intended. He meant just until she had found somewhere else. Purely an interim measure.' She turned to Minnie. 'Don't you think so?'

'I don't know,' Minnie said bleakly, 'I haven't thought ...'

Levina gave a humph, suggesting she doubted this assertion and suspected Minnie of doing nothing since Peter's death but rub her hands together and think gleefully of what a wealthy widow she was going to be. 'All I can say,' she said tartly, 'is it would be extremely selfish of you to remain longer than necessary. You haven't any particular connection to the place, have you?' She looked around the room. 'You haven't exactly put your own stamp on it, have you? To keep it from us would be an act of utter churlishness.'

'Would *you* want to —?' Minnie began, lifting a hand to indicate the house.

'Live here?' Levina snorted. 'Good God, no! I'd be committing professional suicide, moving to a backwater like this. But it's worth money. Not much, in comparison to London prices, but something; and it's part of our inheritance. It would be so much tidier to deal with the estate as a whole, wouldn't it, Taran?'

Minnie bit her lip, not to stop herself from saying something cutting but to restrain the sob that clenched her throat. She had never really felt this was her house. All the things in it were Peter's. She had cared for them because of that. She had valued their provenance in respect of the memory of his first wife. But she couldn't think now of where else she might live. She could barely think of the next hour, or day, without him. The wash of grief that had pushed at her all day was suddenly irresistible.

'I think, if you don't mind,' she said, as firmly as she could but unable to keep a quaver from her voice, 'I will go upstairs and lie down for a while. It has been a long day.' She turned to Taran, who was squirreling the documents away into his briefcase. 'Thank you for taking all the legal palaver on. I really wouldn't be up to it.' She turned to go but a tut of exasperation from Levina reminded her she had duties as a hostess. She turned back to stammer, 'I am not sure if there is food in the house, or if the beds are aired. If you wanted to … I mean, if you planned to …' but she couldn't go on. Her mouth was full of saliva, the red-hot prick of tears behind her eyes was agony. She clapped her handkerchief to her face and rushed from the room.

When she came back down again a few hours later there was no sign of Peter's children but the house had been selectively ransacked. The best of the crystal, all of the silver and most of the china had been taken away. A couple of heavy, bevelled mirrors had been removed as well as a set of original oil paintings that Peter had described as "particularly fine, and an investment." Various trinkets and ornaments were missing from their habitual places. A dark oak chest that Peter had thought to be Jacobean and rather valuable, had gone too. The best wines had been removed from the rack beneath the stairs.

Minnie observed all of this with an odd detachment, absent-mindedly closing cupboard doors and straightening things that had been rummaged through. She drew the curtains closed although it was only late afternoon and still quite light.

She would make tea, she thought. More tea. It seemed like a herculean task but if she could do it, it would seem like something—a small inroad into the morass of bleakness before her. But when she opened the fridge for milk there wasn't any, and she was engulfed by tears again.

Chapter Two—Maisie

It is a Friday afternoon in May, a year after Peter Price's death and funeral.

Minnie's friend Maisie Wilde is expecting her family. Dominic, her oldest, and his wife Pamela are coming from Nottingham with their three children. Daughter Frances, recent recipient of a PhD, and her fiancé Maxim are on the train from Oxford. Gareth, her youngest, is currently at home anyway, on sick leave from the army. It will be the first time they have all been together in the old house since Maisie's own husband's funeral the previous November. Some of them came at Christmas but since then things have changed beyond recognition. Maisie has cleared every last stick and shred of her husband's hoard.

The bedrooms at Old Farm Hall are sparsely furnished with only the bare minimum: a bed, a bedside table, a chair. The two large reception rooms on either side of the hall are entirely empty. The kitchen, however, is as it has always been—minus the slew of junk mail, the tottering piles of newspapers, the rough timber and Clifford's numerous on-going repair projects. The family will eat their supper round the kitchen table and then … then Maisie will break the news.

Frances, Maisie's middle child, arrives first. She lets herself into the house leaving Maxim to pay the taxi driver and bring the bags.

The empty rooms are a revelation to her. She has no recollection of the house other than crammed with broken furniture and boxes of miscellany. She paces the rooms with vinegary awe, walks into corners and alcoves that have never been accessible, admires views from windows that have always been blocked. The house is clean—spotlessly swept and dusted and mopped; the windows shine; the paintwork is free of the greasy, slightly fishy residue it seemed to ooze of its own volition. The amorphous, grey, granular fluff that covered everything, gathered in balls in every crevice and fuzzed the looped mats of cobweb overhead, is banished now. The windows have been opened. Fresh air has been allowed to permeate, exorcising the sullen gloom of disappointment from the rooms. For the first time in years the sun has been permitted to warm the scuffed floorboards and illuminate the faded grandeur of the ornate plaster cornices.

'I don't know quite how to feel …' Frances admits at last, '… mad at Dad for having spoiled all this for us for all those years—I mean, it's so much nicer than I ever imagined—or surprised at *you*, for succeeding so spectacularly in stripping it all bare.'

Maisie puts out a tentative hand—Frances is not a person who welcomes physical affection, as a rule—and strokes Frances' shoulder. 'Don't be cross at your father,' she says. 'It wasn't really his fault, the way things developed. And as for me, well, I've only scratched the surface, really. There's a lot of work to be done yet.'

It is true. There is much to be done in the way of repairs and renovations to bring the house up to anything approaching modern standards of utility or décor. In spite of zealous determination and diligent effort over twenty odd years, Clifford had only managed to affect a minimum of improvements, working in a piecemeal plan that saw many things begun but few completed. Over the years even this limited progress was hampered, then ham-strung, then stifled altogether by his compulsive accumulation of tat and dross that had filled the rooms, rendering access problematic if not impossible. But now that the impediments of dismembered electricals and boxes of junk are cleared, there is no reason why work can't go forward swiftly, and Maisie can afford to do things properly.

But Maisie's pleasure at Frances' approval soon sours when it becomes plain she assumes the pragmatic, no-nonsense strides Maisie has made are preparatory to putting the place on the market and getting rid of it. Maisie has very different plans, but in any case, whatever she does can have absolutely no impact on Frances, who in a matter of weeks, will be married and starting a new life as the wife of the most junior flunkey at the British Embassy in Tokyo.

There is no opportunity to suggest this before Maisie's oldest child, Dominic, his wife and family arrive. Maisie can see immediately that it is not so much the changes that have been brought about in the house—dramatic enough, in all conscience—but the changes in Maisie herself that surprise Dominic most. Well, she can understand that. In the past she was always a homely body, given to plumpness, comfortably clothed in indeterminate woollies and baggy, much-patched trousers. Seen through his eyes, she supposes that she is almost unrecognisable, catapulted from some obscure backwater of contented domestic pottering into a limelight of trendily accessorised ladies-who-lunch. It isn't just her wardrobe that has been transformed thanks to the substantial legacy, it is herself. She is consciousness of having stepped into a whole new life. She feels as bright and fresh as a new-hatched butterfly fluttering with iridescence as she stands on the doorstep, eager to draw her son into her embrace.

Gareth, Maisie's youngest, articulates the words that Dominic's flapping lips can't speak. 'Quite something, isn't she? A changed woman!' he says. 'Let me help with the luggage.'

But even this gives Maisie a qualm. Dominic won't like the idea that he is only catching up on something Gareth has long been party to, and Gareth's attitude to this new embodiment of their mother—sanguine, fully approving—will make Dominic feel even more out of step.

Frances' fiancé, Maxim, has brought a magnum of Champagne and sets about marshalling glasses while the others unpack.

'So thoughtful,' Maisie says, although in fact she has a pantry full of the stuff, ready for Saturday's party, 'and perfect for the *salmon en croute* we'll be having.'

The party is to be a sort of celebration—that the last of Clifford's hoard has been taken away, that her family is all together, that she has new friends to introduce them to. Gwen, Minnie and the other women are coming. They have been a lifeline to her these past few months. Then there is Oliver, who in recent weeks, has been a frequent visitor at the house. Maisie's feelings for him are confused. He is handsome—no doubt about that—with a powerful sexual appeal she finds frighteningly alluring. But he is a Harrington, a family riddled with what are these days called *issues* in which Maisie's late husband had become embroiled. Maisie wonders if she isn't already too closely mired to contemplate further involvement. If Oliver has been a frequent—too frequent?—caller at the house then James has not called frequently enough. He is connected to the Harringtons too but his case is a tragic one, triggering Maisie's inherent empathy and concern. To be honest, she would be lying to herself if she said it was only sympathy she feels for James Armstrong; she likes him enormously—too much perhaps, considering his married status. Her feelings for him are deeper and more complex than the simple animal chemistry that Oliver stirs up in her.

Pamela, Dominic's wife, takes the baby through to the snug little parlour Maisie and the family have always used as their lounge, to change his nappy. She is a spiky, awkward woman, very ready to criticise.

'I hope supper won't be long,' she says as she passes through. 'The girls are famished and you know what Edmé is like when her calorie level is low. What possessed you to think she'd settle in a tent?'

Maisie glances out through the kitchen window over a burgeoning array of green and aromatic herbs that fills the window ledge. Jessica—age six— and three-year-old Edmé are running on the lawn shrieking, pursued by Uncle Gareth. They are to camp out with him. He has already erected a tent borrowed from the Scouts.

'I thought it would be fun for them. She can have Gareth's bed if she doesn't like it,' Maisie says.

'Good luck with *that,*' Pamela mutters. Gareth's room is in the attic, a space with dim eaves and weird wind-whistles.

Maisie slides the baking tray with the glazed salmon parcel into the oven and puts the kettle on to boil for the greens.

I will drink champagne and feed my family and then … then I'll tell them.

Also by Allie Cresswell

Contemporary Novels
Game Show
Relative Strangers
Crossings
Tiger in a Cage
The Cottage on Winter Moss

The Widows Series
The Hoarder's Widow
The Widow's Mite
The Widow's Weeds

The Talbot Saga
The House in the Hollow
The Lady in the Veil
Tall Chimneys

The Highbury Trilogy inspired by Jane Austen's Emma
Mrs Bates of Highbury
The Other Miss Bates
Dear Jane